DETROIT RULES

A CHARLIE STREET Crime Thriller

STREET LAW series
Book 2

LINDA STYLE

"Injustice anywhere is a threat to justice everywhere."

~ Martin Luther King Jr. ~

DETROIT RULES

A STREET LAW NOVEL
Book 2

Not everyone plays by the rules

LINDA STYLE

LMS PRESS

Gilbert, Arizona

LMSPress@cox.net

Detroit Rules

Copyright © 2015 by Linda Style

ISBN: 978-0692481738
1st Edition -- ALL RIGHTS RESERVED

Cover Designer: Rogenna Brewer
sweettoheat.blogspot.com

Editor: Esther Doucet

Formatting: Nina Pierce of Seaside Publications
ninapierce.com/book-formatting

DEDICATION

To my family
Whose love, support, talents, and encouragement
keep me on this incredible journey.

ACKNOWLEDGMENTS

The idea for this book came to me while on my first trip to Detroit over five years ago to stay with a friend…and what an eye-opener it was. But instead of seeing the devastation wreaked on the once-proud city—instead of seeing crime on every corner—I saw a vibrant city and was amazed at the architectural beauty still standing. I was touched by the hope and determination of those making efforts to change things. I became fascinated with the city's history and have spent the last five years sucking up everything Detroit has to offer, and I must acknowledge the hospitality and kindness of the Detroiters who've so generously welcomed me and contributed to my research. Each time I'm in the D, I stay longer and longer.

My deep appreciation to Detroit native Charles Jones for introducing me to this amazing city, and to everyone I've met along the way, from vendors and entertainers at the Eastern Market to servers at the many restaurants I've frequented during my research. I don't know your names, but I remember you and so appreciate the time you took to talk to me. Many thanks to Mark Holmes, limo driver extraordinaire, whose conversation during long drives from the airport covered everything from raising kids to Detroit politics. You gave me insights I'd never have found in any book research. Many thanks to Tony Barchock, one of the first to give me advice on what to see and photograph in Detroit and whose love of the city is evident in his own amazing photographs.

My deep gratitude to my beta readers. You helped immensely in catching things I missed: Robert J. Sadler, former Dallas police officer, Private Investigator, and author of the Michael Grant chronicles, Todd Sheridan, Assistant Attorney General for the state of Arizona, Charles Jones, Criterium Engineers, native Detroiter and fact nerd, Janet Edwards Fensand, sister-in-law and voracious reader, and Tim Sheridan at Smart Productions, LLC, for creating an awesome book trailer. Any mistakes are mine.

I have taken liberties for the sake of the story, and some facts have been subject to artistic license.

CHAPTER ONE

GUILTY AS HELL.

And yet, an aura of doubt filled the room.

He studied the attorney, watched her draw each hand-picked jury member into her web.

The woman inhabited her role as if she were Meryl Streep giving another Oscar-worthy performance… every move skillfully choreographed.

The filled-to-capacity courtroom hummed with expectation as the attorney for the defense, Charlize Street, paused near the witness stand, adjusted her red curve-hugging suit jacket, then took a step back, letting her audience wait just the right amount of time between each perfectly crafted sentence. Each word crisp and clear, every sentence succinct.

She wore a slim, black skirt, ending at the knee, allowing a glimpse of well-toned legs. The deep slit in the back drew his gaze upward to her best asset. Her shoes, while not five-inch stilettos, were definitely tall enough to make any juror with an ounce of testosterone take notice.

And like one of Pavlov's dogs, Remy's hormones responded on cue.

Never mind that she was defending the most notorious madam in Detroit for a gruesome murder that would make Jack the Ripper's carnage seem like a kiddies' birthday party in comparison.

Yet, from the rapt expressions on the jurors' faces, Ms. Street had them right where she wanted. His brother was right. The woman was good. *Very good.*

Exactly the person he needed.

All he had to do was convince her she wanted him. And that, he'd heard, was about as likely as drowning in the desert.

He tugged the neck of his shirt. The acrid scent of too many people in a too-hot room permeated the air like foul exhaust fumes during a Motor City rush hour. Even so, the attorney for the defense stayed cool…in total control.

The defendant shifted in her chair, her gaze cast down, her attitude far different than when Remy had arrested her sixteen years ago working hooker central on Eight Mile.

Madam Lucy Devonshire now hired top-dollar models to do the work for her, but she was still a prostitute. And a murderer.

And she was going to walk.

Thanks to her hot-shot lawyer, Charlize, AKA Charlie, Street, the defendant would be back pimping her girls to horny millionaires within minutes of the verdict.

Cops got the sleaze off the streets and slick attorneys got them off the hook.

But then…what was one more killer on the streets of *Murder City*. Getting rid of one baddie was like swatting mosquitoes in the Okefenokee Swamp.

Remy clenched his jaw. Swallowing his dislike for attorneys was nothing compared to what he was willing to do to find out what happened to Adam.

Nothing compared to what he'd do if he found the son of a bitch responsible for his best friend's disappearance.

In the back of the room sitting next to Hank Hitchens, a retired detective with the Detroit PD whom

Remy hadn't seen in years, Remy drew in a lungful of air. Rolled his shoulders. Focused on his goal—Charlie Street, attorney extraordinaire, defender of the poor…and street slime who thought the law didn't apply to them.

"You involved?" Hitchens whispered and tipped his head toward the bench.

"Nope," Remy mouthed and shook his head.

The older man leaned closer to Remy. "This one's gonna take down a lotta good people."

They always did. When a crime involved Detroit's underbelly of brokered sex, it was inevitable that big names turned up…politicians and cops included.

"All I can say—" the older man said under his breath "—is that bitch better watch her back."

The venom in his tone caught Remy off guard and he wanted to ask which woman was the bitch—the defendant or her attorney—when the courtroom doors burst open and two reporters barreled out. Remy slipped out, too.

He'd seen enough. If Charlie Street could help him, he didn't give a flying fuck if *she* was Jack the Ripper.

Hitch followed on Remy's heels and headed toward the exit, tossing out over his shoulder, "Sorry about Adam, man. He was a damn good cop."

Remy's gut twisted. *Still is.*

He gritted his teeth against a sudden, fierce urge to punch something.

He fucking still is.

Behind him, the courtroom doors banged open, again, and he stepped aside as the first wave of spectators poured out. Christ, everyone from the governor's office on down had a stake in this high-octane case. Once the attorney was outside, the gang of reporters and paps playing bumper bodies on the courthouse steps would swarm her like she was Lady

Gaga. There'd be no way in hell he could talk to her, privately or otherwise.

As the people filtered out, he spotted the attorney behind a bailiff redirecting her to the room between the courtroom and the judges' chambers. The room had two doors, and he was guessing she'd go out the other side to avoid the media circus.

He separated himself from the remaining court groupies and headed to the next hallway, reaching the exit just as the attorney was coming out, ass first, briefcase in one hand and a stack of files in the other.

As she pulled the door shut, he said, "Miss Street, can I talk to you for a moment?"

She froze, her back ramrod stiff. "You just did," she said, still with her back to him. "If you're a reporter—no comment. If you want a consult—" she turned…ice-blue eyes raked over him "—make an appointment."

Crushing the armful of files against her chest, she pivoted, and then made a beeline down the hall.

He bit back a nasty retort and, after a pause, started after her.

Just as he got close enough to say something, a hulking black dude in a too-tight gray suit appeared at her side, as if from nowhere. Remy stopped in his tracks.

The attorney, still walking, took the guy's arm and they headed toward the side exit together.

Remy planted his feet apart, crossed his arms and, hot blood still sizzling in his veins, watched them disappear around the corner.

Yeah. Now he knew which woman was the bitch.

"You sure you're okay?" Dempsey asked as they reached Charlie's car.

"I'm perfect. Couldn't be better." She pasted on a smile, glad the former boxing champ who sparred with students at her brother's neighborhood gym had volunteered to act as her "bodyguard" during the trial.

She did a quick scan of the parking area, pulled the keys from her jacket pocket, and pressed the unlock button on the fob.

Dempsey shot her a skeptical look. "If you say so." The big man opened the car door for her.

"Just another reporter." She dropped her files and messenger bag on the floor in the back, slid into the driver's seat, and kicked off her heels. Wearing new shoes when she had to stand for hours had been a bad pre-coffee decision, and not her first of the day.

She buckled her seatbelt, started the car, and waited for Dempsey to come around on the passenger side. The police had determined the shooting three months ago to be random, a stray bullet, probably gang related, given the neighborhood. And the threat letter she'd received was likely another crank.

She was getting used to those. Most of the cases she worked on made someone unhappy. When her brother first suggested she get protection for the Devonshire trial, she'd balked at the idea. Even if she'd been the target three months ago, having a bodyguard wasn't going to stop a bullet.

But Landon had made a convincing argument that being seen with some well-respected muscle during the trial wouldn't hurt. She couldn't deny she felt more secure with a little heavy duty testosterone at her side, if only to deflect the paparazzi and court creeps.

Like the guy who'd been lurking outside the judges' chambers. If Dempsey hadn't shown up, the jerk would've dogged her, for sure.

Once Dempsey crammed himself inside her Focus, she pulled out and headed to the lot where he'd parked his vehicle. Her stomach growled, reminding her that food was sometimes a necessity.

"How long before the trial is over?"

"Why? You tired of being my escort?"

The big man chuckled. "Easiest job ever. But I got another gig pretty soon, so I was just wonderin'."

"Closing arguments are coming up. After that, there's just the decision. If you have something else to do, go ahead. It's been a long trial, and I'm sure you have more exciting things to do than babysit me." She glanced over. Smiled at Dempsey.

She hadn't taken on a murder trial since she'd been a public defender five years ago. Aside from her pro bono cases, most of the work done by her team at Street Law was investigative.

She tipped her head to the side and rubbed the back of her neck. Damn, she was tired. Trials were exhausting, and she couldn't wait to be finished. But that wasn't going to happen until she'd done everything possible to convince the jury her client was innocent.

Still, given Lucy's profession, it was a tough sell. Not that it mattered. Not when someone's life was hanging in the balance. She'd do whatever she had to do to see an innocent person acquitted.

"You need me for that meeting tonight?" Dempsey asked as she pulled her car in next to his.

"No. I'm good." She forced another smile. "As much as I like your company, Demps, people with secrets don't feel much like talking when there's an audience."

He opened the door and got out. "Yeah, but you don't know—"

"There'll be enough people in the restaurant to intervene if the guy's not on the level."

He gave her a three-finger Boy Scout salute and closed the door.

Tonight would probably be another bust anyway. She hadn't uncovered anything new on her father's case in years and had pretty much quit the search. But she couldn't take a pass on any scrap of information that might help prove her father's innocence. No matter how nervous she was about it.

The evidence was out there, but like Jimmy Hoffa's body, it was just too deeply buried to find.

She drew her bottom lip between her teeth. Twenty-five years ago today. But somehow... someday...she would find who framed her father and orchestrated his murder in prison.

Justice would prevail. One way or another.

On the road, again, she turned on the radio, glad to be going home. There was just enough time for a nap before the meeting.

Humming along with J-Lo, she clicked on her blinker, moved over a lane, then checked the rearview mirror for the upcoming turn onto Michigan Avenue. Seeing a black car closer than she liked, she sped ahead a little to put space between them. But the idiot sped up, too, until he was on her bumper again.

Jerk. In the mirror she could see the person was big. A man. But between the dusky light and his lowered visor, she couldn't see his face. She pumped her brake to warn him to back off. Instead, he accelerated and rammed her bumper. Her head slammed forward.

Her pulse skyrocketed. What the...? She tightened her grip on the wheel, accelerated to pass a car on her right, then slid over a lane to get rid of the maniac. But she saw his vehicle doing the same…and then he was right behind her, again. And closing in, as if to ram her.

What the hell was he doing?

She reached for her phone. *Shit*. It was in her bag in the back, and she couldn't take her eyes off the road to get it. Someone needed to report this idiot. She pumped her brakes again and, this time, he veered sharply left and merged into the next lane. A quick sense of relief swept through her. Good. Stay there, asshole.

But just as she thought it, he sped up next to her, pacing her car at the same speed.

Her heart racing, she gritted her teeth and focused on the road. *Don't look*. That's what he wants. Classic case of road rage. She knew the psychology. He wanted to intimidate her. Scare her. If she flipped him off or called him a name, it would only exacerbate the situation, and it could get even more dangerous.

Tires squealed and she saw his car swerve over. *Oh, shit*. The grating crunch of metal against metal pierced her ears, jolted her vehicle sideways into the path of a semi bearing down on her right. She yanked the wheel left. Her car twisted sideways. Sweat broke out on her forehead. Blood pounded in her ears as she got the car under control.

This guy was totally freaking crazy.

Okay…okay…deep breath, Charlie. Stay calm. She couldn't turn off and have him follow her home, and she didn't dare stop or who knew what he'd do. She slowed. Maybe he'd get tired of not getting the response he wanted and disappear.

But he slowed, too.

Oh, God! He wasn't going to quit.

Her spirits leapt when she spied two police vehicles at a gas station just ahead. Barely slowing, she made a quick right into the driveway and, as she did, she turned to look at the man harassing her.

She needed to know if he was just some angry dickhead taking out his aggressions behind the wheel...or someone who might actually want to harm her.

Like someone who feared exposure at the Lucy Devonshire trial.

Or the man who'd been waiting for her outside the courtroom.

CHAPTER TWO

CHARLIE LEANED FORWARD and shrugged off the power red suit jacket she'd worn for the trial earlier. Her small office in the old former hotel that now housed Street Law & Investigations was perpetually hot, even when the weather wasn't.

It didn't help that one of her clients had been waiting for her when she walked in. She'd had to shift gears from the murder trial and a crazy-ass driver to getting a restraining order on an abusive husband.

So much for relaxing before the meeting tonight.

She stood to see if her legal assistant, AKA receptionist, was at her desk and saw the front door open and then shut. But the partition to the reception area obscured her view, so she couldn't see who'd come in. Damn. She didn't need another walk-in.

She eased into her chair again, picked up the phone, and pressed her assistant's extension. "Do you have time for a restraining order?"

"Sure. I have an hour before I leave for class. Do *you* have time to see a man who won't give me any information? Says it's confidential."

Charlie glanced up and saw the top of the man's head over the partition to the reception area. Some clients were embarrassed to say why they needed her services, and some feared for their lives, but they usually let January know something. If this dude wasn't giving up any information, then it wasn't all that urgent. "Have him make an appointment. And when you're ready, c'mon back."

"Got it."

Walk-ins were a common occurrence at Street Law. People in need didn't stand on ceremony...or make appointments. Most of the time, it didn't matter. January would triage and if it seemed urgent, Charlie would talk to the person to determine how urgent and go from there.

But tonight she had an appointment with a man who said he had information about her father. Anything else that came up would have to wait.

There were only four on her staff; her assistant, January Giordano, two contract employees, Max Scofield, and Gabe Weatherly, and once in a while, a part-time intern. Only Charlie and January were in the office on a daily basis.

Intent on closing up shop so she could change clothes and grab a bite to eat before tonight's meeting, she'd barely scooped up her belongings when January appeared in the doorway.

"He wasn't happy." Her assistant walked over and leaned against the chair in front of Charlie's desk, hands resting on the back, fingers drumming. "But he made an appointment for Wednesday afternoon."

"And?"

"That's it. He wouldn't tell me what it was about."

"What's his name?"

"Initials. R.J.M."

"That's it?"

"I was in a hurry and he wasn't exactly forthcoming."

She could understand January being in a hurry. She was a single mom holding down a job and attending law school in the evening. When not at school or work,

January wanted to be with her little girl.

There's no way she'd be able to do all her assistant did. "Okay, but I have court tomorrow."

"That's why I gave him Wednesday."

"I don't like it."

"Because?"

"Because I don't know if he wants to hire me or give me a load of crap about something."

Her assistant snorted a laugh while reaching to flip her long, blond hair behind her shoulders. "Well, all I gotta say is, if anyone is dishing crap around this place, they better protect their vital parts."

Charlie laughed, felt her muscles relax a little. She hadn't realized how uptight she was.

"Okay. I'll be upstairs if you need me. I managed to spill coffee down the front of my shirt before court this morning, so I have to change before I go out."

"Tonic water. Want me to take care of it?"

"Yeah, sure…and do the interview, the order, and grab the broom and sweep the floor while you're at it." Charlie waved her off. Her assistant was wise beyond her twenty-eight years, had boundless energy and possessed abundant willingness to do whatever needed to be done. Superwoman to the max…and it was going to get her in trouble.

Charlie never failed to be amazed at how she'd managed to pull together such a loyal, dedicated staff who, after just three years together, felt like they were family. January had even helped with the remodeling after Charlie had bought the old hotel as a foreclosure.

One of these days, she might actually finish remodeling. But in the meantime, the only actual enclosed offices were hers and the conference room across the hall. The rest of the place was open, much like a newsroom, with four desks in the middle, two of which were used by Max and Gabe.

And she was going to be late for her appointment if she didn't get her ass in gear.

At the end of the hall at the back of the building, she unlocked the lower door that led to her apartment on the second floor. Reaching the landing a few steps up, the fading sun shone golden through the gauze curtains, fluttering on a soft spring breeze. Seeing movement outside, her pulse jumped. She halted mid-step and ducked to the side of the tall, skinny window.

She waited a moment. Then, heart pounding, she leaned to peer out. Just beyond the vacant lot behind her office, she saw a brown van parked in the alley near the bushes. Again.

She pulled away, her back against the wall. Her chest heaved.

Nothing. It's nothing. Just a parked car. A neighbor.

But no matter how hard she tried to talk herself down, she couldn't shake the eerie feeling that had plagued her since the shooting.

She rubbed her upper arm. All healed now. A random incident, the police had said when they couldn't find the shooter. Teens showing off, or a bullet gone astray from a gang fight—a bullet meant for someone else.

God knew she wanted to believe it. And the logic wasn't without merit. The area where she'd been to visit a client wasn't in the safest section of the city, a point made by one of the officers doing the investigation. His advice… "You live with the rats, you get rat food. Sometimes the poison."

Once again validating her opinion of Detroit's finest.

The same could be said about where she lived. Her office, fairly close to the perimeter of Corktown, wasn't in the best section of town, either.

Leaning one shoulder against the window frame, she peeked outside again. *Gone.* Her blood rushed. *No van. No van!* She closed her eyes and slowly filled her lungs with air. Aside from the road rage guy today, nothing else had happened since the shooting. Nothing at all.

She was overreacting.

Yet, for the life of her, she couldn't shake the ominous feeling that someone was watching her.

CHAPTER THREE

THIS WAS IT. Do or die. The guy would show or he wouldn't. After a quick shower, Charlie pulled on a pair of skinny jeans, took two seconds to decide whether to dress them up or down, and then another minute to throw on a deep cobalt button-front shirt, a black jacket and her black boots.

She drove to Slows in seven minutes and parked on the backside of the building, not too far from the giant mural that let drivers whizzing along Michigan Avenue know they were in Corktown.

Just beyond the razed lots across the street from Slows, the old, gutted, eighteen-story Michigan Central Station stood sentinel, its Beaux-Arts façade like a weary old soldier whose sad dark eyes revealed the knowledge his days were coming to an end. A monolith too big and too broken to fix.

She'd always felt comfortable in the area where she'd grown up, but over the years, seeing the deterioration, the overgrown lots and abandoned, boarded-up homes, she'd become wary. Even if she weren't wary, it would be foolhardy to walk alone. Especially at night.

Corktown wasn't Grosse Pointe, it wasn't even Ferndale, but years ago, the community, settled by Irish immigrants, had been a place where hardworking men and women did the best they could to provide for their families. Her mother's family had been one of them.

The populace had changed over the years, becoming a mixture of whites, blacks and Mexicans, but the neighborhood had always retained its individuality. And despite the deterioration of property in the area, a rash of new restaurants like Slows, and the newer Gold Cash Gold restaurant that once housed a pawnshop, were rising like defiant revolutionaries, ready to fight the crush of blight around them.

The tangy smell of barbecue hit her well before she reached the wall-high, rustic wood door at Slows. Her stomach growled, and every salivary gland in her mouth shifted into overdrive.

Inside, she glanced around. Most nights at the eatery were crazy busy and on weekends, it was standing room only. But tonight, there was no line outside the door, no people jammed in the entry. The place was uncharacteristically empty.

"Hey, Charlie," Timothy greeted her from behind the check-in stand near the entry. The man was so quintessentially Irish, he was almost a cliché. "You workin' late, again?"

He could've tacked on "lass" at the end of his question and the picture would've been perfect.

"Nope," she said, and acknowledged the new hostess he'd apparently been showing the ropes. "In fact, I'm meeting someone here in about a half hour."

"A new boyfriend, is it, then?"

She laughed at his lack of pretense. Tim had a way of making a person feel he was genuinely interested...a trait that made him a great bartender.

"No, and if I ever have one, I'm not going to bring him here so you can pry into his life, too."

One of the waitresses came from behind the horseshoe-shaped bar with a glass of water and motioned for Charlie to follow her.

"If it's not pleasure, then you are workin' late," Tim said, one eyebrow cocked as he went back to bartending a few feet away.

She sat in the back booth facing the entrance so she could see who came in, then glanced to the handwritten menu above the bar, even though she had it memorized. "I'm starving. How about the pulled pork and an Atwater."

"Sure thing," the waitress warbled and went to input the order on the bar computer.

She wished she were working late. Her bills were mounting and her paying clients seemed to be fewer and fewer. The Devonshire case had come when she needed it the most, but it was winding down, and so would be the billable hours.

"Hey, Charlie," one of the other waitresses greeted on her way to a booth on the other side of the bar.

"Hey." Charlie smiled, but kept one eye on the front door. The warm amber lighting added to the ambiance, but from this far away, it wasn't going to allow her a good look at the guy she was supposed to meet.

She knew nothing about the man…other than he'd called two weeks ago, said his name was Smith, and left a message that he knew her father and wanted to talk to her. None of her previous research on her father's case included the name, so she'd thought he was another crackpot.

But then he'd mentioned something no one else could know…other than Charlie and her father. Either the guy was a mind reader or he really did know her dad.

And anyone who had known her dad just might have a nugget of information that could change everything.

She'd played phone tag with the guy to arrange a meeting, then finally, she'd left a message about where and when to meet. He'd sent a text saying OKAY, but she had no idea if he'd actually show up.

She pulled out her cell phone and tried the number again. This time, instead of voicemail, she got a *Not in Service* message. She tried again. Same thing. Crap. A burner. He didn't want to be identified...or traced. Which meant he probably wasn't coming. She halfway hoped he didn't.

All it would do was stir things up again. Get her hopes up.

Her stomach growled. As if on cue, the waitress appeared at her side with a mile-high pulled pork sandwich, coleslaw and a glass of beer. Mouthing her thanks, Charlie snatched up the sandwich. An orgasmic treat for her tastebuds.

Just as she dived in for a bite, the front door swung open and a tall, trim man stood silhouetted in the two-story entry. She froze mid-bite.

His face was in the shadows, but the way he stood, straight and tall, he appeared young. *Okay. Not him.* He was too young to have known her father. An odd sense of relief swept over her.

When the man didn't come any farther inside, she went back to the sandwich, took a giant bite, and then glanced at the TV screen over the bar to watch the news. Although the sound was off, she saw a news crawl about the Devonshire trial.

The newscaster came on and behind him on the screen was an old photo of Charlie— "The accused killer's attorney" —alongside a photo of her father that had hit the papers twenty-five years ago...the word GUILTY emblazoned in the headline.

She chewed. Swallowed. Took a sip of beer. *Assholes.* Her hands shook as she brought the sandwich to her mouth for another bite. Geez, she hated them.

She'd known the second she'd agreed to take the high-profile Devonshire case, the media would dredge up all the old crap to see how much more sensational they could make things. If it wasn't juicy, they'd make it so. News wasn't about news anymore, it was about ratings. Money.

The TV photo reminded her that if the man she was meeting was on the level, it was possible he could provide information vital to proving her father's innocence. In which case, she should be ecstatic…thinking unicorns and rainbows.

Instead, her stomach churned and her head hurt from thinking about it.

It could just as easily be another shakedown. A ruse to get paid for information someone knew she wanted.

Checking the entrance again, she saw the same man still standing just inside, still glancing around. Probably looking for his online date, hoping she was one of the hot college girls sitting near the front windows.

The clock over the bar said she had fourteen minutes to wait. If he came, then whatever was going to happen, would happen. If he didn't show within a few minutes after that, she was outta there.

Just as she decided, she saw the man at the door talking to a waitress who nodded Charlie's way. He glanced over, then turned and sauntered toward her like a gunslinger walking a long, dusty street, ready for a duel.

The distance between the front and the back of the room suddenly compressed as his long legs traveled purposefully forward with smooth precision, one step, then another. The only thing missing was the soundtrack from *The Good, The Bad and The Ugly*.

She glued her gaze to the TV, but she could still see him in her peripheral vision.

When he reached her booth, he leaned against the back edge of the seat across from her.

She didn't move.

After an excruciatingly long moment, he said, his voice low and smooth, "Great commercial, isn't it."

She turned. Her nerves bunched. *What...?* He was the same man who'd been waiting to talk to her at the courthouse after the trial. Staring at him, she took her time to finish chewing. *What balls! What fucking balls!*

"Stalking is illegal," she finally said, then took a quick swig of beer. She set the glass down and lifted her sandwich again.

Even though she forced her eyes to stay on her food, she saw his mouth curve into a grin.

"But—" he slipped into the booth on the opposite side "—we do have an appointment." His grin widened into a full toothpaste commercial smile, his teeth sparkling white against tanned skin.

"Sorry if I'm a bit early."

The new waitress hovering at the booth next to them batted her lashes and gave him what looked to be her best I'm-available smile. With his looks, he was probably used to it.

Charlie slanted another glance at the bar clock. "You are. You don't mind if I finish eating, do you?" Without waiting for an answer, she stuffed another bite of barbequed pork into her mouth, her nerves jittery, like jumping beans under her skin.

He's here. He's actually here. After playing phone tag for two weeks, her nerves on edge the whole time wondering what he had to say about her father, the moment of truth had arrived. And all she wanted to do was bolt for the door.

He waved the waitress over, ordered a Bell's Lager, folded his arms on the table, and watched her chew.

Swallowing, she washed down the suddenly tasteless meal with another swig of beer. "Haven't eaten all day," she said. "Sorry."

"Hey—" he gave her an apologetic look "—I barged

in on your dinner, so I'm the one who should be sorry. In fact," he said, sliding from the booth. "I should go wash my hands and let you finish."

She wagged a finger toward the back of the room on the other side indicating the restrooms.

Wearing dark jeans and a black sport jacket that fit smoothly across his broad back and shoulders, he walked with a military bearing. Mid-thirties, she guessed...and didn't look at all like the man she'd imagined she was meeting.

Based on the phone voice, she'd expected someone more staid, someone more like her mother's new boyfriend, who was as vanilla as a guy could get. The voice she'd listened to over and over again on her voice mail, although probably disguised, had sounded older, his words hesitant.

There wasn't a hesitant bone in this guy's body. And he definitely wasn't vanilla.

Tim, watching from behind the bar, caught her ogling, and gave her a thumbs-up.

She shook her head and mouthed, "No way." But she grinned, anyway. Tim should've been a matchmaker instead of a bartender.

She'd just finished swallowing the last bite of her sandwich when Mr. Not Vanilla returned, stood next to the booth, and scanned the room before he sat again. Even sitting, he was imposing.

She blotted her mouth with the napkin. "How about we start with introductions. You already know who I am, and all I know about you is that you knew my father."

His brows knitted, confusion swirled in his eyes. He looked around like he was making sure no one was within earshot, and then said, "I don't know what you mean, but my name is Remy."

Remy *Smith?* When he didn't offer any more, she

said, "And for the record, I only talk to people who give me their full name."

"Fair enough. Last name's Malone. Remington Malone."

That he'd given her a fake name wasn't much of a surprise. But *Malone?* Her skin prickled at the reminder of a name she never wanted to hear again. A quick flash of heat crawled up her neck. She shifted position, clasped both hands around her glass.

"But Remy's good," he added, his lips tipping up at the edges in an uneven half-smile that softened the tough-guy image he'd projected so far.

"Malone…that sounds familiar to me. Is there a reason for that?"

He shrugged. "I don't know. My father was a Supreme Court Justice, but you're too young to have known him. He's been retired a long time."

Charlie's pulse banged at the base of her throat.

"I'm sorry," he said. "I know this kind of meeting isn't the norm, but I have reasons not to let anyone know I came to see you."

She drew a deep breath. His father, Judge Dancy Malone, also known as the hanging judge, was the circuit court judge who'd sentenced her father. In Judge Malone's courtroom, defendants had been presumed guilty until proven innocent.

But that was years ago, and the judge had retired before she'd started practicing law. Only now, she was even more curious. What could this guy possibly know about her dad? Had he heard something from the judge?

"Okay. So, to save both of us from me asking a lot of questions, why don't you just tell me what you know about my father and we'll go from there."

Pulling back, Malone's brows arched. "Your father?" He raised his hands, palms out. "I'm sorry. I don't have any idea what you mean."

Charlie counted to ten. Why didn't people just frigging say what they had to say? She took a second. Spoke slowly. "From your phone calls, it was my understanding that you knew my father." A muscle spasmed at the corner of her right eye. "If this is some kind of asinine joke—"

"No." He waved both hands. "No. No joke. I really don't know what you mean. I'm not here because of anything to do with your father."

"Then I think you'd better leave before I find someone to help you out." She glanced toward the bar to get Tim's attention. He was looking the other way, so she slid to the end of the booth to get out.

"Wait." He placed a hand on her arm. "It's not a joke. I do have an appointment with you on Wednesday."

She yanked away.

"Now, I realize…" He shook his head, his expression apologetic. "Oh, man. I feel really stupid. You were expecting someone else, weren't you?"

"Someone else? She drew back. Rubbed her forehead. "You're…not …" Oh, shit. If he wasn't the man she'd been playing phone tag with, then who the hell was he?

"No I'm not. And it kinda looks like the other guy is a no-show."

She didn't like the way he looked at her. She didn't like the way he assumed he knew what was going on—even though he was right.

She glanced at the clock. "Apparently. But for all I know, he came in, saw you and left." And she had no way to contact him.

"Why would he do that?"

"Oh, I don't know. Maybe he has reasons not to let anyone know he was seeing me." She scratched her head and dropped against the back of the booth. "Yeah, that seems like a good reason, don't you think?"

"Got me there," he said. "And if that's the case, I'm very sorry. But to be honest, any guy who can't keep his appointments, or at least let a person know he's not going to keep it, isn't very responsible. Or respectful."

"Not respectful? You mean like someone who'd stalk a total stranger and then barge in on her during dinner and screw up everything she'd planned." She took another drink. "That kind of guy?"

The last thing she wanted was to get into a debate with a total stranger on the etiquette of canceling appointments. Especially someone who made his own whenever he felt like it.

He gave a quick, sharp nod. "You're right. I'm a jerk. A slob with no manners whatsoever."

His eyes caught hers in a way that made her blood rush. A little. Not much.

"I deserve the 'Most Uncouth Man in Motor City Award' from Emily Post herself."

She laughed then—releasing the tension that had been building in her all day. Unable to wipe away the smile completely, she said, "If you're waiting for me to disagree, you'll be waiting a long time."

"No, no." He clasped his hands. "No expectations whatsoever."

She sobered. "Okay. What *do* you want? What's so important that you had to track me down? So important it can't wait until Wednesday to see me during your scheduled appointment?"

His face went stone-cold serious. "What I told your assistant is true. I really do need this to remain confidential." He opened the left side of his jacket.

A gun. She raised her brows, eyes wide.

"Sorry. I didn't mean to shock you." He flashed a badge.

Acid rose in her throat. She waited, as she did in court, making sure her voice would be under control before speaking. "Shocked isn't the word I'd use, Mr. Malone." She pursed her lips. "Or I guess that would be Detective Malone…and…Detective Malone, what I am is pissed that you didn't identify yourself immediately."

She leaned forward, elbows on the table. "There's not a snowflake's chance in hell I'll give you any information on any of my clients."

He nodded. "Good. I'm glad you feel that way. Because my job is the reason our meeting has to remain confidential." He glanced over his shoulder, checked out the room again.

A cop. A frigging cop. How could she have missed that?

She'd been so focused on meeting her anonymous caller, she'd totally spaced on Malone's edgy behavior…his scoping out the room earlier. Now, it all made sense. And, she realized on a satisfied note, it probably bothered the hell out of him that she was the one facing the exit and he'd had to sit with his back to it.

Petty. Yes. And it felt damned good.

Facing her again, expression dead serious, he said, "This is about a cold case…and an officer who's gone missing."

An officer who's…? That stopped her. "What do you mean?"

He hesitated, looked as if he was searching for the right words.

He couldn't be asking… Did he want her to— No. Cops didn't hire attorneys to do anything related to their cases. Hot or cold. From her experience, they didn't even like other law enforcement agencies horning in. Besides, it was no secret the relationship between cops and attorneys was sketchy at best.

She glanced around the room herself, making sure no one was within earshot. "Are you sure you don't want to talk about this at my office?"

His eyes brightened. "A much better idea," he said. "Let's go."

She hadn't meant right then, and even thinking about working with a cop set her teeth on edge. She'd made more enemies than friends in the Detroit PD over the years when looking into her father's records, but since taking the Devonshire case, she'd worked hard to smooth things over. A good working relationship with the PD was important and doing something like this could ruin the few inroads she'd made.

Still…this was huge.

And she *was* intrigued.

She looked around him to the front of the bar again.

"He's not going to show," Malone said, as if he'd read her mind. "And that should tell you something." He stood and held out a hand to help her exit the booth.

She didn't need help, but took his hand anyway. It was warm and firm and she kicked herself for even noticing. He was a cop, for God's sake. A damned, frigging cop.

She pulled her hand from his.

His eyelids lowered a little, and he gave her a slow, deliberate smile as he picked up the check. "I'll get this."

Most of the cops she knew hated defense attorneys so much they wouldn't pop for donut holes, much less dinner.

Malone wanted something…and he wanted it bad. She snatched the check from his hand. "Thanks, but you can't. It's a business expense."

And she was going to keep it that way.

CHAPTER FOUR

ON THE WAY to their vehicles, Remy closed the gap between them. He'd gotten her to talk to him. Made progress. But he wasn't kidding himself. She was going to be a hard sell. He knew that much just from watching her in court. Her steely determination would be tough to crack.

At their cars, he said, "I'll follow you." As he might've expected, she drove a practical car, an older model Focus, but when he'd done a background check on her, he saw she also owned a '73 Mercedes 450SL. A nice ride, and he'd made a mental note to ask her about it.

He slid into his Navigator, a black on black department vehicle confiscated in a drug bust, and which gave him some street cred. He waited so he could follow her to the law office. A woman alone at night in the D was a rape waiting to happen.

He doubted she'd think the same, though. He'd met a lot of women like her. Like his ex-wife. Confident. Self-contained. They could handle everything. Qualities he both liked and disliked in a woman. She probably carried mace.

Yeah. Way too much like his ex. Which was a good reminder to watch himself. He didn't want to tick off the one person who could help him. On the plus side, and although he'd heard the attorney rarely took on clients outside her wheelhouse, he'd seen the fire in her eyes when he'd told her it was a police case. Yeah— that was his hole card.

Women like Charlie Street loved challenges.

A half mile later, he pulled into the parking space next to her on the west side of the bright mustard-yellow building. She was out of her car instantly, keys in hand.

He exited his SUV and turning his back to the building, he did a quick one-eighty scan. The law office, a former hotel, was on a corner and faced south to the street, with an overgrown vacant lot, and a seven-foot hedge beyond the small parking area on the west, and an alley, and three boarded-up houses behind the property to the north.

Trees and bushes on two sides. And a dark van parked behind the shrubs.

"No garage?" he asked as she unlocked several locks on the side door.

She turned on an inside light and motioned him to follow. "It's in back, but the renovation is taking longer than I expected, so it's filled with other stuff." She flipped on another light and a room on his left with a glass partition lit up.

Her office, he figured since it had a desk and a full wall of books and file cabinets. Not fancy, which he should've guessed from his previous visit. Taking another look around, he saw four desks in an open area, but since it was only partially lit from the night lights in the office, he couldn't see beyond them. "Looks like you have a lot of space to renovate."

"I do," she said, urging him to follow into her office. She motioned for him to sit while she went behind the desk. Her chair, he noticed, was situated with a clear path to the door. She could get out quickly if needed, but the client couldn't.

He repositioned the client chair to face sideways to

the desk, so he had the wall at his back and a clear view. "You can do a lot with a place this size," he said as he dropped into the seat and made mental note of the exits.

She managed a thin-lipped smile, then pinned him with a let's-get-down-to-business stare. "We're not here to talk about my renovations, so why don't you tell me exactly what's going on, and why you think you need someone to do what the police should be doing."

Nothing like getting right to the point. No putting the client at ease or anything like that. Then again, it *was* after hours and he had interrupted her evening. He'd thought her a hard-ass earlier that day, but she had talked to him at the bar, and now they were here.

She was a master of the unexpected. He hadn't expected her to do either one. Especially since it was late, and he couldn't help noticing the tightness around her ice-blue eyes, the half-moons of darkness below.

Still, he needed to chat first...do a little bonding to convince her to take the job. Because apparently, his wit and charm wasn't going to cut it. "Okay. What's going on is that I need someone to find a police officer who went missing six months ago, and I need someone outside the department to do it because the department has stopped investigating."

Her finely arched brows V'd in the middle. "Isn't that what they do when they have no more leads? Stop investigating."

"When a cop is involved, the department never stops investigating. And that's the problem."

"Six months is a long time."

He nodded, shifted and leaned forward, his arm on the desk. "I know. God knows, I know. The statistics aren't good," he said, brushing a hand through his hair. "But I need to know. What matters is finding out where Adam is—and if someone is responsible for his disappearance."

"Are you saying he might be alive—that he might have purposefully disappeared?"

Remy shook his head. "No. No way. Adam was a multi-decorated cop, dedicated to his job and his family. He would never do that."

"But you do think that after all this time he might still be alive somewhere?"

He looked straight at her. "I can't think anything otherwise. He has a family, a wife and three little kids. They need him."

He saw her eyes soften at the mention of Adam's family, so he added, "He could be hurt and in hiding somewhere...or who knows. He could have amnesia." He shrugged. "Lots of possibilities, and without a trace of him anywhere, we can't assume anything other than he's gone missing."

Her patient expression said she knew he wasn't telling her everything. And she was right. He couldn't. Wouldn't. Not until he had evidence.

"I still don't understand what you expect to come of this. If all the efforts of the Detroit PD can't come up with anything when it's one of their own, why do you think I would be able to do anything different?"

"Because your record for finding missing people is flawless. You're the best in the business." He hauled in a lungful of air. "And I need everything to be completely confidential. No one can know I'm doing this."

"The laws regarding confidentiality are clear, Mr. Malone. For every client."

He leaned back, still looking for the fissure in the granite, a crack in the rock. Everyone was vulnerable in some area. He smiled as he said, "I know, but given the scope of what I want to do, it's still a concern. And it's Remy, by the way. I feel really old when people call me Mr. Malone."

No return smile. In fact, she eyed him as if she thought he was being deceptive, or maybe had another agenda.

"Okay. Well, I'm sorry...Remy," she finally said, her voice firm—polite and professional. "Unless you wish to sue the Detroit Police Department for not doing their job, I don't see a case here."

"I don't want to hire you as an attorney. I want to hire you to investigate."

"And I don't see that as anything other than a waste of your time and money. We would simply be repeating what the police have already done." Her tongue darted out to moisten her lips. "And it's also my policy to work with...a different clientele."

Fuck. He'd expected she might say no, only not so quickly. "But you do make exceptions." He cocked his head, unable to keep his eyes from wandering to the V-neckline of her shirt. She brought one hand up to touch her neck, effectively covering her nicely rounded breasts. Her creamy latte-colored skin looked—

"Rarely," she said, bringing him back on point. "And when I make an exception, there's always a compelling reason."

His blood surged. He shifted position. "I have good reason, and it's as compelling as any reason some people you represent might have."

Her eyes lit up. "Excuse me?"

"Sorry. But it's no secret you're representing Lucy Devonshire, and I can't help wondering why you'd take on a client who's obviously guilty."

"My motives don't matter, Detective Malone. Justice is what matters."

He nodded agreeably. "Right. I get that. Justice is a noble goal, something we all want. But what I meant is that it doesn't seem logical for you to take a case you can't win."

Her eyes hardened like chips of steel. He'd said the wrong thing. Again. "I mean it's gotta be a huge challenge when everything about the murder has been publicized so much. And you have to admit, her profession doesn't exactly make her a sympathetic defendant. Hard to find someone who believes she didn't do it, or have a hand in it somehow."

The edges of her mouth tipped up just a hair. She nodded. "Exactly."

He'd walked right into answering his own question. She didn't believe the client would get an unbiased trial. But did she really believe the woman was innocent?

"I don't take cases based on whether I'll win or not. I represent clients I believe are innocent and who I believe I can best represent. And that's why I can't take your case, Detective Malone. I don't believe I'm the best person to help you."

*What the hell...*he hadn't even fully explained.

"I'm sorry." She stood—the ubiquitous body language for "don't let the door hit you in the ass on your way out."

He steeled his nerves. If she thought he was going to give up and go away that easily, she wasn't as perceptive as he'd thought.

"I'll be happy to give you a list of professionals who have considerable expertise in locating missing persons if you'd like."

What he'd like was to knock her off that fucking white horse she thought she was riding. And then have angry make-up sex with her on the fucking desk.

He forced a smile. "Thanks, but I've done research, and made my own list. I don't need someone to locate a missing person," he said, fighting his basic instincts to take her down a peg.

"I need the best investigator in Detroit to find out

What happened to an officer of the law...and who's responsible. I need someone familiar with the justice system and police procedures...and who can conduct an investigation without drawing attention to me. Someone who can keep their mouth shut." He cleared his throat. "Someone with connections."

The attorney's chin came up. He'd irritated her. She probably expected he'd just accept her answer and go away.

Standing, she shuffled some papers on her desk, and then looked directly at him, her gaze hard and unyielding. "If you need someone with connections—" she said quietly, evenly, as she came around the desk. "—maybe you should talk to your father."

He flinched. *What?* Where had that come from?

She crossed to the door. "Good night, Detective Malone."

Charlie closed the outside door, fastened the chain, bolted all three locks, then turned and sagged against the refinished hardwood. She'd barely let out a long breath when her cell phone rang. She pulled it out and checked the ID.

She clicked on. "Hello Landon."

"Dempsey said there was an incident today."

She let out a long breath. "There was no incident, just a guy who wanted to talk to me."

"You sound tired."

"Tired? Hah. No. I mean yes. It's been a long day. The trial went overtime, the media were like a pack of ravenous wolves, some jerk on way home didn't like my driving, another client showed up before I walked in the office door, and the man I was supposed to meet tonight didn't show, but some other dude did and interrupted my dinner, and now I really, really need a really, really big glass of wine and to fall asleep in front of the TV." She took a quick breath. "On the plus side, no one shot at me."

Landon was silent for the longest time. Then, "This from my totally unflappable sister. I'm excited."

"I'm serious. The trial is almost over and Dempsey has another job, so I told him to go ahead."

More silence.

"I'll be fine. Really."

"You don't know that."

"Unless you can see into the future, I'm gonna go with it."

"Damn. I can never win with you."

"In this instance, I'd rather be right than you."

He sighed, and she said, "I'll keep you posted…and I'll see you at Mom's for breakfast on Sunday."

Hanging up, her heart warmed. Landon was younger than her and yet, somehow, he'd taken on the role of protector. He would make someone a good husband someday.

Back in her office, she picked up her jacket, took her Ruger from the bottom drawer, put it in her messenger bag, and headed to her apartment upstairs, unbuttoning her blouse on the way. Malone had given her a lot to think about. If she was stupid enough to take his bait.

The scenario he presented was another that could have no good end. Investigating the investigators, while supremely tempting, was way outside the mission and goals of the Street Law team.

From the time she'd passed the bar, she'd vowed to commit her life to helping those who, through whatever twist of fate, weren't going to get a fair shake in court because they had no money…or were otherwise disadvantaged.

Equal justice for all. That meant limiting her clients

to those who needed help the most, and it meant wearing a lot of different hats. While the firm represented a select few clients who had legal issues, most of the firm's work involved investigations, finding children in parental abductions, negotiations and, if necessary, extractions. And her crew *was* good, just as Malone had said. The best.

Detective Malone did not fit her clientele profile in any way, shape, or form. He had a good job…and a rich father. He could get anyone he wanted to do his bidding, or at least his father could.

So, why pick her? Why not get his father to pull some strings to investigate his friend's disappearance? Most law enforcement officers she knew had a list of contacts they used to get things done. If a law was bendable, an official bribable, or a snitch available for a price, they seemed to have no qualms if it served their purpose.

Approaching the landing halfway upstairs, she hesitated. This time, before going out, she'd made sure she'd locked the window, and she'd pulled down the old, yellowed shade that had been there since the place was a hotel. Her anxiety may not have been warranted, yet she couldn't keep her palms from sweating and her heart from hammering a hole in her chest.

A loud *bang* downstairs made her jump. Then another *bang*. The door. Someone at the door. She heard a man's voice, but couldn't make out what he'd said.

She went downstairs, her pulse thumping triple-time. It wasn't her brother, she'd just talked to him. And he wouldn't be coming over on a Friday night, anyway. He'd be out somewhere with his buddies, or on a date. A burglar wouldn't knock. And home invaders invaded homes where there was something to steal. She had nothing.

She pulled out her Ruger, set the bag on the floor.

As she moved closer, both hands on the raised gun, she heard a distinctive male voice say, "It's Detective Malone. It's important."

She sighed on a frustrated wave of relief. Unbelievable. Holy freaking unbelievable. What part of *no* did he not understand?

She stood for a moment, hands on her hips, shaking her head. She didn't have time for this. Rising on her toes to look through the peephole, she stopped short, remembering a scenario from a suspense novel she'd read where killers sometimes waited for the peephole to darken so they could shoot into it. Deadly. If you wanted someone dead.

And that was a seriously paranoid thought. Laughing, she shook her head. She must be getting punchy from sleep deprivation. She peered into the peephole and saw Malone, his face distorted in the curvature of the glass.

She walked back to her bag, picked it up, and stuffed the gun inside. If she ignored him, he'd go away eventually.

"Please, Ms. Street. If you won't open the door, then just tell me if one of your neighbors drives a dark-colored van."

Her stomach plummeted. In a flash she was back at the door, fingers flying over the locks. Leaving the safety chain on, she opened the door the few inches the chain allowed. "What did you say?"

"I asked if one of your neighbors owns a dark van. I saw one parked in back and when I started walking toward it, he took off."

She slammed the door, slipped off the chain, let him in, and latched the locks again. "He? You said, *he*. Did you see him? See who it was?"

The detective walked a little farther inside, stopping

near the light in the hallway outside her office. "No, I didn't. The person was large enough for me to think it was a man, but I can't be sure." His eyebrows gathered as he looked at her. "Do you know who it might be?"

It could've been a neighbor before. Still could be. If it was, no one in their right mind would sit there and wait for some stranger to walk over. Not at this time of night...not in this neighborhood. It would be normal to take off if you saw a man walking toward you. "No," she said. "I don't, but I've seen the van before."

"It's obvious it bothered you. Do you have any idea who it might be? An old boyfriend, maybe?"

"No." Nipping at the soft flesh inside her bottom lip, she shook her head again.

"If you don't know who it is, then how do you know it's not an old boyfriend?"

"Trust me. It's not an old boyfriend."

"Someone you have a problem with, then. A former client?"

Seeing his gaze drop to the vee where she'd opened the top of her shirt, she touched the silver Celtic knot pendant at her neck, her pulse quickening. "I don't have a problem with anyone, client or otherwise. But I have seen the van there before."

He looked away and they stood quietly for a moment, she feeling as if he were cross-examining her—and him looking very official as he did it.

"It probably *is* a neighbor's car, and I'm probably still a little skittish after what happened a few months ago."

Frowning again, he said, "What do you mean? What happened?"

He didn't know? If he'd done his research, he would know about the shooting three months ago. "Nothing, really. Just a kid prank that spooked me. And the brown van...now that I think about it, I really do think it belongs to a neighbor. I'm just not used to seeing anyone parked back there."

An awkward moment of silence hung between them, until he said, "What kind of kid prank?"

When she didn't respond immediately, he said, "If it involved the police, I can find out easily enough, so why don't we quit wasting time."

"It was one of those wrong place at the wrong time things. I was leaving a client's house near Six Mile and Chalmers, there were gunshots—" she cleared her throat "—and a boy died. The police chalked it up to a random act, teenagers partying."

"But?"

"No buts."

His gaze narrowed. Granted, she wasn't very convincing, but then she didn't have to be. It wasn't any of his business.

Except she did let him in, and she did ask about the van.

"I don't think about it except when something happens to make me remember, and then, sometimes, I get a little spooked. My imagination kicks in, and I start wondering things. Like if I'd seen the van somewhere before."

"You think…or you did?"

She shook her head. "No, I'm sure it's just my imagination. There are probably dozens of vehicles just like it and if I've had a long day…" She shrugged. "I'm fine."

Looking at her like a parent trying to pry the truth from his teenager, Remy waited, his gaze locked with hers.

She glanced away. "Really. I'm fine," she said, rubbing her upper arm. "Today has been a long day. I'm just super tired and need some sleep."

He studied her for another couple seconds. "Okay. I'll leave then, but if you think there's a problem, just give me a call." He handed her a card with a number written in on the bottom. "That's my personal number. And, if at any time, you'd like to hear the rest of what I have to say about my friend's disappearance, I'd really appreciate the opportunity to tell you."

Her nerves crawled on the outside of her skin. She'd probably let him stay all night to stand guard if he pressed. But he didn't. He just stood there looking as tired as she felt. And yet he'd come back to ask about the van. He was doing his job...being concerned about her safety.

Crap.

"O-kay," she finally blurted, then let out a slow sigh. "I can see you're not going to give up, so let's do it now." She walked into the work area, buttoning her shirt on the way, pulled out a chair at Max's desk, and set her purse on the floor beside it.

Max Scofield was her go-to investigator and although he had an office elsewhere, he rarely went there, preferring to use his desk at the Street Law office instead...social animal that he was.

The detective followed her and sat where she indicated at Gabe's desk. He glanced from left to right, then nodded toward the photos setting front and center. "Nice dog," he said. "A good watchdog?"

"I'm sure she would be, but Gabe doesn't let her out of his sight."

"Gabe? Another attorney for your firm?"

She nodded, but didn't feel like explaining. Gabriel Weatherly, a former Navy SEAL, was an attorney, but he had many other skills far more important for the work he did for her on contract.

Steepling her hands, she leaned back in the chair. "So, what else did you want to tell me?"

"Well, first of all, thank you. I really didn't think you'd listen to me, again." He gave her a quirk of a smile.

"But I am, so go on."

It was obvious he wanted to direct the conversation, and she could feel his resistance. He didn't like anyone to have the upper hand.

"Right," he said, his eyes never leaving hers as he reached to his inside pocket, pulled out a photo and handed it to her.

Two boys, about ten years old and one, she was pretty sure, was Malone. He had the same lazy-lidded eyes and well-defined lips...a wide, friendly smile that even at his young age could've charmed a prime rib from a hungry pit bull.

He leaned forward, hands on his knees. "That's Adam on the right. I'm on the left."

She glanced, then handed it back.

"We were more than friends," he said, brushing the photo with his thumb before pocketing it again. "He was like the brother my own brother wasn't. His family like the family I wished I'd had."

Really? She arched a brow. Malone was raised in a prominent, wealthy family, and he wasn't happy about it?

"That doesn't mean I didn't have a great family, but my mother died when I was ten and nothing was the same after that. Or maybe things were the same, but I didn't notice anything wrong before because she was the buffer." He shrugged. "After she died, my dad worked even more hours and my twin brother just kept doing what he always did...excelling in school and sports. They just went on with their lives."

He swallowed. "Adam's family filled the gaps for me. If it weren't for them, I might not be here today."

He looked to the side, definitely uncomfortable with revealing so much. Knowing what he was willing to do for someone he cared about melted a little of her resolve.

He drew a deep breath. "I owe Mr. and Mrs. Bentley. I owe them—and Adam—my life. If Adam is out there, I need to find him. His family deserves to know what happened. Where he is. They need closure."

Don't we all.

And I need to know I've done everything in my power to find him."

Exactly.

His gaze came back to hers. "And before you suggest again that I have my father pull strings to have the department reinvestigate, let me tell you I tried that. It's not an option. And second, I believe the department has deep-sixed this for a reason. I have it from a good source that Adam was working undercover on a deal going down with The Partnership."

He drew a paper from his pocket. "This is a list of people who could be involved. Or most likely know what happened."

Charlie took the paper, then dug her tortoiseshell reading glasses from her purse. Five names were on Malone's list. The first four were known members of the Detroit mafia, AKA The Partnership. The mafia from days of old was long gone and in its place a new partnership had emerged with members from different criminal groups, most of whom were well educated and white collar. But just as deadly. With ties to La Cosa Nostra, The Partnership was not to be messed with if you valued your life.

Seeing the last name on Malone's list, Charlie's breath hitched.

She read the names again. Was the detective playing her? Trying to get her to help him by feeding her some crumbs of hope? She'd been down that road so many times she was frigging hoped out. If Malone thought for one minute he could manipulate her…

"How did you come up with this list?"

"Research."

"Most are the usual mob suspects whenever anything big goes down. I could've made the same list without researching squat."

"Maybe." Remy angled his head. "But I have files of information, some of which came from the Detroit PD."

"What about the last name on your list? He's an outlier." She handed back the paper. "Do you have a file on him, too?"

Remy glanced at the paper. "I do."

"Does he work for The Partnership?"

"That I don't know. I just got the name a few days ago, did some preliminary research and I'm waiting on results."

"I thought you said you had a file."

"I do, but it's not complete. Why do you want to know about him?"

"No reason." The name was the same as a man she'd been trying to find for years. A man who seemed to have vanished into thin air after testifying against her father at his trial. Joey Drakar. If Joey Drakar was involved in Adam Bentley's disappearance, he must've resurfaced in the past two years—after she'd stopped looking for him. If he'd returned to Detroit, she didn't need the detective's information to find him. If Malone could find him, so could she.

"At least tell me you'll think about it, Ms. Street." He stood, as if ready to leave.

"I will. I'll think about it." She rose, too. Folded her arms over her chest. "Where did you say you saw that van, again?"

He peered at her from under his brows. "Do you mean the one you said belongs to a neighbor?"

She shifted her feet. "The one I thought *could* belong to a neighbor. I didn't say I was sure it did."

He held her gaze. "I saw it in back. Behind the hedges. But, like I said, whoever it was took off." He waited a second and then added, "I can hang around if you'd like. Sleep on the couch in your office." He nodded toward the black faux leather unit against the wall, which had no arms and was only two cushions long.

She didn't know which was worse, that he knew she was lying...or that she was feeling vulnerable. "Thanks. I appreciate the offer, but I'll be fine."

The jangle of her cell phone made her jump. As she took it from her purse, she glanced at the caller ID. Her mom. Relieved to get out of the current conversation, she answered and took a couple steps away from the detective.

"It's late. What's going on?" Head down, she paced in the other direction.

"It's only ten-thirty. It's not late," her mom said, her voice sharp.

She could picture her mom standing there with her arms crossed, her current favorite posture since she'd met Wayne and decided to become a new person taking charge of her life.

"I'm not one of those seniors who eats dinner at four in the afternoon and goes to bed at nine, you know."

Although Malone's eyes were cast down, she knew he was watching her. Evaluating. Deciding his next move to get her to do what he wanted.

"Yes, I know. But it's late for you to be calling."

"Late for who?"

Charlie gnashed her teeth. Since meeting Wayne, her mom had changed so much it felt as if she'd had a personality transplant. The woman had gone from being a pleasant, helpful mother, to a self-absorbed pain-in-the-ass know-it-all.

"As surprising as it might seem, I don't fall asleep

in my soup at dinner and I can actually stay awake long enough for the late news."

"I didn't mean anything, Mom. I have someone—I mean…I'm working, and I can't talk right now."

"It's Friday night. You shouldn't be working. You should be out having fun."

"I will be as soon as I'm done."

"You can take a few minutes for your mother, can't you?"

"Of course. But just not right now. We'll have lots of time to talk tomorrow." When her mom didn't respond right away, she added, "You wanted me to help you with the refinance papers."

A long pause. Then, "What time are you coming?"

"One. That's the time you said to come. Don't you remember?"

Another long pause, then, "Of course I do, and I'm tired of you asking if I do."

"Sorry. I didn't mean—"

"You never do. I have to go." Her mother clicked off.

Surprised at the abrupt end of the call, it took Charlie a second before she said, "Okay, talk tomorrow. Bye." She touched the "end call" icon and stood for a moment, letting her blood pressure calm before saying, "Sorry. Family stuff." What she meant was *men-o-pause*.

Malone nodded, then shrugged and started for the exit. Once there, he said, "So, you'll think about it, then."

Also not a question. "Yes," she said, following him to the door. "I'll think about it." But there was no way in hell she was going to do it. What would be the benefit? She'd feel guilty taking his money when, given the time elapsed, his buddy was probably dead. No one's life was hanging in the balance.

He didn't want to hear that, but he had to know it.

But she *was* curious about his list. One name in particular. Joey Drakar. Still, for all she knew, Malone could've added Drakar's name to his list because he knew it was one she hadn't been able to track down. If he'd done a background check on her, he knew about her father and that she'd investigated his case for years and come up empty. He didn't act like he knew, but any skilled detective would have done his research.

She rubbed her temples. Too many questions. Between her anonymous caller and Malone's list with a connection to the very person whose testimony convicted her dad, she didn't know what to think. Except that any new information could be the critical piece of evidence in finding out who framed her father—and who was responsible for his death. The two things combined almost seemed an omen of some kind.

Man, taking Malone's case was all too tempting. He'd mentioned a police cover-up. If there was one, the people of Detroit should know. And finding Drakar, the only person who was there the night her father was arrested, could be a game-changer. Joey Drakar was the only person who knew what really happened that night.

But using information from a client's case for her own purposes wasn't ethical. Not only that, it would lead to getting her hopes up, again, and for what?

No matter how many times she'd debated the issue with her family over the years, the question was always the same. Her father was dead. What difference did it make if he was framed or not?

There was no professional reason for her to take the detective's case. The Detroit PD had already investigated his friend's disappearance. If there were police issues, Malone should be taking it up with the police department's Internal Investigations unit. And if Drakar was out there, she could find him on her own.

There was no logical reason for her to represent Malone.

And yet...she was one hundred percent certain, she'd regret it if she didn't.

CHAPTER FIVE

REMY SCOPED OUT the area behind the Street Law office before sliding into his vehicle.

Nothing. A couple of cats chasing each other. Or a rat. That was it. Still, he wasn't comfortable leaving her alone. The attorney had been uncertain about the van, didn't know if it was a neighbor's vehicle or not, and she'd seemed reluctant to tell him anything more.

Even though she'd said she was fine, she'd jumped like a frightened kid when the phone rang. Her hand shook when she'd answered. She'd tried to hide it, but he could see how edgy she was when he left. If she was fine, he was Santa Claus.

The van had taken off when he'd approached it earlier, and, yeah, it could have been a neighbor ready to go somewhere. But in his book, it was suspicious behavior.

A few minutes later, sitting behind the wheel, he pulled his coat collar up, little defense against the chilly night air, and saw lights go on in the middle window on the second floor in the attorney's building. Saw a slim shadow pass by.

Difficult to make out who it was or even what gender, but not in his mind's eye. He pictured Charlie Street in her bedroom, slowly unbuttoning the last few buttons on her shirt, button by button, her long mahogany hair falling softly over her breasts.

If he hadn't been in her office on business, he may never have left. Despite a personality disorder that made her want to save the world, criminals included, there was something about her he liked. She was different. Intelligent. Edgy.

He hadn't had a woman challenge him in a long time. Damn, he got hard just thinking about it.

The shadow disappeared and the light went out. Good. He slouched in the seat, rubbed his hands together. He was there for one reason only…to find out what happened to Adam. And he needed Charlie Street, the investigator, not the woman, to help him.

It pissed the hell out of him that she wanted to blow him off. If all he needed were an adequate attorney or investigator, he'd have been out of there faster than a man discovering his date had herpes.

But he didn't need just anyone. He needed someone with her skills to do what he couldn't. Someone who was always poking into police records to get information. No one would question her sniffing around again, only this time it would be for a different reason.

It was perfect. Would've been if she hadn't shut him down without even hearing him out.

For the second time he'd left her office feeling like a kid who'd been told to leave the room. But even as pissed as he was, knowing someone had taken a shot at her, he couldn't just dismiss the van when he saw it. In the end, it had worked to his advantage.

He hadn't gotten a yes, but at least she was going to think about it. In his experience, that was as good as a yes.

All he had to do was push her over the edge.

Charlie awoke with visions of her daddy still in her head—and he was whispering the name, *Joey Drakar. Joey Drakar.*

She'd tossed and turned and during the night must've kicked the covers to the floor. A fine sheen of sweat covered her body, naked except for her panties. Her head swirled with all she had to do—a trial to continue on Monday and the Stratten investigation to get started, and those were only the most recent things on her list.

So why should she feel guilty about not taking Detective Malone's case?

The pain in his eyes when he'd shown her the photo of him and his friend had been almost palpable. No matter how stoic Malone pretended to be, she saw it, and she'd wanted to shut it out, distance herself from feeling anything. But he'd blindsided her, reminded her of her own losses, enough that she'd felt his pain as if it were her own.

Another good reason to stay planets away from Malone. Investigating the same people she was sure had something to do with framing her father couldn't help but open up all the old wounds.

She'd spent nearly all her extra time during law school studying her dad's court files and had come up empty. Even the little extra time she'd had when working as a public defender, she'd spent trying to find some shred of information that might prove he was innocent. And had never found a single thing.

How much more time was she going to spend trying to fix the unfixable?

Rolling over in the queen-sized bed, she grabbed the extra pillow and covered her head. But Joey Drakar's name kept playing over and over…and Malone's eyes, dark with pain, kept staring at her. Damn. She might as well get up and do something.

She tossed the pillow, flicked on her bedside lamp, got up, pulled on one of her brother's old T-shirts, and then walked to the spare bedroom two doors down from hers, the only light in the long hallway coming from the night-light in the bathroom.

She'd avoided going through the boxes of her father's things her mother had recently given her, but not because she wanted to forget her father as her mother did. She'd avoided it because the memories were too painful.

She'd gone through her father's things several times over the years, and the contents had never shed any new light. But even as painful as the memories were, she'd never give them up like her mom had. It was all she had left.

And all these years, she'd thought her mother felt the same. Her mom had been inconsolable when Charlie's father died, said she didn't know how she could live without him. Charlie had thought her mother was going to die, too. From a broken heart.

Eventually, Diana O'Meara Street had come around, pieced her life together, had a good career as an elementary schoolteacher and, finally, twenty-five years later, she'd retired, started teaching art classes, and begun dating. And then, after one month with Wayne Peterson, her mom said she was done living in the past and had given Charlie all of her father's belongings.

It was as if her mom wanted to erase Alejandro Montoya Street from her heart and mind forever.

Charlie heaved a sigh. Sometimes she almost wished everything people believed about her father were true. At least that way, she could stop thinking about it whenever something came up to remind her. Stop feeling guilty.

How ironic that Malone thought she was the best

person for the job when she couldn't even solve her father's twenty-five year old murder.

She clicked the wall switch in the spare bedroom. A shadeless lamp on the floor in the corner cast a garish slash of light against the wall, leaving the rest of the room in deep shadow.

Like the master bedroom, the guest room had been drywalled and taped, the oak floors and woodwork refinished, but both rooms still needed painting and new light fixtures. And window treatments.

If she took Malone's case, she might have some money after paying bills to continue refurbishing. It would also float her during the time she did pro bono work. At the closet, she turned the knob on the lone light hanging from an electrical cord. That needed replacing, too.

The boxes she wanted were stashed next to the door, so she pulled out two of the smallest and brought them to the table. Staring at the containers, a heavy dread washed over her. This…these few boxes…was all that was left of her father. One man's life contained in a half dozen cardboard boxes.

Her throat felt scratchy as she swallowed and opened the flaps on the first box, labeled "Gym & Miscellaneous." The contents were mostly loose documents, sales slips, and old newspapers.

She sorted the papers into piles, one for invoices and receipts, one for newspapers and clippings, one for letters, most of which were from Charlie and Landon to their dad during the brief time he was in prison. She'd written a letter every single day.

Her hand shook as she picked up one of the letters. Landon's five-year-old printing was neat and precise, his drawings rendered in scroll-like designs, his artistic talent already evident.

She didn't have to look at her own letters to know

what they contained. Charlie's drawings were mostly girly hearts and flowers. She'd wanted them to be pretty, she remembered, to cheer her daddy up and to let him know how much she loved and missed him.

On the back of each envelope she'd printed, "I miss you, Daddy. Please come home." Then, in smaller printing under her name, she'd written, "I am sorry, Daddy. I love you. I love you. I love you." She'd drawn little tears between the hearts at the end.

She'd ended every letter with the same words. "I'm sorry, Daddy."

The same words she'd screamed at him when the police dragged him away.

She'd never seen him again. Even though her mother had said her dad missed her when he was in jail, when they brought home her father's effects, the letters were all there...unopened. Her father had never read them...never even knew how sorry she was.

Pain constricted in her chest. She was still sorry. And she still missed him. More than she could ever have imagined.

It wasn't freaking fair. She crushed the letter into a ball and flung it back into the box, cursing the people responsible. And the God who'd never answered her prayers and had let an innocent man suffer and die.

She swiped at her tears with the back of one hand. She was ten when she'd realized she was on her own. Kim, her best friend, had been hit by a drunk driver and dragged down the street under the car. Kim had died and the drunk, who'd hired the best attorney money could buy, got a DUI. A slap on the wrist and a fine.

Until then, she'd thought the God she'd been raised to believe in had His reasons, but He'd taken the two people who meant the most to her. And He kept taking. Next had been her grandmother and then Mimi, her sweet little dog. It wasn't fair.

God wasn't fair.

And He'd made it perfectly clear…if you wanted help, you had to help yourself. So she did. College, law school, buying the hotel, it was all her. She'd had no help other than student loans.

She picked up a doll-sized pair of leather boxing gloves and held them up. Her father's Seventh Street Boxing Gym, run by her uncle Emilio until Landon was old enough to take over, made no money. But it was there, a part of her dad she never wanted to see go away.

Unlike her mother, Charlie had loved going to see her dad at the gym, liked joking around, and she even liked the teasing she got from the guys. She still did.

She set the tiny gloves aside and glanced at some invoices, among them a handwritten receipt for a loan that said "Paid in full." *Ten thousand dollars*. The date was after her father's death, but there was nothing to identify who had paid it or what it was for. Since the gym had no mortgage, neither she nor Landon had been involved in the finances. Her uncle took care of everything.

She placed the receipt aside and slumped against the back of the chair, closed her eyes. Papers. Boxes of papers. That was it. She stared at the box for a moment. Then she leaned forward and in one broad sweep of an arm, she sent the pile into the wastebasket next to the table. Deep breath. Her pulse accelerated. Good. Yes. *Very good*.

She found another stack of newspaper clippings that had no significance to anything she knew of and chucked them, too. When she finished, the box was empty, and feeling a strange sense of accomplishment, she straightened. Tomorrow, she'd go through another box and do the same thing.

Arching her back, she stretched her arms over her head. Maybe now she could actually get some sleep. As she stood, she saw a folded piece of paper on the floor and knelt to pick it up. Unfolding it, she recognized the handwriting as her dad's.

It was a list of names, a few she recognized—former boxers, none of whom were still boxing, and at the bottom was another name, Merceury, a name she'd come across once before and had checked out. And like most everything she'd looked at to see if it had any significance, she'd found nothing.

She stuffed the paper and the little boxing gloves in her pocket. Detective Malone had Joey Drakar's name on his list, maybe he'd know something about the other name, too?

She went back to her bedroom, set the paper and the gloves on her nightstand, shut off the light, and then forced herself to the window, her heart doing a *rat-a-tat-tat* in her throat. She had to know. Hands clammy, she lifted the edge of the old sheet she'd hung over the bottom half of the window and peeked out.

A lone street light cast a yellowed glow over much of the parking space next to the building, but toward the back where the van had been, it was too dark to make out anything. All she saw were trash cans and, at the corner of the building, a black SUV.

Black SUV? She drew back. *Malone?*

She glanced at the clock on the nightstand. Four a.m. Had he been there the whole night? Had he seen the brown van again? Whatever his reason, he obviously didn't want her to know he was there.

Only she did, and a warm sense of comfort washed over her. Was that what it would be like to be married? To have someone with her all the time? Someone who made her feel safe enough that she might even be able to sleep soundly...

Except now that she'd seen Remy, she doubted she'd be able to sleep at all. Early spring nights were still cold. She couldn't leave him sitting in his car the rest of the night.

She rummaged through her purse for the card he'd given her at Slows, picked up her phone, went over and peered out the window—just in time to see him drive away.

She stood there for a moment. Smiling. He must've decided the threat—if there'd even been one—was gone. Or he'd moved to a different location.

Sliding into bed, the smooth sheets felt like a gentle caress against her skin. She closed her eyes and envisioned strong tanned hands stroking her body, caressing her, reaching down between her legs.

Two years since she'd been in a relationship and her body was letting her know it. Otherwise, why would she even consider fantasizing about Malone? A cop, who, while ruggedly good-looking, wasn't even handsome. He looked fit, but not muscular. He dressed well, but his clothes were hardly GQ material. He was fairly average in about every way.

And yet, the man stood out in a crowd as if he'd climbed on a pulpit wearing nothing but a smile.

Her father'd had a similar charismatic effect on people and, now, thinking about it, Malone reminded her a little of her dad…a passionate man who didn't know how to care just a little bit. When something was important, he got involved, pursued it to the end.

Malone had that same energy, that same intensity about him. He wasn't going to quit pursuing the disappearance of his friend, no matter what.

Just as she'd once vowed she would never quit searching for the person who had framed her father.

Only she had. It was a matter of survival, both mentally and financially.

But now, knowing Malone had information and not acting on it was like knowing there was a cure for cancer and she had to keep it a secret.

It would eat at her. Drive her crazy.

What she needed to know was if Malone really did have useful information...and that he wasn't just blowin' smoke to get her to take his case.

CHAPTER SIX

"WHEN, EXACTLY, DID your daughter disappear, Mrs. Linski?"

The fiftyish woman on the other side of Charlie's refinished thrift-store desk glanced to her clasped hands, then back to Charlie.

"I don't know. Six weeks, maybe. I called the police as soon as I heard from the school she was gone. They told me because Ella had ran away before and the police wouldn't be real quick to do anything. Except it's been a month since I talked to the police and I don't think anyone is even lookin' for her anymore."

Charlie nodded. If she had a penny for each time a client complained about the police, she'd be able to retire, or at least experience the thrill of buying a pair of Louboutins.

The woman mopped her forehead with her sleeve.

"What's your daughter's name, Mrs. Linski?"

"Ella. She never liked her name, but—"

"Did the school notify the police about Ella's disappearance before you did?"

"They told me they did."

"When did you say you last spoke with someone from the police department?"

The Detroit PD dealt with hundreds of homicides every year, but the murders of four young girls in the past two months had the community in panic about a possible serial killer at large. Under the circumstances, it was hard to believe police response to a missing teenager wouldn't be lightning fast.

"I haven't talked to them since they told me they had no new information."

Dark purple crescents under the woman's eyes suggested she'd spent many sleepless nights worrying about her daughter. She looked as tired as Charlie felt, having barely slept last night thinking about Malone and his missing friend. And Smith, obviously another crackpot, about whom she wasn't going to waste another thought.

"That was right after I heard she went missing. They said…" She choked, unable to finish.

Charlie took a box of Kleenex from her drawer and handed it to the woman. She would've liked to give the worried mother something to pin her hopes on, but from what she'd heard so far, hope would be hard to come by. In six weeks, if the girl was a runaway, she was long gone. If there was foul play, the time period for finding her alive was next to nil.

Reaching for a tissue, Mrs. Linski continued. "The police said they're doing everything they can, and I should just be patient, and she'll probably come back."

The woman's eyes pooled with tears. "I know I wasn't a very good mother or she wouldn't have been in the group home in the first place. But she was coming around, and the last time we talked, she t-told me…" She bowed her head, her voice almost inaudible. "Sh-she said she loved me. She never said that before. Not since she was a little girl, and I—" She dabbed at her nose with a tissue again. "—I was sure she was going to make it this time."

On the last word, Mrs. Linski released a deep, chest-hitching moan and tears flowed unchecked down her ruddy cheeks. Her shoulders shook as she threw her arms on the desk and collapsed over them, her body bouncing with each uncontrollable sob.

Charlie swallowed, her throat tightened.

She touched the distraught woman's hand. "I'm sorry about your daughter, Mrs. Linski. What is it you wish me to do?"

The woman hiccupped out one last sob, straightened, and then blotted her cheeks, revealing fingernails bitten to the quick. She raised her chin, lips thinning as anger and determination visibly rose to the fore. "It's just Sandra. Not Mrs… I'm not married."

"Okay, Sandra. What is it you wish to do?"

"I told the school I wasn't going to forget it. I told them I was coming here. They didn't seem happy about that, said I should leave it to the police. But I can't…not when they aren't doing anything."

A complaint she heard all too often. Inaction by the police was generally because there was no new information to go on, but few parents would accept it as fact when their child's life was hanging in the balance.

"I-I want to find Ella," she said, looking at Charlie as if she should know. "I read about you in the paper before, how you found that senator's son who was missing for a long time, and the police couldn't find him either." She took a breath, her features hardening. "And I want to find out why nobody is doing anything. File some charges or something."

If only it were that easy.

"Everyone says you can find anyone."

Charlie suppressed a grin. It always came back to that. The investigative part of her business had developed organically after she'd spent years investigating her father's records, and after she'd located and rescued an abducted child who'd been missing for over a year—and whose father happened to be a state senator.

The irony was that she'd been working for Reston, Barrett, and Brown representing the senator over an allegation of misuse of state funds, something totally unrelated to the abduction and, during the investigative stages, discovered information that led to the child's whereabouts.

The publicity surrounding the case had propelled her into the limelight as the John Walsh of Michigan, a title she'd never live up to, but one that suddenly broadened her life's mission. Not long after, she'd left Reston, Barrett and Brown to do what she'd always wanted.

"People think because we're poor and had problems that I don't care," Sandra Linski went on. "But that's not true. I love my daughter. She's just got in with the wrong kids. That's all. She's a good girl. She really is."

Way too familiar with the story, Charlie nodded her understanding. Sadly, most of her clients had a similar lament. No money, kids getting in with the wrong group, drugs, runaways, absent parents, parents on crack or heroin…it all went together.

The cycle of poverty fed on itself and without some kind of intervention, would continue to do so. Mothers would cry over lost sons and daughters, fathers would escape into drugs, flee from responsibility they weren't equipped to handle, or go to jail. Families would descend deeper and deeper into poverty hell— Children would run away, disappear, and even die.

The unfairness of it sucked. A few people, through some lucky fluke of intellect or sheer determination— or with the help of a dedicated mentor—made it out. Far too many didn't.

"If I can pay a little at a time—"

"Don't worry about that. Right now the important thing is to see what I can do to help you." *If anything.*

The woman's eyes narrowed, as if she hadn't heard correctly, and then a second later, filled with relief. She blinked back a new rush of tears. "Oh, thank you, Miss Street. I heard you were a good person and they were right. I can't thank you enou—"

Smiling, Charlie held up a hand. "To start, we need a record of everything that happened. And any other information you have."

When it came to missing persons, the results weren't always what parents or loved ones hoped for—and it was Charlie's policy to ensure clients were informed of all contingencies beforehand.

Most of her cases in which a child went missing involved parental abduction, a different investigation than a teen runaway. And this one, from what the Linski woman said, didn't tick all the teen runaway boxes. The girl had disappeared from the group home just when it had looked as if her life was coming together. Charlie had no idea how much of the woman's interpretation of events was accurate, though.

It would be normal for a parent to place blame, but the disappearance of a sixteen-year-old girl, even a serial runaway, should be cause for concern in any city. The Detroit PD should be all over it, but sadly, it wouldn't be the first time a case got ignored.

"I'll tell you whatever you need to know. I'll give you whatever information I have. But I don't know her friends or anything. Ella never told me too much and neither did the people at the group home. I told the police that right off. Officer Glover said they'd do everything possible, but then I never heard from him again."

Officer Glover. Charlie recognized the name. She'd heard it in connection with some scandal. A police investigation, maybe. She blanked on it, but made a mental note to check it out at some point.

"That's important information, Sandra. I'm going to have you meet with my legal assistant so you can tell her everything. She'll have a few questions for you, too. Once we take a look at all the information, we'll know how to proceed and we will be in touch."

"Mom? You here?" Charlie opened the screen door at her mother's turn of the century home in Corktown. The inside door was wide open. She made a mental note to tell her mother that no matter how nice the home renovations in the community were, leaving her door open was an invitation to burglars…and other sleazy characters.

"Mom? It's Charlie." She heard low voices. Odd. She hadn't seen any other cars in front where she'd parked.

"I'm in the kitchen, dear."

And obviously not alone. Her mother hadn't mentioned having anyone else over for lunch, but maybe Landon had stopped by. Or Wayne. No. Not Wayne. She got a sour taste in her mouth just thinking about him. That would definitely curb her appetite.

Charlie's brother had expressed the same thoughts she'd been having about her mom's new boyfriend being too controlling. She had to make time to talk to her mom about it, but she wasn't looking forward to it. Her mother's mood swings these days were erratic to say the least.

The scent of apples and cinnamon wafted as Charlie made her way through the living and dining rooms to the kitchen at the back of the clapboard house. Like most of the renovated homes in Corktown, which had been designated a Historic District in the 1970s, the old wood floors, doors, and woodwork had been sanded and refinished, the electrical and plumbing systems updated.

Wherever possible her mom kept the original fixtures—chandeliers, doorknobs, kitchen cabinets and the old claw-footed tub. Any replacements were replicas of the original. Her mother had maintained the turn-of-the-century feel in furnishings and décor, but Charlie couldn't help wishing her mom had kept the comfy furniture they'd had when she and Landon were growing up.

Going through the archway into the kitchen, the smell of cinnamon started her salivary glands working overtime. Apple pie, she decided as the scent got stronger, and hoped she was right. Her mom's apple pie was the best in town, and she couldn't wait to dive into a warm slice.

Then she saw Malone.

Her mouth went dry.

The last time she'd seen a cop in this kitchen, she'd been eight years old. And the police had been taking her father away in handcuffs.

Her mother hurried across the room, coffeepot in one hand, a slice of apple pie on a plate in the other. "I was just pouring some coffee. Would you like some, too?" her mother chirped, her tone syrup sweet.

Once she was able to breathe, again, Charlie faced Malone sitting at the round oak table. "What are you doing here?"

Her mother's mouth dropped open. "Charlie!" She set the pie and coffee pot on the table.

Malone's lips drew into a tight smile as he deferred to her mother for an answer.

Feet apart, arms crossed, Charlie glanced from one to the other.

When her mom hesitated, Malone said, "It's business."

"What kind of business?"

"Please sit, Charlie," her mother urged.

Every nerve in Charlie's body vibrated. "I'm sorry, Detective, but anything you have to discuss with my mother, you can discuss with me...as her attorney."

"Excuse me!" Diana stepped between Charlie and Malone, her long copper-colored ponytail swishing in Malone's face as she did.

Her mother wore jeans and a black Detroit Eastern Market T-shirt, and in no way did she look old enough to be the mother of a thirty-something daughter and a twenty-eight-year-old son. Getting married young and having children before you were twenty had its advantages.

"I don't know what's going on with you, Charlie, but I don't need a lawyer." Diana raised her chin to look at her daughter, who stood a half foot taller than her mother's mere five-feet two inches. "I'm perfectly capable of speaking for myself."

When her mother was mad or determined, she reminded Charlie of the little bantam rooster her grandpa had kept in their back yard when Charlie was little. Still, her mother was so naïve, it was hard to believe she'd grown up in the city.

"Nothing is going on," Charlie answered. "I just don't think it's wise for you to answer questions without knowing why they're being asked."

"*You're* the one who doesn't know what's going on, not me," her mother huffed. "And *you* would know if *you'd* asked instead of jumping to conclusions."

Charlie counted to seven. Took a breath. "I did ask...the minute I walked in, and the answer was, 'It's business.' And when a cop says that, it means you need a lawyer."

"Well, that's all wrong. I called the police to report something and Detective Malone came out to talk to me about it."

"What?" Charlie crossed to her mom. "You called

the police? What happened? Are you okay?"

"Of course I'm okay. I don't know why I even called."

"What happened?"

"Nothing. I thought I saw something and got nervous. But it was really nothing."

Charlie took the chair next to Remy. "Whatever it was, you thought enough of it to call the police. That's not nothing."

Diana shrugged. "I thought I saw someone watching the house and called the police." She sat across from Charlie, folded her hands in front of her on the table. "Then, when I realized I was wrong, it was too late. Detective Malone was already here."

Charlie nodded. Her mother hadn't been spooked for a long time. Not since she'd started dating Wayne— the one and only good thing Charlie could think of about her mother's boyfriend. "You saw someone where?"

"It's okay," her mom said, frowning. "I was wrong. Let's just drop it."

Right. Charlie knew from her mom's icy tone that it was best to do that. At least for now...while the detective was still there. She took a deep breath, turned to face him. "So...I guess you're done here, then."

"Not until he has some pie," Diana said.

"No, thank you, Mrs. Street." Remy levered to his feet. "Your pie sounds delicious, but I do have to leave. I'm still on the clock." He headed for the door.

Once he was out, Charlie's mom glared at her as if to say, 'see what you've done.' Someone else might have withered under her mother's penetrating gaze, but Charlie had her mother's genes and sometimes it came down to a test of wills.

Only this time, her mother was right. She *had* been rude to Malone—the man who'd sat watch outside her house during the night. The man she wanted to talk with to see if he knew anything about the other name she'd found.

She bolted to her feet and dashed out the door. Malone was halfway down the street before she caught up with him. "Detective."

He turned, his steely gaze flicking over her.

"I'm sorry I was rude."

"Really?" His shoulders seemed to broaden as he stood there. "Why am I not convinced?"

"I said I was sorry."

"Okay. You're sorry." He turned and continued walking.

"Please wait." She touched his arm. "I'd like to talk to you for a minute." She hurried to get around him before he reached his vehicle.

He stopped, eyes glinting as they locked with hers. "I don't know, Charlie." He rubbed his chin. "You might need to make an appointment…and if you're going to ask me any questions, I should probably lawyer up first."

What an ass. Maybe she deserved it, but still… "Okay, you made your point. I apologize…again. I jumped to conclusions, and I'm sorry."

He grinned sappily, as if he knew he'd won the round. "Apology accepted." Then he continued on to his car, parked a couple houses down. No wonder she hadn't noticed.

She followed.

At the vehicle, he pivoted to face her, leaned a shoulder against the driver's door. "What's on your mind, counselor?"

His smug look galled her and it was all she could do not to wipe it off with a karate chop that Gabe would be proud of.

"What kind of vehicle did my mother see that worried her?"

"I think you should ask her about that."

Double ass. "Okay, there is one other thing. You showed me a list of names you'd collected when looking into your friend's disappearance. Most of them are known members of The Partnership, but your list doesn't include another name that's come up for me a few times now and I wondered if you've ever come across it. The name's Merceury." She spelled it out.

"Merceury? Last name?"

She shook her head. "I don't know."

He shrugged. "No, I haven't heard it before."

His 'no' squashed the kernel of hope she'd been trying to ignore. The empty void in her chest told her she hadn't been successful.

"I can check it out for you."

"Thanks, but I've done that already. Nothing comes up."

"Must be an important case."

"It's...not a case." She moistened her lips. "But all my clients are important." She turned to leave, but felt Malone's hand on her shoulder and stopped.

"We could help each other out, you know."

His hand was warm. Solid. "How so?"

He came around. "If you help me find out what happened to Adam, I can help you find Merceury."

"It's not...that important."

"It was important enough for you to come after me."

She coughed. Cleared her throat. "I did do that, didn't I."

He smiled, brows raised. "I have different resources. I know people you don't. People who know other people."

"Snitches."

"Some," he said. "But I have other contacts as well."

"I would have to talk to people. Maybe some within the Department."

"Yes, but it could be for another reason. You're working on something pretty big right now."

"The tradeoff isn't exactly equal."

"Payment in cash."

Her interest piqued.

"I would be a paying client. Surely you need one of those once in a while."

No question there. No question he'd done his research, either. It was obvious he knew about her history of representing pro bono clients. "I'm expensive."

He shrugged. "Not a problem."

Right, money was never a problem for someone born with the whole silver service in his mouth.

But he had a point.

CHAPTER SEVEN

REMY PULLED THE files he'd collected with anything related to Adam, most of the information culled from public records, police files, interviews with prominent people he'd vowed not to expose, and a few snitches—packed them into a briefcase, and locked it. High potency stuff. It wasn't likely the information would get out of his hands, but he wasn't going to take the chance. Lives would be at risk. Two of his contacts had already been snuffed—and not in a pretty way.

At his desk, Remy glanced at Captain Pendergast, who was in his office and talking with someone in a suit. The guy looked like I.A., which was consistent with rumors that Internal Affairs had been investigating a couple cops purported to be on the take. The captain wasn't looking very happy about the meeting, but then he hadn't looked happy about anything since Remy had come on board.

The time on his cell flashed ten a.m., a half hour before his meeting with Charlie Street. Just enough time to return a few calls. One, he noticed, from his dad, who'd already warned Remy to lay off looking into Adam's disappearance.

He hadn't seen his dad for almost a year before Adam went missing, and, fool that Remy was, he'd actually thought his father might've mellowed a little.

Hell, yeah. And he'd make police chief next week.

He shoved the phone into his jacket pocket and headed out the door.

Two men and the receptionist were already in the Street Law conference room when he arrived. He tightened his grip on his briefcase.

Someone closed the door behind him and when he turned, a biker chick barreled past him. Realizing his mouth was hanging open, he snapped it shut. It was Charlie.

Only her hair was midnight black, short and spiky like a rock star, and she was wearing lots of leather, tight black pants and a jacket with studs. High black boots...and more makeup than she usually wore...red lipstick and the dark eye shadow made her look like she was ready to star in a porn flick. Not the kind of look he usually liked, but...damn, she looked hot.

Charlie motioned for him to sit, and then introduced the others. Max Scofield, a PI, who readily popped from his seat to shake Remy's hand, and Gabe Weatherly, an imposing man who, even without standing, looked to go at least six-four. His job with the firm wasn't explained, but Charlie made it clear that as a former Navy SEAL, the man had skills. Remy remembered the dog photo had been on Gabe's desk.

They shook hands, and lastly, she introduced January Giordano, the pretty blonde he'd met a few days earlier.

"January is in her last semester of law school at WSU," Charlie said. "She's my legal assistant and she's indispensable. We wouldn't exist without her."

He nodded. So, okay, he knew everyone. Now what?

The counselor stood with her feet apart and her arms crossed. "When representing a case like yours, Detective Malone—" She looked directly at him. "—I like to keep the team in the loop at all times, so if I need something, I don't have to waste time explaining again and again."

She relaxed her stance when she turned to the two guys. "From what I've seen so far, I don't think we'll need you, Gabe, but I can't be sure." The ex-Navy SEAL shrugged.

"And Max, your work will probably be minimal, too. At least with the PD. I'll know more on that score as we get into it, but I do want your input. All of you."

She turned to the wall behind her, pressed a button. The hum of an electric motor geared up and a giant white board dropped down from a slot in the ceiling.

"Let's get started." She picked out a marker from the top of a file cabinet in the corner and went to the board.

Remy cleared his throat. "Sorry to interrupt, but if these guys aren't going to be working the case—"

She turned, eyes hard.

He tipped his head in Max and Gabe's direction. "— if they're not active on the case, the information stays between you and me."

In a blink, she was back at the table and closing her file. "Okay. I guess we're done here."

Remy flinched. "What do you mean? Done?"

"You don't want to work with us, so we're done."

What? *Damn.* He cleared his throat. "Incorrect. I want to work with you, but maybe I haven't expressed the importance of what I'm doing. The need for total confidentiality. If word got out, it could put several people in harm's way."

Charlie's expression never changed, but he saw the tightness in her mouth, as if she wanted to counter his protest, but then decided against it.

"As you know, all who work here are bound by confidentiality laws, Detective, regardless of the job title. Legally and ethically."

"And you can guarantee that?" He glanced at the others, again. "No disrespect intended."

Back straight, she continued to pull her things

together. Casual. Nonchalant. "There are no guarantees in this life, Malone. Other than the proverbial death and taxes. If you want me to represent you, I will." She moistened her lips. "But you'll have to trust me." She turned to her team. "Trust us. Otherwise, we're through here."

Both Gabe and Max stood, ready to leave.

Shit.

As if reading his mind, she said, "I know trust isn't automatic, especially for those in your profession. I am, however, acutely aware of what's at stake here, as I am in every case. I wouldn't have someone working for me that I didn't trust implicitly."

"And you've never put trust in someone who screwed you over in the end?" He had. Many times. Including his so-called loving ex-wife.

Charlie visibly stiffened. "I think you'll see in a very short time that there's nothing to worry about."

Gabe and Max waited.

Scratching the two-day stubble on his chin, Remy realized what she'd just said was giving him a way to save face. She was right about the trust thing. In his profession, blind trust could be deadly. You assume the worst…and shoot to kill.

And he'd asked her to do this. It was dumb to have cold feet now. Especially because if things went down as he thought they would, everything would come out in the end, anyway. "Okay," he said.

She looked at him from under her brows. "Okay what?"

"Okay, let's do it."

He saw her mouth tip up on one side just a hair, and then she reached up, pulled off the wig and then withdrew a few hairpins to let her a soft tangle of curls tumble down around her shoulders. She turned to her crew. "I'll brief you on the other stuff when we're finished with Detective Malone."

When Charlie turned back to him, Remy was sure his mouth was hanging open again.

"Okay," she said. "Let's get down to business."

Charlie blocked a jab from Shamar, her martial arts training partner, but the next swing came even faster. She anticipated the left punch, grabbed his arm at the elbow, shoved her leg behind his and pulled hard while she turned into his body. In one quick motion, she bent over, yanked his arm to bring him across her body to land flat on his back with a one-hundred-and-eighty-pound thud. The canvas under her feet vibrated with the takedown.

"Excellent!" Gabe applauded. "You're a quick study, grasshopper," he said, mimicking the master in the old *Kung Fu* television series.

She held out a hand to her training partner, a teen from the neighborhood who was working with her brother at the boxing gym. "Thanks, Shamar. You're a good sport."

The boy grinned from ear to ear, as if he'd been the one to take *her* down. "I do my best," he said, shaking out his arms.

As he started to walk away, she asked, "Can you come again on Thursday?"

The teen looked surprised. "Sure. If you want me to."

"I do. That would be great."

"Okay," the boy said and headed out, again.

Wiping the sweat from her neck with a gym towel, she said, "Thanks, again," and turned to Gabe, her go-to person for self-defense. "You, too. I wouldn't have any real skills if you hadn't convinced me I needed to up my game."

She'd learned basic self-defense early on, thanks to hanging out at the boxing gym with her uncle and brother while growing up. But after being robbed at the casino a few years back and working several dangerous cases, including rescuing the senator's son, she needed more than the basics and had since developed some killer skills in Wing Chun Kung Fu.

Gabe was an expert in the art, a major Chinese martial art based on the theory of surviving an attack by being a better attacker than the assailant. The focus was on personal protection and street survival. Exactly what she needed. So…she'd agreed to do it, as long as Gabe would be her teacher.

Self-defense wouldn't stop a bullet, but there were other benefits. Part of the training was spiritual. Learning to open and focus the mind. And using that internal channel to calm mind and body. That's what she needed now, because being calm gave her a keener awareness—the ability to recognize a threat sooner—and deal with it proactively. Before she was in harm's way.

So why had she been so rattled the other night? She'd seen the car before…seen lots of cars parked in the back alley off and on. But her gut said "danger," and all the calming exercises, logic and rationalizing didn't override her gut.

"So, are you going home, or to the office," Gabe asked, a tease in his voice.

"Funny." She glanced at the second ring where a couple of teenaged boys were still sparring and her brother was hanging on the ropes, coaching from the sidelines. She tossed the towel in her gym bag and took out a Tigers' hoodie. "Actually, I think I'll hang around here for a few. I need to talk to Landon."

Gabe nodded and turned to go. He wasn't a talkative guy, but during their many training sessions she'd managed to engage him in a conversation or two. Nothing deeply personal, though, and she doubted he'd feel comfortable enough to talk about whatever it was that had him bound up so tightly. She could literally feel the undercurrent—a repressed energy so intense it vibrated from him in waves like the proverbial simmering volcano that might blow at any time.

Didn't matter. After the shooting incident a few months ago, Gabe had held vigil at the Street Law office, and if she hadn't known earlier, she knew then that he was the kind of person she could count on no matter what. Whatever his past, whatever was going on inside the guy, wasn't her business. She respected his privacy, just as she wanted others to respect hers.

Picking up her bag, she waved to get her brother's attention and signaled him that she was going to his office.

Once there, she sat to read email messages and nearly ten minutes later, Landon came in.

"Hey, Sis." He plopped into the chair behind his desk and clasped his hands behind his head. "I was watching you with Shamar. You're a wicked woman on the mat."

She grinned. "I do my best."

"So, what's up?"

"What? Can't I come in and talk to my baby brother without a reason?"

Landon arched a brow. "Call me skeptical."

"You're skeptical."

"Funny. As in *not very*. And I know you don't have time to sit around and shoot the breeze. I just hope it's not what I think."

She slumped in the chair, her answer obvious.

"Mom?"

"You need to talk to her. I can't do it. She's weirding out on me."

"Crap." Landon rolled his eyes, folded his arms over

his chest. Finally, on an overly dramatic sigh, he said. "Okay. What else?"

"That's it."

He gave her a side glance. "That's it?" Pause. "Seriously?"

"Isn't that enough?"

Scrutinizing her through squinty eyes, he leaned forward, elbows on the desk. "You stayed here ten extra minutes to tell me I need to talk to Mom." He scoffed and shoved back again. "You don't stay anywhere for an extra ten seconds if you don't need to."

She shrugged, palms up.

"You could've called or texted me."

She shrugged again. "Dang. Can't you just talk to her and not give me the third degree?"

Landon chortled, "Third degree? Really? Now I know something's wrong."

"You don't know shit," Charlie said, launching to her feet and feeling as stupid as she must've sounded. Maybe he was right. Maybe she was more bothered than she wanted to admit. Landon always saw right through her. Dammit.

"I'm outta here." She snatched her gym bag and started for the door.

"Okay. But I'll find out anyway. You know I will."

She stopped. Heaved a heavy sigh and turned back. "It's no big deal. Not really. In fact, it'll probably turn out to be nothing in the end, but—" She cleared her throat. "I have a new lead on Dad's case."

Landon stared at her, as if unable...or unwilling...to absorb what she'd said. His lips thinned. "A new lead. What the hell does that mean?"

"I said it was probably nothing. It's just a person I tried to find before and couldn't."

He kept staring, waiting for more information. An explanation.

She couldn't give him one. She'd breach confidentiality. All she could tell him was that the name of the person she'd been trying to find for years had finally surfaced. She couldn't tell him the name was on Malone's suspect list of persons he thought might be involved in his friend's disappearance. The list that included members of the Detroit mafia.

Landon stood, squared his broad shoulders. "You're going to forget it, though. Right? I mean, you know what happened before."

She took a moment before meeting his gaze.

"I can't forget it."

CHAPTER EIGHT

REMY PULLED INTO the circular drive at his father's home in Grosse Pointe Shores—the mid-point between the prestigious five points located on the southwest side of Lake St. Clair. He parked and then let himself in through the side door to the kitchen. Get in and get out unscathed. That's all he wanted from the evening.

"It's about time." Caroline, his dad's cook, stepped away from the stove. She smoothed the front of her apron and hurried over to give him a giant bear hug. "You've stayed away too long."

The woman had been in his father's employ since Remy's mother's death. She'd been hired to pull together food for the guests who'd come to the house after the funeral and his father had kept her on. The judge had never liked having anyone cook his meals except Remy's mother, but there was no way he was going to do it himself.

"Maybe," Remy said. "But dinner invitations from my father are hard to come by if you don't work for him."

As a kid, Remy had hated that his mother had been replaced so easily but before long, Caroline Sellik had become his only ally in a house full of enemies. That's how his adolescent brain had seen things, anyway.

"Still think you'd make a damned good lawyer."

"Maybe," Remy said as he grabbed a mug for the coffee he smelled brewing. "But I'm a much better cop."

Caroline took his cup, filled it and handed it back. "You're early. Dinner isn't until seven."

"I know. I was told to come early." His dad wanted to talk, and Remy was pretty sure he knew what about.

Caroline's eyebrows rose. The grandmotherly woman had always been there to console him when he was a kid and he and his father had a disagreement, which seemed to be all the time. She'd also been Remy and his buddy Adam's go-to person for snacks after school. And for giving them a heads-up when his dad came home from work and they were playing loud music in Remy's room.

"Would you like a biscotti or something with your coffee?"

Remy laughed. "No, Ma'am. A shot of whiskey might take the edge off, though."

"That may be more necessary than you think," she said. "He gets crankier every day."

"Well, it's good that you're here to keep things running smoothly." He gave her another quick hug and headed toward the library where he knew he'd find his dad. Remy had been gone a long time, first for college, and then when he'd worked for the Boston PD. When he decided to return, he'd thought maybe the old man would've mellowed a little, but no such luck.

The double doors to the library were open and Remy stood for a moment at the door. Everything, from the gleaming patina of the exotic Peruvian walnut doors to the gilt-edged mirrors, was exactly the same as when Remy was growing up. Everything shiny and perfect—and very expensive. Even the family room had been a showcase...not a home.

His dad was lounging in a leather easy chair in front

of the fireplace, a drink in one hand, a cigar in the other. Remy double-tapped the door.

Without turning, the judge said, "C'mon in."

As he went over, his dad stood.

"How're you doing, Son." He reached out a hand.

Remy switched his coffee to his other hand. "Good. Real good. Parker here yet?"

"No." The judge strode to the bar, his back straight as a rod, his broad shoulders square as ever. "He's got some event with Whitney first, but he'll be here for dinner. What can I get you?"

"I'm good with coffee for now."

The judge picked up a crystal whiskey decanter, glanced at Remy. Refusing anything the judge offered was the same as an insult. Such a small thing, but if he wanted to get out quickly... Remy held out his cup.

Pouring, his father said, "Okay, then. Have a seat. Let's talk."

"When's the wedding?" Remy asked, sitting in the matching leather chair facing the massive Chicago brick fireplace, hoping his dad would follow his lead and talk about his brother. Any conversation was better than the one he knew his dad wanted to have.

"I should be asking you about that." His dad sat again. "I barely talk to your brother since he's been engaged. If he wasn't running the firm, I'd never see him."

Physically, his dad had barely changed in the years Remy had lived in Boston. If it weren't for the shock of silver hair, it would be hard to tell his old man's football days at Yale were more than a few years ago. People always said Remy looked more like his dad and his twin brother more like their mother. Another one of life's little ironies.

"I haven't talked to him in a few weeks, either." Like his father, Parker was still pissed that Remy hadn't finished law school and joined the firm as expected.

"But... I know what you've been doing," the judge said, his words clipped and a little slurred. "And I don't like it."

His old man wouldn't like it if Remy were the first man on Mars. Unless he'd personally orchestrated it.

Remy bit back a crisp retort, sipped his coffee and opted for ignorance. "I'm not crazy about the assignment either. I thought working homicide would take less of my time, not more. It's keeping me busy twenty-four, seven."

His dad glanced over, the change in Remy's assignment obviously news to him. But he waved a hand in dismissal. "You know very well that's not what I meant. Detroit is a big city, Son, but you should know from growing up in this house that when it comes to the inner circles, it's a very small town." He knocked back the rest of his drink. "Sticking your nose in where it's not wanted will have serious consequences."

"Heard you the first time, Dad. I'm just doin' my job. Being a good cop...keeping my nose clean."

The judge went for another drink and this time Remy followed and held out a glass for a straight shot.

"And the woman? Is she part of your job?"

Remy shifted his stance, schooled his expression so he didn't give away his surprise. Why, when he was with his father, did he always feel like a little kid being called out for doing something wrong? "What woman do you mean? I see a lot of women. For different reasons."

His dad peered at the ice in his glass, swirled the liquid for a moment. "You know who I mean. The lawyer. That woman is a troublemaker."

He'd been careful not to be seen with Charlie, but obviously, not careful enough. Hitchens, maybe? His dad's old friend had seen him at the courthouse...or maybe someone saw them at Slows? "Just doing my job, Dad. No big deal."

His dad seemed to weigh the response, but whether he believed Remy or not, Remy couldn't tell.

After a moment his dad said, "I heard the chief may be cutting some jobs. Might be a good time to think about joining the firm with your brother."

The subtext was clear. The judge had more connections than the Internet, held more favors than Mother Teresa. He could get Remy fired any time he wanted. The chief of police had warned Remy if he kept pursuing Adam's disappearance, he'd make it happen…and he'd made sure the judge knew it.

Remy hoisted his drink. Smiled. "I'm a little old to be going back to school, and I have no intention of leaving law enforcement regardless of where I work." He shrugged. "If I can't work in Detroit, I'll go somewhere else."

He watched the muscles in his dad's jaw dance. The judge wanted him here. The only reason he'd put in a word for him to get the job with the Detroit PD was so Remy'd move back home. His dad wanted both his sons in the city, working together at Malone and Malone. And right this minute, the judge was supremely pissed that his threat wasn't working.

The small victory wasn't working for Remy either. As a kid, he'd idolized his dad. All he'd ever wanted was for the judge to understand he didn't want the same things as his brother, and that it was okay to want something different. He'd wanted his dad to be a dad. Something that he'd finally resolved was never going to happen.

The judge held up the bottle of Jack and squinted to see how much was left. "Fine. Just remember what I said about consequences. You're not the only person who could be affected."

His dad had been retired for years. Nothing Remy did could have any effect on his dad. Unless he meant

Malone and Malone. Was he afraid of losing business? How could his looking into Adam's disappearance affect his father's business? And even if it did, they were talking about a man's life.

Remy swung around. "I'm doing my job, Dad, and that's it. What I do *always* affects people's lives."

A long moment passed before his dad produced a smile and said, "Just making sure, Son. Just making sure."

"Sorry I'm late," Parker said, coming around the corner. "The event lasted longer than I thought it would and then I had to take Whitney home. I've got some files from the firm to bring in, but I'll be right back." He took a few steps to go, then turned, looked at Remy, then their dad. "Everything okay?"

The judge waved him off.

When Parker left, Remy clenched his jaw and faced his dad. "If you have something else to say, just say it."

The judge strode to the fireplace, set his glass on the mantel. He stood there quiet for a moment, then raised his head. "I know you want to find out what happened to Adam. I understand. You were good friends. But you have to let the right people do their job. What I said about consequences can't be stressed enough. You piss off the wrong people…" He raised both hands letting Remy finish the rest of the sentence.

What his father wasn't saying was clear. One of Remy's snitches, Willie Boyle, AKA the Rabbit, because he was continually twitching his nose, had been tortured, shot in all extremities and had his bones crushed before a double tap to the head. Not too long after talking to Remy.

But it was hard to determine who 'the wrong people' were. Within the PD, Police corruption, gross negligence, and ties to the mob were all on the table. Remy was even cautious about what he told his dad because it could get back to the chief. Remy didn't know who he could trust within the department.

As Parker came into the room again, Remy's phone blasted the theme song from the *Law and Order* TV show, the ringtone he'd picked for Charlie. It was a text with the time for their next meeting. Perfect. Pocketing the phone, he said, "I'm really sorry, Dad. I'm not going to be able to stay for dinner."

Parker raised his hands, eyes questioning.

"Sorry, Kid," Remy said, using his favorite nickname for Parker, who was two minutes younger than Remy.

He turned for the door.

"Remember what I said, Remington. Don't be pigheaded," his father said. "Let the police handle police business."

He kept walking, thought his old man had finished. But as he was about to escape, the judge added, "And make better choices in women."

Charlie finished rereading the transcripts of her dad's trial and, again, went over the little bit of information she'd collected on Joey Drakar. She didn't know what she expected this time that would be any different than the last, but she'd felt compelled to go over it again. Finding nothing, she closed the file and shoved it to one side of her desk.

It was always the same…and yet she couldn't help feeling as if she'd missed something. There had to be a flaw in the prosecution's case. There was always a flaw when someone had been framed.

And because of Joey's immediate disappearance after he'd testified, she'd always believed the answer she needed had something to do with him.

Joey had been one of the teenagers her father had taken under his wing, taught him to box and gave him a part-time janitorial job at the gym. After her dad's fingerprints had been identified at the crime scene, the police interviewed everyone her dad knew. And Joey's story about seeing her dad come back to the gym late at night with blood on his clothes, and then later, seeing him stuff a bag into the trash, was all the police needed to get a search warrant. The rest was history.

But it was apparent to Charlie that her father's attorney, a barely-passed-the-bar public defender, had let the prosecutor run away with the trial. He'd been so intimidated he'd hardly managed to put up a defense. After that, Joey's testimony locked in the prosecutor's case tighter than the doors that had imprisoned her father for the brief two weeks before he was murdered.

She'd never found any real evidence to prove her father was framed, but her belief in his innocence was infused in every fiber of her being. Would a murderer devote his life to helping at-risk teens find direction and meaning in theirs? Would a murderer tuck his children in at night and read them bedtime stories? Sing them lullabies? Would he go to church every Sunday?

No matter what evidence had been mounted against her father, nothing could sway her from the belief that he was innocent.

A motor noise in the parking area outside her office window alerted her. She checked the time. Not quite seven. Malone was early, and she wasn't prepared. Even though she wanted to ask questions about Joey Drakar, she had to remember it was Remy's case they were working on. He was a paying client.

Charlie got up, smoothed the front of her shirt on the way to the door, and before answering, glanced quickly at her hair in the mirror.

CHAPTER NINE

REMY WAS ABOUT to knock a second time when the door opened.

"I wasn't sure what door I should use," he said, surprised to see her in casual clothes…skinny jeans, black boots, double layered navy and white T-shirts that hugged her curves. Why he was surprised, he didn't know. It was after hours.

"This door is best after six," she said, motioning him inside. "We lock the front then, except for the two nights we're open late."

He followed her to her office, appreciating the view. On his one-to-ten scale, Charlie Street was a twelve. At least from his current vantage point. But he wasn't there to ogle her assets, no matter how appealing they might be. He was there to answer questions that would help find Adam.

As they sat—she behind the desk, him in front—she said, "I've gone over everything you gave me. We're working on potential leads, but I need to clarify what actually happened."

He nodded. "Everything I know is in the files I gave you, but, go ahead."

Her brows crinkled in the middle. "We know Adam was working undercover on the same job for nearly two years," she said. "He disappeared approximately six months ago and your notes indicate the police investigation stalled about a month later. Do you know why?"

He shrugged. He'd told her everything the first time they'd talked about it, and he was sure they'd talked about it during the group meeting. "No more leads. It's all in the file."

Her voice was crisp when she said, "I know what's in the file."

And she apparently knew that in order to get as close to the truth as possible, you had to ask the same questions over and over. Invariably, something new would turn up. He knew that. And now he knew what it was like to be on the other end. "Adam wasn't the only one on the inside."

"So, if we move forward, we could possibly put someone else in danger."

"Possibly. Everything is possible. I don't want to mess with anyone's set-up. I just want to know where Adam is and who's responsible for his disappearance."

"I know I mentioned this before…as a cop, you know the stats."

Yeah, he knew the odds of finding Adam alive. Anger burned like battery acid in his gut every time he thought about it. He cleared his throat. "His family needs to know."

Thoughtful, she fingered the papers in front of her. "Revenge is never an answer."

"Revenge?" He scoffed, but couldn't help smiling. He eased back in the chair. "I'm a cop, Charlie. A good cop."

Her eyes came up to meet his. "Just saying…"

A baited comment if he'd ever heard one. "What else do you need from me?"

She flipped open a file to her right and pulled out a sheet of paper. "I need the status of each person on this list and what type of contact you've made." She handed him the list.

He'd committed the list to memory a long time ago and he knew she probably had, too, but he went ahead anyway. "The first four are with The Partnership. Tony Carlozzi is Falcone's underboss. I've made no contact. The woman's name next to Carlozzi's is his girlfriend's sister, who I've heard hates Carlozzi and has tried to get her sister away from him."

Charlie pulled back. A slow smile emerged. "Good." She held out her hand and he handed back the list. "You think Carlozzi is involved in Adam's disappearance?"

"If the Detroit mafia is involved, Carlozzi's involved."

"And you think this gangster's girlfriend's sister..." She glanced at the list. "You think Gina Martingale knows something about Adam's disappearance?"

"No. But I think she can be convinced to find out because she's worried about her sister. Carlozzi's a scumbag with a Napoleon complex. He likes the hands-on method to keep his women in line."

She dropped the list on the desk. "And the rest?"

"Manny Warzynski does some jobs for the underboss. Manny likes to drink and he likes to talk. Albert (Knuckles) Tucci is the street boss."

"And the big dog...Frankie Falcone?"

"Not much information gets out on Falcone. He's a ghost. He's so protected, I doubt SEAL Team Six could get to him."

She arched a brow. "You underestimate my guys."

"I'm realistic."

"Okay." She smiled, but it was half smile, half smirk, as if humoring him. "The others?"

"Nothing on Vinnie Zizzo."

"Zizzo is the new cleaner," she said. "Someone screws up, Falcone sends Zizzo to clean up the mess."

How did *she* know about Zizzo and he didn't? He

edged closer to her to look at the list. "You sure?" Dano Tangretti was replaced?

"I worked in the public justice system for a long time. I heard a lot of stories from a lot of snitches." She waited a beat. "Still do."

He knew she'd worked for the Wayne County Public Defender's Office. Knew everything about her that was public record—and more. But he didn't know what was in her head. "So, you have a snitch list of your own?"

"Something like that."

"Dirty cops, too?"

Her gaze, no longer ice blue, but deep cobalt, came up to meet his. Stormy. Intense.

"No one I can blackmail for information, if that's what you mean."

She was sharp. Street smart. He smiled to himself at his private pun.

"What about Drakar?" she asked. "What do you know about him?"

"Not much. His juvy records were expunged. His name came up in connection with Johnson, but from an unreliable source. Just added Drakar's name last week."

Her eyes darkened even more. "Do you know where he lives?"

"Nope, just where he lived as a kid. The last time Drakar was in the D was in '88, so it's likely my source was looking for drug money."

"What about Johnson?" She glanced at the list. "Nick Johnson? I've never heard of him."

"Bartender at the Devil's Den. No record. Not much history. Supposed to be from Miami, been in town for about two years."

Her eyes narrowed as she said, "The police investigation shows Adam was at the Devil's Den on the night he disappeared."

"Yeah. Johnson could be the last person to see

Adam."

"And?"

"And nada. It's all in the file. The police investigation got nothing. Zip. Zero. Zilch."

She took a huge breath, letting it out slowly through her nose like she was doing some kind of breathing exercise. "Did you talk to him?"

"I was warned off."

"Do you plan on talking to him?"

He shook his head, gave her a questioning look. "I can't get close to anything on the original investigation. Not if I want to keep my job." He frowned, angled his head. How many times did he have to go through it? "That's your job now."

"Okay. Just making sure we're on the same page."

Yeah. Making sure he knew his place, sitting back all casual, as if talking about something as innocuous as the weather.

"And how is Johnson connected to Drakar, again?"

He straightened. Man, she annoyed him. She'd probably want a medical report before she ever hit the sack with someone…and then question the results. But this was business. Her way. That's why he'd hired her. "My source said they were cousins or something. I can't be sure though. The tweeker only talked when he needed a fix. But he said if we found one, we might find the other."

Her eyes raised to his. "Pithy."

"No. Junkie sociopath."

Charlie's pulse quickened. If Remy's source was right and the two men were related, Johnson could know Joey's whereabouts. Her nerves dancing under her skin, she leaned forward. "Okay, tell me everything…down to the smallest detail on Johnson and Drakar."

"That's it. I got Johnson's name from Adam's last partner who got it from a snitch looking to cut a deal. I ran both names and got nothing."

Made sense. She'd stopped actively looking for Drakar years ago because she hit the same brick wall.

"Okay. I'll get Max or Gabe to pin down the snitch."

"Can't. He was found in an alley trash barrel the day after he talked to me."

"Murdered?"

"Eventually. His throat was slit."

Which meant he was tortured first. She cringed just thinking about it. As a public defender she'd seen her share of gruesome. She'd had to provide a defense for monsters like the serial killer who'd tortured his victims before burying them alive. She'd been forced to endure photos of his grisly crime scenes, listen to hours and hours of his depravity. She couldn't imagine what it would be like to be on the scene, seeing things like that every day. And yet, Malone didn't even flinch talking about it.

"He wasn't the first. One of the other snitches ended up the same way." He took a breath. "And another is missing."

And would probably show up in the same condition. "Apparently the assassin likes his job," she said, searching Remy's eyes for some sign of emotion. He had to be thinking that his buddy, Adam Bentley, may have met the same fate, but the muscles in his face didn't move.

"Any leads on those hits?" she asked, even though she knew the answer. No one really cared when gangsters and junkies offed each other.

He shook his head.

"What about Adam's wife? When did she last see him?"

He gestured to the file. "Adam was undercover for

two years. During that time, their contact was limited. I talked to her first. She said she'd given him an ultimatum. Change jobs or she was getting a divorce."

Easing against the back of her chair, Charlie could relate. No one wanted to be second in a relationship. Not one of the guys she'd dated in any serious way had been able to understand her dedication to her job. "I'll talk with her."

Remy shook his head. "Nope. Susan and Captain Pendergast's wife are good friends. Talk to her and everyone will know what I'm doing. My job will be toast."

"We're discreet."

"No," he stated soundly. "I've talked to her. She doesn't know anything about Adam's disappearance. And she's a smart lady. She'd put the pieces together...what we're doing. I can't risk it."

Charlie took a breath. Reminded herself to be patient. He was a cop, used to doing his own investigations and he had rules to follow. Unlike her team. Still, Remy had to know a new interviewer could pick up things others hadn't. Some small clue, something Adam might've said that others too close to him might've overlooked. Others like Remy.

"Okay," she said. "It's obvious there's a lot of work to be done just to get new information. We've retraced the documented police investigation and found a couple areas that could have been looked at more thoroughly. So, we're working on that. I'll let you know as soon as we get anything concrete." She placed her hands on the desk and stood.

Remy launched to his feet. "You'll let me know?" His forehead furrowed. "No...I want to know everything you're doing...as you're doing it. I want to know who you're talking to, when, and why."

A muscle at the edge of her eye twitched. A fucking

control freak. But then, what cop wasn't. She drew in a long breath.

"Of course. And as soon as we have something, I'll be in touch."

Charlie shook out the medium-length, blond wig and held it up next to the longer, ginger-colored one. Jessica Simpson or Amy Adams? Britney Spears or Emma Stone? Or as her dad would've said, Marilyn Monroe or Rita Hayworth. He'd loved old movies and used to let her stay up late to watch with him. He never knew she'd only pretended to like the movies so she could spend more time with him.

It was that bond that made her dabble in acting while in college. She never would've guessed then that her brief acting stint in a local little theater would be so useful later on. She pulled her long hair into a high ponytail, flattened it upward and put on the skull cap. She tried the red wig first. No, tonight she needed to bring it. She needed flat-out sexy. She pulled on the blond wig and fastened it with hairpins, making sure it was tight enough not to move.

At her closet, she flicked on the light. On the floor was a duffle bag containing some stripper tassels and other paraphernalia, given to her by one of her first clients at Street Law. She kept the bag as a reminder that fate works in many ways.

On the right side was her normal street wear, and on the left, her alternate personality clothing, as January liked to call the costumes Charlie wore on the job. Some were sexy in silky, satiny fabrics that draped smoothly over her curves, and which required five-inch strappy stilettos.

The next level down, her Rita clothes were sexy, too,

but more subdued, like the black jersey wrap dress with plain black stilettos. Four inch.

And still sexy, but going totally in the opposite direction, one of her favorites…a short, spiky rock star wig and lots of tight leather and boots hung next to the soccer mom garb, the librarian, and the biker chick. January had accused her once of liking the acting jobs too much. Hah. She was right. It was more fun pretending to be someone with no responsibilities instead of the person who needed to pay the bills and make sure her mother didn't go off the deep end.

Perusing the dresses, she pulled out a silver jersey sheath that looked more like a body stocking than a dress. Perfect. A little makeup, longer eyelashes, some jewelry and…voilà. She slipped her fake ID into an evening purse, grabbed her dressy leather jacket for later and she was ready for the Devil's Den…or the devil himself.

Going downstairs, she reminded herself that tonight was exploratory, a way to establish a presence so Nick Johnson would begin to think of her as a regular. Someone with whom he wouldn't mind sharing information. She had a tendency to rush things, so she had to remember to slow things down, take her time.

Downstairs, she went into the garage. After the scare with the van last week she'd cleared out the space next to her dad's old Mercedes so she'd have room for the Focus. Once inside her car, she flicked off the interior light so when she opened the garage door no one could see her. The tinted windows helped. Pulling out slowly, she checked the mirrors to make sure the brown van hadn't returned. She hadn't seen the vehicle since the night Remy had played watchdog.

On another night she'd seen a black SUV turn the corner and wondered if Remy had taken it upon himself to patrol the area…maybe thinking he could win points to get her to take his case. But then he'd never mentioned it afterward.

Pressing the remote to close the garage door, she smiled. For a cop, Remington Malone was...okay. More than okay in the looks department. If it wasn't for the cop thing, and the fact that he was a client, she might've considered seeing if his other skills were more than okay.

A tight pull deep in her belly told her it had been too long. Malone would be willing, of that she was sure. She could peg a guy's interest within sixty seconds and with Malone, it had been even less.

She hoped to hell she was better at keeping her thoughts to herself than he was.

CHAPTER TEN

FORTY-FIVE MINUTES LATER Charlie was perched on a stool at the Devil's Den waiting for the Cosmopolitan she'd ordered and staring across the bar at a pair of watermelon-sized boobs encased in a sparkly T-shirt so tight she could see nipples. Thankfully her adolescent prayers for triple Ds were never answered.

"Nick won't be here for another half hour," the woman chirped to the one and only waitress, also wearing a T-shirt three sizes too small. Then she turned to Charlie. "You waitin' for someone or lookin' for someone?" She slid the Cosmo across the scarred bar surface with two fingers.

"Waiting." Charlie glanced to the end of the long stretch of wood where two middle-aged men were staring at the overhead TV. "And I'm hoping he looks like his picture."

The Devil's Den was a working man's bar, the kind where the damp, yeasty scent of beer greets you before you enter, and you know most of the patrons are regulars. One of the oldest bars in the city, even the furniture seemed imbued with the stale scent of cigarettes and beer. The Den was closed in, dark, and, even though there were only a dozen people in the place, noisy. A few round tables filled the space between the bar and the booths and unlike all the sports bars, there was only one small TV.

"Well, good luck with that," the bartender said, her expression a statement that she'd been there, done that. She wore a necklace with a shiny penny on the end that kept getting lost between her boobs. When she turned, Charlie noticed she had a booty to match the boobs. All her own, she decided.

"I know." Charlie sighed. "Sometimes I think I should just forget it, but I want to get married someday and have kids, so…" She shrugged. The having kids part was true. She'd discovered early on when working undercover that the closer she stuck to the truth, the easier it was to play the part. No lies or a ton of fake details to juggle in her head.

"I hear ya, sister. But you keep at it. You'll get lucky sooner or later. I did, but there were a lot of bullfrogs in the swamp to go through first."

Charlie and the bartender, whose name she learned was Penny, short for Penelope and the reason for the necklace, talked for another ten minutes about online dating and the merits of staying single. As they were talking, a man with short, ash-blond hair and who looked to be in his forties joined Penny behind the bar.

"Hey, Nick," Penny greeted, motioning him over. "This is Nick," she said to Charlie. "It's his shift now, and if that creep doesn't show, my boy here'll give you an extra drink on me."

Charlie's blood rushed.

"Sure thing, Pen." Nick's eyes sparked with interest, his gaze hovering between Charlie's thighs and her neck.

Just the effect she wanted. If Nick Johnson was related to Joey Drakar as Malone suggested, it was possible she might actually find out something about…

No. That was not why she was here. She was on the clock for Remy…finding his former partner. *His best friend.* Johnson was the last known person to see Adam

Bentley. This had nothing to do with Joey Drakar.

Still…

When Penny was gone, Johnson did some bar maintenance then came back to her. "How long before you give up on the jerk?"

Smiling, she fluttered her lashes. "About fifteen minutes ago."

He laughed. "In that case, I'll get you that drink." He moved closer, eyes locking with hers. "What's your pleasure?" His voice came low. Smooth.

Excellent. She lifted her glass, still half full. "Cosmo, but I better not." She held his gaze, but the sudden skitter of nerves in her stomach reminded her she hadn't flirted with anyone in a long time. She had to get in character, make it real. Think as she would if she were really interested.

In real life, Nick—depending on what came out of his mouth when he spoke—might be flirt-worthy. He was above average looking, lean and nicely muscular. Not quite as tall as she generally liked…or as nerdy. Based on his behavior so far, Johnson's brain seemed to have only one working part.

The man's dark gaze slid from her eyes to her mouth…to her throat…and to her boobs, again, his lips lifting in the kind of smile that said he wanted to do her right there on the bar.

She shuddered. Sweat broke on the back of her neck and the wig suddenly felt like a heavy rug.

Still smiling, his gaze came back to hers, one brow raised. "Cosmo it is."

As he moved down the bar to pour, something about him struck her. She'd never met the man before, yet he seemed familiar. Which probably had to do with the fact that he and Drakar might be related—cousins, Remy had said. The thought sent a shiver of excitement up her spine.

Her breath caught on the thought, the idea that, after all this time, she could possibly find Joey Drakar. Or was it wishful thinking? Was she imagining a resemblance because Malone had said the two guys might be related?

Her memory of Drakar was a twenty-five year old blur of someone she'd seen at the gym and who, in her eight-year-old mind, looked like all the other gangly, pimply teenagers who worked out, got sweaty and hung towels over their heads.

Johnson could have been one of them, too. He could've even come with Joey...except she didn't remember any blondes. She'd known who Joey was because he'd helped her dad, doing some odd jobs for him.

Johnson gave her a knowing look from the end of the bar and immediately her muscles jumped. She drew her gaze away. Damn. If she kept doing that, she was going to give herself away. She was definitely out of practice. Except for the cheating husband watch she'd done last week, she hadn't worked undercover in over three months.

Her shrink said it was perfectly natural to be a bit edgy for a while, because, whether the shooter had meant the bullet for her or not, the reality was impossible to ignore. She could simply be going about her life, taking a walk or driving a car, or whatever, and then in an instant, she could be dead. Like her father.

She drew a long breath, then let it out, counting each time as she'd learned in her one and only yoga class five years ago. She was about to do another round when Nick brought her drink. "It's one of my best," he said. "With the expensive stuff."

She raised an eyebrow.

"Penny won't mind."

"But I mind." She softened her voice to a teasing whisper. "I'm an independent girl, and I know most gifts have strings attached."

Nick held her gaze even though he moved slightly to the side toward a man who'd just come in and sat a couple of stools away. Then he pointed a finger at her as if shooting a gun and said, "Back in a minute."

She lifted her glass, deciding her next move. She was here to establish a presence, not become a fixture. It was time to go. But she had to talk to Johnson one more time to set things up for her next visit.

A few more people came in and after receiving their drink orders from the waitress, Nick went about his bartender duties, his gaze catching hers between pours.

Giving him another seductive glance, she looked away, catching a glimpse of the man on the barstool a few feet away. Well built, dark stubble that was almost a beard, longish hair.

His eyes met hers.

Shit. She turned her back to him, her pulse thudding wildly at the base of her throat. Her hand shaking, she gulped down the rest of her Cosmo. Had he recognized her? Would he give her away?

In the fraction of a second it took to think it, she felt a warm presence at her side.

"I like the look," he said, his low bass voice as smooth as French silk.

She came around. Forced a tight smile. "You mean the look that's asking what the hell you're doing here?"

He shrugged, lifted the glass he held in one hand. "Having a drink." He moistened his lips. "And I'm guessing you're either going to a costume party, or into some kinky role playing."

Before she had a chance to answer, Nick was back. "You okay?" he asked, looking at Remy and then back to her again.

She flicked her hair behind her shoulder. "For now." She turned to Remy. "He's got about fifteen seconds to explain."

Remy's expression switched from challenging to confused, but he held her gaze.

She didn't think Remy was stupid enough to blow her cover, but couldn't overplay it, either, or Nick would get the impression she was excited her date finally showed up. She had to make it appear to Nick she was more interested in him than the date.

Nick lingered for a half second, then said, "I'll be just a few feet away." He glared at Remy who didn't even look his way.

When he was gone, she rounded on Remy. "Like I said, you've got fifteen seconds."

His taut expression said he'd love to rip into her with a few choice words, but instead, he scrubbed a hand over his stubble, then took her hand in his, his expression dead serious. "Same as you, Charlie." He pressed his lips together, then released her hand. His voice suddenly going to a whisper, he added, "I'm just trying to find out what happened to Adam." His eyes met hers. "Any way I can."

The raw emotion in his eyes caught her off guard. She knew what he was going through, and seeing it so openly expressed was…painful. She would have liked to tell him it would get better, that the pain would fade and life would someday go back to normal.

But that would be a lie. You could never forget.

"Okay." She huffed out a breath. "Then let's get on the same page. You're my online date, and I'm not impressed. I'm going to make goo-goo eyes at Nick, and you're going to take a trip to the little boy's room." She fluffed her hair, again, and glanced at Nick. As he looked her way, she moistened her lips, waited a moment, then turned back to Remy.

"Very good," Remy said, nodding his approval. "He's gonna need a bib to catch the drool."

"Great. Now go hit the john."

"How long?"

"Three to five."

Nick took notice the second Remy swung his feet to the floor. He didn't even wait for her date to be out of sight before he came over.

"Want me to get rid of him?"

"Now why would I want you to do that?" She fluttered her lashes again.

He leaned forward, one arm on the bar. "Because he's not your type."

She arched a brow. "Oh?"

"And *I* know what you want."

She closed the gap between them…lowered her voice, "You sure about that? I'm hard to please. I can't get what I want just anywhere."

His eyes lit up, apparently getting the message. "What's your pleasure?"

Taking her time, she straightened, crossed her legs, making sure they were exposed up to the thigh, then leisurely brushed back her hair. She glanced around, as if checking to make sure no one was within hearing range, then leaned in. "My pleasure? I'm just an all-American girl lookin' for a guy who brings me candy," she said. "A lot of it."

Nick's eyebrows shot up, his expression uncertain, as if trying to decide if she was for real.

She laughed. "Can you help me out or not?"

When he didn't respond immediately, she shrugged. "I didn't think so." She glanced toward the restroom, lifted her glass.

"No…" he said. "That's not it. I mean, yes, I can. But some things take a little time."

She reached for his hand, gave him a coy look. "Then I guess I should thank my date for picking this place to meet."

Nick's chin lifted, he straightened and she could almost see his chest puffing up.

"You know…" she said. "It's been a while since I've been here, but I don't remember seeing you before. How long have you worked here?"

The smile disappeared. After a brief pause, he said, "A while. A year maybe."

She acknowledged with a nod. "That's why, then. Where did you work before?"

He leaned on the bar again. "What difference does it make?"

"A lot," she said. "I don't want to get involved with someone who's going to disappear on me." From the corner of her eye she could see Remy returning and she still hadn't gotten any information.

"I've been gone for a while," Nick said. "But I've got a pretty good memory, and if you ditch the date, I bet I can show you some places you've never been."

As Remy got closer, she gave Nick another sultry look. "I bet you could."

"Okay," Remy said, sidling up next to her, his hand on her arm. "You ready for that late movie?"

Nick was already on his way to service another customer, so she shrugged and got up to leave with Remy. As they started for the door, Nick said, "Come back soon. That special order you wanted should be here in a couple of days."

Charlie glanced over her shoulder. "Absolutely."

Once out the door, Remy said, "I think you missed your calling." He was talking as they walked, but his eyes were scanning like a high-tech camera on motor drive.

They hurried down the street past a gaggle of hooded teenagers and rounded the corner. "Just part of the job," she said over the traffic noise. "I'm parked up the next street at the Casino."

"Me, too," he said as cars whizzed by, their bright lights flicking in her eyes like strobes at a disco. "But I—"

Car tires suddenly screeched, the growling sound of a motorcycle, and the *pop, pop, pop* of gunshots, people shouting...screaming...and in the same instant, Remy plowed into her like a truck, knocked her off her feet and slammed her into the wall. She went down, her head hitting concrete. Stars flashed.

CHAPTER ELEVEN

SIRENS WHINED IN the distance, voices, loud and hushed, faces loomed over Charlie...one big mishmash of sound and light that made her head swirl. With the wind knocked out of her and Remy's full weight on top of her, she couldn't tell if she...or he...had been hit. His head rested on her shoulder, but she was moving and he wasn't.

"Remy!" She pulled to the side to look at him, but his head was turned so she couldn't see his face. "Remy! Are you okay?" She pushed against him, adrenaline racing through her like a freight train.

"Don't move, miss." A woman's voice. "I called nine-one-one. You should wait for them to get here."

Charlie glanced around to see who the woman was talking to. Another person was sprawled on the ground near her...and he wasn't moving, either.

Her heart pounding, hands trembling, she reached to lift Remy's head. Touching his cheeks, her fingers slipped against something wet and warm. Blood. *Oh, God!*

"You could be hurt, miss. Best not to move until an ambulance gets here. I used to work in the ER and that's what they always said."

"Are you a nurse? He's hurt. He needs help." Her head spun as she gave one last push and wiggled to the side, slipping from underneath Remy's dead weight.

Sirens blared louder and louder, lights suddenly flashing in one continuous arc around her and people yelling and screaming and Remy was hurt...because of her. She pushed to get up, but fell to her knees.

"Wait, ma'am!" A male voice now. "We'll get you to the hospital in no time. Just stay still." A heavy hand landed on her shoulder.

Moments later she and Remy were bumping along in an ambulance, Remy on a gurney and her sitting at his side, heading to Detroit Receiving.

She was fine as far as she could tell, but the police, who'd arrived at the same time as the ambulance, insisted she get checked out medically.

"Is he going to be okay?" she asked the EMT monitoring her pulse. Another tech was on the other side, apparently taking Remy's vital signs, and someone had wrapped a bandage around his head.

"Looks that way. Just a flesh wound as far as I can tell. He might have a headache for while though."

"Really." She grabbed the tech's arm and shifted to the side to see around him. "If he's okay, then why is he still unconscious?" Every muscle in her body felt like rubber bands stretched to the limit.

"I'm not."

Snap!

She turned. Remy's eyes were closed, but he was smiling. She sagged with relief...swallowed a gulp of air. "It's about time."

He wiggled a finger for her to come closer.

She leaned in.

"No one can know," he whispered. "We have to get out of here."

The police had looked at her fake ID, but she didn't know what identification Remy had on him, or if any officers had recognized him. He did look different...his hair was longer and the beard covered his face some. No one had questioned them since the extent of their injuries was undetermined. She wasn't worried for herself because if they wanted to question her, they'd be questioning Charlene Krenshaw.

She leaned even closer, her mouth near his ear. "Are you okay? Can you move?"

He nodded. "Stay on my right and follow my lead when we stop."

No sooner than he said it, they pulled into the hospital Emergency drive, the back doors flew open and a handful of blue jackets rushed the ambulance. The EMT who'd taken her vitals helped her get out while the other two handled the gurney down the ramp. When they stopped momentarily to talk to the staff at the door, Remy grabbed her hand, rolled to the side and slipped off the cart.

"Hey, wait. You can't get up yet," the tech standing next to the cart yelled.

"C'mon," Remy said, pulling her along toward the parking lot at one side of the building.

"No, you can't leave. You're hurt," someone shouted. "We need information—"

Moving as fast as she could, which, even though she'd taken off her shoes, wasn't very fast because she was still a little dizzy, she said to Remy, "You're hurt. Maybe we should stay?"

"I'm fine and we're not staying. I'm going to call a cab," was his grim-faced reply.

Continuing around the building, they came to the front entrance to the hospital where he led her inside and down the hall toward the restrooms.

Two nurses walked by, expressions curious. Charlie tugged at her wig, made sure it was still secured tightly. She caught a glimpse of their reflection in a glass window as they passed...her hair sprouting wings as she tripped along in bare feet, carrying her five-inch stilettos, blood on her silver dress and Remy with a head bandage. They were quite the pair.

Her gaze darting from side-to-side as they went, she said, "What about our cars? We should take a cab to get our cars, and then find out what happened."

He stopped dead and she stumbled into him. He grabbed her upper arms with both hands as if he might shake her.

"What happened is that you shouldn't have gone to the Devil's Den alone."

"Excuse me?" She pulled back, frowning. "Aside from the fact that it's none of your business where I go, I'm in the investigation business. I do this all the time. I can handle myself. I have skills."

Remy laughed. "Skills? Sorry sweetheart. You mess with any one of those guys at the bar and they would eat you for breakfast."

Heat radiated up her neck. She stiffened. "Well, thank you for your confidence in my abilities," she said through gritted teeth. "Is that why you hired me? Because you thought I was incompetent?"

His face went from pink to red. A muscle danced near the corner of one eye and the veins in his neck looked about to pop. He crossed his arms.

"You know, when people hire me, they sit back and wait for me to do my job. I investigate and then bring them the information. It's as simple as that. I get hired to do a job, and I do it…whatever it takes."

"Charlie, if I hadn't seen—" He stopped suddenly, clamped his mouth shut, waited as another person—a janitor—went by.

Oh, my God. Her heart skipped a beat. He'd seen the shooter and had shoved her out of the way. He'd saved her life.

A chill ratcheted through her. Another case of being

in the wrong place at the wrong time? Or was someone
trying to kill her?

After retrieving their vehicles from the Casino parking
ramp, Remy followed Charlie home and parked next to
the garage while she parked inside. He slammed the
door, locked his vehicle and stalked inside the garage.
He was only trying to tell her how dangerous it was,
that she should be more cautious.

He'd felt the same way in the bar when she'd been
talking to the bartender. He was a cop, trained to
protect. He'd feel the same damned way if she was his
partner. No point in taking chances, putting yourself in
danger. That's all it was. He wasn't kidding when he
said she wasn't any match for guys who could be
connected to the mafia. But, apparently, he'd insulted
her by saying so.

Still, she was right. He'd hired her to do the job. He
just didn't know now if he could let her do it.

As she climbed from her vehicle, he tipped his chin
toward the old Mercedes under a clear plastic tarp.
"Nice ride."

She looked at him for a long moment, clicked a
remote and closed the garage door. "It belonged to my
father."

Apparently the trip from the garage to her place had
cooled her down. "Does it run?"

"One week a year."

He raised an eyebrow.

"The Dream Cruise."

"Seriously?" Every year, for a week, car aficionados
hauled out their vintage vehicles to cruise miles and
miles on Woodward Avenue. Old geezers, rednecks,
the golf club crowd, bikers, Gen Xers, teens…all came

out to participate and watch the parade of vehicles. Some brought lawn chairs, food, and even portable barbeques to tailgate like they were partying at a football game—with plenty of adult beverages to go around.

He couldn't picture her in that crowd.

"Seriously." Her eyes brightened as she raised the clear plastic covering the vehicle and reverently touched the front fender. "You act surprised."

"I am." And he felt a little dizzy, too, like he wanted to lean against something to keep from falling.

"Why?" She turned to him, arms crossed. "Because cars are a guy thing?"

"No, because you're Charlie Street, a one-woman-wrecking crew, who doesn't have time for anything but work."

She motioned him to follow as she went inside. "Well, you know what they say…looks can be deceiving."

He was pretty sure he had her pegged. But then, every time he saw her, he learned something that contradicted his preconceived ideas about her. "Seems a shame to only take it out once a year," he said, following her. "But then, I guess it's not a car you'd want to park on the streets anywhere near here, either."

"Exactly." She motioned him forward. "Let's go upstairs to talk. The renovations are only partially finished, but…" she nodded at his injury "…it's still more comfortable than the office."

"Lead the way," he said, amazed that suddenly she seemed so relaxed. Not edgy at all. What had he said or done to change things?

Once upstairs, he had to stop for a second to let his head clear, again. Then she led him down a hallway to the front of the apartment, pointing out on the way the would-be floor plan once it was finished. The two bedrooms, one with its own ensuite bath, were at the back of the building, then another bathroom, in case he needed one, she said, then an empty room, and in the front, a large, open loft-like area that housed the completed kitchen, living, and dining room. With soaring ceilings and tall narrow windows, it was a great space.

"Nice floors." He noted what appeared to be newly finished oak flooring. "Original?"

She nodded. "It was a grand old hotel built in the late 1800s and I'm keeping as much of the original structure as I can...floors, chandeliers, sinks, doors, doorknobs..."

"All that stuff piled up on one side of the garage."

She pivoted to face him. "You're observant."

He smiled. "Job hazard."

She motioned for him to sit. "So, what did you observe tonight? What's your assessment?"

He picked a squishy black leather barrel chair to sit. She sat on a matching couch—all very contemporary and modern—and flicked off her shoes.

"I heard one of the uniforms say it was gang related," he said.

"That's what they always say."

"You think otherwise?"

"I think it's the second time I've had shots fired around me. And if that bullet hadn't hit you, it would've hit me." She glanced at his bandaged head. "I have to thank you—"

"Just part of my job." He shifted position, not wanting to take credit for something he did on instinct. "The guy behind us wasn't as lucky."

She studied him for a moment. "I heard a nurse say he should make it."

"And the media will say he's critical, his life hanging by a thread and if he dies, someone will be responsible for his murder…and be sure to tune in for more details."

"Oh, for sure." She nodded. "If it bleeds, it leads…and then make it worse."

He chuckled, surprised they actually agreed on something. "Bottom line, we're only guessing. The target could've been you, could've been me, or the other guy. Or…just life on the street."

She picked up a TV remote setting on a square black leather hassock, which apparently served as a coffee table, then flicked on the television and went to WDIV where Devin Scillian was in the middle of the 11 p.m. news. "One man is in critical condition after gunfire near the Devil's Den earlier tonight. Two others, a man and a woman were injured and taken to Detroit Receiving, but left the hospital without making statements."

"Apparently none of the cops recognized you," Charlie said.

He rubbed his chin. "Yeah. A four-day beard and a little extra hair is all it took." He reached up and pulled off the fake hair length attached by small clips under his own hair, and set it on the coffee table. "I didn't recognize any of them, either."

"The police are looking for both the man and the woman," the newscaster went on. "Captain Wade Pendergast said they have no suspects, but the shooting may be gang related."

"Which means they won't be looking very hard for the shooter," Charlie said, focused on the TV.

"They'll look for leads. If they don't have any…" He shrugged. "If the shooting victim survives, they'll question him, see if there's a reason someone wanted to take him out, and go from there."

"But they won't spend much time looking for us if they think the shooting is gang related. They'll focus on that. Once they fix on a suspect, that's it, they work to prove guilt." She directed her gaze at him.

He heard the subtext loud and clear. She believed her father innocent and the police were to blame for not finding the real killer. She had no evidence, of course, and he couldn't blame her for thinking what she did. She wasn't far off about the police focusing on a person of interest. When evidence pointed in one direction, so went the investigation. The likelihood of changing course once the department identified a viable suspect was slim. Ninety-nine percent of the time, they were right.

"Not necessarily," he said, struck with a sudden need to defend his profession if not his peers. "There's standard procedure we all have to follow, but not every cop works the same."

"Oh?" Her eyebrows rose. "Have you ever gone against standard procedure? Done something you felt you should do regardless of the outcome with your superiors?"

He crossed his arms. *Hell, yeah. All the time—if it was necessary.* "I am right now."

She shook her head. "No, you're not. You hired me to do it for you."

"There are…" He was about to say there were reasons for that. But she was right. That's exactly what he'd done. "This is different."

"How?"

"It just is. You'll have to take my word for it."

She held his gaze for the longest time, as if deciding whether she could, should, or would take him at his word. She didn't trust him. He doubted she'd trust any cop. She'd implied more than once she thought he was unyielding, that he saw things as black and white and wouldn't risk going against protocol, even if he believed it was right.

She was wrong, but in the end, it didn't matter what she believed as long as she did the job he wanted.

"Okay. Let's go down one road at a time," he said. "Say you were the target; who would want to do that—and why?"

CHAPTER TWELVE

"GOOD QUESTION," CHARLIE answered.

Waiting for her response, Remy thought about the same question for himself, and the answer was obvious. Someone who wanted him to stop looking into Adam's disappearance. There were several people on that list. Chief Bouvaird had his reasons.

But going against the chief's wishes would only get Remy fired.

The chief had talked to Remy's father about it, and his father was worried the publicity could ruin his chances in the political arena. But that wasn't going to get him a bullet either.

That left the person responsible for Adam's disappearance, which brought him back to the beginning again. He'd taken precautions going to the Devil's Den, even with his appearance. He hadn't told anyone, and he hadn't been tailed.

No one knew he was working with Charlie, so he could cross off that scenario.

But someone could've followed Charlie. And that could be anyone if it was related to one of her cases. Including his.

She seemed preoccupied with the news, but then flicked off the TV, got up and walked to the industrial-style kitchen on the other side of the room. "Something to drink?"

"Sounds good?"

"Beer, wine, soda, water, juice. I also have a full bar."

"Beer works."

She stood near the counter which looked like it might've been made of concrete. The kitchen was all stainless steel and stone, edgy and efficient. Like her.

"How do you feel?"

"Fine." He shrugged. "It's only a flesh wound."

"But the ER tech gave you something, didn't he? Should you be mixing meds and alcohol?"

"It was a mild painkiller. No big deal. One beer isn't going to do anything."

Her expression said she wasn't sure, but she opened the refrigerator, pulled out a couple bottles of some local craft beer, came over and handed one to him along with an opener. After setting hers on the side table, she pulled off the blond wig and the skull cap that covered her hair, which was tacked to the top of her head. She seemed completely at ease. Not self-conscious in the least about her looks.

It was a refreshing change of pace from many of the women he knew or had dated.

She took out a few hair pins, shook her head and her hair spilled down around her shoulders. She ran a hand through the tangled curls.

His hormones replied. He downed half the beer, eyes not leaving her for a nanosecond.

"What?" she asked.

"You look good with your hair like that."

Her brows came together. "Like what?"

She did that thing again with both hands in her hair, fluffing it out. "Not in a ponytail—" he managed, ignoring the wake up call to his vital parts. *All wild and messy, looking like she'd just been—*

She moved to sit on the couch again, pulled her feet up under her, bringing the short dress farther up her thighs. She took a sip of her beer.

He guzzled the rest of his.

"I can think of a few." Her eyes met his then broke away.

It took him a minute to realize she was answering the question he'd asked earlier about who would want to take shots at her and why.

"A few. Just one is bad enough, but a few?"

"Job hazard," she said, repeating his earlier words. "A couple of ex-husbands who don't think court-ordered custody applies to them...and I guess there might be a person or two who doesn't like my representing an ex-prostitute."

He frowned. "Hardly a reason to kill someone."

"Ex-husbands don't think rationally. Especially those who may have been physically abusive to their wives and family to begin with."

"I meant the Devonshire case. People may hate the woman and think she's guilty, but no one is going to take shots at you simply because you're representing her."

"Oh?" She looked at him from under her brows. "If someone were in Lucy's little black book of clients and the publicity would ruin them, they might be very inclined. And the killer who actually murdered the congressman could think I've got information that's going to expose him at some point in the trial."

He took the last swig of his beer. Did she really believe that woman was innocent? "Do you have information to do that?"

Her brows rose. "Confidential," she said, relaxing against the back cushion. She brought an arm up to rest on the pillows next to her. "Remember?"

He did. And he liked her professionalism...even though his own had long since departed. Once he'd started thinking about how sexy she looked, it was hard to concentrate on anything but how her breasts rounded just above the scooped neckline of her dress…how her ice-blue eyes seemed even bluer than he remembered.

"I do." His voice sounded oddly distant. He started to say something else, but suddenly lost his train of thought. She was right. The meds and the beer…not a good idea. "So, that's it? No other possibilities?"

"Isn't that enough?"

"More than. How about those who don't make the confidential client list? Not everyone in your life is a client."

Her forehead furrowed. "Maybe—" she hesitated, then shook her head. "—no. No one else."

That was a bad cover-up. She'd thought of someone, but changed her mind about telling him.

"Speaking of us," she said. What about you? Any enemies?"

"I'm a cop. I arrest people. Put them in jail."

"I mean like someone who doesn't want you to find out what happened to your friend."

"Yeah…there is that." He held up a hand and counted on his fingers. "We have the chief of police, Captain Pendergast, and my father. But they're not people who would take me out because of it. The only person who would do that is the person responsible for Adam's disappearance."

"Or the person who hired him."

"That, too." Which left them nowhere.

"Well, think about this," she said. "If it was someone who wanted to take you out, he could've done it when you were alone somewhere. And same for me. Why tonight, when we were together?" Both brows raised. "And there was more than one shot."

"True. But no one could've known we'd be together. I didn't know it."

She gave him a sideways glance. "You didn't know I'd be there?"

"Nope. Surprised the hell out of me."

"You're sure of that? One hundred percent?"

"Pinky swear." He shrugged. "Then again, no one ever knows anything one hundred percent. But one thing I'm sure of is that we don't know any more than when we started."

Her expression became thoughtful. "No... I think we do." Her eyes caught his.

Waiting for her to finish, he saw a flash of reluctance. "What is it?"

She stood, went to the big windows that were covered with what looked like dark sheets. She pulled one side open and peered out. Turning back to face him, she said, "Joey Drakar."

"Joey Dra—"

"He's the common denominator between us."

"What do you mean?"

She came back and sat on the couch facing him. "I..."

He waited.

She cleared her throat. "Joey Drakar was also on my list of people to check out in my father's case."

He frowned. "Sorry... You lost me."

"I think it's safe to assume you would have researched everything about me before hiring me, and that you know about my father."

"I did, and yes, I do, but I don't know what that has to do with anything now. What happened with your father was years ago."

Another long pause.

"Well, I don't believe my father was guilty. Never did, and I've spent a lot of time looking into it. I never came up with anything, but I know there's something there. If I can just find it."

He knew that, too. "And?" He shook his head. He'd checked her out thoroughly before hiring her. Had he missed something?

She went on quickly without a breath, as if wanting to just say it and be done. "When I was going to law school, I was actively investigating my father's case. I did a lot of digging and I pissed off a lot of people during that time. Chief Bouvaird and the mayor to name a few. Anyway, years ago...back before my dad's trial, Joey Drakar was one of the neighborhood teenagers my dad had taken under his wing at the gym, and it was Joey's testimony that convinced the jury my father had—"

Her breath hitched.

"Look—" he said, taking her hand "—maybe we should talk about this later."

"No. Now. We need to do it now. She hauled in another long breath and launched to her feet. "I never got the chance to talk to Joey because he disappeared around the time my father was murdered. When I was old enough, I started asking questions about what happened that night. I spent a lot of time investigating and always came up empty. A couple years ago, after making no progress, I stopped investigating...but I never stopped needing to know what happened. And when I saw..." Her voice cracked.

"When you saw Drakar's name—" he finished for her and nodded. Yeah, he got it.

"That's one of the reasons I didn't want to take your case, and now I know I shouldn't have. It's a conflict of interest. I can't do it without wanting information for my own reasons, so I really need to think...about withdraw—"

"No." He shot to his feet, eyes meeting hers, trying to decipher his own schizophrenic feelings about what she'd just said. He wavered as he stood...waited a second to steady himself, then, eyes still on hers, he said evenly, "So, what you're saying is now that you have what you want, a new lead on your father's case, you're going to blow off mine."

Her mouth pinched.

His head began to swirl even more. He shifted, unsteady on his feet, so he sat again. "Look, Charlie," he said, keeping his voice even, "I don't care if you're investigating ten cases that overlap. We're making progress."

"Getting shot at isn't progress."

"Someone is worried enough to want to stop us."

She pulled her gaze away.

"Permanently," he added.

"But we don't know that for sure."

"I'm sure. I'm damned sure!" More now than ever. "We were asking questions in the place where Adam was last seen. That's a pretty good indication that we're onto something." He touched the bandage wrapped around his head. "We're close, Charlie. Really close. I...we...can't quit now."

She turned away, silent for the longest time, then, shoulders straight, she faced him again, chin raised, resolve in her eyes. "Okay. So you agree the best way to find out what happened to Adam is to find out who wants to stop us from doing so."

"Agreed."

"Then we need to go back to the beginning...talk to the guy who told you Joey Drakar was the last person to see Adam," she said.

"Adam's former partner? Or the snitch he got the information from and whose mangled body was found floating in the Detroit River."

"Oh, no." She raised a hand to her mouth.

Remy nodded. "Yeah. Bad luck."

For a moment, she just stood there looking at him.

"For him, or for you?"

He drew back. "What's that supposed to mean?" He launched to his feet, and swayed to the side, dizzy. He grabbed the arm of the chair, steadying himself as he came upright.

She gave him a strange look, took a step closer. "I... Nothing," she said. "I didn't mean anything. You better sit."

He jerked away, wavered and almost lost his balance. "No, it was *something*. It was you thinking I don't give a rat about the guy because he was some lowlife bottom feeder." He poked a finger in the air at her. "But you understand him and feel sorry for him because he got a rotten break in life and it's not his fault."

Her mouth flattened. She crossed her arms. "No, that's not what I was thinking. But if the shoe fits..."

Damn. Did he appear that much of a hard ass that she really believed he didn't care? And what difference did it make if she did? He stepped closer, his face only inches from hers. "You think you're the only one with a conscience? The only one who cares about justice?"

She reached out, one hand on his arm, the other on his chest. "You'd better sit," she said. "Before you fall."

"I wouldn't be a cop if I didn't care, but if you saw the stuff we see every day, you'd learn some people aren't—"

She snatched her hands back, as if she'd just touched something foul, eyes instantly afire. "Some people aren't what? Aren't worth the effort?"

"No. That's not what I meant. And stop putting my thoughts into your words. You have no idea what I'm thinking. And for the record, I don't know anything about your father's case...or whatever you're talking about that you think is a conflict of interest."

She backed away. He closed the gap again...just

short of bumping into her. "But I do know about snitches like Willie Boyle, and, yeah, you're probably right. I'm more concerned about not getting information from him than the fact that he's dead. The guy's dead because he earned it. Not because he was a snitch, but because he's a sorry excuse for a human being, a guy who beat his wife like she was his personal punching bag, kicked her in the face so she's spitting teeth along with the blood, and no one can do anything because she won't press charges.

"Even if she did, a restraining order isn't any good if he kills her. His kids have been in the ER multiple times for unexplained injuries…and that's not counting the rape and assault he did time for. No one could've saved this guy, Charlie. So no, I'm not sorry he's isn't going to hurt anyone again. But I am sorry if it keeps me from finding out what happened to Adam. Very sorry."

He stopped for a breath. Thought he saw her eyes soften. "That's the only thing I care about right now. We're on to something, so we can't stop. That's what they want…to scare us into quitting. And if they can do that, the bad guys win."

She stared at his bandage, tipped her head up. "That injury is more than a scare."

The world swirled around him. "It is. And that's what tells me—" he closed his eyes to stop the room from turning, then opened them again "—we're making someone really nervous."

He had the feeling he was repeating himself and each word seemed drawn from a swirling reservoir. He swayed, arms stabbing air to grab onto something and next he knew, she was flat against him, chest against chest, her arms around him, bracing his body upright with hers.

On contact, his mind went blank, all thought

replaced by the fastest hard-on he'd ever gotten.
So…he kissed her.

CHAPTER THIRTEEN

REMY'S LIPS WERE warm and soft and Charlie melted into him, returning the kiss with equal fervor. Except her response came from raw desire. His from the effects of meds and alcohol.

She pulled back. "You'd better sit."

"You think? I'm kinda liking it right here."

"Well, you won't be thinking the same way when the meds wear off."

She walked him to the couch. "I don't believe we're going to get anything more accomplished tonight, and you can't drive home." She pressed two fingers against his chest, gave him a slight shove and he dropped onto the couch like he'd been sucker punched.

"You know," he said, grinning. "You're probably right." The grin switched to a frown. "The shooter might want to finish the job."

A shiver ran across her shoulders. "And you could stop someone if they wanted to do that?"

His mouth crooked up on one side and he raised his eyes to hers. "Maybe not. I guess that would be the time for you to use your 'skills.'"

His attempt to placate her made her smile. "Okay," she said. "I owe you one, anyway."

"Man, how did I get so tired all of a sudden?"

"Either you're a pansy-ass drinker, or they gave you

something stronger than Tylenol. Could be both."

He looked about to protest, so she said, "I'll get you a pillow and some blankets, and then look at your injury."

Going down the hall for the emergency first-aid kit she'd received after enrolling in an EMT and CPR class a few years back, she was sure she could take care of a simple flesh wound if necessary. Her first-aid kit had bandages, Iodine, and antibiotic cream. If he needed more than that, stitches or something, she'd have to get him to an ER somehow.

Except, a few moments later when she returned, he was dead asleep on the couch. In his shorts. She lifted his head to put the pillow underneath, careful not to bump his injury, and noticed a tattoo on his left arm, a symbol of some kind…and as she knelt beside him, it was impossible not to notice the rest.

No ginormous body builder muscles popping out all over, or washboard abs, but his muscles were substantial and well-defined. His abs—above low-riding black briefs—nice. Flat. Her pulse quickened as she drew her gaze down the length of him.

Damn. She'd had fantasies about guys like him, could easily have one right now. For real. Just reach out, run her hands over his chest, down his stomach…and keep going. He was out so cold, he'd never even notice.

She moistened her lips. Her breathing deepened. She raised a hand…then grabbed the blanket.

Yeah. It was official. She was a sex-starved slut!

She tossed the blanket over him, drew a deep breath and then pulled the first-aid supplies to her side.

Reaching to take off his bandage, she saw a scar on his left cheek, near his chin that she hadn't noticed before. With a few days' growth on his face, it was more obvious. He surprised her. Not the scar so much.

He was an active guy...and a cop. There were many ways to get a scar, but the tat?

Guys like him, guys who grew up in Grosse Pointe—the son of a judge who was about as far right as Hong Kong—didn't get tats. A guy like Remy who grew up in the closed world of staid old families with power and prestige—didn't get tats. Not unless he belonged to some white supremacist group. But that would be way too farfetched. But the symbol wasn't any she'd ever seen in her criminal justice studies, either.

Remy was an unusual man, not quite what he appeared. In fact, she had to wonder what made him become a cop instead of following the predetermined path guys from moneyed families usually followed. Why hadn't he become an attorney and joined his father's firm? She could only imagine what his father, the judge, thought of his career choice.

Not that it mattered.

She lifted the end of the bandage, but the rest was stuck to his forehead with dried blood, so she dabbed it with a wet cloth first, moving closer as she unwound it. Seeing the deep gash above his right eyebrow, her breath caught.

A little to the left and he would've been dead.

A little more to the left and she might be dead.

No. Not might. She would be. That shot had been meant for her. She was as sure of it as she was that her father was innocent and had been framed for murder.

Someone wanted to keep her from investigating, and Remy was right, they were getting close enough for that someone to be very worried. But was it about Adam's disappearance, or something else? Was it the shooter who'd missed his mark three months ago, or someone else? How many unhappy people were there on the other side of her hard-won cases? Or even those she

couldn't save when she was a public defender and they
wound up behind bars. And crazy ex-husbands...and
wives...politicians worried something might come out.
Or someone whose career swindling people had come
to an end?

It could be any one of those. And the only way to
know was to keep doing what she was doing. Find out
who their shooter was. And there was only one way to
do that.

Make herself a target.

Remy squinted against the bright light shining directly
in his eyes. It took a few seconds to realize he was on
Charlie's couch in her living room, and the light was
coming from a hole in the sheets she had hung over her
windows. If the sun was that bright, he was late for
work.

He pulled to a sitting position then snared his pants,
neatly folded on the end of the couch, and pulled his
phone from the pocket. Nine o'clock, three missed
calls...and he had a head banger of a headache. Even
though he'd had only one drink, he felt like he'd been
on a three-day bender.

A quick glance around told him he was alone. The
place was morgue quiet with no sign of his host. Not
even the scent of coffee. With great caution, he pulled
to his feet, but even then his head swirled and his
stomach pitched. Crap. He stood still for a few, waiting
for his equilibrium to settle down. Sunday, he
remembered. Okay. Unless he had an emergency call,
he didn't have to go anywhere. Not immediately.

As he waited, his head stilled and the nausea
subsided enough for him to move. Very slowly.
Remembering the brown van he'd seen parked outside

before, he shuffled to the window to see if it had returned. Was it a neighbor or someone keeping watch? Maybe someone who liked to take pot shots at people? Hard to tell unless he made contact...which he would if the guy showed up, again.

At the window, he pulled back the sheet, and immediately saw the tail end of a dark van disappearing behind a trashed house on the right. Charlie said she'd seen a dark brown van there before she and Remy had met, so he probably wasn't the shooter who'd fired on them last night. But whether the shot had been meant for him or Charlie or the guy who'd been hit, was anyone's guess.

A sharp pain stabbed in his head, making him waver. Oh, man. Just thinking made his brain hurt.

He spied a coffeemaker on the counter and shuffled his way across the living room to the kitchen. Picked up the pot. Dang, the thing looked brand new, never been used. He searched the cabinets for coffee and found nothing but dishes and a few spices.

What the heck. Didn't the woman eat? He checked the stainless steel fridge and spied a bag of coffee. *Thank you, God.* Moving like a snail so his head didn't bang any more than necessary, he filled the pot with water, doled out what he thought might be the right amount, and then leaned against the counter to wait it out.

Where *was* Charlie? She couldn't be sleeping. Not her style. She was a doer, a go-getter, a one-woman show. A *sexy* one-woman show. Especially in that costume she'd worn to the bar. As he took a cup from the cabinet above the coffee pot, he envisioned her in his bed. But, oddly, the costume didn't do it for him. She was much more attractive without all the makeup and hooker clothes. In fact...without any clothes...he was sure.

"Sleep well?" a low female voice—not Charlie's—caught him mid-fantasy. He swung around. The young blonde with the unusual name and who resembled one of his favorite actresses—a name that escaped him at the moment—emerged from the hallway.

"Yeah. I did." It was Charlie's receptionist, except her hair was different than when they'd met before. Not the ponytail she was sporting today. "Sorry," he said, indicating his state of undress. *Scarlett.* That was the star's name. Scarlett…something.

"Not a problem. Charlie had to leave, but she said you should help yourself to whatever you can find to eat."

Hah! "Very generous of her."

"I know," she said. "Sad isn't it. I think she lives on Starbucks and Slows's barbeque." She tossed a set of keys at him and he nearly fell over reaching to catch them.

As he straightened, he said, "January…is it?"

"Yes. You're good to go…whenever."

She was obviously not up for conversation. But as she said the words, he heard light footsteps in the hall and a second later a little girl with dark curly hair and big brown eyes appeared.

"Mommy, what are you doing?" The child looked at Remy, her expression curious. "Are you Auntie Charlie's boyfriend?"

Unsure how to answer since he was in his skivvies and either way, whatever he said, it wouldn't be good. He looked to January.

"He's just using Auntie Charlie's apartment for a little while, Sweetie. And you shouldn't be asking those kinds of questions from people you don't know."

Eyeing Remy, the child asked, "What's your name?"

He wanted to go over and grab his pants from the table, but it would only prolong the discomfort.

"Remy." He bent down to shake the child's hand. "What's yours?"

Eyes wide, the little girl looked at her mother. "He's not a stranger now, so is it okay to tell him?"

The look in January's eyes said no, but she nodded, anyway.

"I'm Kacey," the girl said, reaching out a hand. "And I hope you get to be Auntie Charlie's boyfriend because Mommy says she really needs one."

"Oh, boy," January said, turning the child around and giving her a gentle nudge. "Go back downstairs. I'll be there in a minute."

When the child left, he grinned. "Awkward."

"It'll be a heck of a lot more awkward if you don't get your pants on and get out of here before Charlie's mother arrives."

Judge Dancy Malone closed the library door and then went to sit at his treasured Louis the VIII desk.

"I'm tellin' you because we go way back, Judge Malone. If you want to keep the peace, you'll do something, if you know what I mean."

Police Chief Leon Bouvaird stood hat in hand in front of Dancy's desk and looked as though he'd been dropped onto an alien planet instead of the judge's library. "You sure? Last I heard he'd put it to rest."

Bouvaird fingered the brim of his hat. Eyes cast down. "Someone's askin' questions, again."

Dancy drummed his fingers on his thigh. "Someone? Does this someone have a name or are we playing twenty questions?"

The chief's face reddened. "You know damned well what I mean."

The judge laughed. "Calm down, Leon. No one is

doing anything you have to worry about."

"I wish that was true." The chief paced one direction, then another, still rolling his hat in his fingers. "I got four murdered girls in four months, which means a possible serial killer on the loose. There was another shooting near the Devil's Den and two of the victims disappeared. I don't have time to mess with all this other stuff. You need to get things under control.

"People who hang out in bars and run from the law usually have something to hide. Why are you so concerned?"

The chief's face hardened, his mouth turned up in a sneer. "I don't give a rat's ass about some street scum getting shot. I hope he bled out in an alley somewhere so he wouldn't cost the city a dime. What I care about is seeing my grandkids grow up and that's not gonna happen if I don't keep things running right in this town. That means certain people keeping their nose outta where it doesn't belong."

"Certain people, Leon? Why don't you quit the crap and say what you mean."

"I only know what's reported to me and if other people hear about it, I'm going to get the heat. We gotta keep people happy, if you know what I mean."

Dancy squelched his disdain for the simple-minded police chief. A guy who got all worked up about things that could be handled easily shouldn't be in a job of authority. He made a mental note to talk to the mayor about that, then leaned back, hands steepled. "I'll take care of my family, Leon. And I suggest you take care of yours."

Bouvaird puffed up his chest, lifted his chin. "I remember you sayin' that before, but nobody seems to be listenin'."

Dancy stood, pasted on a smile to cover his disgust, then walked around his desk. With a hand on the chief's shoulder and the slightest bit of pressure, he urged him toward the door. "That's right. I said it before…and I'm saying it again."

Turning to look at Dancy, the chief returned his hat to his head. "I got a lot riding on this, too, Judge. So, make us all happy. We don't want any bad stuff going down."

Dancy suppressed an outright laugh and patted the man's shoulder. Was that supposed to be a threat? "Take it easy, Leon. You're going to end up with an ulcer. Just leave it to me."

The grimace on the chief's face said he probably already had an ulcer and nothing was going to make him stop worrying like an old lady. Dancy all but pushed him out the door.

Idiots. All of them, including his son. He gnashed his teeth. Would Remy never learn? He'd been a problem since his mother died, always going his own way, never listening. He was sick and tired of it. But what he felt was nothing compared to what would happen if Remy persisted in his naïve quest.

He jammed a hand through his hair. If Remy didn't listen, he'd find out what happened to his friend…but not in the way he wanted.

CHAPTER FOURTEEN

AT THE PRECINCT, Remy rose from his desk and followed Adam's former partner to the john. Coming up behind Sean Glover before he went inside, Remy said, "We need to talk."

Sean's gaze darted, checking if anyone was within earshot, and then, under his breath, he said, "We talked. I have nothing more to say."

Remy motioned him into the washroom. Sean didn't budge. "I can't, man. I told you everything I can." Sean stepped to the side to go around, but Remy blocked him.

"A minute. That's all I ask. Adam deserves that much from his partner of seven years doesn't he." Remy shot a glance around. He didn't want to be seen questioning Sean any more than Sean wanted to be seen talking privately to Remy. "Or maybe Adam doesn't deserve anything more? Maybe he was a shithead partner and you don't give a fuck what happened to him?"

Neither one was true, but if playing the guilt card would get him what he wanted, he'd do it. And a helluva lot more.

Sean edged sideways, tucked his chin. "Not here. The Lafayette. One hour."

Remy tipped his head, agreeing, then moved past

Sean and punched open the door to the john. Another cop, Terence Frey, a rookie, stood on the other side, eyes wide and looking guilty as a thief.

Frey lowered his gaze. "Sorry," he said and hurried away.

Sean and Remy exchanged glances. If the kid heard them, they could both be in deep shit. "He's new," Remy said. "He heard me mention Adam's name. No big deal."

Sean tagged Remy on the arm. "Later."

Remy went inside and at the sink, leaned down and splashed cold water on his face. As he rose and reached for a paper towel, he saw Captain Pendergast's reflection in the mirror. He swiped the scratchy towel over his face.

"A guy from I.A. was nosing around yesterday," the captain said. "You know anything about that?"

Remy turned. "No, Sir. Why would I know anything?"

"Because you're a troublemaker, that's why."

Remy almost laughed. The last thing he wanted was for Internal Affairs to get involved. I.A. could screw up everything he was trying to do. He raised his hands. "Nothing to do with me, Sir."

"Then I guess you can explain this?" He handed Remy a manila envelope addressed to him and which had an I.A. return address.

He felt like asking the captain if he'd been demoted to mail delivery, but took a big breath and opened the envelope. "Just a date for the deposition on Duncan's DUI."

The captain's mouth pinched.

Remy took a step to exit, then said over his shoulder, "Sorry to disappoint you, Captain."

"Sorry might be your last word in this department if you don't start producing. Your job is to solve crimes and close the files and, lately, I've seen little of that."

"I'm working on it, Boss. Can't make up evidence," he said, although he knew a little fabrication was common practice with some of the cops he worked with, and he was pretty sure Pendergast knew and even condoned it. Backing out was a common practice to lower the stats, and it was well known the chief of police wanted cases closed and didn't care how it was done.

A man planning a run for mayor had to look good on paper, regardless if the information was true or not.

The majority of the Detroit PD were good guys, good cops. Clean cops operating with their hands tied due to work overload and no money budgeted for anything. But there were dirty cops out there, too. Some who believed the end justified the means. He'd witnessed the captain looking the other way, but he didn't know where he drew the line. How far would the captain go to keep his job secure? To do the chief's bidding? The mayor's?

As he walked away, he felt the captain's glare on his back. Pendergast never liked having to hire Remy since he'd already had someone picked for the job. But when your father is good friends with every power broker in the state...and he wants something...he gets it.

Yeah, he was going to regret the comment to Pendergast, but he'd do regret later. Right now, he didn't have the time. Back at his desk, he went through his notes on a few other cases and determined what he had time to do before meeting Sean.

He was just clearing out when his cell phone buzzed—an email message from Krista in HR, a cop wannabe he'd been sweet talking to get information from Adam's personnel file. He'd met her at the casino and convinced her if she'd get him Adam's personnel file, she'd be helping him expose major corruption, like an undercover agent. It had been so easy it was scary. He'd given her a newly created e-mail address that his former college roomie, geek extraordinaire, had said was untraceable.

The message from Krista said, GOOD TO GO. EMAIL OR HARD COPY?

He responded E-MAIL ASAP, pocketed the phone, closed his PC files and headed out to meet Sean.

Remy arrived at the Lafayette early, ordered a Coney dog and chili-cheese fries, then instead of sitting at the counter, he took his food to a two-seater against the wall. The scent of French fries and spicy chili reminded him of his first time in the city without an adult. He'd been twelve and Adam was a year older. Even then, his best friend'd had a sense of adventure and daring that was sure to land him in trouble someday.

Adam had been hanging out in the D for several months and convinced Remy he needed to get away from suburbia and see how the real world lived. What Adam really wanted was to score a little weed and he didn't want to go alone. They'd scored, smoked a few joints, hit a coney establishment near the old Tiger Stadium on Michigan and Trumbull and chowed down, laughing like idiots the whole time.

He'd never been in the city without his parents before that day. He and Adam had gone back many times and not just to score. For Remy, the D was an adventure, a whole new world that he and Adam had shared. They'd been closer than brothers. A lot closer than he and Parker had ever been.

Between bites, he pumped up his email from Krista. The file was large, so he decided to wait until he got home to read it, but Krista's message set off a few alarms. WE SHOULD REPORT THIS STUFF TO CNN. PEOPLE SHOULD KNOW.

Geezus, she wanted to be another friggin Snowden. And he didn't know if she was talking in general, or if she'd found something she thought should be reported.

He texted back, THANKS. PLEASE DON'T DO ANYTHING WITHOUT MY OKAY. YOU COULD RUIN THE WHOLE OPERATION. I'M COUNTING ON YOU.

"Hey."

The man's voice made him turn. Sean stood a few feet away at the counter getting coffee. A moment later, he eased into the seat across from Remy.

"Let's make this quick. I'm busy today," Sean said. "But for the record, I want to know what happened to Adam as much as you do, so don't give me that shit anymore." He took a drink of his coffee. "And I can't tell you anything more than you already know."

Remy's pulse jumped. He shoved away from the table. He'd see about that.

"Can't or won't?"

Charlie fingered the files strewn across her desk—Malone's and two others she was working on. Max had been following the ex-husband on the Stratten custody case and had documented his findings. And January had obtained new information about the group home where Sandra Linski's daughter had been staying.

She had other clients besides Malone, but she always came back to him...drawn like the proverbial moth to the flame. Because some of the people involved in Malone's case were intertwined with the people in her father's, it was proving way too easy to get caught up in the hope dangling in front of her.

The mere thought made her weary. Hadn't she done enough?

For years she'd followed every lead, no matter how small or how seemingly insignificant, and found nothing. Why couldn't she leave it alone? All she was going to get was more heartbreak.

She shoved the file aside. She had a satisfying job, one that needed her full attention. She needed to focus on what she could do, not what she couldn't. Her clients believed in her…believed she was committed to getting them what they deserved. Which she was.

But no matter what she told herself, her thoughts kept straying to the night last week when someone had taken shots at them. The night Remy had slept on her couch. The night he'd kissed her.

Despite the fact that he was a cop—and so not the kind of guy she'd ever be interested in— he'd looked mouth-wateringly sexy…and after that kiss, she could've jumped his bones in an instant.

But that was her sex-starved libido doing the thinking. The rational part of her brain was asking whether Remy really hadn't known she'd be at the Devil's Den…or had he followed her? Was he going to be the client from hell, always second-guessing her, demanding to know what she was doing and how things were going? It had looked exactly that way.

Except she hadn't seen him or even talked to him since he'd come to the office last week, so it appeared he was literally doing as she asked. Letting her do the job and waiting for her to get in touch with him when she found out something new.

Good. That was good…except that she kept thinking about him.

She went back to the Linski file. January had gathered more information from the woman about her daughter, including the group home's incident reports on the girl's behavior. The reports noted the teen's bad attitude and the fact that she'd threatened to run away.

No documentation that could be a clue to where she might go…or who she might've gone with. No notes on any of her friends at the home or even anyone with whom she'd had problems.

Most noticeable was that the reports didn't gibe with what the girl's mother had told her—that her daughter was doing better and was looking forward to coming home. If that were the case, why would she run away? Obviously someone wasn't being truthful.

Charlie held up the report she'd looked at earlier and still felt as if she was missing something. Rereading it, she saw nothing unusual. But she sensed it…and when her gut began to give her messages she couldn't explain, it was almost always best to follow up on it. Go to the source.

Getting January on the phone, she remembered she had a meeting with the judge and the prosecutor on the Devonshire case in a couple of hours, probably to talk about another plea bargain. "I need to schedule an appointment with the Phoenix Rising group home director for later in the day," she said. "See if you can make it as soon as possible."

"Already done," January said. "You're meeting with the director, Gregory Ustinov, this afternoon at three fifteen."

Three fifteen? Charlie glanced at the clock.

"The deposition is at nine," her assistant continued. "And then you have the meeting downtown at ten thirty."

Her assistant was more efficient at seven a.m. than Charlie was two hours after coffee…on her best day. "Great. Thanks. Now tell me what's going on with you." Having worked with January for almost three years, she'd learned the woman amped up her productivity when stressed.

Silence. Then…finally…"Nothing. Just a little trouble with maintaining a low profile."

"Do you want to talk?" They were busy, but she'd make time if necessary.

"I'll let you know."

"Promise."

"Yep."

"Okay then. Give me a heads-up when we're ready for the deposition."

They hung up and Charlie stood to peer toward the front desk to see if January had her five-year-old daughter with her. She always brought Kacey to the office when she was worried her ex might've found her. Craning her neck, there was no kid that Charlie could see...but she saw someone else walk through the front door.

Malone.

Her blood pressure spiked. She dropped into her chair, hoping he hadn't seen her see him. Her phone buzzed.

She picked up. "I'm busy."

"He says it's urgent."

"What's urgent?"

"Didn't say, but we are representing him. Right?"

"Yes, but he can't just pop in whenever he feels in the mood."

A long pause.

"Are you okay?"

"I'm fine," January shot back. "So, you'll see him then? He's nervous as a cat on a high wire."

Charlie let out a long breath. "Let him know I have five minutes and that's it."

"Done."

Moments later, Malone entered her office.

"I have other appointments, so please make it quick." She barely raised her head and kept reading the file.

"I know. Five minutes." He tipped his head to the chair. "Do I have time to sit?"

"Five minutes and you're wasting some of it."

He dropped into the chair, leaned forward, elbows on his knees. He jammed a hand through his hair. January was right, he was wired. He'd switched his usual black sport jacket for a leather biker type, and wore faded jeans and a black T-shirt. Wired…and hot.

"I have new intel on Johnson."

She pushed back, sat at attention. "From?"

"Not important. What's important is that Johnson may know more than we thought."

"Okay…" She folded her hands in her lap.

"Johnson's connected."

"Nick Johnson. The bartender." Her tone was flat. "How?"

"Don't know."

"When we were at the bar," she said, "Johnson agreed to get me some drugs, but that can't be the connection. Anyone can get drugs without going through the mob. Who's your source?"

Remy crossed his arms. She stared at him…waiting. After a long pause, he finally said, "I talked to Sean Glover again. Adam's former partner. He said Adam spent a lot of time at the Devil's Den. Sean also confirmed Adam was undercover with The Partnership. Using his alter ego, he set himself up with them by amassing huge gambling debts, got a loan to pay off his debts, then got in deeper and deeper until he was doing business for them."

"Okay. We knew he was working undercover and suspected it was with the mob. Now that it's confirmed, how does that help us?"

He leaned forward, eyes brightening. "That's not all. There's a mole," he said, contained excitement in his voice. Then, in one swift motion, he sprang to his feet, swung his arms wide. "It helps us because…if we find out who the mole is, we might be able to uncover what happened to Adam."

"I thought we eliminated that because we didn't want to put any other undercover guys at risk."

Remy bobbed his head. "We did. But the mole is with the FBI." His brows lifted and he produced a wide white grin, as if this was some big aha moment. "This guy was there! He would have to know what happened to Adam."

"The FBI?" She snorted. "Well, great. Let's just hustle on over and get the information then."

Remy's expression flattened.

Seeing his disappointment, she cringed. "Sorry. I didn't mean the information isn't good. But it's no secret the two agencies aren't exchanging valentines."

He looked at her as if he'd just seen something he didn't like, shoved his hands in his front pockets. "Right." He turned to go.

"That's it?"

He stopped in place. "My five minutes are up."

Heaving a breath, she came around the desk and stood in the doorway. "Do you know anyone with the feds that *might* give us some kind of clue?"

A long moment passed…his gaze riveted on her, as if trying to figure out something. Finally he said, "No, but it's another source. Whoever the mole is, he knows what happened to Adam. We also know this is big, probably crosses state lines. That's more information than we had before."

That was true. "And you have some suggestions?" Stupid question. Of course he did. He couldn't seem to stop wanting to take over her investigation. Hell, she should just let him. Less for her to do. But she didn't work that way.

"Yeah. Find out who the mole is. If we can get some intel on who's joined The Partnership, say…within the last couple of years, we can narrow it down."

"Johnson," she said. "You mentioned he's

connected to the mob. Do you know that for sure? Because if he really is involved, then he'd be a source. He'd know who was new to the organization within the last couple of years."

"Exactly."

Her heart skipped a beat. It was the first real opening they'd had to get solid information. She dusted her hands together. "Okay, that's it then. I'll make another trip to the Den. Johnson liked me…promised he'd get me some drugs."

His eyes met hers. "There must be another way. Something less dangerous than going back to the place where someone decided to use us for target practice."

"We weren't at the bar when that happened. We were around the corner."

Malone raked a hand through his hair.

Damn. She moistened her lips. Why did he care how she did her job? Anytime you worked with people and one party was unhappy, there was a chance something unexpected could happen. It would be the same for him. But his concern seemed genuine. Maybe he was worried that if something did happen, he'd feel guilty because he'd hired her?

"I always take precautions," she said, although she didn't know why she felt obliged to tell him how she did business.

He looked at her askance.

"Trust me. I always have a plan B. I know what I'm doing where my own safety is concerned."

He studied her face, probably wondering if she was telling the truth, because he obviously hadn't seen Max.

"Okay. Good," she said before he could respond. "We're clear then. I'll let you know if I get anything."

She stepped aside. "And if that's all, I've got appointments to keep."

CHAPTER FIFTEEN

AT THREE O'CLOCK Charlie entered the main door to the admin offices of the Phoenix Rising Group Home, a building that looked like it might've been a school or a hospital at one time.

A musty scent, like wet clothes left in the washer too long, permeated the air. Mold. She'd learned a lot about mold when representing a pro-bono client in a lawsuit against a slumlord last year.

January had received a lot of information from Sandra Linski, plus whatever records she'd had in her possession. Sandra had also signed a consent to get police records, too, but that was slow in coming. Learning what happened from the source might provide new information, but mostly, she was interested in why the Linski woman's information didn't agree with that from the group home records.

Crossing the worn concrete floor in the entry, Charlie made her way to the reception desk, where a woman about her own age was immersed in whatever was on her computer monitor, and introduced herself. The woman, dressed in a white tailored blouse and something black on the bottom, looked up, but didn't speak.

"I have an appointment with Mr. Ustinov at three fifteen."

"Oh, right," the woman said. "Please have a seat."

She gestured to the school chairs lined up against the wall across from her desk. "Mr. Ustinov is running a bit late today."

On the woman's left was a bank of windows through which Charlie saw a concrete courtyard devoid of trees, shrubs or places to sit. Some children hung together in groups of three or four, a few others clung to the walls, as if trying to be invisible. From her research, she knew the residents ranged in age from about nine to eighteen.

One of the smaller girls, alone and hugging the building, caught her eye for a moment then quickly turned away.

"Miss Street," a low, deep voice came from a hallway to her left.

A man with a head of thick black hair and equally black eyebrows who wasn't much taller than she walked toward her. His dark suit was top of the line and he filled it out well. Some designer name, she was sure. Black, tasseled loafers completed his ensemble.

"I'm Greg Ustinov. Nice to meet you." With a swish of an arm, he indicated a room a few feet down the hall. "Please, come into my office." He went ahead of her and opened the door. "Have a seat," he said and then went around to the other side of a large ultra-modern desk of glass and steel. He stood behind it, smiling, apparently waiting for her to sit.

"Thank you for seeing me on such short notice." Charlie sat at the same time as he, observing the fine artwork on the wall behind the desk, the plush easy chairs on one side and leather couch on the other, a stark contrast with the sparse décor in the reception area.

He nodded. "It wasn't a total surprise since Ms. Linski had mentioned she was going to talk to you."

"Good. Then you know my questions are going to be about what happened with her daughter, Ella."

He nodded, his expression sad. "Nothing that hasn't

happened before. Only this time she hasn't been located and returned."

"She's gone missing before? I don't recall seeing that in the reports."

"It's there. We're required to report all incidents."

"I mean the police reports."

"Oh, right. That's because, on those other occasions, she was located shortly afterward. There was no reason to report it to the police."

"Well, I'm a bit confused and maybe you can help me out. Sandra Linski tells me everything was going along fine with her daughter, and she thought things were such that Ella would be able to come home soon. She didn't mention most of the things I read in the incident reports."

"Our policy is to notify the parents of every incident, but if we can't reach the parent…" He gave a slight shrug, raised his hands, palms up. "We can only do so much without parental cooperation. It can be very difficult when there's only one parent."

His icy attitude made her skin prickle. "That's not unusual, is it? I mean with the kids that are here. Statistically, many troubled children come from single-parent households and knowing that, I'm sure your staff are well trained to deal with all their issues."

He stiffened. "Yes, of course. Every employee is certified, but as you might imagine, the work can be difficult at times."

"So, what happened to Ella? Why did you wait twenty-four hours past the required time to report the incident? And did you or someone else question the other children to find out if anyone knew where she might've gone?"

Ustinov pursed his lips. "I was not here when it happened, but it's all in the report. If you don't have a copy—"

"I have a copy, thank you. But as you know, reports only go so far. They usually include only what's necessary. I would like to talk with some of the students she was closest to. It's possible they may know something that's not in the report."

"That's *not* possible. Not without parental permission. And if you'd read the files we already gave you, you'd see the police have talked to some of the other girls."

She'd read the files and they included very little. And why was this guy being such a dickhead? She frowned. "Excuse me. Are you saying you don't want to help us find Ella Linski?"

He stiffened. "That's a ridiculous suggestion, Ms. Street. Of course we want to help. If you can get me a list of your questions, I'll be happy to share all the details we are allowed to share without the client's permission."

"Good." Charlie jammed a hand into her messenger bag and pulled out the papers January had prepared. One with several questions and another with Sandra Linski's authorization for records. She handed them to Ustinov. "The questions and an authorization from Ella Linski's mother for you to share all the information, and a request for the records from the time Ella entered the facility."

Without so much as a glance at the documents, Ustinov nodded for her to set them on the desk. "I don't know what you're looking for, Ms. Street. If your client thinks she's going to get some money based on negligence, it's not—"

"Are you a parent, Mr. Ustinov?" Locking eyes with his, she narrowed her gaze. "I would guess not, because if you were, you'd understand my client simply wants to find her daughter and she's willing to do anything to make that happen." She rose to her feet and pressed one hand on top of the papers on his desk, fingers splayed, eyes never leaving his. "That's all my client wants, and I'm trying to help her. I expect you would like that, too, not only as the director of this fine facility, but as a human being. And the only way we can do that is by uncovering information that might lead us to where Ella might've gone."

His mouth pinched.

"Capisce?"

And his eyes looked as if about to pop from his head. A vein bulged on his suddenly rose-colored forehead.

"I understand, *Miss* Street. It is Miss, isn't it?" Without waiting for a response, he went on. "I know about you. I'm familiar with your work…and how all you lawyers drag your opponents through the mud to win your cases."

The accusatory tone in his words was nothing new. *Bastard.* She shook her head. Frowned. Feigned confusion. "Opponents? I'm sorry… I assumed we have the same objective here. Finding Ella Linski." *Cold mother-fucking bastard.*

He blinked, eyes suddenly alert, as if it just dawned on him that he may have said the wrong thing—and that he'd been antagonistic instead of helpful…as a good group home director should be.

"Yes. Yes, of course," he said. "We want to do everything we can to help find the Linski girl, but I can't allow you to disrupt things for the other children who are still here and making progress. We regret that the Linski girl ran away, but now we must leave the issue in the hands of the police so we can continue to provide the best services possible to those who are still here and need us." He gave her a smarmy, gotcha smile. "Surely, you can understand that."

Charlie forced a smile. "Surely." Just as she turned to go, she added, "And understanding the need for

speed on incidents like this, you'll *surely* have those
questions back to us as soon as possible."

The smarmy smile returned. "Oh, you can be sure of
it, Miss Street. As soon as possible."

After leaving Ustinov's office, Charlie went directly to
the front desk and told the receptionist she had a long
drive back to her office and would like to use the
restroom.

The woman pointed down the hall. "At the end, near
the back door."

On her way, Charlie noticed the back door led to the
street on the side where she parked. "I'll just go out that
way, when I'm finished," she said, then pressed on
without waiting for an answer.

She took note of some kids in the courtyard on her
way to the restroom and once inside, she was happy to
see the bathroom had a window…even though it was a
typical horizontal bathroom window and above her
head.

She glanced around. Toilet…sink…and a metal flip-
top wastebasket. The wastebasket might not hold her
weight…and the rounded top hard to stand on, but the
sink was a long stretch to the window, and the toilet,
definitely too far away and too low.

Taking a deep breath, she shoved the waste
container to the window, kicked off her heels, put one
foot on top, then raised herself up so both feet curled
over the cover. Balancing on top of the can, she smiled.
All right! You got this, girl.

But as soon as she thought it, she wavered and, arms
flailing in the air, one foot slipped off, and just about to
fall, she caught herself with a hand on the window
ledge.

Her pulse raced as she steadied herself. She pulled a few breaths until certain of her balance, however precariously, and then raised her head and peered outside.

The same children were milling about. She was hoping, if anyone was close enough, she could open the window and talk to them. But across the courtyard she saw a woman, about Charlie's mother's age, approaching the girls from the left. Wearing black leather pants and a tight, white T-shirt and black vest, the woman wasn't dressed as one would think a teacher...or a counselor would be. But then, Charlie didn't always present the image people expected either. Current position a good example.

A smaller girl who looked to be about ten and with hair so short it looked like someone had buzzed a razor over her head, stood apart from the others. She was far enough away from Charlie that if it would be difficult to make contact without getting the attention of the others. She'd have to come back. Or maybe send Max. He was an expert at getting into places and ferreting out information.

Finished, she jumped down, put her shoes on, flushed the toilet, washed her hands, went out, and exited through the back door.

A chain-link fence separated the walkway from the courtyard where the children were hanging out, and the leather-clad woman was now standing across the courtyard under the patio overhang talking with one of the older students. Charlie didn't see the smaller girl anywhere.

So much for getting information they didn't already have. She'd have to wait until they got all the records before she'd know how to move forward.

Waiting was always a pain and she seemed to be doing a lot of it lately. She kept walking. After a few more feet, she heard a rustling sound…and quick footsteps. Not seeing anyone, she slowed, took a few more steps toward her car when a small voice said, "Psst. Lady. Did the police find Ella?"

Her gaze darted. She spotted a child's form slip into the shadowed recesses of the building next to her about fifteen feet away. Squinting, all she saw was the girl's outline in the corner of the building, and the toes of the kid's scruffy once-white tennis shoes. The girl in the yard with the shaved head had the same shoes.

"Don't look at me." The same voice. "Don't come over."

The girl was outside the fence and obviously didn't want anyone to know…probably afraid to trust anyone, but interested enough in Ella to risk getting caught. Charlie opened her purse, took another step and made herself stumble, dropping her purse and spilling its contents all over the sidewalk. Kneeling to pick up her things, she kept her head low and said, "No, we haven't found her, but we hope to soon. Were you friends with Ella?"

A long pause. Then, "She was nice to me."

Charlie sensed the hesitancy, the distrust. A feeling she knew well. "Did you know Ella was going to run away?"

Another pause. Then, "No. But everyone wants to run away."

O-kay. Can you be more specific, Ms. Street? "Do you know where Ella might have gone?"

She waited, but got no answer. Still crouched, she picked up the cosmetic bag, then a notepad, and after taking as long as she could to pick up the rest of the contents…and still no response…she brushed one of her business cards into the bushes next to her. She said under her breath, "I'm going now, but I'm trying to help find Ella and bring her home to her mother. If you know anything, or just need to talk to someone, you can call me anytime. I help lots of kids and my number is on that card I just put under the bush."

Straightening, Charlie flipped her hair behind her shoulders and started for the car. The last thing she wanted was for the kid to get in trouble for talking to her, and she was sure that was what would happen if she gave away the girl's presence outside the gate.

More movement, and then, "Lady..." The same voice, again.

"Ella didn't run away."

Hearing quick footsteps again, she glanced to the corner of the building. Gone.

CHAPTER SIXTEEN

REMY PRESSED THE security buttons to the massive iron gates at his father's home in Grosse Pointe and was reminded of how much his mother hated the place. For all he knew, being forced to live in a community where she was practically blacklisted was the reason she'd committed suicide.

As far as the world knew, Sarah Malone had died of cancer. It never ceased to amaze Remy how someone in his father's position could manipulate almost anything he wanted. Even the truth about his wife's suicide.

Remy and Parker were told the same lie their father had told the press. Remy hadn't known the truth until years later when he'd needed a copy of her death certificate. He'd been stunned. Even now he could feel the anger that had raged inside him. He'd hated his dad for not telling them the truth. He'd blamed him for not being there to save his mother, and he'd cursed his mother for leaving…for being so selfish. For not caring enough about him to stay.

Every time he saw the gates, he was reminded of his loss. And every time he came through the gate, he knew it would be another tug of war between him and his dad.

Today's summons would be about something his old man wanted him to do. Or something he found wrong in what Remy was already doing. There was little in between. If Judge Dancy Malone had his way, Remy would be reporting to him instead of the chief of police. Yet despite it all, he couldn't help wondering if maybe this time would be different. Maybe this time his dad just wanted to see him, no strings attached.

Caroline was at the front door before he'd finished parking in the circular drive and climbed from his vehicle. The woman was a saint. She'd run interference for him as a teen, warning him whenever his father was in a foul mood, and since he'd been back, she continued to do so, despite his protests that he was an adult now and could handle his father's moods just fine.

"Don't tell me," he said, raising a hand, when he reached the door. "But I appreciate the thought."

Caroline's lips compressed. She crossed her arms over her chest as he passed by and went into the foyer. *Oh, man.* He knew that look.

"I was going to tell you what I heard about that woman you're seeing, but I guess you'll find out eventually," she huffed behind his back.

He stopped short. Turned. "Who said I'm seeing anyone?"

She lifted her chin. "No one. No one said you were seeing someone. I just thought when your father and his friend were talking about you and that attorney—"

"Never mind." A muscle near his eye twitched. He didn't need to hear any more, but stepped closer, lowered his voice. "Thanks. I didn't mean to be a jerk, and I appreciate that you want to help me." He was about to reiterate, 'but, I don't need it anymore,' then stopped, realizing whatever he said wouldn't make a bit of difference. He touched her arm. "Sorry."

He tipped his head. "In the library?"

She nodded, her expression still defensive.

"Got it." He winked, went to the big double doors to

the library off the foyer and, steeling his resolve, knocked once before opening it. He stepped inside. "Hey, Dad."

His father rose from his usual spot in the leather chair next to the fireplace, shoulders rigid, purpose in his eyes. "Son." He stuck out his hand.

No matter what the reason for being summoned, Remy always got a handshake...a pat on the shoulder.

"Glad you could make it, son." He indicated the bar with a tip of his head.

"No thanks. I'm on duty and can only stay a few minutes."

"Okay, have a seat. This won't take long."

Remy obliged, but perched on the edge of the cushion. A fire burned in the fireplace, everything cozy and warm on a chilly spring night. Remy's rental apartment had none of the amenities he'd grown up with, but he had privacy, which he wouldn't have if he'd taken his father up on his offer to live at home when he'd returned to Detroit. Even staying in the carriage house as his father had suggested was too close.

The judge settled next to him, leaned back, his expression serious. Remy was reminded of *The Godfather* movie, how the patriarch quietly oozed authority. All his dad needed were some jowls.

"What's going on with you and that woman?"

Remy's gut knotted. "Excuse me?"

"I hear you're still seeing that investigator...the attorney."

His dad knew her name, but it was his practice to diminish people by referring to them by their job or in some other way. "You *hear*?" He'd been cautious about their meetings, but obviously, not cautious enough. "From anyone I know?"

"Does it matter? What matters is that you're stoking some dangerous fires."

"I think what I do and who I see on my own time is my business."

"I agree, one hundred percent. But others see it as more than that." He knocked back the rest of his whiskey.

"Like Chief Bouvaird?"

His father scoffed and waved his hand in dismissal. "That pissant. Fuck him."

Remy knew his father disliked the chief's "working man's mentality"—and he also knew the chief was simply the messenger.

"If not Bouvaird, then who?"

"Geezus, Remy. Don't be so damned obtuse. Nothing you do is going to change what happened to Adam, but if you keep stirring the fucking pot, you're going to pay the consequences. Both of you. You want to be responsible for that?"

He clenched his hands. "I don't know what you're talking about."

"Your friend has a history of pissing off the wrong people, and…" He paused, took a breath, blew it out.

"And?"

"And…she might not be so lucky the next time."

The next time? Did he know about what happened last week? There was no way. Unless… Remy's pulse soared. Or did he mean her earlier escape from a bullet? He shot to his feet. Staring down at his father, he cleared his throat, leveled his voice. "Next time?"

His dad stood, their faces only inches apart. He cocked his head. "You are aware of her history, are you not? Someone shot at her a few months ago."

He gnashed his teeth. "Acutely aware." He also knew that the case had been closed out. No way to tell if the shot was meant for her. But someone knew.

"What I'm saying is that what you do affects us all."

So, *that* was it. His old man was afraid that somehow

what Remy was doing would affect him—not the fact that his son could be in danger of losing his job…or even more severe consequences. But one thing he said made sense. Whoever took a shot at Charlie, the first time…or the last…might not miss the next time.

What Remy didn't know was whether his dad, in his own manipulative way, was warning him that Charlie was in danger because of him—or was the judge warning him because what Remy was doing could affect his political aspirations?

But even more important, who was so afraid of what they might uncover that they would stop at nothing to keep them from it? It had to be someone the FBI and the Detroit PD undercover unit had on their radar. Someone big.

Frankie Falcone big. The head of the snake.

Interesting that Remy and Charlie—a detective and a PI—were making the mob nervous. They had to be damned close or Falcone wouldn't be putting the pressure on.

Remy's adrenaline spiked. Whatever it was, Adam had been involved. And no matter what the threat, they couldn't quit now.

He just had to figure out how to keep both of them alive to do it.

Fresh from her after-work shower and garbed in no more than panties and bra, Charlie laid the costume on the bed. Red dress; blond wig; silver stilettos; handbag big enough for her gun; fake identification; large, sparkly earrings…and her watch. She couldn't forget the watch she'd found at the Spy Store online. She could record with it and take photos.

The red dress fit way too tight, but it was perfect for

her doppelganger, Charlene Krenshaw. Tonight all Charlene had to do was get Johnson to trust her enough to reveal his ties to the mob and then give her the names of any new guys within the last couple of years…information that could get him whacked. And that would be letting him off easily.

Oh, yeah…piece of cake.

If she was a mind-reader.

Remy could have totally messed up her first meeting with Johnson, but it had turned out okay in the end, once she'd figured out a way to make coming back a done deal. Drugs. But now she wanted a whole lot more, and she was going to do everything in her power to get it.

If she could stop procrastinating and get dressed. Good grief. What was wrong with her? She'd taken on a lot of scary jobs—even one in which she helped bring home a child who'd been kidnapped by the non-custodial father and taken to Afghanistan. But none of her earlier jobs had made her this jumpy. Every nerve in her body seemed on fire.

Gabe had suggested one night when she was unusually jumpy, that the shooting three months ago had affected her more than she wanted to admit. He might be right. But using herself as bait was, all by itself, a pretty good reason to be scared. And yet, it was more than that.

The possibility of messing up something that might help exonerate her father literally made her nauseous.

And thinking about it wasn't helping.

Okay. She imagined herself in costume, blew out a breath. *Okay. The most effective way to do something is to do it,* she recited a quote she'd heard somewhere to try to get into character. Or better yet—she looked in the mirror. *There is only do and do not. There is no try.*

But tonight, she wasn't channeling Yoda either.

She sat on the edge of the bed, her thoughts drifting to the same place they'd been far too often lately...to what it would be like to live like a normal person with a normal life, maybe married...and with some kids. Or at the very least just having someone there who cared. Someone who gave a shit what happened to her.

Really, that's all she needed. Someone who cared. Someone other than her mother and brother.

She sighed. Not likely that was going to happen with the company she kept. And even if she did find someone, how long would it be before it fell apart? Her brother said it was a self-fulfilling prophecy on her part, that she subconsciously picked guys who were unavailable, guys she knew she wouldn't end up with.

It was true her record was lousy. Like Sam, a workaholic, who she'd later discovered was married. And Zach, who was married to his buddies...and Brandon, who'd been trying to climb the corporate attorney ladder when they both worked at Reston, Barrett, and Brown. He'd actually thought he could get her fired and take her job. Poor bastard.

And there was Allan. Sweet Allan Chenowith, now Michigan's Attorney General and much of the time, her nemesis. There'd been a period when she'd actually thought it would work with Allan and they'd had a good year together. She should've realized the relationship had disaster stamped on it from the get-go.

And there was Heath. They'd been two strangers passing in the night. He'd changed her life, and she would never forget him.

Maybe Landon was right. Maybe she did pick the wrong guys. So, screw it. Screw them all. She didn't need anyone except the people she worked for...the people who needed help they couldn't get anywhere else. They were the only ones who mattered.

The only ones who needed her.

She fingered the red dress, stood, and then slipped it over her head.

Her phone rang and glancing at the caller ID, she saw it was Remy. Dang. Nibbling her bottom lip, she set the unit down and let it ring until the voicemail kicked on. If she talked to him, he'd want to go to the Devil's Den with her. When the voicemail kicked in, she heard, "We need to talk. I'm across the street and can see your lights are on, so I know you're there. I'm going to stay here until you talk to me."

Shit. She punched the return call button. When he picked up, she said without preamble, "I'm getting ready for a date, so make it quick."

"I didn't mean talk on the phone. I wouldn't be here if that was all I wanted."

"The message said *talk*."

"Screw the message. I need to see you now...before we go any further on the investigation. It's important."

"You have more intel?"

"No, just something we need to discuss."

She let out a long breath. Her first impression of him was correct. He wasn't a quitter...and that meant she better get it over with, whatever it was. "I don't have a lot of time—"

"I know. Five minutes."

"What?"

"Isn't that the usual?"

Jerk!

Without waiting for an answer, he added, "That's all I need. Five minutes."

She doubted it, but said, "Side door."

Five minutes later, he was sitting in her office, ogling her boobs like he'd never seen a pair. She folded her hands on top of the desk and waited.

"Nice," he said. His gaze raised slightly to look at her face. "Must be a special date."

His mouth twisted a little in a way that made her think he didn't like the idea. And for some strange reason, she liked that he didn't like it. "They're all special."

Glad she hadn't put the wig on yet, she waited for him to have his say. Except he continued to study her, and she continued to decipher his mood. On the phone, it seemed whatever he had to talk to her about was urgent. Now, not so much.

She glanced at her watch. "I really *don't* have a lot of time." From her previous visit to the Devil's Den, she knew Johnson's shift began at six p.m., but she didn't know what time it ended. It was now after eight.

He scrubbed a hand across his chin, then his eyes lit, as if he'd just deciphered a secret code or something. "You're going to the Devil's Den, again." It wasn't a question. He launched to his feet. "That is so—" he sucked in some air "—so dangerous." He pivoted, then, hands raised, said, "Do you have any idea what you're getting into?"

"Yes. And yes. That's what I do. All...the...time. And, I repeat, it's what *you* hired me to do."

"I know." He sighed. "Believe me, I know...and it was stupid on my part. Now I realize I can't have you investigating something that could have serious consequences...And that's why I can no longer retain your services."

She blinked. Leaned forward. *What?* "You're—" she let out a laugh of disbelief "—you're firing me?"

His brow furrowed. He nodded. "Yes. I'm firing you."

He couldn't fire her. Not when she was on the verge of getting information that might... She pushed to her feet and came around the desk. "Okay, let me get this straight. You just took weeks convincing me to take the job, and finally I agree, and now you're firing me because it's too dangerous, even though it's what I do all the time—and what you hired me to do."

He straightened, shoulders back. "Yes. I didn't reali—"

"Okay. I know it seems like not much is happening, but it is. We're all working on it. Me, Max, and Gabe. And things always seem to go too slow at first…seems like things aren't happening. But they are, and right now, the guys are piecing information together. The Johnson lead is a good one and I've already made the connection. It's—"

"It's done. I'm done."

Blood pumping, she stepped forward, her face only inches from his, thanks to her five-inch stilettos. "What happened?"

His eyes widened. "Nothing. I'm just done."

"Well, I'm not."

His expression went from adamant to puzzled. "If I fire you, you're done. Finished. You can't investigate a case you don't have."

She crossed her arms and when his gaze went to her boobs again, she glanced down to see her strapless gown exposed more cleavage than she needed at the moment. Hiking up the top of her dress with two fingers on each side, she said, "Really? I've been investigating cases I don't have for years."

"Okay. But not this one. I don't want to be responsible for…" He turned away.

"For what? Finding out what happened to Adam? Because that's what I'm doing. And we're making excellent prog—"

"Dammit, Charlie." He swung around. "I don't want to be responsible for something happening to… I mean, the guys we're dealing with. If we keep messing with them it's highly likely something will happen. Especially if you go to the Devil's Den." His eyes softened and he reached out, held her at arm's length. I—I don't want to see someone I...I know...get hurt. It would kill me if that happened, again."

"What do you mean 'happened again?'"

He released a long breath. "What happened to Adam...he was like my own brother. And if something happened again to someone I care about—" He cleared his throat, his hands fell to his sides. "I don't want *you* to get hurt, Charlie. I can't be responsible for putting you in harm's way."

His words ran together in her head. Someone he cared about? Cared about her, or cared about not being responsible? She could understand both, but they meant different things. And at that moment, she knew what she wanted it to mean.

"That's it," he said, taking a step back, putting a foot of space between them. "That's all I wanted to say."

Wow. For a second she couldn't breathe. She was going in totally the opposite direction. She hauled in a long, deep breath, then slowly let it out. "You're firing me because you don't want to be responsible if something bad happens to me. Okay. I get that."

But it wasn't that simple. Not only did she have a good lead on Remy's case, she had the first new lead in ten years on her father's conviction for murder...a lead that might actually help her find out who framed him. She had no choice but to continue. For herself.

She waited for Remy to say something more, but he just stood there, an astonished look on his face, like he didn't believe it would be that easy to fire her.

"So, we're done here, then," she said, moving beyond him toward the door.

The pressure of his warm hand on her shoulder stopped her. He turned her around, his eyes narrowed. "That's it? You're okay with that?"

She glanced at his hand lingering on her bare skin.

She moistened her lips as she brought her gaze to meet his. "Do I have a choice?" Her words were low and throaty and from the look in his eyes, he was getting the message, or thinking the same thing. *If he wasn't a client...*

Desire unfurled deep inside.

He brushed his thumb across her shoulder and, their eyes still locked, she added, "Very okay."

His pupils dilated. Her pulse quickened. His nostrils flared. Her breath caught and they both lunged forward, chest to chest, mouth to mouth, tongue to tongue, their kisses rife with desire...and raw need. He pulled back. "And this is okay, too?"

She chuckled. "You just fired me. You're not a client anymore."

CHAPTER SEVENTEEN

HE KISSED HER again, and again, backed her to sit on the desk, deepening each kiss as he moved against her. She spread her legs so he could fit between them. The dress was short and if she inched it up just a few inches…

She wrapped her legs around his hips, curled her arms around his neck, bringing him so close she could feel his heart hammering against her chest.

"I want you," he murmured, his mouth moving over hers. "So much." His breathing deepened, he slid his tongue between her teeth and she eagerly opened her mouth to his thrusts, her senses spinning from repressed desire. She needed this. She so needed it.

But not like this.

She pushed the thought away and ran her hands through his hair, tipped her head back as his mouth followed the line of her neck to the base of her throat, his hands tugging the spaghetti straps off her shoulders.

Her breathing stalled as he bent to kiss the tops of first one breast, then the other. The sensation of his warm lips on her breast sent pre-orgasmic twinges downward. His mouth met hers again, his hands at the back of her dress…unzipping.

Then she heard that stupid voice again. *No. Not like this.*

The last time she'd had sex with someone who didn't mean anything to her, she'd vowed never to do it again. Physical gratification was great in the moment, but she always felt worse afterward. Every single time was the same, the result of some deeply ingrained psychological brainwashing from her Catholic childhood she was sure.

But how she got that way didn't matter. How she felt did. All filling the physical need ever did was make her more aware it wasn't what she wanted. She didn't know *what* she wanted, but it wasn't the empty is-that-all-there-is feeling that sent her into a funk for three days.

"What?" Remy said, easing back to look at her.

"What do you mean, what?"

"You're having second thoughts."

Tilting her head to look at him, she said, "You're a mind reader, too?"

His chest heaved as he scrutinized her face. "I felt it. You pulled away."

She glanced at their position, her legs still wrapped around his hips, the straps of her dress hanging below her shoulders, her boobs hanging out, and her lips on fire. "Not from my vantage point."

"Mentally. You pulled away mentally."

"I didn't know there was an intellectual requirement. Usually it's pretty mindless."

A strange smile quirked up one side of his mouth. Then a puzzled frown formed and he gently pulled up one strap of her dress and then the other. "Yeah. It usually is."

Holy crap. Was he blowing her off? She'd offered him a freebie and he didn't want it? She didn't know whether to be offended or relieved. The moment lost, she quickly came back to the fact that she would miss Johnson at the bar if she didn't hustle. She released her legs and when he stepped back, she stood and reorganized herself, and gentleman that Remy was, he zipped the back of her dress for her.

"Thanks," she said, strangely at a loss for words.

"I'm sorry."

He *was* blowing her off. She shrugged. "For what?"

He shrugged, too. "I don't know. For not finishing what I started?

"It's okay. It's fine. I have someplace to be and I'm late already."

He looked as if he wanted to say something else, but then he just went to the door where he stopped and turned, posture suddenly rigid. "You're going to the bar anyway, aren't you?"

She could almost see the fumes rising. Understandable. He was a man in authority and she was telling him to stuff it. "I am. But not for the reason you think."

And why the devil was she explaining anything to him?

"I don't get it," Remy said. "What other possible reason could you have for spending any time at all that hole in the wall?" He waved a hand up and down her body. "Wearing that…that… 'rape-me' dress."

She raised a brow. "Really? 'Rape-me' dress? Is that why you nearly ripped it off a few minutes ago? It was the dress?"

He shoved his hands in his front pockets. "I'm not talking about me…or what happened. I don't know what happened, but it has nothing to do with you going to the Devil's Den investigating a case you're no longer entitled to investigate."

"I told you…it's not what you think. I'm not going there about Adam."

He swung around, threw his hands in the air. "Not about Adam. What else then? Oh, wait...I know. You've got the hots for Nick the bartender." He slapped his head. "How did I not see it that the night we were there? And he's such a great guy, he's even going to score some crack for you. Or was it H? Yeah, I get it now."

Her eyes clouded, as if she wanted to blast him back, but she didn't. Instead, she moved past him. "I can't tell you. It's another case...totally unrelated to yours."

As she moved away down the hall toward the stairs to her apartment, he grabbed her arm. "Am I supposed to believe that? You have more than one client whose case requires you to go to the Devil's Den to investigate? It can't be the Devonshire case, because I know Lucy and her girls are too high class to even step inside that sewer."

She raised her chin, mouth zipped tight as a freaking zip-lock bag.

Geezus, she made his stomach knot. If she wasn't going to the Den on his case, she had no reason to tell him why she was. It was none of his business. Which didn't make it any less dangerous. Whatever reason she had for going, it wasn't a good idea. Not unless she had backup. "Okay. I'll go with you. I could use a shot of Jack."

She rolled her eyes. "Really? What's with you, Malone? It's not about—"

"I don't give a rat's ass what it's about. It's a dangerous neighborhood. You know that, and the next time could..." He swallowed. "You could get hurt."

A curious expression drifted across her face. Then she said, "I always have backup."

"Backup?"

Her expression switched from curious to incredulous. "Max or Gabe. Anytime I go on a potentially dangerous job, I alert one of them and they go in either before me or soon after." She shook her head, gave a small laugh. "I can't believe you'd think I'd—"

"No. I don't...I mean didn't...I just wondered...I mean, last week—" *Fuck.* Last week he was too busy flaunting his machismo to pay attention. "Who was there last week?" He hadn't noticed anyone, but then he'd been so off his mark seeing her dressed as she was...

"Max went in before me. When you showed up, I signaled him it was okay to leave."

Heat filled his chest, crawled up his neck to his cheeks. He wanted to do a belly slide out the door. She was smart. Brilliant. She knew her business...had been doing it successfully for several years. He knew that, knew how respected she was for her expertise, but from the first moment he'd hired her, he'd done what he usually did, press his authority, push back before he got pushed, act like he knew it all. Like the alpha wolf vying for position.

He was an idiot.

But he still didn't believe she had other cases that would take her to that rat hole.

"In fact, I was just about to call M—"

"Forget it. I'll be your backup."

"You fired me."

"I take it back."

A half block from the Devil's Den, Charlie watched Remy drive away in the makeshift taxi, then adjusted the micro-processor-controlled receiver nestled in her ear canal and the tiny voice transmitter on her watch that was also a mini-cam. She loved the Danish-made spy equipment that allowed them non-visual contact. Remy would be able to hear the conversation and would know if anything went wrong...and he'd also know when to call and say her mother was sick. Then he'd play taxi driver again.

She hadn't wanted to do it this way, but since she couldn't stop Remy from following her, it made sense to join forces. He *was* a detective, after all. From what she knew, he was equally skilled as Max and Gabe. Why he'd felt a sudden need to protect her, she hadn't a clue.

Rubbing her temples, she almost wished he'd fired her for real, because in those few moments when he had, she'd realized she could forge ahead on her own. She'd be free to investigate her father's case without it interfering with Remy's. But he'd reversed his decision...and she needed the money.

Still, it was only fair to tell him. And she would. When the time was right.

Entering the Den, she saw Nick was working and he spotted her before she reached the bar. Smiling, he motioned her to sit on the end near where he filled the drink orders. She supposed he wanted her close so he could talk to her without it seeming like he was shirking his job.

"You look hot," he said as soon as she slid onto the stool. "I hope you ditched that loser who was with you before."

She glanced over her shoulder. "You see anyone with me?"

He angled his head. "You got another date showin' up?"

She flashed a sultry smile, eyelids at half mast, which was easy to do with the fake eyelashes. "No. I came to see you because you told me to come back," she said. "Alone."

She quickly noted who was working and how many people were in the room—one waitress, two customers glued to the television above the bar, and a loner at the table in the far corner. She'd hoped coming on a weeknight it would be less busy and Johnson would have more time to talk to her.

When he just stood there looking at her she said, "If you're working, I'll have a glass of house Merlot."

Flashing a lizard-like smile, he went to pour her a glass of wine and came back again. He leaned forward on the bar. "I got a present for you, but you'll have to wait until I'm off shift at midnight."

"That might be kinda tough. I'm a working girl and need my beauty rest."

He lifted a shoulder. "Up to you, babe…and your needs."

She looked away and placed her small purse on the bar. "I have needs." She batted her eyelids again. "But I'm a girl who thinks it's a good idea to know a little more about the guys I spend time with." Turning to look up at him through her lashes, she said, "That's always a good idea, don't you think?"

"Goes both ways, sweetheart. One chick came on to me the other night and five minutes after we left the bar, her gorilla-sized old man came after me." His eyes bulged. "Man, I don't need any trouble like that."

"No husband." She waved her ringless hand. "Not even an ex."

He placed his hand on hers. "No one who looks like you is going to be without a guy unless it's by choice. You must be particular."

She gave him the big-eyed innocent look, used her small, breathy voice. "I guess that's true. But it's because the last guy I dated lied about everything. Told me he wasn't married and he was. Another guy I met at Vinnie's next door told me he could help me make lots of money, but it turned out he was an undercover cop and thought I could help him since I was friends with some mob boss's girlfriend."

"What was her name?"

She shrugged. "I don't remember. "Angel, maybe."

"Angela, I bet. She's Carlozzi's girlfriend." He raised his chin, shoulders back, apparently proud of his mini-store of knowledge.

She feigned stupidity, again. "Is he the mob boss?"

He leaned closer, glancing to the back of the room. "Yeah...almost. And you better not be talkin' too loud about him, if you know what I mean."

"Well, I don't know. I don't know anything about that mob stuff, but this guy thought I went to school with her, and I didn't. It was her sister and besides, that was really a long time ago and I didn't actually know her...not like a friend or anything. No one can remember all that high school stuff, anyway."

She fiddled with her napkin. "But I wish I did know her so I coulda made some money." She brought her chin up, eyes widening, as if just realizing something. "Hey, how do you know Angela's name? Was that detective in here asking questions, too?"

He shrugged. "Maybe. Or maybe I just heard it around. You know. Stuff gets around when you work at a place like this."

"You know anything like he was talking about...to make extra money? She moved forward. I could really use some extra money. But I don't sell nothin' personal." She gestured to her body.

"Even if I did know something, which I don't," Nick said. "Those guys don't just take people in and give them money. You gotta earn their trust. Not many outside guys get to be family...unless Carlozzi or one of the other top wiseguys gives the thumbs up."

Hanging on his every word, she said, "Wow. You *know* that?"

His chest puffed up. "No...not like that. I just heard. Like I said, you hear a lot when you work in a place like this."

Her phone vibrated in her purse. She glanced at the clock, keeping track of the time so she could signal Remy to call her before Nick ended his shift. She wasn't about to meet Johnson after work as he'd suggested. "Well, anyway, now you know why I don't trust anyone until I get to know them really well."

He pointed to the neon Budweiser clock on the wall and winked. "We got a couple hours. You can get to know a person pretty well in that time."

She laughed stupidly. Felt stupid. While she liked some of her alter egos, and especially liked acting sultry and sexy—it was an act as far from her own persona as the next galaxy. Acting like a vapid fluffhead was tough, and she never felt like she pulled it off. But after an hour with Nick, and in between his servicing other customers, he'd spilled his guts, so she must've done something right.

Except the information he'd told her wasn't exactly a good lead into conversation about undercover detectives. Instead he'd segued into a story about how his father had run out on his mother before he was born and how he'd been in foster homes, group homes and juvy, and hadn't seen his real family for years. If it weren't for an older guy who took him under his wing and made him believe he could be someone, he'd probably be a lifer now…or on death row somewhere.

But he didn't give her a damn thing she could use to ask about a mole working for the mob. What she had, though, was enough information to know Johnson was connected. It was a start. Something she could build on. Maybe the next time she'd get him alone and spike his drink with sodium pentothal.

For now, best to depart and leave him wanting more. When Johnson turned to look at her, she again noticed the similarities between him and his supposed cousin,

Joey Drakar. Several things were similar, but mostly it was the way he walked and gestured. Joey had spent a ton of time at the gym, and even though she'd been a little girl, she remembered him. Nick and Joey had to be related. And she wanted more than anything to find out if Nick knew where his cousin lived.

But for now, she was here to find out about the mole, the federal agent who was her only lead to what happened to Adam Bentley. She was not here to find out if Johnson knew the whereabouts of Joey Drakar. Unless it just happened to come up.

"I didn't live up to what he saw in me," he continued talking about the guy who had helped him. "But I survived. And I didn't end up in prison."

"I'm sure he's happy about that."

"Not really. He's dead." His gaze dropped to her boobs. "But I'm sure I can make *you* really happy about it."

Glad he was off the childhood reminiscing and wanting to get him back on her track, she said, "I'm sure you can, but like I said, I don't trust people all that much. Especially guys who promise me stuff and then don't deliver."

He puffed up his chest. "Baby, you've been hangin' with the wrong dudes. Those guys were just blowin' smoke. I'm the real deal. I de-liver."

She fluttered her lashes. "Yeah? Impress me."

He frowned...sucked air through his obviously capped teeth, then glanced down the long bar. "See those men at the table in the back corner?"

She nodded. They'd come in fifteen minutes ago and joined the loner at the back table while Nick was going through his litany of childhood exploits. He'd stopped yakking immediately to bring them drinks. Stayed and talked for a long time.

"Wiseguys. They got connections."

She shrugged. "That supposed to impress me? If they got connections, maybe I should go talk to them."

"No...because they come here to talk to *me*. They don't know shit. They're not even on the food chain yet, so they do all the gruntwork."

Not being on the food chain meant they must be fairly new to the organization. It took time to become a *made man*...a full-fledged member of the mafia. They had to prove their loyalty and that meant not only doing stuff no one else wanted to do, it meant doing things a normal person wouldn't. All to show unconditional loyalty.

Lashes lowered, she slid a surreptitious glance toward the men. If they were the bottom rung, one of them could be her mole. But they sat in the shadows and it was difficult to see their faces. She could wander back to the restroom to get a better look, but Johnson might wonder if she did it right away.

When he went to refill a drink for a customer, she adjusted her watch and clicked a couple of photos. With the low lighting, it wasn't likely the images would turn out, but it was all she had.

Seeing the time, she realized Nick would soon get off work...and she had to split. "Anytime," she signaled Remy to call her.

Five minutes later, Remy still hadn't called and Nick came back. "I got the eight ball you wanted back at my place. That impress you?"

She pasted on an expression of interest, laced with doubt. "Maybe. But how do I know you're telling—"

Her phone buzzed and almost simultaneously, the William Tell Overture ringtone played out in her purse. "My mother," she said, and after answering was surprised to hear an old woman's voice. "I'm sick and I need you to come and take me to see a doctor." She made a face, took a deep breath as she hung up. "Damn.

My mom is sick and I gotta go."

His mouth flattened. "Yeah? That's too bad." He leaned closer, elbows on the bar. "Or maybe you got somethin' else going on?" In the blink of an eye, he snatched her phone.

Her heart leaped to her throat. She reached to take it back, but he held it away. Studied it.

"Let's see. Recent calls...that should show me—"

"It will show you I talked to my mother, and that's none of your business." She grabbed for it, but he kept moving back.

He grinned. "Worried I might find something?" He pressed the button. Glanced at the display.

Her chest squeezed as the phone lit up.

He tapped an icon. Turning to look at her, he frowned. After a long moment, he smiled. "Just teasin', baby. Can't you take a joke?"

When he came closer she snatched the phone. "That's not funny. And like I said, who I talk to is none of your business." She stuck out her bottom lip in a pout, pressed the recent call button herself to see what he'd seen. An icon of an elderly woman and the name Mom popped up. *Thank you, Remy.* Breathing again, she pressed the messages icon, listened and said, "Yes. Can you please send a taxi to the Devil's Den." She gave her name, the cross streets, and clicked off.

"Whatareyadoin'?" Nick said, reaching for her phone. "You're riding with me."

CHAPTER EIGHTEEN

WITH REMY AT the wheel of their quickly created taxi, an old car Remy borrowed from a friend and on which they'd stuck a TAXI sign on the side, they hit the entrance ramp onto the 75. "My place is the other way," Charlie said.

"We're taking the long way. I want to make sure you aren't being tailed."

"How would that happen? No one knows where I am and no one would recognize me even if they knew."

He looked at her askance. "I did last week."

"That's because you followed me."

"I didn't follow you. But the point is, I'm not taking any chances."

Okay. She was good with that. "Did you hear my conversation with Nick?"

"Most of it. We can check mug shots and if you can ID the goons that work for Carlozzi, we might have a lead on the mole."

"It was dark and I didn't get a good look. I took a couple digital images, but the lighting was bad, so I won't know till we pump them up if they're any good."

Remy was silent after that, disappointed, she was sure. She had to admit, she was disappointed, too. She'd thought she could get more from Johnson, but instead came away with a feeling she was missing something.

She might've learned more if she'd taken his offer to give her a ride, but even with her skills and a gun in her purse, she didn't want to chance being alone with him. "But now we know they hang out at the Devil's Den, so I can make another trip."

A buzzing sound came from her purse. A text. She pulled out her cell; the message was from Lucy Devonshire. Odd. Lucy never texted her—or called for that matter. Lucy was the most blasé client Charlie had ever represented and seemed resigned to the fact that she was going to be convicted regardless of her innocence. Understandable since it wasn't easy to make a case for someone with Lucy's dark and admittedly sleazy background. She opened the text. CAN'T TAKE THIS CRAP ANYMORE. I'M LEAVING TOWN.

"Shit." Shit, shit, shit. She texted back. YOU CAN'T LEAVE. YOU HAVE TO BE IN COURT ON MONDAY. She pulled up Lucy's number.

"What's up?"

"Wish I knew," she said, waiting for Lucy to answer. After the third ring, voicemail picked up. "Lucy, listen to me. I know this whole thing is scary, but you can't leave. I don't know what's wrong, but don't do anything until you talk to me. Call me back as soon as you can."

Charlie shoved the phone into her purse. "Dammit." Lucy was going to screw up everything they'd done if she gave even the slightest sign that she might be a flight risk.

Remy glanced over. "Something happen?'

She looked at the time Lucy had texted. Two hours ago when Charlie's phone had been on mute. If Lucy was going somewhere, she'd be long gone. "I hope not." That's all she could say. She couldn't tell him anything without violating client confidentiality. She may already have done so by letting him hear the message she'd left for Lucy.

After driving a circuitous route for another fifteen minutes, they ended up at a townhouse in Royal Oak.

"And we are…where?" Charlie asked as they pulled into the garage and the door came down behind them.

"My place. I requested some information on Johnson, and I want to see if it came in."

"You know," she said, getting back to the job he'd hired her for. "I just don't get it. If the feds are involved, why isn't the chief doing something to get the same information we're trying to get? The only reason I can think is that they already know who the mole is. And maybe they're working with the feds?"

Remy shut off the motor.

"But if they are…if they want to take down Falcone, what difference does it make who does it, or what they nail him for? A murder conviction is better than a drug convict—" Charlie bit off her words mid-sentence. She glanced at Remy who simply sat there, hands gripping the wheel.

"Sorry," she said. "I didn't mean—"

"Yes, you did." He looked at her, eyes steely, expression hard. Then he faced the road again. "And you're thinking I should know it, too." He closed his eyes for a second. "And I do," he said so softly she almost didn't hear him. Then, *bam*, he slammed his palms against the steering wheel. "Geezus, do I know!"

He leaned his head back against the headrest, blew out a long stream of air. "I know the odds of finding Adam alive are next to none." Each word was a near whisper, again. "But the odds are against a lot of things that turn out not to be true…and I will continue to believe that this will be one of them. Until I *know* different." His voice rose a little on each word, intense with conviction.

"I have to believe there's still a chance. Just like I do with every kid or any other person who goes missing or is in trouble. Because if I don't, the urgency is gone and then it's only about finding a body, not a person. A person who's a friend...a husband...a father...and a son."

The pain in his voice was palpable. She covered his hand with hers. He missed his friend, missed him deeply.

Like she missed her dad. After years and years, Charlie had finally accepted her father's death, but she'd never accepted how it happened. Never stopped missing him.

Maybe some of what Remy said was the same for her, why she felt such a need to prove her father's innocence. Because if she believed he was guilty then he wasn't the man she believed he was—a friend to the boys he worked with...a brother, a son. A husband and father.

Which brought her back to the fact that Joey Drakar had been one of those boys, and Nick Johnson might know where his cousin was.

Removing her hand from Remy's, she said, "I have to tell you something."

He opened the car door. "Fine, but let's go inside. I need a drink."

She did, too. A stiff one.

"It's a place to sleep," Remy said when they entered his rental unit. "And that's about it."

Charlie glanced at the small space, most of which was visible from the entry. Living room, dining room straight ahead and an L-shaped kitchen on the left, bedroom and bathroom to the right.

"If it works," she said, shrugging.

It did. He liked that his place was small. Less to

worry about and no upkeep. "I'm hardly ever here, so it's all I need." He motioned for her to sit on the brown sectional sofa he'd been willed by his brother after he'd bought a houseful of new furniture in preparation for his impending marriage.

She sat, crossed her legs and did a circle thingy with one foot. "I do need to get back to my place to review the conversation with Johnson and look at the photos...see if anything fits into the puzzle." She reached down and slipped off one shiny red shoe, then the other.

"You could get a nosebleed wearing shoes that high. Or a broken ankle."

She laughed, relaxed, it seemed. "I like them. They're so...feminine."

They were that. The spiked heel accentuated the long length of her well-toned legs, making her calf muscle more pronounced. But it wasn't just the shoes that made her legs look so hot. She was curvy, but lean...and muscular, and he'd put money on her working out with weights or doing some kind of fitness activity on a regular basis. And yet, she *was* feminine. She didn't need shoes to prove that in any way, shape or form.

He liked looking at her. "I need a drink. You?"

"Sure...whatever you're having."

"That would be a shot of Jack."

"Fine."

He glanced at her askance. *Seriously?* "There's also some beer, and...beer."

"Hmm. So many choices...but I'm good with whiskey."

All righty, then. He went to the kitchen, separated from the dining area and living room by a breakfast bar with stools, got the bottle of J.D. and a couple glasses, and carried them back. "So what pieces of the puzzle are you trying to fit together? Maybe I can help?"

"I don't know," she said. "It's actually more like a piece of the puzzle is missing."

He sat on the couch next to her, set the bottle of whiskey and two short glasses on the glass-topped coffee table, another hand-me-down from his brother. For just a fraction of a second he wished his place were bigger, fancier, and filled with comfortable furniture, the kind of place a guy would take a woman when he wanted to cook dinner for her, ply her with wine and seduce her. "Go on."

"I've been thinking if the digital images can be cleaned up enough for me to identify someone from photos Johnson pointed out as members of the mob, we can make contact with Johnson again and see if we can get some names. Then make contact with the mole and get him to tell us everything he knows about Adam. But—" she turned, her expression all business as she looked into his eyes "—realistically, I don't think that's going to happen. There's no way any deep undercover agent is going to give up information that could blow his cover." Her eyes still holding his, she said, "That's the missing piece. That's what we need to make happen?"

She was right. Even if they could get the guy to sing like a mockingbird, Remy wasn't going to do anything that would put another officer's life in danger. He knocked back the shot and as it burned a path down his esophagus, he pulled air through his teeth. He shook it off, then noticed she was staring at him with a quizzical frown.

"That good, huh?"

"Oh, yeah." He grinned, then laughed out loud. "Yeah, that good."

She knocked back her shot, too, then ran her tongue across her lips and closed her eyes, as if savoring every last drop. Damn. Was she really that tough or was she trying to show him how tough she was? No, he decided, as she turned and gave him a satisfied smile. Charlie Street wouldn't feel a need to prove anything to anyone.

From what he'd observed, she didn't give a flying fig what anyone thought of her. The woman had ice running through her veins. Nerves of steel. If she had any emotions at all, she was a master of disguise. He doubted anything would really bother her.

"I see what you mean," he said, getting back to the conversation. "The mole isn't going to give it up. He knows what we'd do with the information...and he'd get dead."

"But," she said as she set her glass on the coffee table, her face lighting up, "if we could get someone else, someone the mole would trust, to get the information and then tell us, we wouldn't jeopardize the guy's position within the mob." Her eyes sparkled as she looked at him. "That's it!" She took his hand. "Thank you. You just helped solve the puzzle."

"Well, I don't know what I did to help, but I really like the results," he said, grinning and glancing at her hand on his. Then he drew his gaze upward. The dress she was wearing was cut so low, it was next to impossible to keep from appreciating the sweet curves escaping the top of the skimpy dress.

She flipped his hand away, then turned and reached for the bottle to pour herself another shot, exposing a nicely curved backside.

Leaning against the pillows behind her, she took another drink. "It wasn't what you did, it was that you said, 'he knows what we'd do with it.' That made me realize he wouldn't have to give *us* the information. Our mole can give the information to someone else...someone he trusts and knows isn't going to use it against him. And then, we get the information from him."

"Perfect. And that someone would be?"

"Nick Johnson."

He pulled back. "The bartender at the Devil's Den?" He stood. "No way."

She rose along with him, her expression taut, his automatic 'no' apparently not to her liking.

"I meant, why would anyone tell Johnson anything? He's a small-time punk. And even if he could get the information, why would he give it up?"

She brought herself up to her full height, which he guessed must be five-feet, eight or so, but without her tall shoes, she no longer met him eye to eye. "He will give it up—" she said "—because he likes money."

"Bribe him."

"And because he doesn't want to go to jail for selling me drugs."

"What? When did that happen?" She sounded like she was making it up as she went along.

She paced a couple of steps, then stopped by the patio doors to the balcony and peered out. "It didn't. I had to leave because my mother was sick. Remember?" Her eyes met his. "But he told me he had an eightball for me and the next time I go to the Den, I'll make sure we make the deal." She smiled big and wide. Sexy. Inviting.

And he was reading all kinds of shit from nothing except her excitement at having figured out a way to make it work. There were beaucoup problems with the plan, but he wasn't about to stomp out her fire.

"Okay, then." He walked over to stand near her, pulled the blind, unlocked and opened the patio door to let some of the balmy spring air clear out the stuffy apartment. "Sounds like a plan."

A breeze drifted inside and she raised her head, took a deep sniff of the air. "Oh, can you smell that? Is it lilacs?" She opened the screen. "There must be lilacs outside."

He followed her out onto the small balcony. It was one of those dark nights where the clouds covered the moon and the sky was a blanket of black, the only light being small lamps around the walkway and trees in the courtyard below. Now that she mentioned it, he smelled the perfume in the air.

"Are they tall bushes with purple or white flowers?" He leaned forward, arms on the balcony railing, and gestured below near the corner of the building where there were more lights. "Like those?"

She leaned on the rail next to him and peered down. "Exactly like those. We had lilacs by our house when I was growing up and I remember my grandmother putting vases of them in every room." She drew in another huge gulp of air. "I love the scent of lilacs."

"You know, my mother used to do that, too," he said. "I'd forgotten."

"You didn't forget. The memory is still there."

"Yeah, guess so, but I haven't thought about it in a very long time." He hadn't thought about a lot of things from the past. But being with Charlie seemed to bring it out.

"I know what you mean," she said. "I worry sometimes that I'll forget things about my dad and, eventually, everything will just fade away like a long ago dream." She looked down. Pensive.

Interesting how she talked about her father as if he was just gone and wasn't a convicted murderer who'd been offed in jail. But it was the first spontaneous information she'd shared with him, and he could tell it hurt her to even talk about it. Yet she trusted him enough to do it.

He took her hand. "The loss of a parent, it's…" He stopped, his chest squeezing. "No feeling I've ever had compares to that." He turned to her. "It's tough. Really tough."

As their eyes met and held, all the lust he'd felt earlier morphed into an overwhelming need to comfort her—and maybe himself, too—let her know he knew her pain. Regardless of the man her father had turned out to be, she'd loved him.

And he wanted to kiss her.

So he did.

She kissed him back, long and deep and hard. He was about to say they should go inside where they could get comfortable on the bed, when he heard a *click, click, click.*

Charlie drew back. "What was that?"

More clicking and a flash of light. His arm still around her, he pulled them back to the door, eyes scanning. "I don't know." He'd barely said the words when he saw an object flying through the air in their direction. He shoved her back into the apartment, threw her to the side on the floor and landed on top of her— just as the object hit the glass door and exploded.

Shards of glass rained down on them, smoke filled the room, and a poof of flames erupted on the balcony outside the doorway. Fire! "C'mon," he shouted, jumping to his feet and helping her up at the same time. He pushed her forward into the hallway, then grabbed the fire extinguisher from the wall. "Close the door after me so the fire doesn't spread," he said. "Call nine-one-one." And with one arm over his face, he charged back inside, spraying the extinguisher ahead of him.

The smoke was worse than the fire and it took only seconds to get the flames under control. He went back and opened the door.

"You okay?" Charlie asked, entering again. "I couldn't call because my phone is in my purse."

"I'm okay. It's fine. Fire's out." He tipped his head outside at the charred boards where they'd just been standing. Kissing.

"Can you tell what it is?"

"Looks like a simple firebomb." He turned to look at her. "That's a good thing."

"Oh, great. I feel so much better now." She sent him a withering look from under her brows. Fluffed her wig.

"You should. At least we know it wasn't a hit. A professional would be more thorough."

"A warning?"

"Possible."

"For?"

He shrugged. "I don't know. I haven't been back in the D long enough to make too many enemies outside the department."

"Who then? The same bad actors who've been taking pot shots at us?"

"That would seem the most likely, except this was amateur stuff. So, nope. I don't think so. The mob doesn't give warnings with kiddie cocktails. They'd break a leg or cut off a finger."

His attempt to reassure her and lighten the moment produced a scowl.

The high-pitched whine of sirens filled the air.

"I better leave." She grabbed her shoes and her purse. "I don't want to blow my cover."

"Yeah. Except—"

"No. I really do need to go." She started for the door. "I'll get a cab around the block."

"No. Here—" he pulled out the *Taxi* keys and tossed them to her. "But don't go home. Go to someplace safe."

CHAPTER NINETEEN

SHE DIDN'T KNOW why Remy thought her place wasn't safe. Whoever bombed his apartment wasn't looking for her. And even if someone had seen her, she was in full costume. No one would recognize her. But if she'd stayed at Remy's when the police came, she'd have to identify herself and they still had her name from the incident after they'd been to the Devil's Den. It would come out that Remy was with her that night and from what he'd said, that wouldn't be good.

At home, entering from the garage, the night lights were on in the hallway as usual, but as she got farther inside, she saw illumination coming from another room. *Her office.*

Strange. She'd turned out all the lights when she left. She was certain.

Adrenaline surged through her as she pulled her Ruger LC9 and a tiny keychain flashlight from her purse. She slipped off her shoes, set down her purse, and then, gun raised and back flattened against the wall, took a few more steps. Creeping forward one silent step at a time, she stopped just before the door to her office and peered inside. The desk and file drawers were hanging open with papers sticking out and strewn all over the place.

She swung around her gaze darting. The dim

fluorescent night lights cast eerie shadows over the vacant desks, file cabinets and chairs, and every little creak sounded like a shriek.

She inched forward. Everything in the outer office was the same as when she'd left. Whatever the person wanted, he'd obviously thought it would be in her office. She clicked on the miniature flashlight, then spotlighted the windows and doors for signs of entry. No broken windows, no broken locks. She switched off the light in her office and went to check the interior garage door. No signs of a break-in anywhere.

A professional job? Except a professional wouldn't leave *any* sign he'd even been there. Her office would look untouched.

Unless whoever it was wanted her to know. Or had been interrupted.

At the base of the stairway to her apartment, gun still in hand, she unlocked the door and tiptoed up the stairs. At the top, she listened. Hearing nothing, she slowly turned the knob. Still locked. Her pulse beat triple time as she unlocked the door and swung side-to-side, checking as Gabe had taught her, then again inching her way forward to make sure each bedroom was clear, then the bathrooms, and living room. Seeing nothing out of place, she heaved a sigh, went back for her shoes and returning, triple locked the door behind her.

She stood for a moment, back against the door. God, she was tired. The only thing someone might look for in her office was Lucy's client list, which Lucy refused to let Charlie use in the trial because she was "fond of her clients" and wanted to keep them after the trial was over. Charlie had agreed, but only if she could keep the original list herself and if the trial looked to be going the wrong way, she would have to use it.

Right now, Lucy's defense was circumstantial evidence. No one had seen her at the scene of the crime and she had no connection with the victim other than he'd been a frequent customer.

Maybe whoever had been there had searched Lucy's place, too? Or threatened her. Could be why Lucy wanted to run.

Walking farther inside, she placed her weapon on the kitchen counter, then tossed her shoes and purse on the floor near the couch, flopped down, pulled off her wig, and loosened her hair.

She should report the break-in. Except that it didn't appear to be a break-in since all the doors and windows were intact, and nothing appeared to be gone. If she reported it, she'd have to answer questions and go through all the reasons someone might want to ransack her office. And that wasn't something she wanted blasted on the morning news. Not in the middle of the most sensational trial in years.

On the other hand, the fact that someone had been in her office, going through her things, totally creeped her out.

Ready to scrounge up a badly needed drink of some kind, she heard a muffled ringing sound coming from her purse. The only people who'd call her at nearly midnight were her mother, her brother...or one of her crew at Street Law. Taking out the phone, she didn't recognize the number that came up and let it ring so her voicemail would pick up. If it were important, they'd leave a message.

After a long pause, a man's voice said, "*Stop what you're doing or you're going to get hurt. You are in grave danger.*"

It was the same voice as the man she was supposed to have met at Slows last week. She clicked to pick up the call, but it cut off. Damn. She pressed the callback number and got nothing.

She hurried to the front window and pulled the edge

of the sheet aside. The dusky amber glow of the old street lights gave the deserted road an eerie feel, as if it were a scene in old noirish detective movie.

Just then, a car cruised around the corner, one headlight slightly brighter than the other and moving slower than most traffic would normally go. A big car; long, dark windows, Oldsmobile, maybe—circa 1970. But even as it cruised by and kept on going, she couldn't tell for sure what make it was. She leaned a shoulder against the wall, heart pounding against her ribs.

She glanced at the phone number again and pressed the return call button. Still busy. What did he mean? What was she doing that was dangerous? Working for Remy to find his friend was the most obvious since the mob was involved in whatever sting Adam Bentley had been involved in. But Lucy's call meant trouble, too, and this call could be related to either one. Except the man on the phone was the same man who said he knew her father…and that had nothing to do with Lucy or Adam Bentley. Or maybe it did? Maybe the whole thing about him knowing her father was a ruse. But why?

Even more confusing, she couldn't tell if his message was a warning or a threat.

Of the cases she'd worked in the past two weeks— the Linski case, the Devonshire case and Remy's—only one was even remotely related. She'd talked to the stick-up-his-ass group home director and asked January, Max and Gabe to find out everything they could about the staff and the group home, but hadn't done anything else yet. She went over her conversations with Nick Johnson, every possible scenario. Maybe he was on to her somehow…thought she was a cop and blabbed to the two goons in the bar. But Johnson only knew her as Charlene Krenshaw and had no way of knowing her cell phone number to call her.

The fact that her office had been searched was probably the best clue. Someone wanted something and thought it might be here. But the only information she could think of that someone might want was Lucy's client records. Despite Lucy's desire to keep the list secret, maybe it was time she took a good look at it.

She heard a rustling sound at the interior door. "Who's there?" Her brother had a key. Maybe he'd come over after getting her earlier message saying she needed to talk to him. "Landon, is that you?"

No answer.

Quickly, she retrieved the gun, crossed to the door, and stood to the side with her back to the wall. She held out her weapon cop style. Then she waited, her pulse pounding in her ears.

The knob rattled. She heard a thud, like someone hitting the door, then a scratching sound. A thief? Her anonymous caller? The scumbag who tossed her office?

Whoever it was, she doubted they'd want to get caught...or shot. "I called the police," she yelled. "And I've got a shotgun ready to blow your fucking head off."

After what seemed an eternity, she heard car tires squeal. She hurried into the far bedroom and glanced out the window. Nothing. She went back to the front window. Nothing there, either.

Still carrying her gun, she went to the door, quietly unlocked and opened it. The lights were still on in the stairwell, and she saw nothing...except at the bottom of the steps was a legal-sized manila envelope.

Odd. Any legal papers she received were always delivered to the front office and almost always required a signature. She started down the steps, then stopped. If it wasn't something work related, what else could it be?

Whoever delivered the envelope might be lurking

just outside the door…might have been in her office when she was looking around. A chill rocketed up her spine. First the phone call and now this.

Someone was watching her…and waiting. But for what? If the person had wanted to hurt her, he would've had ample time while she was in her office.

Curiosity won over good judgment and she crept to the bottom of the stairwell, checked to make sure the locks were secure, picked up the envelope and sprinted back upstairs, two steps at a time.

No label on the envelope. No return address. Taking no chances, she pulled a pair of surgical gloves from a kitchen cabinet drawer, put them on and pried the clasp. She peered inside, surprised to see a photo, and eased it out of the envelope.

As she pulled it out and saw the black and white image, her mouth fell open. It was a photograph of Charlie with her father at Boblo Island. He'd taken her to the amusement park for her fifth birthday. Just her and her daddy.

Odd that she'd never seen the photo before. But she remembered the day as if it were yesterday… remembered waving at her dad as she rode the big horse on the carousel, laughing at him sitting in the bumper cars, his knees almost at his chest.

She could tell by the fine cracks in the surface of the photo that it was an original, not a copy. Touching a finger to her father's face, she forced herself to breathe past the tightness spreading across her chest, the ache of loss as fresh as when it happened.

Whoever had left the photograph obviously wasn't out to hurt her…and she was grateful for the photo. But who would've left it for her so secretly, and why?

"Not a clue," Remy said, back straight, shoulders squared as he faced the captain. "Everything I know is in the lieutenant's report." Thankfully his townhouse was in a burb and none of the cops who'd answered the call knew him. But it hadn't taken long for the captain to hear about it. "Kid stuff. No big deal."

"That's not what I wanted to talk about." His boss's expression was grim. "Sit."

Remy preferred to stand—stay eye to eye, on equal footing—even if the captain outranked him. He nodded for the big man to sit and they both sat at the same time. Remy crossed his arms. Waited.

The captain sucked air through his teeth, a sure sign that what he was about to say wasn't good. "We got a report on a floater downriver."

Another snitch? The captain wouldn't make a special point to call Remy in for that. He clenched his hands.

"No ID. The DB's decomposed. Unrecognizable." The captain looked at his desk. "We don't know anything...won't know until we can get the reports, but—" He brought his gaze to Remy's. "I thought you should know."

Despite a sudden adrenaline spike, Remy remained calm, raised his head. "Really? Why is that?"

The chief's eyebrows quirked together. "Why? Whaddiyamean, why?" His voice rose. "I thought you should know—"

"DBs turn up on the streets every day. Why should I know about this one?"

"There was evidence of anchoring. Legs and ankles. Probably got cut loose somehow in the current."

Remy pulled a deep breath, nostrils flaring as he fought to control the growing fire in his chest. Anchoring was generally associated with the mob. Other criminal groups had different MOs. He bolted to his feet. "So, you think it's Adam. Right? You wouldn't have called me in if you didn't."

The captain's eyes hardened. "We're done here, Detective Malone. I'll let you know more when I do. Now get back to work. Reports are due in the morning and you have several outstanding cases the chief wants to see resolved."

Remy nodded, swung around, charged from the room and headed for the john, his breath coming in big gulps, and still he couldn't get enough air. Inside the room, he dropped back to lean against the door, Pendergast's words pounding like a hammer into his brain. *Floater…floater…floater.* Unrecognizable. Anchoring.

As he stood there, chest heaving, the possibility registering. No! He shook his head. No! No! No, no, no!

It wasn't Adam. He pulled up. Shook himself out. The captain was worried, that was all. Worried Remy would uncover something that would make the captain—and the department—look bad. The chief wouldn't like that and he'd think Pendergast couldn't handle his job.

Yeah. Bodies turned up all the time. Pendergast had other reasons to tell him about this one. Make him think things that weren't true. Throw him off. And the easiest way to do that—to get him to quit looking for Adam—was to tell him they'd found his body.

That was it. Had to be.

But he wasn't going to quit. Not until he knew without a doubt what happened to Adam. Not until he found the person responsible.

"I don't have any idea," Diana said, staring at the photo Charlie brought over the next morning. "I do remember that day, though. It was a daddy-daughter day and your father took you to the park for your birthday."

"I've never seen it before, either," Landon said, stuffing a forkful of cheese omelet into his mouth. "This is really good, Mom."

The smell of coffee, bacon, and cinnamon scones on Sunday morning in her mother's kitchen harked Charlie back to her childhood and mornings rushing around before school to find lost shoes and misplaced homework, and Diana making sure they had food in their stomachs before they went out the door. No matter how broke they were, her mom always managed to make sure they never went to school hungry.

"Maybe Emilio would know? Your father and his brother were inseparable back then. Maybe he went along and took the picture."

"Where were you? It was my birthday. How come you weren't there?"

"It was your choice," Diana said. "Your father asked what day you wanted for your Daddy day that week and you picked your birthday."

Charlie heard a note of wistfulness in her mother's voice. "It was just as well since I was taking care of your grandmother."

"You want me to call Emilio?" Landon asked. "Or you could just bring it to the gym the next time you come."

"I have a meeting with my staff later today, and I have to be in court tomorrow."

"I can take it, and ask him," Landon offered.

Charlie wasn't sure she wanted to let the photo out of her hands. It was nearly thirty years old and the only one she'd ever seen from that day. "Maybe I can work it in." It was possible Emilio would know. Her uncle had been the family patriarch, watching over Charlie, Landon, and their mother after her dad died. He'd been their rock, had managed the gym for years, and still worked as the accountant, paying the few bills they had and reconciling the other accounts. The building was paid for, so aside from building maintenance, equipment replacement and taxes, anything they made from the boxing club membership was profit. Little as it was.

"Okay, I'm glad that's settled," Diana said. "Wayne is coming over for brunch, so don't eat all the scones, Landon."

Charlie and Landon exchanged glances.

Landon nodded at Charlie. She cleared her throat. "Uhm...that reminds me, Mom. We've been meaning to talk to you about Wayne."

Her mother, standing at the stove preparing more food for her newfound love, turned to face them, her haughty expression a reminder that she was the mother and they were the children. "Talk to me about Wayne?" Her brows furrowed. "What about him?"

"We...Landon and I think you're moving too quickly with Wayne."

Diana crossed her arms. "Moving too quickly?"

"Yeah, you know...you've only known him a couple of months and already he's got you selling the house and packing up for who knows where, and—"

"I beg your pardon." Diana huffed. "Wayne doesn't *have* me doing anything. We're in love...and we're talking about the future." She raised her chin. "Our future together."

"But, Mom—" Landon said. "You gotta admit, things are progressing at lightning speed. You barely know the guy and he's asking you to sell your house and—"

"And get married. He wants to marry me."

"He doesn't even know you," Charlie chimed in. "More importantly, you don't know him."

"I know what I need to know."

"You haven't dated in twenty-five years," Charlie continued. "You don't have the experience to see when someone is playing you. I'm not saying he is, but you have to be aware of the possibility. Those dating sites are filled with players...guys who want something from you and then when they get it, they're gone."

"He wants to love me. What's wrong with that?" Diana held up the photograph, again.

"But do you love him?" She looked her mother in the eyes. "Do you love him like you loved Daddy?"

Her mother's spine went rigid.

"Stop it, Charlie." She frowned. Her chest heaved. She waited, tapping her foot. Finally, she came over, sat at the table with Charlie and Landon, still clutching the photo. "I've spent the last twenty-five years loving a dead man. A man who did something unthinkable and left me with two little kids to take care of. I need a life."

"But do you love him? Like Daddy?" Charlie persisted.

Diana's eyes met Charlie's. "Your father was my first love and that's something a person doesn't ever forget. But Wayne and I love each other on a more—" she looked away "—adult level. We're realists. It took me a long time to see I was wasting my life...and I'm not going to waste another single minute."

She rose from the table. "I need to start living. And so do you, Charlie. It's time for you to realize your father is gone. He's dead and you need to stop searching for something you'll never find."

Charlie gaped at her mother. She flew to her feet. "You can't possibly believe that. Tell me you don't believe Daddy was guilty of murder." Her voice shook. She looked to Landon for support.

Her mother pulled in a breath. "I believe it's...it's a possibility. I've heard things and I know things about the past that you don't know. But, that's not the point. Either way, it doesn't matter. He's gone and I'm here and I deserve to be happy. So do you. You need to forget what happened."

No. No. Shaking her head side to side the whole time her mother was talking, Charlie repeated under her breath, "No…no…no…" Tears filled her eyes. "No! You're wrong! He didn't do anything. Someone framed him and he was brutally murdered. We can't forget that. Ever."

Landon's hands landed heavy on her shoulders, urging her to sit. "C'mon," Landon insisted. "Or maybe we should just go."

Diana scoffed. "Can't forget? I've been telling myself the same lies for twenty-five years, but Wayne made me realize I was simply telling myself those things so I wouldn't have to face the truth. And once I did, I could finally let it go." Diana's face crumbled, eyes glistening with tears which she swiped away with her shirtsleeve. She looked at the photo, again, then shoved it at Charlie. "When I could finally let go and see the truth, it freed me to start living again. And that's what I'm doing."

Charlie clutched the photo to her chest, hurt and anger raging like a fiery volcano inside. But she couldn't move.

She'd argued with her mother too many times and anything she'd say in anger would have the opposite effect she wanted. She said softly, "Well, the truth isn't what you think it is. I don't believe he did anything wrong and I will never believe it. But if believing Daddy was guilty allows you to move on and have a so-called happy life, then I guess that's what you have to do. But, please, can't you at least wait until you find someone mo—"

"Wait?" Diana snapped, her chin jutted at Charlie.

"How long? Should I wait another twenty-five years? I'm fifty-eight years old, for God's sake." She stopped suddenly, waved her hands, a gesture she always used when they were kids to smooth things over. Now, she was calming herself, and her voice was whisper-quiet when she said, "I'm just glad I came to my senses while there's still some life left in me."

She stepped next to Charlie and touched her arm. "I wish you could do the same, sweetheart. I want more than anything for you to be happy, too."

Charlie wrenched away. "I am happy. I'm very happy. But I won't ever believe Daddy was a killer so I can forget about him and move on. Salving my conscience with lies doesn't work for me. I may have stopped trying to find out who was behind framing him, but I will never forget that somehow there's a way. And when I do, I'll prove he was innocent and you'll regret everything you said."

Her mother shook her head, her mouth now a firm line. "No. Regret is for the things you didn't do. Not the things you do. What I regret is that I didn't go on living. I couldn't change what happened, but I could've done *so* many other things. I was in denial. You're in denial, Charlie." Her voice softened. "You can't change what happened by looking for evidence that's not there…any more than I could by spending all those years alone."

Diana swung around. "I wasted so many years…years I'll never get back. That's my true regret." Her mother's voice cracked again.

"I'm trying to move forward…to have a life again…and be happy. Wayne has made me realize I deserve that, and I'm not going to let another hour, minute, or second pass me by."

Diana took Charlie's hand in hers. "You need to stop flailing at windmills, honey. Or you'll end up sad and alone—" she moistened her lips "—like me."

Sad and alone? Charlie stared at her mother. That wasn't true. Her mother was busier than anyone Charlie knew. She was just saying those things to move them away from the truth that Wayne was a bad influence. Charlie raised her chin. "Okay. Fine. But if it turns out badly, don't say we didn't warn you."

"That's just it," Diana said on a wry laugh. "It may turn out badly. Life is like that. But I'd rather love someone for however long it lasts than live without love. I may not feel the same way about Wayne as I did your father, but it's a helluva lot better than feeling nothing."

She reached out again, touched Charlie who was standing legs apart, arms crossed. "And I hope with all my heart that someday you'll feel the same."

CHAPTER TWENTY

"SORRY, GUYS. I HATE to call you in on Sunday, but I have court in the morning and some things are becoming urgent."

Charlie left the door to the conference room open so January could hear Kacey, who was occupied with toys in the children's playroom next to the reception area. She went over and took a seat between Max and January sitting on the near side by the door. Gabe glowered at them from across the table.

Last week after her futile meeting with the director of the group home, she'd asked January, Max, and Gabe to dig up all the information they could on both the group home and the staff, and in particular, the director, Gregory Ustinov. She'd also asked each one to review the information collected in the Adam Bentley case, update her on their progress and give her their independent assessments. Fresh eyes helped.

Her assistant passed around cups of coffee while Max flipped through a file folder. Gabe simply sat there, watching. Waiting.

Still shaken after spending the morning at her mom's, coffee was the last thing Charlie needed, but she took it anyway. *Focus on the work at hand.*

After picking up the mess in her office last night, she hadn't been surprised to find there was nothing missing

Lucy's records were protected on a duplicate flash-drive under lock and key in Charlie's safe deposit box at the bank, and there wasn't anything else of interest to anyone, just a lot of files with coded case numbers. So it would be difficult to know whose file they were looking at without a whole lot of research.

"So, who wants to go first?" she said, eyeing Max.

"I guess *I* do." And with his typical good-natured smile, Max shoved the file toward her. "The group home has been around for nearly forty years, has undergone a few transformations, and has had a number of directors. In the beginning, the facility housed orphans, both boys and girls, then it was a group home for kids with behavior problems, girls on one campus and boys on another. About ten years ago, the facility switched to girls only."

Charlie remembered a lot of the kids her dad used to work with had come from Phoenix Rising or Passages, another group home a little farther away. Drakar had been staying at Phoenix Rising right before her dad began working with him.

"Ustinov has been the director for the last three years. And there's an assistant director, a woman named Veronika Combs. She's Russian, but married a guy from England, and is here on a work visa. Ustinov is also from England. A little preferential hiring there." He sipped his coffee. "The assistant director's husband went back to England, and she and the director spend a lot of time together outside of work."

"Okay," Charlie said. "I don't need to know their personal relationship unless it has some bearing on the case."

"Ustinov," Max continued, "signed the incident reports for the missing girl, but one of the aides said he never reads the reports, so he probably doesn't even know what's in them. The assistant director reads the reports and clears it for his signature. It looks like the home followed procedure on everything related to the girl's disappearance."

He cleared his throat. "However, the Combs woman was picked up a couple of months ago on a drug charge. She claimed to have found it on the premises and didn't know who it belonged to. The case was dismissed for lack of evidence."

Hearing about their background and possible relationship, Charlie had a better understanding of why Ustinov had seemed so defensive when talking about Ella Linski's disappearance. He may have been protecting his assistant.

"Beyond that, I made friends with the receptionist and when Ustinov was gone, I talked with a few of the girls. Most weren't surprised that the Linski girl ran away, and some didn't even know her. They also looked scared to death to talk to me. One said she doesn't make friends because everyone leaves and they never come back." Max looked at Charlie.

"Makes sense. It's not a resort. Why would anyone want to go back?"

He shrugged. "Kids make friends. At school, camp, or wherever. Didn't you ever have friends at school or camp that you wanted to see again after you were gone?" Max gave her a quick scowl, then looked away. If she didn't know Max as the most steely guy she'd ever met, she might've thought what she'd said hit a nerve.

"That's it," he said. "All we got, and it's not a whole lot to help find our runaway."

"Okay. Thanks." Charlie sighed and motioned to January, ready to move on. But, thinking again, she then turned back to Max. "What exactly did the girl say about making friends?"

Max looked at his notes. "To be exact," she said.

"No one really pays attention to who comes and goes because kids leave all the time and never come back. Why make friends when you never see them again?"

Charlie frowned. "Sad. Not the best environment for behavior modification."

"Not unless they figure on making the kids so miserable they'll do anything to get out and not come back," January chimed in.

Max said, "I checked the past year's police reports to see how many runaways we're talking about and found nothing. So, she must've been talking about when kids are discharged to go home. If there were other runaways, they must've been found and returned before a report was necessary."

Exactly what Ustinov had said earlier. "Okay. Thanks." She nodded at January, who reported she'd gone through all of the information on the Adam Bentley case and found nothing different than what they already knew.

"But..." she said. "I went over some public information on Johnson again since he was Adam Bentley's last contact, and I noted he lists his schools as Holy Redeemer, which is a Catholic school, and Michigan State. I checked both and couldn't find a record of him at either one."

Holy Redeemer was familiar. More than familiar. It was the same school Joey Drakar had attended. Which made the relationship between him and Nick Johnson more likely. Some families liked to live near each other, have their kids grow up in the same neighborhood.

Finger-combing her blond curls, January squelched a yawn. "Oh, sorry." She held up a hand and took a sip of coffee.

"They're about the same age and probably went to the same school at the same time," Charlie said, thinking out loud. "Drakar and Johnson."

"Is that significant?" January asked.

"Just an observation." Again, Charlie had forgotten. This wasn't about her, but it was increasingly hard to keep the two cases separate. Because if it was true the two guys were related, Nick Johnson probably knew about the gym and that Joey was hanging out there. It was possible he'd even talked to his cousin about the night her father was arrested and—

"Charlie?" January waved a hand in front of Charlie's face.

Yeah. She was getting off track again. "Okay... Thanks, January."

Gabe cleared his throat and shoved a hand through his shock of dark hair, his unfathomable chocolate-brown eyes deep pools of gorgeous. He had the same larger-than-life presence that Remy had, the kind that made you listen when he talked. The kind that made you want to know what dark secrets lurked behind the façade.

Gabe had made it known when he signed on with Street Law that he was a loner, a private person. She hadn't figured out what that meant, but he'd never once talked about the women in his life, or anyone else for that matter.

Gabe said, "I talked to a contact who's peripherally connected to a woman Adam was seeing when he was undercover. Gina Martingale. The intel, if we can believe it, is that the sting Adam was working on involved human trafficking."

Charlie's mouth fell open. "That's huge. Gina is Angela Martingale's sister."

"Angela is Carlozzi's girlfriend, so, yeah, it's huge," Max added.

"Being the mob underboss' girlfriend is huge?" January asked.

Charlie didn't know if January was being

purposefully obtuse or really didn't know what she meant. "Human trafficking. That's why the feds are involved." She rubbed her chin. "That clarifies a lot of things."

And Remy wasn't going to like it. This was much bigger than just another local drug sting...or another gang murder in *Murder City*. "Specifics, Gabe?"

"No," Gabe answered. "The sister didn't know any details...just that it had something to do with moving a lot of people around and some didn't speak English."

"Okay, then. Good work everyone. I'm not sure where this leaves us but I'll let you know after I study it some more. Anyone got anything else to contribute?"

"Well," January said. "If they're into human trafficking with illegal immigrants, they may be working with coyotes who bring them across the border. I've also heard traffickers pick up street people who won't be missed."

Charlie smiled, liking the progress she'd seen in January since she began working for Street Law. Her assistant wasn't just collecting information anymore, she was deciphering it as well. "Right. And either way, they have to have a place to house them. And someone has to know where those places are." Charlie rubbed her temples again, her mind spinning with possible scenarios.

"Okay, continue with whatever leads you can find on both. For now, I have to get my act together for tomorrow." Tomorrow and her final arguments on the Devonshire case. She also had to talk to Remy.

"Oh—" January said "—I meant to tell you, the prosecutor's office called and said Chenowith will call you back in an hour or so."

"On Sunday?" Allan Chenowith never worked on the weekend that she could remember.

"Yeah." January shrugged and at that same time

Kacey appeared in the doorway. "Can we go get ice cream now, Mommy?" Kacey's dark corkscrew curls bounced from side to side.

"Sure, Sweetie. I'll be right there." January's eyes lit up whenever her little girl was around. She adored the child. And it was easy to see the little girl adored her mommy, too.

Charlie's heart warmed just watching them, and it made her insides go all mooshy. How wonderful would that be...having someone who cared about you, no matter what. "Okay, get out of here, guys. It's Sunday. You're not supposed to be working."

Gabe gave her a sidelong look.

Max gave her one, too. "Practice what you preach much?"

She would if people let her. "Thanks. Maybe I will. After I hear what the prosecutor has to say." Collecting her files, she said good-bye to everyone, then headed upstairs. Her cell phone rang. She answered and kept walking.

"Hello, Allan. What's up?"

She and Allan had met at Wayne State and began dating. Their ill-fated relationship had been over before graduation, but their paths seemed fated to continually cross. They'd remained friends and had even worked together, she as a public defender, he as a prosecutor. He'd risen to the top in record time and although they worked well together, it seemed they were always on opposite sides. Still were.

"Better get a strong drink ready. You're not going to like this."

She was already going into the kitchen to do exactly that, regardless of what he had to say. "Quit being so dramatic, counselor. Just spit it out."

"One of the jurors has been compromised."

"Fuck."

"Yeah. I know. It appears he was meeting with people from the congressman's family."

Allan didn't elaborate. Bribery could be involved…coercion…or nothing. Who knew? She sighed.

But then, aside from this being the never-ending trial, which most of the time was a good thing for a defendant, this little delay could work in her favor. Especially since she didn't know where the devil her client was at the moment.

"Okay. I'll see you tomorrow, then." It would be short…a continuance until they could get a new juror. Or maybe the judge would start all over. Damn, she hoped not. She clicked off. She didn't just need a drink, she needed a double shot. Straight. Her client suddenly decides to leave town and now this.

Had someone threatened Lucy? Bribed her to run? Or had someone decided to take justice into their own hands?

"You can't win, Remy," Judge Malone said. "Believe me, I know."

Remy glanced at the photos his father had tossed to him over the desk in his father's library. "You had me followed?" He lifted the photos taken of him and Charlie on his balcony. Her face was shadowed and she was in costume, unrecognizable, he hoped. Looking at his dad, he shredded the photos, one strip at a time, letting the paper fall onto the desk.

His dad leaned back in his chair shaking his head, his expression saying his son was dumber than dirt, an idiot. Too stupid to live. Remy was familiar with the process.

"No, not me. I don't need to do that since you've

managed to get other people doing it. People who let me know by sending me this garbage." He gestured to the shredded photos. "You've gotten the attention of people I'm indebted to. People I need to back my campaign for office."

"And?"

"And they want me to help you rethink what you're doing."

"What I'm doing? You mean going out on a date?"

"I'm only going to say this once and then you're on your own. "What you're doing is creating a problem that must be resolved. If you continue, I'm afraid I can't help you anymore."

"Help me, anymore?" Remy stepped back, released a harsh breath. "If I remember correctly, I asked for your help and you blew me off."

"I told you what I needed to tell you so I wouldn't have to make a trip to identify your body at the morgue."

Remy almost did a double-take. For the first time since Remy could remember, his dad actually seemed as if he were worried about him. "Then tell me who's telling you to keep me quiet. Besides the chief, who we both know is just another pawn in the whole political scheme of things.

The judge rolled his head back and laughed. "We're all pawns, son. We just have to learn how to make our own moves. Smart moves that keep us in the game."

A game? A burst of adrenaline coursed through him. He waited a beat. If he spoke now, he'd regret it the minute the words spewed from his mouth.

"This is not a game, Dad. It's about a man's life."

"No, it's about many lives. What you're doing affects all of us. Me. Your brother. The business. And my upcoming campaign."

Remy stared at his dad. *Unfuckingbelievable*. "Is

that what this is all about? A man's life is expendable as long as all the other parts keep working as you want them to." He swung around, scrubbed his hands over his face. "Good God, Dad. Adam is missing. His parents and his wife and kids need to know what happened to him."

His dad launched to his feet, hands fisted, his face getting redder by the second. "Damn it, Remy. Give. It. Up!"

Remy gritted his teeth, his insides seething as he glared at his dad.

Not backing down, the judge glared back. But after a long moment, he looked away, straightened and smoothed the front of his shirt. "Look," he said, his voice quieter, but no less firm. "I'm as sorry about Adam as everyone else is, and we all know what happened to him. Everyone but you. And you're not doing anyone any good by persisting in this folly."

Looking at his dad, Remy felt as if he were seeing him for the first time. Here was a man he'd idolized as a kid, a man who suddenly seemed a total stranger. "Folly?" Remy all but hissed the word. "I can't believe you said that."

"You don't know what you're doing, son. You don't know the kind of people you're messing with."

Remy rubbed his temples, suddenly bone tired. And empty. As if all the blood had been drained from his body. "No, that's where you're wrong. I know exactly what I'm doing and who I'm messing with." He turned to leave.

"Wait," his dad said, coming from behind the desk, then crossed the room and stood next to Remy. Looking Remy in the eyes, he held out a hand. Remy hesitated, but his dad pulled him close, hugged him, and said, "Good-bye, son."

He just stood there, arms dangling at his side. He

couldn't remember the last time his father hugged him. If he'd ever hugged him. And deep in his bones, he knew it would be the only time.

"I gotta go," Remy said. "Thanks for the father-son talk."

CHAPTER TWENTY-ONE

THE STUBEN WAREHOUSE…Charlie checked the address again on her phone GPS app to make sure she had the right place.

Remy's email had said, MEET ME AT THE STUBEN WAREHOUSE. A place that made her breath come short and her palms sweat. Had Remy done some deep digging into her past and wanted to make a point? As far as she knew, Remy didn't have time for anything except his job and ferreting out those responsible for the disappearance of his friend.

She glanced around. The abandoned structures in the industrial area near the desolate Packard Plant all looked alike, gray, windowless crumbling shells sprayed with colorful graffiti. One building had ZOMBILAND written across the top in letters large enough to see a mile away. She'd heard the old Packard building had been the first in the U.S. to use reinforced concrete, but she wasn't sure about the other buildings nearby and had to give kudos to anyone brave enough to climb to the top of the building to show off their art.

Charlie considered the eerie-looking structure in front of her, shaded on one side by a much larger building that also looked abandoned. The setting sun cast long distorted shadows in front of her and glinted off jagged shards of glass beneath vacant windows. She saw no visible address, but this had to be it.

She'd studied the building and its layout dozens of times in the past...on paper...and on the Internet, but she'd never been here or ventured inside the place where her father supposedly killed a man. But just because Remy wanted to meet her here didn't mean it was related to her dad. Lots of criminal activity went down in areas like this.

Like so many other businesses that had floundered, the Stuben Warehouse had been empty and fenced off for at least the past five years, a haven for graffiti vandals, paintballers, and scrappers who'd gutted the building of wiring and building materials.

No one around now that she could see, though, and waiting, she walked around the exterior in front, her heartbeat quickening. There was no door in front of the building. It would be easy to go in, see where it happened. She closed her eyes against the inextricable pull.

Was this the kind of closure she needed? Go to the scene. See where it all happened?

Maybe her mother was right that she needed a reality check—face her demons, accept that she was never going to find the answers, and move on. How many times had she told herself that very same thing?

Seeing an opening in the fence wide enough to walk through, she slid the strap of her messenger bag over her shoulder and across her body, and stepped through the opening. The sleeve of her leather jacket caught on one of the sharp fence wires. Dammit. She stopped, moistened a fingertip, and brushed at the scratched leather.

Her gaze drifted upward. Her nerves tensed.

She wanted to go inside, and yet she didn't. What did she expect to find? There would be nothing here after so many years, no evidence of any kind. What was the point? Maybe the point was just doing it. Maybe once she went inside that would end it for her. Maybe she'd be done with trying to find answers that weren't there. Weren't anywhere.

Maybe she didn't want that.

A stupid thought. Of course she wanted to end it. She just wanted to end it the right way. Prove she was right.

She took a breath, switched her gun from her messenger bag to her pocket, pulled out her phone to get some photos. She walked forward. Stepped inside. Just as she took another step, she heard a car door.

Remy. Thank God. She released her breath, unaware she'd been holding it. As much as she wanted to do this, her better sense told her not to do it alone.

"I'm inside," she called out, taking a few cautious steps amid the debris. Hearing a cough, she swung around.

Gasped.

Her stomach plummeted. Ten feet away, Nick Johnson stared back at her. "What…what are *you* doing here?"

He smiled.

"You—" Her thoughts raced as fast as her heart. She looked at her phone "—you sent the message?"

Still smiling, he said, "It's easy to get fake email addresses."

Did Nick know who she really was? He had to, didn't he? Otherwise why would he pretend to be Remy? Pocketing her phone, she clicked on the recorder. Placed her hand on her gun. "Why? What do you want?"

"I didn't think you'd come if you knew it was me."

She glanced from one window to the other, taking quick exit inventory. "I don't understand."

"I like you better as yourself," he said, swaggering toward her. "Without the wig."

She stepped back.

Stopping, he raised a hand, cast a glance back toward the door. "Sorry. I don't mean to scare you. I came here to warn you. No one can know I'm talking to you." He shoved his hands in his front pockets, bounced from one foot to the other. "I know who you are," he said, shifting again, his movement jerky, like he was ready to jump out of his skin. "And what you're doing is…it's dangerous. You need to stop. If you don't, it's going to end ugly."

"What do you mean? How did you—" He knew who she was, so why was he warning her? What did he think she was trying to do?

"I can't tell you anything more. You just have to stop. Because if you don't, you're going to get hurt just like that other guy."

Like the other guy? Adam? Did Johnson think she was an undercover cop? Was that what he meant when he said he knew who she was?

He shoved a hand through his hair, revealing a spider tattoo on the underside of his forearm.

"Like what other guy?" She thought back to their conversation at the bar. "Do you mean the detective the police asked you about?"

His head bobbed up and down…he glanced to the door and back to her again, kept shifting his feet, jamming his hands in his pockets one second then rubbing his face the next. He was wired…had to be on something.

"Yeah, yeah…and the others," he mumbled, raised his hands to the back of his neck and dropped his chin to his chest, his voice barely audible. "You gotta stop or the same's gonna happen to you."

She tightened her grip on her gun. "Is that a threat?" Staring at him, her nerves pinged under her skin. She couldn't draw her gaze away, and as she stared, the tattoo on his arm seemed to grow larger and larger. An image flashed through her head—Joey, raising his hands when he was in the ring. Her heartbeat accelerated. Her pulse pounded in her ears.

How did she not see it before? The spider tat encompassed a large dark birthmark, just like the one Joey had. The odds of both Joey and a cousin having the same tattoo was a lot greater than the odds of them having the same birthmark—and the same tattoo.

Nick wouldn't have known who she was no matter what she was wearing, but someone else might have figured it out.

Joey could have figured it out.

Her breath caught.

What was it Remy had said when she'd first asked about Johnson? *If you find one, you might find the other.* She'd thought it meant they might be hanging out together, but that wasn't it at all.

Nick Johnson wasn't Joey Drakar's cousin. Nick Johnson *was* Joey Drakar.

He knew who she was and he was warning her. Or was he? Either way, she was in danger and she had to get out of there. But then Joey could disappear all over again. She needed information from him, and if she could keep him talking, she might get it.

When he didn't answer, she said as evenly as she could, "What did you say, Joey? I didn't hear you."

"I said, no. It's not a threat. But I'm tellin' you, if you don't stop what you're doing, they're gonna—" His eyes widened, apparently realizing she'd called him Joey. And he'd answered.

"I don't like *you* better as yourself," she said, advancing toward him, her mind still reeling. He was Joey…that's how he figured out who she was. He didn't think she was a cop or an attorney helping a cop, he knew she was Alex Montoya Street's daughter. And all she could think was, "Why, Joey? Why did you testify against my father when he was so good to you? And where have you been all these years?" Good Lord, had he been in the city all along as Nick Johnson?

Fury seizing in her chest, she stepped closer. He edged one back. His gaze darted, sweat broke on his forehead. "It was never supposed to go down that way," he said. "Alex…your dad…he was getting too close to the operation, and he would have exposed them all. They threatened my family, made me say what I did. I had to go away. I even had to change who I was to come back when my mom was sick—"

"Who threatened you? Who would be exposed?"

He kept backing away, nearly tripped over his own feet. "I can't say. I-I don't know. It was small stuff back then. Drugs and kickbacks and shit. Now it's like really huge." He turned and, hands in his front pockets, hustled to the door. She followed on his heels.

"You're the reason my father went to prison and was murdered. His life ended because of you. At least give me the name of the person who blackmailed you!" She caught up, stopped a few feet back. "Don't you feel anything about what you did? My father was an innocent man. Someone who treated you like family." Her voice rose, each word more vehement than the last. "You might as well have murdered him with your own hands."

Stopped at the door, Nick slowly came around to look at her, his eyes gray and flat, like shark's eyes with no light reflection in them. No feeling.

"Yeah, I used to think about that all the time, but—" He shrugged. "I had no choice. I'm sorry."

Sorry? A choked scream rose in her throat. The horrible injustice of it all ripped what was left of her heart to shreds. She wanted to pound on him. Stab and torture him. Kill him.

Forcing herself to breathe, she managed, "If you're really sorry, then tell me who was involved? It's not on you. No one else will know. Just me. I *need* to know."

For a moment, he just stood there, conflict flashing in his eyes. Then he lifted his chin, straightened, as if he'd just remembered he was a tough guy. "I can't. It was small business back then, but now, it's huge," he repeated. "Just talking to you could get me whacked. Believe me, you don't want to mess with these people. Ever."

He edged away, ready to go out the door again.

"Joey, wait!" When he kept going, she pulled her gun. "Stop or I'll shoot." She drew back the slide to check the chamber.

He froze at the sound. Turned, eyes bugging out of his head when he saw she really had a gun.

"I need more than that. I need names."

His shoulders slumped, he closed his eyes and released a long breath, as if all the air suddenly evacuated his body.

"Ask your friend's dad...the judge," he finally said. "He knows all about it."

"What?"

"That's it." He raised his hands and backed away. "I'm done. And if you tell anyone anything about this, you might as well shoot us both right now because we'll end up in the river, anyway."

Two seconds later as he was getting into his pickup truck, he called back to her, "Don't come to the bar again. They know who you are, too."

Watching the bartender speed off, Charlie put her gun away and clicked off the recorder in her pocket. Johnson—Joey Drakar—said *they'd* blackmailed him to testify against her dad. *They*, meaning the mob? And while Joey hadn't actually said the men he'd pointed out at the table at the Devil's Den were the ones who killed Adam Bentley, it was clear to her that "the other guy" Johnson mentioned was Bentley. It had been fairly clear to her all along the mob was behind Bentley's disappearance. Now she was sure of it.

But even as nervous as Joey was, he'd had enough smarts not to give out any names.

He didn't have to. She knew. But, in court, what she knew and what she'd deduced was worth about as much as the pitiful building she was standing in. And what did Judge Malone know about the any of it?

She recalled Judge Malone's words to her father at the sentencing, words she'd read in the trial transcripts many years later. The passing of time made it so easy to see the man had clearly been biased. Or maybe paid off? Was that what Johnson meant?

The urgency to go inside tugged at her. All these years, she'd stayed away, couldn't bear the thought of even going near the place where her father supposedly killed a man. Maybe it was time.

Picking her way through the debris, she heard another noise outside, a car door slammed. She started, dashed through a door and across the room, hid behind a wall of crumbling concrete and bricks, found a hole about halfway down, and crouched to peer through it. Could be someone walking by. Kids who liked to vandalize the old buildings in the area. Destroy things. Light fires.

Thugs sent to kill her.

The sound of footsteps crunching through the debris echoed throughout the empty building, the only noise except for her heavy breathing which could probably be heard in Canada on the other side of the Detroit River. Her hands trembled and even though she wasn't cold, she shivered like it was ten below zero.

Focus. Clear your mind and focus. Gabe's voice rang in her head. Mental training was the foundation for the martial arts skills of Wing Chun that Gabe had taught her, and was just as important as the physical. She ran through the mantra, calming herself so her hands no longer shook. More noisy steps, then a man's shadow filled the light at the end of the hall.

Her heart raced, she glanced behind her and weighed her options in case she needed to flee. She peered one more time at the doorway.

He stepped inside.

Remy?

"Charlie? You here?"

What the hell… She stepped out from behind the wall. "Are you following me, now?" She shook her head. "Or, I should say, following me, again. Or still." Even as she spouted the words, waves of relief swept over her.

Remy frowned. "No, I got a voice mail giving me this address and a message that you might need help. I think it was one of your staff. I know the area. Got worried and came as fast as I could."

"What?" No one knew she was coming here. Not a soul. And no one on her staff would call Remy. Gabe or Max would drop everything and come themselves if they thought she was in trouble. "Someone left you a message?"

"Yeah." He glanced around. "Not the best place to hang out. What's going on?"

She rushed over next to him. "Is the voice mail still on your phone?"

"Sure." He got out his cell and after pulling up the message, handed her the phone.

Listening, her jaw tightened. The message was brief, just as Remy had said. And the voice sounded unmistakably like the one belonging to the guy she'd been playing phone tag with for weeks now. The guy who'd recently told her she was in danger. The man named Smith.

She hit the call-back. Not in service. Another burner. She brought her gaze to Remy's, debating what to tell him.

He needed to know what Johnson had said about Adam. He didn't need to know what Johnson had said about her father. Or his. Not until she knew exactly what Johnson was talking about.

"That was not a message from anyone on my staff. I don't know who this person is, but it's someone I've talked to before. I don't know what his agenda is. And I also received a message—an email—from you saying I should meet you here. That's all it said. I was familiar with the building because of…some other stuff. When I arrived, Nick Johnson showed up."

She gave him a censored account of what happened…that Nick was somehow on to her and had sent the email; that he'd warned her, saying what happened to the other detective would happen to her if she didn't stop what she was doing.

Listening, Remy ground his teeth together so hard she could see the cords in his neck pop out. A nerve twitched near his eye.

"Other than your cover being blown, it doesn't change anything," he said. "Except we have a better idea how important whatever Adam was working on is to someone. And we're a threat."

Nothing she didn't already know. And a pretty good hunch they weren't going to find Adam alive. "Right. My staff has a new lead they're following up on as we speak. I'll let you know if it turns out to be anything."

"And the guy who called to tell me to come here?"

She kicked a pile of rubble with the toe of her boot.

"I don't know. He obviously wanted you to find me, so I have to believe he knew what was going down…and he's not out to harm me."

"Not necessarily. He could be your stalker, and stalkers can be very dangerous."

It wasn't something she hadn't thought of herself. "Or it could be the mole?"

"Possible, but I doubt it. He's not going to jeopardize his cover."

"Right."

"Or maybe someone wanted both of us in one place." Remy smiled as he said it, but the subtext was clear and the hair on the back of her neck prickled. *A setup.*

"I don't know what this guy's agenda is, but it couldn't have anything to do with our investigation because I talked to him before you and I ever met."

"Giving credence to the stalker theory."

"I don't think so. Stalkers follow a pattern. His previous contacts haven't been typical stalker behavior." She shrugged. "And if that were the case, it's my problem, not yours."

"Have you reported it to the police?"

"It's not a police matter. It's personal."

"Okay. Now I'm confused. But—" He indicated the doorway with the sweep of an arm "—why don't we get out of here and talk in a more comfortable environment. C'mon. I'll follow you home."

"Not yet. I want to walk through the building first."

"Did you see the sign outside?" He gave her a sidelong glance. "It's not safe."

"Lots of things aren't safe. That doesn't mean I'm not going to do them."

"Okay…" he said, following her as she walked back into the hallway where she'd been earlier. "When I read the address, I ran a check on the building. It's owned by a corporation called Quadrastar. You know anything about them?"

"No, but I know what happened here twenty-five years ago, and if you ran a check, I imagine you do, too."

"I do."

"So humor me. I need to do this." She pushed a box aside, headed toward a door at the end of the hallway.

Moving in step directly behind her, Remy said, "Then we better hustle. It's not going to be light for long."

Stopping, hands on her hips, she rolled her eyes. "I can handle it, Malone."

"I know. But *I* need to go with you. Humor me."

CHAPTER TWENTY-TWO

THEY WALKED DOWN the first corridor, walls crumbling around them, piles of plaster, broken glass, rusty pipes, and plenty of empty beer cans littered their path. Apparently the building was safe enough for someone.

As they went deeper into the structure, the windows were fewer, and the light grew dimmer. Shining a flashlight he'd brought along, Remy also noticed the farther they went, the better shape the walls were in, and the debris wasn't as thick. Apparently the tough punk vandals didn't like the dark.

When Charlie turned down yet another corridor, he asked, "Do you know where you're going, or are you winging it?" The building was three floors, four if you counted the basement, and covered nearly a half block. Back in the day it had been a commercial linen company and launderer for hotels and businesses, and cheap labor toiled long hours to make less than enough to live on.

As the labor laws changed and hiring illegal immigrants became an issue, the payoffs rose and staying in business cost more than using the place as a warehouse. But even that failed when the city's economy took a dive. Then the whole country went to shit. Like all the other empty businesses and homes in the inner city, the Stuben Warehouse had become another pile of trash.

"I've studied the blueprints for this building dozens of times," Charlie said. "But I'm quickly discovering the actual layout doesn't conform to the plans." She turned another corner.

He heard a noise—a shuffling sound—and flashed a beam of light down the hall. About thirty feet ahead, a dark form, a man it looked like, was on the floor slumped against the wall, legs straight out front. Something furry skittered over the guy's stomach and ran toward them.

Charlie shrieked and jumped back, bumping into Remy. He grabbed her arms. "Just a cat," he said, looking to see where it went. "Or a rat."

"I hate rats. And where there's one, there's more." She broke from his grip, eyed the man on the floor, and said softly. "You think he's dead?"

They walked toward him, but before they got too close, the man stood, turned, and disappeared into the doorway next to him. "If the rest of the building is still in decent shape, there's probably a homeless colony living in the bowels of the building. He probably went to warn them."

"Let's go see," she said, then took off after the man.

"Wait, Charlie. It's not safe." She kept going, so he took off after her. She stopped just inside the doorway. Another empty room, but it had a door on the far wall to his left, probably the one the guy went through. A window high on the wall let in enough light to see more debris, rusty metal pieces, broken glass and empty food cartons, evidence that people had been staying here. The pile of empty pizza boxes shifted as if alive. More rats. Charlie visibly shuddered.

"Look." Charlie pointed to her right where the dusky rays of a setting sun shone through the window. "Over there. Can you put some light on that wall?"

Shining a beam against the wall opposite them, he

saw hooks of some kind. "This place was a factory for years and then a warehouse." They stepped closer. A loud bang sounded behind them. Together, they swung around. The door had slammed shut. They glanced at each other. "I hope you've got a key," he said, a lame attempt at cutting tension.

"I don't, but I've got this." She reached into her messenger bag and pulled out what looked like a small Ruger.

"Whoa." He backed up. "You know how to use that?"

She gave him an are-you-serious look. "You're joking. Right?"

He wasn't, but he nodded. "That's me…the joker."

Then, before he could ask the obvious questions, she said, "Ruger LC9, seven rounds in the mag and one chambered."

"Any extra magazines?"

"One." She grinned, then tipped her head toward the door.

He pulled his jacket aside exposing his weapon, and when she glanced over, he said, "Smith and Wesson M7P40, 16 rounds, 15 in the mag, one in the chamber. Fully loaded with two additional mags."

Her brows rose.

"I've shot Expert, three years running. Sniper training, top of my class."

"Impressive." She grinned as she put her gun away. "I doubt I'll need this. I'm sure he's long gone."

At the door, she tested the knob. "It's stuck…or locked."

He reached over and tried it himself. "Yep. Stuck or locked."

They crossed to the other door. Also stuck. Or locked.

She crossed her arms. "What do you think?

"I think he wanted a chance to get away and warn his friends." Wishing door locks were as easy to blast off as it looked in the movies, he glanced around for something to use to pry open the door. One of the rusty metal pieces in the debris pile to his right looked as if it might work.

"Want me to shoot the lock off?"

"If you had a shotgun, maybe. That's door is four inches thi—"

Voices suddenly sounded behind them…from outside the window. Remy turned just as a round grenade-like cylinder came flying through the window. It landed at their feet and on impact, hissed and then emitted a blast of fog. *Gas*.

"Cover your mouth and nose and get down," Remy ordered as he kicked the canister away and to the far wall. Crouching low, he pulled out a hankie to cover his nose and mouth and moved over next to the pile of metal. He grabbed the longest, flattest piece and, using it as a crowbar, jammed it between the door facing and the doorjamb, pushing sideways as hard as he could. It didn't budge.

Charlie—holding a scarf over her mouth and nose—grabbed onto him from behind. With her hands locked on his arms and her added weight and muscle, the lock finally popped. "Let me go first," Remy said, pulling out his Smith before opening the door. "And stay close." Almost before he got the words out, she grabbed the back of his jacket and held tight. Eyes watering, he stepped into the hall outside, Charlie directly on his heels, both of them coughing and wheezing. He pulled the door shut and motioned her down the hall away from the fumes. He had no idea what kind of gas it was, but he wasn't taking any frigging chances.

"I'm guessing that wasn't a homeless guy," she said, coughing.

"Yeah. It was a se—" Two shots rang out. He jerked back, his free arm flattening Charlie against the wall next to him. She reached for her gun again.

"On your right," she said, her voice a hoarse whisper. "Ten yards. Three o'clock. Behind the half-wall."

"Can you cover me?" he whispered back.

"Like a blanket."

"Okay. On the count of three, send a couple shots to that high window on the other side. That should give me enough time to get to the corner. If not, fire another round or two into the window next to it."

"Got it."

He crouched low. "One. Two. THREE!

Charlie's first shot shattered the window. Shards of glass flew everywhere. He crossed the hallway and, safely on the other side, crept forward. She fired another round above him and one to the window closest to the corner—three rounds total. More glass shattered. With his gun raised and back against the wall, Remy turned the corner.

Crack, crack, crack.

Charlie fired once again, then stopped when she heard Remy's answering shots. Then more shots rang out, another round and another, followed by a hail of bullets, some sounding different than others. Different calibers. Maybe even a shotgun.

Her chest seized as the obvious hit her. There was more than one shooter.

Nick Johnson—Joey Drakar—had set them up. And Remy was outnumbered.

Gunfire still sounding on the other side of the wall, she hunkered down, crossed to the opposite wall and crept forward. She'd gone only a few feet when the gunshots quit. She stopped. Listened.

Her chest rose and fell with the hammering of her heart. Not a sound. Nothing. Except the flinty smell of gunpowder heavy in the still air.

Her breath caught. A sharp jolt of fear stabbed in her chest. No! Oh, God, no! That couldn't happen. She wouldn't let it happen. She blinked, the light so dim, all she could see were shadows.

The smell of concrete dust and burnt charcoal clogged her nostrils, but she swallowed back a cough, tightened her grip on her Ruger and inched forward.

A half dozen steps more and she could make out the end of the wall where three quarters of it were missing, forming a crescent moon shape. More light spilled in from somewhere on the other side. Her heart clanging against her ribs, she pressed forward to the end of the wall, took a deep breath, did a drop and roll around the corner, gun raised, and aimed. At Remy.

In a semi-crouched position, he reached out and yanked her over.

Breathing heavy, she scoped the area. "How many? It sounded like a war zone."

"I think we scared 'em off." He turned to her. "Awesome backup."

"Right." She snorted. "It was over before I got here."

"Good thing. That gun's not much good in a shootout."

She'd heard that before, but never thought a shootout would be in her realm of duties. "So, they're gone?"

"Yeah, but I'm guessing not for long."

CHAPTER TWENTY-THREE

SPRINTING TO HER car, Charlie said, "I didn't get a chance to check out the site."

"Yeah," Remy said, taking giant steps alongside…after stopping to pick up a few spent cartridges from the scene. "I'm thinking another time might be better."

She tipped a grin. "Right. We need to have a heart-to-heart with our favorite bartender."

"Johnson is a punk wannabe gangster. He may have set us up, but he's a soldier…a puppet. He does what they want and gets paid. I didn't get a good look, but our shooter had a long ponytail."

"So, it wasn't Johnson."

"Not unless he dyed his hair black and was wearing extensions. But—"

She stopped a few feet from her car. "But what?"

He angled his head to look at her, lifted his shoulders in a shrug. "I don't know. There was another shooter besides the guy I saw with the ponytail. Only he wasn't shooting at me. I think he was helping me."

"What? Helping you?" They simultaneously opened the doors to their vehicles.

"Get in and follow me."

"To?"

"A safe place while we figure out our next move."

"Okay. Any ideas where that might be?"

He pondered a moment. "The *House*...the station."

"To report what happened?"

"No, not yet. The parking garage. Just get in and follow me. We'll talk later."

She did as asked and as soon as they were on the highway, her phone rang. It was Remy.

"We have to assume they'll make another attempt," he said. "And we probably have a very small window of time before that happens. We need to disappear for a little while and figure out what to do."

"Got it." Going to the police station was a brilliant idea. And he'd been amazingly competent under fire back at the warehouse. But what he'd said about another shooter possibly helping him...that was crazy.

Once inside the precinct garage, they parked both cars and went into the building where on the next floor, she stopped to use a bathroom in the hallway.

"Stay in there while I go talk to someone," he said. "I'll do a triple rap on the door when I'm back." He didn't say what he was going to do, but ten minutes later she heard the signal.

Returning to the garage, he asked for her keys and a few seconds later another officer showed up, and he introduced them. Sean Glover, Adam Bentley's former partner, took Charlie's keys. His name sounded familiar, but she was pretty certain she'd never met him before.

"You got this?" Remy asked.

"Got it," Sean said, glancing at Charlie and back to Remy again. "Burn rubber and kill time."

No, never met him. She would remember a black man with startling blue eyes, for sure.

"Great. Then leave it in the impound section and keep the keys," Remy instructed. "I'll call when we're ready to pick it up."

Sean made a clicking sound, gave them a thumbs-up, then slid into Charlie's Focus and sped away, tires squealing as he exited the garage.

"We need a little time while the cartridges are tested and run through the system to see if there are any matches," Remy said. "And I want to be sure we're not followed when we leave here." He extended an arm toward another car. "Our new ride."

The new ride was a big badass black Chrysler 300 with dark tinted windows, confiscated in a drug bust, no doubt. "You can just take any car you want?"

"Generally, no. But we're good on this one."

Once inside Remy revved the motor. "Lots of extra power in the event we need it," he said, then drove them out a different exit and a few turns later they were on East Jefferson.

"Nice ride." Charlie ran a hand over the smooth leather.

"The only one available. And it's faster than the Escalade if we have the need...for...speed." He emphasized the last words.

"Highway to the Danger Zone..." she sang a few bars of the theme song from the old *Top Gun* movie and Remy joined in for the refrain. Laughing, she said, "Oh, man. We are sooo bad. We'd get egged on a karaoke stage."

But she really didn't give a damn, because when she laughed, it felt so good...a welcome release from the adrenaline-induced tension that'd kept her nerves on perpetual red alert.

Watching the mirrors for anyone following them and seeing nothing, she eased back against the seat, suddenly bone weary. They were heading east and the evening sky seemed blacker than black through the dark windows. "Where are we going?" she finally asked, but not really caring. She was relaxed and comfortable in her driver's capable hands.

"A safe house. We need to regroup."

She angled her head to look at him. "Seriously?"

He grinned. "Not a safehouse…a safe house."

"Hmm. Okay. With adult beverages, I hope."

"I'll make sure."

They were both quiet then, and she nodded off for what seemed only seconds, but the next she knew, they were out of the city and Remy had pulled into a long curved driveway that led to a huge mansion. He stopped at the iron-gated entry, pulled out his phone, pushed some numbers and the gate swung open. But instead of continuing to the entrance, he turned off his headlights and took another road leading behind the big house, stopping in front of what appeared to be a garage.

"This is it," he said. "About as safe as we can get."

"Oh-kay. And we are where?"

He lifted a hand for her to wait, then got out, came around the front of the car, scoped out the area, then came over and opened her door.

"It's clear," he said. "We're good."

Once out of the car, a full moon lit the yard well enough to see the structure wasn't a garage, it was an old carriage house, but bigger than the house she grew up in. Trees and shrubs surrounded the cottage, with stone pathways leading in different directions through dense gardenlike foliage.

"You didn't answer my question."

"Grosse Pointe. We'll be safe here. Trust me."

Grosse Pointe being on the east side of Alter Road, the dividing line between the haves and the have-nots—the dividing line between the blight of the city on one side and mansions with iron gates and alarms, literally, on the other—she believed him. "How'd we get so lucky?"

He looked away. "It's my dad's house," he finally

said. "But no one ever comes out here. The carriage house has been closed up for a long time."

His dad's house? They were hiding out in Judge frigging Malone's carriage house? She pulled back, unable to hide her astonishment. How freaking ironic was that? What were the odds...

He motioned for her to follow. At the door, he moved a fluffy green potted plant aside and picked up a key. "My father goes to bed early, but just to be on the cautious side, we should use candles and the night lights. We can stay here the rest of the night, figure out a plan and be out of here in the morning. He'll never know we were here."

Unbelievable. Judge Malone's house was the last place on the planet she wanted to be. But she had to admit, it was probably the safest. Who'd ever think to look for her at the home of the man to whom she'd written dozens of letters asking him to please help her daddy?

The judge had never answered. Not once. And then he decided her father's fate. Life behind bars.

"C'mon in," Remy said, taking her hand. "Be careful until I get us a little light." He shined a flashlight in front of them, then led her to sit on a couch covered with plastic. Once her eyes adjusted, she could see Remy's outline moving about, opening shutters above the main windows to let the moonlight shine inside.

"Okay, now a few candles—" he continued moving "—and maybe a fire in the fireplace to take off the chill."

"What about the smoke?"

"It's gas. My mom wanted to keep the original wood burner, but put in the gas for safety when the place was used as a guest house."

His mom. He'd never mentioned anything personal to Charlie before...except when talking about Adam when he'd hired her. She rolled her shoulders to get out the kinks. Remy seemed to have things well in hand. He was right. Going home right now wasn't an option. This was safe, and she was glad to be here.

Truth was, she'd been scared to death at the Stuben Warehouse, running on pure fear the whole time. A little down time would be good. She took out her phone.

"Don't tell anyone where we are."

"I'm supposed to be in court in the morning. I need to talk to January." She held out the lapel of her leather jacket, swept a hand over the rest of her attire...her boots and leggings. "Not exactly court worthy." She pondered a moment. "She can bring me something in the morning."

"If not, Caroline can probably get you something. Her daughter is about your size."

"Caroline?"

"My dad's assistant, AKA, cook and housekeeper. I texted her that we're here and she's making us something to eat." He came over and sat next to her.

"But if she works for your dad?"

"She won't say anything."

Must be nice. Remy probably never thought a thing about having servants. And why would he. For him, it was simply how people lived. Charlie couldn't help remembering her grandmother's work-worn hands, fingernails dry and cracked from cleaning houses from the time she came across the border at thirteen, until she died three years ago.

"It's okay. January goes to the office early on Mondays. She'll pick out something court appropriate."

It was late, though, so she decided to text rather than call. If January was awake at this hour, she was probably studying, and the call might wake Kacey.

While she texted, Remy went about lighting more candles and placed them on the coffee table.

"Caroline should be here soon," he said when she hung up. "In the meantime, I'm the bartender. What's your pleasure?"

His low, sexy tone made her aware she'd been watching his every move. She wondered if she should tell him how hot he looked in his jeans and biker jacket and that she'd be more than happy to tell him her pleasure. They were both adults. He was attractive, and sexy and based on their last encounter on his balcony, she was pretty sure the feelings were mutual.

Poor timing, though. They had things to figure out. Like how not to get whacked.

Remy rummaged through some cabinets in the kitchen behind a butcher block counter and came up with a couple of wine glasses and two bottles of wine, both red with very old dates on them and expensive-looking labels. He uncorked one bottle and just as he began to pour them each a glass, there was a knock at the door.

"That would be our food," he said, going over.

The older woman who entered wore a scowl, but carried a red thermal bag emanating a tantalizing aroma. She was middle-aged with tousled brown hair streaked with silver and wore dark exercise pants and a matching jacket, and she was obviously not pleased to have been called out at such a late hour.

"Leftover lasagna, salad and bread," she said, giving Charlie a once over and taking out a well-wrapped container and handed it to Remy. "It's very hot, so be careful."

She sounded more like a mother to Remy than his father's cook or housekeeper. Remy gave a huge smile and wrapped an arm around her. "You're amazing, Caroline. And we really appreciate it."

The woman crossed her arms and stood there as if waiting for an explanation. For a moment, Charlie thought Remy might give her one, but then he said, "Everything is fine. Don't worry. I'll explain later, but right now, we have work to do."

"At this time of night?"

He shrugged. "Happens all the time in our line of work. We just needed a place to do it where no one would interrupt. It's fine, Caroline. We'll be gone before the old man even gets out of bed."

The worried expression didn't disappear, but she headed for the door anyway. "If you need anything else—"

"We're good," he said walking with her. At the door, he thanked her again and gave her a pat on the shoulder.

At first Charlie thought Remy was giving Caroline his charming routine, but then she realized he really was fond of the woman. She studied him as he went to take the food out of the containers. The man was an enigma. Not at all what she'd expected from a cop. And at that moment, she liked him a whole lot more.

When he returned, she said, "Can we get some paper? A tablet or something? I'd like to do a little dot connecting." She wished she had her laptop, or even her notebook. All she had was her cell phone and the battery was almost gone.

He found some paper and a pad of Sticky Notes, got the fire going and they ate lasagna and drank wine while talking and jotting down information, making separate lists for what they knew for sure and what they only suspected. What they really needed was the information her crew had collected because some of it seemed to fit with what Nick Johnson had said.

The room had heated quickly and they both removed their jackets and shoes. Working together, they laid out each Sticky Note and drew arrows from one occurrence to another. What they knew for sure was that Adam went missing while undercover and the last known person to see Adam was Nick Johnson. Like Adam, Johnson could easily have been the last person she and Remy had seen if the shooter tonight had been successful.

The cold reality sent a shiver of goose-bumps over Charlie's skin. "What did you say earlier about more than one shooter at the warehouse?"

"Yeah. Someone else was there, and I can't be sure, but it sure seemed like he was helping me." He scratched his head. "It's strange. Very strange."

"Johnson? Maybe he didn't set us up and really was there to warn me? Then when he realized what was happening—"

"Possible, but I doubt it. He'd be signing his own death warrant."

"A squatter, then…some homeless person who was protecting his turf?"

"Also possible. But how many homeless people can afford a gun? Or would be willing to die for some stranger? Whoever it was probably saved my life. And he was pretty good with a weapon. Almost as soon as he started shooting, Ponytail backed off." Remy raised his hands. "Beats me." He turned back to their notes.

The second thing they knew for sure was that for whatever reason, the Detroit PD had stopped their search for Adam only a few weeks after he went missing, and no one, including Adam's former partner, wanted to talk to Remy about it.

The third thing was that the chief had made a point of telling Remy to lay off his investigation…under threat of losing his job. And, four, they'd been in the line of fire three times, so it was obvious they were getting close to something and were considered a threat.

Five, Charlie had an anonymous caller who claimed to have information regarding her father, and the same man had alerted Remy that she would be at the warehouse today. Six, they'd learned the FBI was involved and had an undercover agent on the same job Adam had been working on.

Seven, Nick Johnson had admitted to knowing mob members and he'd gotten Charlie to the warehouse to warn her...or he'd set her up.

"And—" Remy said, "—don't forget the brown van."

"Which began before I agreed to take your case."

"Right. So that means we could have two different scenarios and we aren't sure which is which. One involves our investigation to find Adam. And the second, we have no clue what it's about." He turned. "Or do we?"

She swallowed, ran her tongue over her teeth. "Anything else that might be on the table involves my clients and that's—"

"Confidential. I know." He leaned against the back of the couch, his forehead furrowed. "We can be fairly confident someone in The Partnership doesn't want us to uncover what happened to Adam. Whether there's more going on with one of your cases, we don't know. But we can't ignore it. There has to be a connection because of the phone call I received telling me where you were going."

Yeah, like someone keeping continual surveillance on her since she'd been stirring up stuff about her father's case from the time she got out of law school.

Turning to her, one arm on the back of the couch, he said, "You mentioned you recognized the voice...that it was the same person you were supposed to meet at Slows the night I was there. Does that also involve a client?"

"No. It...it involves something else."

"Your father. You mentioned him when we first met. You thought I was the man with information about your father."

She nodded. "Right."

"And you're not going to tell me anything more?" He pulled back, his expression incredulous. "If he's the same man, whoever he is, he probably saved your life. If I hadn't received that message there's a good possibility you might be dead. That means he had to have known you were in danger. Maybe he knows who wanted to kill you? So, how did he know that? How did he know me? And why would he want to warn you?"

"Maybe he didn't want to warn me. Maybe he was part of the setup. Maybe he works for whoever wants to hire him." She jammed her hands through her hair. "I've even thought it could be someone my brother asked to guard me since the shooting three months ago."

Geez. She hadn't planned on telling Remy about Smith, but now it seemed necessary. "The man I was supposed to meet at Slows that night had contacted me in the same way he did you…left me a phone message that said he had information about my father. He didn't say what it was, but he wanted to talk to me about it. I had no idea who he was or why he'd even contact me, other than maybe he knew I had spent a lot of time investigating my father's case."

Remy cocked one eyebrow.

"I believe someone set my father up, framed him for a crime he didn't commit, and I've spent a lot of time trying to find something to prove his innocence. But I'd pretty much stopped investigating over a year ago because, while I've gone through every shred of evidence available, I always come up empty handed." Not to mention the toll it had taken on her jobs. And her personal life.

"It was all to no avail. But then this guy called, and if he had information about my dad, it might be something that would help…and I had to know." She sighed. "We never connected, but on one other occasion after that night at the bar, he called again and told me I was in danger. And that was it. I have no ideas on who, what or why."

She closed her eyes briefly and inhaled long and deep.

"Wow," Remy said, blowing out a whistle. "Just, wow."

"Unless…" she said, pulling her feet underneath herself. "Unless this man, Smith, knew my father years before when he was in a gang." She turned to look at Remy. "And though my dad got out of the gang, maybe Smith didn't. Maybe he went on to bigger things and he's still involved somehow and that's how he knew I was in danger. That kind of information gets around on the street."

Remy's expression turned pensive, and she wondered if she should have kept silent. She hadn't yet mentioned that Nick Johnson was really Joey Drakar, the person whose testimony put her father behind bars. Seeing his response, she didn't know if she should tell him what Johnson said about his dad, either.

"Okay. This guy, 'Smith', heard it on the street."

"Or he's involved somehow with the mob…maybe deals with them?"

"So, some street goon who knew your father knows you're on someone's hit list and he wants to protect you because?"

"Because…I don't know. I'm just tossing stuff out there. Maybe he and my dad were good friends. Maybe he owes my dad a debt? Gangs are like family, with their own set of rules. Some things are sacred. Loyalty. Friendship. Unless you get crossed."

His brows met in the middle and he gave her a look that said she might be certifiable.

"You're a cop. You know that."

"And I don't give a damn. They're criminals. They steal, beat people up, hook kids on drugs. They kill people. They don't get a pass because they have some fake gang loyalty or code to follow. I don't care about any of that. What I care about is that this guy knows what you're doing and where you'll be, and we need to know how he knows and why he's stalking you." He looked deep into her eyes.

"Right. I think he knows what's going down and, for some unknown reason, he's letting me know."

When she thought about that, it made sense. A lot of sense. A light went off in her head. "That's it." She smiled wide. "That's the connection!" Her pulse danced through her veins. "He knows what's going on, so we talk to him and find out who's behind it all. Easy, peasy."

"If we knew where to find him."

"The next time he contacts me, I set up another meeting."

"If he contacts you."

"He will. I'm sure of it. And it gives us another avenue to pursue. We now have two people we can lean on to get the information." She smiled big again, and raised a hand for a high-five.

After a slight hesitation, his hand met hers with a *smack*, but then instead of drawing his hand back, his fingers curled around hers...and he pulled her closer.

Even after a long day, the faint scent of his cologne lingered. Masculine. Sexy. And stoking the long-smoldering embers of lust deep within. Her passion ignited, she leaned in and kissed him. Really kissed him. She needed a man's arms around her, his body close to hers. Naked. But it wasn't just any man's body she needed—she needed Remy's.

CHAPTER TWENTY-FOUR

THE TOUCH OF Remy's warm lips on hers roused a desire so intense and so deep it felt as if extracted from the very marrow of her bones. His hands slid around her shoulders to her back, pulling her to him, pressing her closer, allowing her to feel his need and desire.

She should stop. No good could possibly come of this. But that was her rational, logical side making a rational, logical attempt to convince her she was going to make a fool of herself...a futile effort she crushed almost as soon as it surfaced.

The kiss went on and on, teasing, tempting, drawing a soft moan from deep in her throat. She molded her body into his, her breasts against his chest. Desire coursed through her, and she could feel the firm tight need in him straining against her.

Every sinew of his body that touched hers said he wanted her, and she closed her eyes and reveled in the in the salty taste of his mouth, the ragged draw of his breath, the masculine scent of his body. His kiss, slow and gentle, his tongue tracing the outer edges of her lips, made her want him even more and when he pulled back, her mouth burned with need.

He stood, tipped his head toward the bedroom, and when she smiled her yes, he picked her up like a feather, carried her into the room, and deposited her on the down-filled comforter. She felt like a fair maiden being dragged off by a pirate who intended to pillage her body. Or was that wishful thinking? Mostly, it was what she wanted to do to him. The guy had more restraint than she did, that was sure.

He unbuckled his belt, let his jeans fall to the floor, and lay beside her, facing her, the hard press of his need throbbing against her hip, making her pulses leap. With one finger, he traced a line down the front of her shirt, so she lifted up and was about to pull it off when he stopped her. "Let me," he said, then gently touched her cheek with his fingertips before reaching down and pulling her T-shirt over her head.

She wasn't cold, but she shivered under his gaze. He reached around and unsnapped her bra, took it off and flung it aside. Then he bent to her and cupping her breast in his hand, outlined the circle of her sensitive swollen nipple with his tongue. He sucked it in for a brief moment, then moved to the other side and did the same. She moaned as he made his way up to her neck again, and then to her lips where all gentleness stopped and he ravaged her mouth with a kiss that left her breathless.

Within seconds they'd both shed the rest of their clothes and, as she looked at him, an unbelievable ache of longing filled her. He must've read her mind because the next thing she knew, their mouths and bodies were meshed in a fiery web of passion. She arched toward him when he reached down to spread her thighs. She cared about nothing except him inside of her.

He twisted away for a second, reached to open a drawer in the nightstand, said, "Yes!" and took out a packet. "I hope to hell these still work," he mumbled as he put on the condom. Right now, she couldn't care less, but liked that he'd thought of it.

She reached out, her hands on his lower back, his

flesh hot and tingling beneath her fingertips. On his knees between her legs, raw desire flared in his eyes. He drew his hands down her sides, as if memorizing her shape, and making her need even more intense. Then he lowered himself over her and entered.

He groaned, barely moved, and when he did, she felt his restraint.

"Hey," she whispered. "We have the rest of the night."

"Music to my ears," he whispered back.

Hearing the tender agony in his voice, a tremor inside her thighs and groin vibrated with need.

He stroked slow and easy until she couldn't stand it. Raising into him, she urged him on, harder, faster, and within seconds she climaxed in a downpour of fiery sensations so intense she hardly noticed he'd done the same.

They stayed entwined for the longest time it seemed, and then Remy drifted off to sleep. She floated in languid contentment thinking how alive she felt. It had been so good and so natural, as if they were made for each other. An adolescent thought for sure. But if there was one thing she knew about Remy, he didn't do things lightly and it both reassured and bothered her. But right now, all she wanted to do was lie back and enjoy.

For this one moment in time, she had nothing on her mind except more hot sex with a hot man she really liked, and she planned to wake him in a few hours to enjoy their lovemaking all over again.

She trailed a finger down the side of his arm where he had the tattoo.

"That's nice," he said, surprising her that he was still awake.

She noticed the skin was bumpy.

"Battle wound," he said, before she asked. "I thought a tattoo was better than an ugly scar."

Oddly, her scar from the gunshot wound was in a similar place. "Good idea to cover it up. How did it happen?"

He hesitated. She felt his breathing deepen.

"Stupidity," he finally said. "A kid I didn't want to shoot. Instead…" He cleared his throat. "Instead, I learned a lesson."

She didn't know what to say, except, "I'm sorry."

He didn't respond, and it was obvious this was not the time to ask more questions about it. Like, did the symbol have meaning? Like—did he shoot the kid after all?

She trailed a finger down his arm again.

"You've got all night to stop doing that," he said, lightening the moment

"I think I'm up for the task."

"Good." He laughed. "I may need a few minutes, though." He pulled her into his arms. "But I'm very good at cuddling."

She snuggled closer. She wasn't, but she felt different tonight. Everything felt so easy. So natural.

"You know," Remy said, his voice soft. "Being in this place reminds me of when I was a kid, my twin brother Parker and I would come down here to hide from my dad." He laughed. "He'd always find us, though."

"A twin brother. How cool."

"Not identical. But it *was* cool. Sometimes."

"Your playhouse was bigger than the house my family lived in when I was growing up," she said, reminded of where they both came from…how different they were. "We lived with my grandmother for a while, too."

"Uh-huh." He nuzzled her neck. "That's nice. I wish I'd known my grandparents, but—" He paused, his body tensing. "They were all long gone before I was born."

"I'm sorry," she said.

"It's okay. I never knew them. It's nothing like when someone you love dies."

She rolled to her side.

He gently touched her cheek. "I'm sorry. What I meant was that with my grandparents, it was simply a fact I knew all my life. With my mother, it was a total shock."

Charlie pulled to a sitting position and wrapped her arms around her knees. He'd told her earlier his mother died, but he hadn't elaborated on it.

"She committed suicide."

For a moment, Charlie didn't know what to say. "Oh, no. I'm so sorry."

Remy pulled to a sitting position, too, propped up on his hands behind him, knees bent. He told her how his father had lied and it wasn't until years later Remy had learned the truth on his own. Hearing how he adored his mother and was devastated at her death, how he'd used the carriage house to escape and be alone, wrenched Charlie's heart. They had more in common than she'd thought. She knew his pain. Intimately.

"I'm sorry if staying here is bringing back such sad memories."

"No. Oddly, it's not. Not bad memories I mean. Actually, it feels good." He glanced at her, a hint of a grin curving his lips. "It feels very good."

They talked for most of the night being both serious and silly, but best of all, they weren't professionals doing a job, they were just two people enjoying each other's company, finding out what made each other tick. Finding out how different they were, his life one of affluence, hers from the other side of the tracks, one filled with love, the other not. He'd had everything money could buy, but had missed out on the most important part. Even Remy's brief marriage five years earlier had met with disaster.

When Remy put his arms around her to finally fall asleep, Charlie felt safe, like she might actually be able to sleep without keeping one ear open. She hadn't experienced that feeling since she was a child and her parents were together.

Way back when, theirs had been a happy, secure family and, for the first time since she was a little kid, she thought it might be possible to feel that way again.

Remy quietly lowered his feet to the floor. He'd been lying awake for an hour, his mind in transit. It was almost sunrise, and though he'd like nothing more than to savor the moment, they had to act quickly.

He grabbed his scattered clothes and crept from the room. After dressing, he went to the kitchen in search of coffee. It was unlikely there would be any, but after searching the cabinets, he found a few packets of instant coffee, the kind you get in a hotel room. Better than nothing. Charlie would insist on going to work, but he wasn't letting her out of his sight.

It was his fault she was in this mess. Chances were she'd be safe in court since as far as he knew, there'd never been a mob hit in the courtroom. But they needed a plan for when she finished.

He heated water in a teapot, went to the bathroom and on his way out, noticed lights on in the main house. Probably Caroline up early to make breakfast for his old man...who even after all these years knew nothing about the woman and still treated her like a servant. Why Caroline had stayed working for him for so long was a mystery.

Reaching for a cup in the cabinet next to the stove, he heard his phone ring. He grabbed it quickly, muted the sound, and put it on vibrate so it wouldn't wake Charlie. His father's number showed on the caller ID. The clock on his phone said it was five a.m. He didn't answer and let it transition to message mode.

When his coffee was ready, he sat on the couch and listened to the recorded message. "I need to talk to you. Now!"

As he was reading, the phone vibrated, indicating another call. His dad. He picked up and before he had a chance to answer, his dad launched into a tirade on how Remy was screwing up any chances he'd have to win an election and seconds later, there was a loud banging at the door. Remy hurried to unlock it and had barely turned the knob when his old man burst into the room.

Charlie awoke to voices. Shouting.

Groggy, she shook her head. Had the hit man found them? Was Remy in danger? She glanced for her clothes, strewn everywhere since they'd been in such a hurry. She was glad she'd hadn't been stupid enough to leave her gun in the other room and drew it from her purse holster. Wrapping the sheet around her naked body, she crept to the door to listen.

"Dad! Stop talking," she heard Remy shout.

Holy shit. Judge Malone was out there. In a flash, she put the gun away, threw on her clothes and shoved her hair into a ponytail, ready to meet the bastard if necessary. Her ear next to the door, she could hear them talking, but their voices were lower now and she wasn't able to make out much of it. Then it was quiet. Was he gone? Was the coast clear? But then, clearly, as if they were right next to the door, she heard—

"Dammit Remy, you just can't get it through your head who you're dealing with."

"Oh, I get it. I get it exactly. I just can't believe a senate seat is worth all the lives these people destroy?"

She heard a snort of disgust, then laughter. Not Remy.

"You are stupidly naïve, son. Do you think taking out a few low-level gangsters is going to change anything? It's called natural selection. Only the strong survive and if you don't get with the program, you won't be one of them. Losing your job won't be a problem if you get yourself and that bleeding heart friend of yours killed."

Another loud bang, as if someone knocked something over. Then another strange laugh, the kind you make when something is so horrible it's almost funny. Was it Remy?

"Losing my job?" Remy's voice again. Another strange laugh. "No, it's you who doesn't get it. Do you think I give a damn about this job? The *only* reason I'm here, and I mean the *only* reason, is to find out what happened to Adam. And when I do, I'm gone." He scoffed. "I admit, when I first came back, I had a crazy thought that things might be different and that maybe—"

After a long pause, she heard Remy say in strong, even tones, "Forget it. None of that matters. But I *will* find out what happened to Adam. There *will* be justice. And I *will* do everything in my power to keep anyone from getting hurt."

He was still talking, but the words she kept hearing were, 'And when I do, I'm gone.' She took a breath. Okay. She never expected anything from this. Why would she feel disappointed now? It was a surprise, that's all.

She looked at the time. Court in two hours. She snatched Remy's car keys from the table, then slipped out the sliding patio door.

CHAPTER TWENTY-FIVE

"GOING SOMEWHERE?" Remy's voice disrupted Charlie's concentration as she listened to the voice mail from January.

On the patio, car keys in hand, she shook her head. "There's better reception out here," she lied, holding up her phone…which didn't explain why she had his keys. "I received a message from January about the case, but didn't get it all." She pressed the star key for the message to repeat. Waiting for it to begin, she handed him the keys. "They were on the floor."

She listened to the message again. "She's bringing me some clothes, so I'll have to get there early to change." She peered inside. "Company gone?"

"Yeah." He nodded. "Unexpected. But no big deal. He won't tell anyone where we are."

She wondered earlier why he hadn't asked for his father's help, but after hearing them argue, it was pretty obvious. "We won't be here long, anyway."

"I found some coffee."

"Good. I'm going to need to clean up a bit before going to court. Is that possible here, or should I go someplace else?"

"The shower works. If there aren't any towels, I can ask Caroline to bring some and whatever else you need. Now that the judge knows we're here, we can relax for a little while."

Relaxing sounded wonderful, but not likely to happen. She headed inside. "Where's the coffee?"

He went to the kitchen, held up a packet of instant coffee. "Not the greatest, but better than nothing. I'll ask Caroline to bring the real thing when she comes," he said, pulling out his phone.

While he did that, Charlie looked over the notes they'd laid out on the table. Wondered if the judge had seen what they were doing. "We didn't add a couple of things," she said.

Finishing his call, he came back. "What?"

"Max got some intel that the job Adam was working on might involve human trafficking."

"Reliable?"

She shook her head. "Just a guess, but another avenue to pursue. We're following up."

A knock sounded at the door. Caroline again, only this time with towels and soap, coffee and some scones and croissants. Remy thanked her and then motioned for Charlie to sit and have something to eat.

"I don't have a lot of time," she said, settling on the couch.

He sat next to her, gave her another strange look. "Did I do something wrong?"

"No...why?"

"Because we've just spent hours making love and sleeping together and you're acting like...like I'm a—"

"A client?"

His mouth quirked up on one side. "Yeah...like that."

She raised her chin. "But you are. I have other clients as well, and I need to get back to doing what you all hired me to do." She picked up a scone.

He grabbed her hand, made her stop moving, his eyes met hers. "Our lives are in danger. I get that. We have business to attend to. I know that. But we can't ignore what happened."

"Why not?"

"Because it happened." He shoved a hand through his hair. "I just…want to make sure you're okay with it."

Why wouldn't she be? It was a few hours of great sex. She didn't need it to be anything more than that. Did he think she did? Well, he was wrong, she *could* ignore it. Do what she always did. She pulled herself up, back rigid. "I'm fine. Last night was…great. I enjoyed it. I didn't think it would affect our business relationship, or…"

Remy's brilliant blue eyes darkened to storm-cloud gray. He dropped her hand like he'd just learned she was infected with a deadly virus. "It won't." He turned…handed her a napkin. "So, we're good, then."

She forced a smile. "We're good. And I really do need to take a shower."

Charlie had left Remy at the door to the empty courtroom when she went to meet the prosecutor in another room next to the judge's chambers. Apparently the alternate juror was sick and the trial was going to be delayed until the woman was feeling better or they could get someone else. Judge Grant hadn't even bothered to come in since the trial had been scheduled for the entire day. The delay was great news. She still hadn't heard from Lucy and hoped to hell her client hadn't skipped.

The whole thing had taken less than fifteen minutes. Even Remy, sitting on a bench next to the door, was surprised to see her back so soon. They didn't speak until the others had left. "That's it, until they can reschedule," she said still standing at the door and scanning the hallway.

Earlier, driving in, they'd talked about what their next step should be, given that someone wanted to kill them. They drew no conclusion. She also had to do something about finding Lucy, who was going to spend the rest of her life in prison if she so much as took a fast step near city limits.

"I have some ideas," Remy said, finally. "I think we should go back to my dad's. It's a safe place to regroup. Someone would have to scale the security gate to get inside. If they did, all the bells and whistles would go off."

"Okay." Like Remy, she kept her gaze moving, scanning the area, her nerves like needles under her skin.

"We're good with the different vehicle. Anyone watching will still be looking for your car or my Escalade. As long as no one sees us leave, we should be okay. I haven't picked up on anyone, but we need to be cautious."

Although people walked by, they kept moving, except for a man now standing near the stairway. He was in a dark blue coverall, and she could see an emblem on his shirt pocket...a uniform of some kind. He looked directly at her, stared for a moment, then turned away.

"Maintenance," Remy said. "Saw him mopping down the hall earlier. He's just checking out the goods." His gaze shifted downward.

Lech...Both of them. She swung around, away from the maintenance guy's unabashed stare. The dress January had brought her when they met at McDonald's a few blocks away was a jersey wrap with a plunging neckline and fabric that clung to her body like snakeskin. Nothing proper about it. The only courtroom worthy thing was the color. Black. The four inch heels on the ankle boots didn't help. Fortunately, she didn't have to appear in front of a jury looking like one of her client's hookers.

"I've been thinking about our departure and came up with a plan. If you have something better, let me know," she said.

"Okay. Shoot." His eyes skimmed over her body again…appreciatively.

And damn if it didn't make her blood run hot. He wasn't a man who kept his desire under wraps, and apparently, she wasn't very good at keeping hers there, either.

She moistened her lips. "I called Dempsey and he should be here any minute. I'll have him wait while we go inside. If anyone is watching, they'll think he's waiting for me as he's been doing during the trial. You can go in first and then go out the door on the other side, go down the hallway to the restroom. When you come out, continue in the opposite direction. About three quarters of the way around the building, there's another exit. Go out, get the car and bring it around to the east side."

"Got it."

"I had January bring me a few extra things, so after you go, I'll wait a few minutes, go inside myself and use the room next to the judge's chambers to change clothes. I'll come out the back door to meet you. If anyone is watching, they'll be watching this door and Dempsey. If anyone tries to get inside, Demps will stop them. If anyone is watching right now and sees me wearing a dress, they won't be looking for someone with short spiked hair and wearing jeans."

Remy gave her a two-finger salute. "Okay, boss."

She bristled at the subtext in his comment. He was paying her to do a job, but he *wasn't* part of her team as his familiarity implied. "Once Dempsey gets here, we'll chat briefly, and then move."

A few moments later, her bodyguard came through the front doors, his too-small suit looking as if it was going to split its seams like the Hulk at any moment.

"Thanks for coming," Remy said, reaching out a hand. "I'm Remy."

Dempsey nodded his acknowledgment as they shook hands and Charlie quickly ran through the plan. Once inside, it would take her about three minutes to change and another few to get out of the building. She told Dempsey to wait at least fifteen minutes before taking off.

Finished explaining, she signaled Remy and he disappeared into the room. She pretended to laugh and talk to Dempsey for a moment, then went inside herself. The room next to the chambers was used as a waiting room, and as long as no one else was inside, she was good to go.

Finding the room empty, she went in, locked the door, and dumped out the clothes from the disposable plastic grocery bag—black rock star wig, a black silk shirt, some hoop earrings, a long maroon neck scarf, and a removable nose ring. Hurrying, she changed into the jeans she was wearing yesterday, minus the leather jacket and boots, which she'd left in Remy's car along with her messenger bag and gun. She tucked her hair into the short, spiky wig, donned the jewelry, folded the dress and shoved it into a large manila envelope, tossed the plastic bag into the trash, and she was outta there. Three minutes, tops.

Remy was waiting at the east exit just as they'd planned. He did a double take when she slipped inside, eyebrows rising. Turning back, eyes on the road, he stomped on the gas and took off.

First thing, she called her office to get Max and

Gabe on a 'locate Lucy' detail and then explained what had happened and that she'd touch base with them as soon as they had plans in place.

She was about to hang up when January said, "One more thing. We checked real estate records for Tony Carlozzi and it looks like most of his property belongs to a corporation called Quadrastar."

"Quadrastar. That sounds familiar," she said, more to herself than to her assistant.

"Because I mentioned it earlier," Remy chimed in. "When I ran a check for the Stuben Warehouse address, the records showed the building was owned by Quadrastar, Inc."

"Did you dig any deeper?" she asked January.

"Not yet."

"Okay. Do it and get back to me."

"I like the new look," Remy said when she hung up. "The nose ring in particular."

"My favorite accessory."

He snorted.

An hour later, they were back at the carriage house and once inside, she turned to Remy. "All right. Where were we?"

"Right where we left off." He shrugged off his jacket. "Sort of."

What a tease...and even knowing that, she had to smile. "Right." And where we left off was figuring out a way to find a missing cop while the bad guys are trying to kill one of us. Or both. For the same reason. Or different reasons."

He arched a brow. "I'm sure that made sense somehow, but my brain is fried."

"And it's only nine a.m." She grinned. "What I meant was that someone might want to take *us* out because we're getting too close to finding out what happened to Adam. Or they might want to take out only you, because then I'd no longer have you as a client. Or someone might want to take me out because of a client I happen to be representing in court. Someone who doesn't want to be exposed. Someone who tried to bribe a juror."

"You don't know that's what happened. All you know is that someone on the other side was in contact with the juror. Nothing more. Right?"

"Why else would they be consorting outside of court?"

His brow raised again. "Consorting?"

"Consorting." She glowered at him.

He was quiet, apparently considering her reasoning…or wanting her to shut the fuck up.

Then he said, "In police work, we look at the evidence and make decisions based on what we see. We don't decide guilt or innocence or someone's motives."

"And in the investigation business, we need to figure out motive in order to find answers to the crime."

He pondered that briefly, then said, "If we put the two together, we might come up with something."

"And—" She dropped onto the couch, removed the nose ring, and took off her boots. "That's why you're a cop and I'm an attorney. You see black and white and I see all the little details—all the shades of gray—and keep looking. Oil and water."

"Cliché."

True. She threw the nose ring at him. "Okay…back to our little problem."

He walked to the kitchen counter, brought back the plate of scones and croissants they hadn't eaten earlier, then sat next to her. He picked up a scone, paused for a moment, then said, "The most significant evidence points to someone wanting to keep us from finding out what happened to Adam."

"By evidence, you mean Johnson sending me a

message pretending he's you to get me to the warehouse and someone else sending you a message to go there for who knows what reason."

"Right. Since the people pulling Johnson's strings are getting real serious, it's probably safe to assume he knows more than he's let on."

"Johnson," she said. "Good assumption." She glanced over. "He's the only real shot we've got."

He nodded. "Right. We have to make him talk."

"Right.

The phone rang and Charlie nearly jumped out of her skin. Her caller ID showed it was January. "Hey, what's up?"

"I'm going to email you the list of buildings owned by Quadrastar," January said. "And I'm waiting on the Corporation Commission for a list of Quadrastar's owners."

"Great." She clicked off and rubbed her temples. "January's emailing me the list of buildings owned by Quadrastar.

"Coffee?" He picked up the thermal carafe, eyes questioning.

Chewing a quick bite of blueberry scone, she nodded.

He waited until she finished chewing, then asked, "And the list is for?"

Suddenly feeling like there were so many puzzle pieces they'd never figure it all out, she sighed, then stretched her arms over her head, pulled off the wig and then bent over, head between her knees. "I don't know," she said, her voice a hollow echo from below.

Her head hurt and she didn't want to think about any of it any more. At least for a little while. "It's just another avenue to pursue. Maybe someone important is attached to the corporation and we can put the pressure on him to do something." She had no idea what. All she knew was that she wasn't going to leave a single stone unturned. "And right now, my head hurts thinking about it all."

He set his coffee cup on the table, then went behind the couch where she was sitting. "Lean back."

As soon as she did, she felt his long fingers weave through her hair, massaging their way to her temples where he made slow circular motions. Her stomach tightened, the rush of warmth between her legs telling her it wouldn't take even a nanosecond to forget everything that was going on. Not with him touching her that way. Gentle, yet firm, circling around and around...

She closed her eyes, savoring the light pressure of his strong hands massaging her temples, then her neck and her shoulders.

Remy leaned down, his mouth close to her ear and said, "I know an even better way to get rid of a headache."

CHAPTER TWENTY-SIX

IT WASN'T A long list, ten properties. The Stuben Warehouse was on the list, as Remy had previously said. There was nothing on how long it had been owned by The Partnership…or who had owned it twenty-five years ago when a man was murdered in the building.

"Anything good?" Remy asked, looking over her shoulder at what she was doing on the phone. He came around and sat in the overstuffed chair next to her.

"Not really." After lying in bed savoring more great sex, both she and Remy had showered and dressed and were waiting for Caroline to bring them some lunch. Pretty nice. Just make a call and food comes to you. Something she could easily get used to.

And that, Charlie Street, is how corruption begins. People wanting things they can't get simply by working hard. "Nothing I recognize, anyway. But…there is a building name on the list with a name similar to one I've seen before. The Mercury Building."

"Never heard of it."

"We probably haven't heard of most of them since they will likely have the names of the occupying business attached to them."

"So the list is incomplete."

"It's a start. You don't know where something might take you unless you keep digging. "Do you remember, the name that I asked you about when we first met? I showed you a list that I'd found in my dad's possessions that had the word Merceury on it— Merceury with another 'e.'"

"Yeah. I drew a blank on it."

"Well, what if my dad was just a horrible speller and what he really meant to write was Mercury?"

"You lost me."

"Sorry. I'm just thinking out loud. What if Merceury is the Mercury Building? If it is, then I know something I didn't know before. What if the common denominator here is the Detroit mafia…The Partnership? I believe my dad was set up and the mob was behind it. Just as they're behind Adam going missing. One has nothing to do with the other except if Merceury is misspelled and really means the Mercury Building, it could mean the mob *is* involved. It could mean I may have a new lead on my father's case."

Remy visibly bristled. "Great…except we're working on finding Adam, not your father's twenty-five-year-old murder conviction."

"Right. And my team has been on it twenty-four seven. But I can't ignore the things that have happened during the investigation…like the call you got out of nowhere from the same person who'd been telling me he knows something about my father."

She bit the skin inside her lower lip. She would have to tell him eventually. "There's something else I discovered at the warehouse that makes those things even more important." She hesitated. Cleared her throat. Geez. Just freaking say it. "Nick Johnson is an alias. Nick Johnson is really Joey Drakar, the man whose testimony put my father on death row."

Remy angled his head, as if he might have heard incorrectly. "What?"

"The last person to see Adam is the same person who testified against my dad, someone I've been trying to find for years. The same people are involved." She swallowed, her mouth suddenly bone dry.

"Johnson...is the same guy who testified against your father?" Remy said, his tone incredulous. She could practically see the wheels in his head turning as he absorbed what she'd said.

"Yes. Johnson is Joey Drakar, a gang kid my father was trying to help. He used to come to the gym, so I saw him around a lot. When we were in the warehouse I noticed Johnson had the same tattoo his cousin Joey did, a spider that sprang from a large birthmark. Having the same tattoo might not have tipped me off, but the chances both men would have the same birthmark..." She shook her head. "Uh-uh."

"I was a kid back then and Joey Drakar was a pimply-faced teenager. He's changed his looks, his hair color, and maybe he's even had some surgery, but as soon as I saw the tattoo, I knew. I'd wondered why something about Johnson seemed so familiar, but I brushed it off to the fact that he and Joey were cousins and would have some of the same characteristics, but-"

"Nick Johnson is Joey Drakar?" Remy repeated, as if he hadn't heard the rest of what she'd said.

"Do you remember what you told me when we first started...what the snitch told you about Nick Johnson?"

He looked at her for a moment, expression blank. "No."

"If you find one, you might find the other," She said. "That was good intel—if we'd known what it actually meant."

"Why didn't you tell me about Drakar?"

"Why didn't I—?" she sputtered.

"Okay, okay." He waved a hand. "I got it. You didn't want to pollute one case with the other."

Finally.

After a long stretch of silence, he exhaled a big gush

of air. A look of resignation crossed his face. "I have something I should've mentioned, too." He cleared his throat. "Maybe…maybe we don't need to look for Adam anymore."

"What?" Her eyes went wide. "What do you mean?"

"The captain told me the other day that a body washed up downriver. It could be Adam, but we won't know until DNA results come back."

Her stomach plummeted. "Oh, no. I'm so sorry. But maybe—"

"No. I can kid myself that it's not him, but it's pretty hard to do after all this time. And now there's—" his voice cracked.

There's a body— Charlie silently finished his sentence. Words he couldn't say. A lump formed in her throat. She knew, and she ached with him, wished she could help. But acceptance was an elusive thing, even knowing it would be for the best. "It's still the same, Remy. The person responsible for Adam's disappearance is probably the person trying to kill us."

"And probably the person responsible for Adam's death."

"But you don't know for sure if it was Adam, so it really doesn't change anything. Even if it is, you still want to know who's responsible. Right?"

He pinched the bridge of his nose between two fingers. "Right."

Good. She pressed a hand against his arm, then got on her phone, texted January again and asked her to follow up getting addresses for every building on the list. Just as she sent the message, her phone screen went black. Damn. "My phone just died and I don't have the charger cord with me."

"Mine's almost gone, too," Remy said, snatching the unit from the coffee table. "I'll see if I can get Caroline to find a cord we can use. My father has all kinds of electronic equipment and doesn't use any of it. Maybe there's a laptop or something." He texted, then put the phone down.

"If not, January can bring my phone cord in the morning. But…"

"But?" He glanced at her.

She didn't want to say it, but she had to. "Do we need to worry about your father telling someone we're here?"

A scowl formed. "Whatever problems we have, he's still my dad."

Okay. Remy might believe that his father wouldn't rat them out, but she wasn't so sure. She would've been wary under any circumstance, but remembering what Johnson said in the warehouse about the judge cast another layer of doubt. Still, Remy seemed confident, so she had to go with it. "Sorry. I had to ask."

She checked her phone again. Still dead. The recording was probably why the battery was gone. She wished she could remember Johnson's exact words. He'd said something about Remy's father being "in on it," but she'd been so rattled, she couldn't be sure. Johnson could've been deflecting, a common tactic among criminals…and sociopaths. But she had to hear it again before saying anything to Remy.

"Nick Johnson knows more about what happened to Adam than he told me," Charlie said. "I'm sure of it. We have to get him to talk."

Remy's mouth quirked up on one side.

"What?" she questioned, hands palms up.

"It's hard to picture you forcing someone to talk. Although…you are kind of a badass chick with a gun. How do you propose we do that?"

"You're the cop. You should have lots of experience at that."

His chin came up.

"I mean...you know what to do."

His gaze bored into her.

"You guys do it all the time. You're trained to interrogate and get people to confess."

He crossed his arms. "Are we still talking about Johnson...or something else?"

"Something else?" She went still. "What do you mean?"

"I don't know. It's a feeling I get whenever something comes up about my job. You get defensive."

"Defens...what...I—That's ridiculous."

The look in his eyes said it wasn't. He shrugged. "Okay. It just felt that way."

Her mother had told her the same thing when she'd disagreed with her. But it wasn't what they thought. She was just passionate about...things. "I suppose I get a little intense, sometimes, but it's nothing personal." She'd moved on with her life...buried all that long-ago anger at the system. She'd had to.

But somehow, when she was with him and talking about some subjects, all the old anger, the painful, hollow feeling of loss, kept boiling up like hot lava in a volcano about to explode.

"Johnson," she blurted. "Back at the warehouse, he said some things that made me think he knows what's going on with the human trafficking Adam was investigating. Maybe there's a reason he was the last person to see Adam. Maybe Johnson set Adam up, just like...like he did us." Like he did her father. "We really do need to make him talk."

"We?"

"Us. You and me."

"Not without backup."

"We have help. Max and Gabe."

"Professional help."

She drew back. What did he think? That because

they were investigators her team wasn't trained? "You disappoint me, Malone. You may have checked my background, but you obviously didn't do your research on my team. Max is a former Marine sniper, and a SWAT cop from Chicago who went rogue and turned PI. Gabe is a former Navy SEAL, and an attorney…and both have killer skills in martial arts. Is that professional enough for you?"

He scrubbed a hand over the two-day growth on his chin and cheeks.

"I think I know your problem," she said, leaning against the back of her chair.

His head came up. "*My* problem?"

"Yeah. You can't stand not being in control. No wonder you like working alone."

He glared at her for a second, then produced a big hearty laugh. "Said the pot to the kettle." He raised his feet to the coffee table, lounging back, hands behind his head. "You know what…you're absolutely right. And I like it that way."

She put her feet up, too. "And I have a job to do. I'm going to need a car and a bunch of money." If Remy wasn't going to help her squeeze Johnson for information, she'd do it alone.

CHAPTER TWENTY-SEVEN

THE OBVIOUS QUESTIONS were, where would the mob house people for human trafficking? Who was in charge? And did they sell the victims or use them for ransom? Or both?

The list of buildings owned by Quadrastar was extensive, and now with the addresses, she was able to pinpoint the location of each building. A few were major Midtown properties, others were apartment complexes, and some looked to be smaller businesses and even individual homes. With such significant holdings, The Partnership could easily influence city politics. But not if someone exposed a racket like human trafficking.

Adam had been a threat. She and Remy were a threat.

An hour later, they were still sitting on the couch, legs extended and with the laptops Caroline had commandeered on their laps. She pulled up another page of addresses for buildings owned by Quadrastar and, one by one, plugged them into Google Maps. The homes were of particular interest. Two were in the most blighted area of the city, as were two warehouses that appeared to be empty. Two homes were farther out near Eight Mile Road.

"I worked on a human trafficking job a few years back in Boston," Remy said. "It's going to be more than we can handle."

"We're looking for evidence, Malone, not single-handedly trying to take down the Detroit mafia. If we get the evidence, we take it to Chief Bouvaird."

Remy rubbed his chin. "I don't know. It's hard to know who to trust, especially when I've been warned off the case. I've felt all along there's department cover-up on some level. Could be anyone. Captain Pendergast. Or even the chief."

She got that. In spades. With so many government officials convicted of crimes over the years, it was hard to trust anyone in power. "The mayor, then, or the FBI. I'd think they'd be delighted to get evidence on a case they're in on."

"You'd think. It's still dangerous business and if we're dealing with human trafficking, that's organized crime on a grand scale."

Charlie drew to the side to look at him. "I worked on a Korean sex trafficking case a couple years ago. My team also rescued three children from a Middle Eastern country, another from France and two in Mexico, so I do know a bit about who might be involved and how dangerous it is."

"An abducted child is a lot different than dealing with drug lords and other organized crime syndicates. Drug cartels, like the big South American drug cartels, work with American and Russian organized crime groups. We have no idea who's involved. This is big business," he said. "The cartel the mob is working with will be using coyotes to bring people across the border and hand them off to other people who move them to their next destination. If they don't get waylaid by *bajadoros*."

She sent him a questioning look, then continued to search the Internet for information on crime syndicates. She was familiar…just not as familiar as he was.

"*Bajadoros*," he explained "—steal hostages from the coyotes who transported them into the States."

She knew the term, but didn't interrupt. While he continued, the information popped up on her laptop and she went on reading about illegal immigration, coyotes, drug cartel involvement and the Devil's Highway. Most illegal immigrants were from Mexico or Guatemala, but there were others…Syrians and Asians…all willing to make the highly dangerous trek across the U.S.-Mexico border through some of the most treacherous territory in the U.S. in terms of the criminal element and the landscape.

She knew someone once who'd come through The Devil's Highway, a desolate stretch of land three hundred miles long from Mexico through the Arizona desert that had claimed many lives.

Interesting, but they were a long way from Mexico, and what they needed to do was get information from Johnson, hand it over to the police and let law enforcement deal with whoever was involved. What *she* really needed to do was listen to the recorded conversation she'd had with Johnson at the warehouse. If she could get a simple cell phone cord to charge her battery, she could do it.

Remy had asked Caroline to look for an extra phone cord at the house, but so far, she hadn't come up with anything. The woman had brought two extra cords with the laptops, but neither fit Charlie's phone.

"We should visit a few of these places," she said, going back to her list of properties owned by Quadrastar. "I can send Max and Gabe to a couple of them and we can check out some others."

"Depends on what Johnson says." He paused. A moment later, looking at his monitor, he said, "I've got an address for Johnson. I don't know if it's current or not, but it's all I can find. I'd like to know what he did that he had to change his whole persona and hide out for so many years."

"He told me it was too dangerous for him to stay here after testifying, so he'd had to leave. He didn't say why, but I have a feeling the mob didn't trust him. If he lied on the stand about my father, they may have been afraid someone would get him to turn and admit the truth."

"Which is?"

"I don't know. All I know is that he lied. My father didn't kill anyone."

"What was your father doing at the warehouse?"

Another thing she didn't know...not for sure. "Court documents show he testified he was given a message that his brother Emilio was at the warehouse and was hurt. When my father arrived, he found the body, thought it was Emilio and turned him over. It wasn't Emilio, but he tried to revive the man and when he couldn't, he got scared. He said he knew it didn't look good, so instead of going home, he went to the boxing gym, showered and put his bloody clothes in the trash.

"According to the transcripts, Joey Drakar had been hanging around outside the gym and was sleeping on a bench when he heard some noise, then saw my dad covered in blood. He saw him go inside, then come out, dump something in the trash, and leave. When Joey checked the trash barrel he saw the bloody clothes and called the police."

"What happened then?"

The air seemed to disappear from the room, and suddenly she couldn't draw a breath. The only person she'd ever told about what happened that night was her brother. But even then, she hadn't told him the whole story.

Words choked in her throat when she said, "The police found his clothes in the trash barrel at the gym, so they came to our house...and arrested him."

He turned to her. "Were you there?"

Her hands trembled on the laptop keyboard. She pulled them away. "I was."

Remy's expression softened. "Wow. How awful. I'm sorry." He placed a hand over hers. "That had to be tough, especially for a kid."

Tough for everyone. She remembered her mother crying all night long. All day long. "It was." Blinking away the sudden tears in her eyes, she went back to her search on the computer.

A long moment passed before he said, "Who was the victim?"

"Just a guy with no connection to my dad that I could tell. He worked at the warehouse."

Remy's brows furrowed. "Was it owned by Quadrastar back then?"

"Looks like it."

"So, there's a connection somewhere. We just need to find it."

She looked at Remy. "A connection to what?"

"To the vic and Quadrastar. There's a reason the guy was whacked."

What? One minute he was accusing her of not focusing on Adam's case and the next, he was doing the same thing. But if he was questioning *anything* on her father's case, she sure as hell wasn't going to stop him.

She scrolled down to another page and went so fast, she nearly missed a familiar address. Her heart skipped a beat. She typed the address into Google Maps, watched it come up. "Oh, wow."

Remy was back on his laptop. "What?"

"I have an address for the Mercury Building. It's the Phoenix Rising Group Home."

"The Partnership owns a group home?"

"Quadrastar owns the building, but I'm guessing they rent it out."

They exchanged glances.

"You thinking what I'm thinking," Remy said.

She doubted it. She was thinking maybe the man who was killed in the warehouse had discovered something. Maybe that's why he was murdered. She could make up a dozen different "what if" scenarios from that one thought. Including...

Ella Linski. Sandra Linski's daughter went missing from the Phoenix Rising Group Home.

"What?" Remy's brow furrowed.

"Oh, nothing," Charlie said, her blood rushing. Wow. Could it be? But Quadrastar owned lots of properties. All they had was a vague connection.

"Were you thinking the group home could be involved somehow?"

"Yeah...sick as that would be."

"There's safety in numbers," Remy said after Charlie continued to harangue him about renting a car so she could find Johnson and talk to him. "It's why uniformed officers never go on a call alone."

"Do you think he'll say anything in front of a cop? I don't."

"No, but I think he might finish the job he started."

"That's not happening. I plan to get his attention real quick." She pointed to her gun on the table.

"Then I'll stay back and cover you," Remy said. Looking at her, his emotions ran the gamut from a desire to drag her back into bed to an urge to flee. Either way, he couldn't shuck the sudden need to be with her. To protect her. He scoffed at the thought. Protect her like some kind of action hero saving the fair maiden in distress. Which she clearly wasn't.

Unlike many of the women he knew, she wasn't a person to spill her guts five minutes after meeting someone. Charlie went the opposite direction. She was all business. A good idea, but they'd lost that round on the first kiss. Maybe even before.

She wasn't as invulnerable as she wanted to appear. The armor cracked a little when she'd told him about her dad. She truly believed in the man's innocence and she was so convincing, he almost believed it could be true. Why not. It wouldn't be the first time an innocent man was set up.

"Johnson's hours are usually seven to eleven on weekdays and eight to closing on weekends. So, we either catch him at work, before or after, or at his residence," she said, apparently okay with going as a team.

"Work is out. No one will expect us to go to his apartment. We have a different vehicle, so I'm not worried about anyone recognizing it."

"Provided that address is actually where he lives and he hasn't moved or met with a bad end since he screwed up the hit at the warehouse."

"I think it's the ponytail guy who screwed up. Johnson was gone before I arrived, so I think we can assume he's still around."

"Okay, let's do it," she said. "But we have several hours to wait…even if we get there early."

They exchanged hot glances. She shook her head.

"Right. We need to eat, find a way to charge our phones, and make sure we're topped off before we leave."

"Done. I changed out my mag when you were in the bathroom." She grinned at him. "And we need a plan. Do you know if Johnson lives alone?"

"No one else is listed at that address in the records I looked at, but we can't be certain, and we don't want to encounter any other people who could mess things up."

"If we wait for Johnson to leave for work, we can

take him to a place where we can interrogate him." She ran a hand through her hair, then smoothed it back and held it up off her neck before letting it down again. "Someplace no one would expect us to go."

"Someplace without neighbors…where no one would see or hear us."

"What about the boxing gym?" she said. "It's late enough that no one should be there…and there's a big metal garage in the back."

"Too risky. It has to be someplace isolated. More than likely they'll be watching the places we usually go."

"And yet here we are at your dad's."

"True." Someone could be out there now.

"But they'd be watching for the Escalade."

"Right," Remy agreed. "We'll take the back road. It's well hidden. If anyone is watching, they'll most likely be at the front gate."

"So, what about going to Johnson's apartment? If anyone else is there, we can leave and wait for him to come home from work and catch him in the parking lot before he has a chance to go inside."

They agreed. Johnson's apartment was one of the least likely places anyone would expect them to go.

"Okay," Charlie said. "Sounds like a plan. And if we can't get Johnson to talk, then what? If we go about our daily business, which I will need to do on Monday, we'll be open targets."

Remy nodded.

"What about police protection?"

"And tell them what? That we're on the mob's hit list because I'm still investigating Adam's disappearance?"

"At some point they're going to know."

"After we have the evidence to take these guys down…and that hinges on getting Johnson to talk."

"I repeat...if we can't?"

Unblinking, he looked at her. "Then we're screwed."

CHAPTER TWENTY-EIGHT

AT SIX P.M., Remy parked down the street from the Wilton Apartments, a seedy-looking building that had showed up on the Quadrastar list. Johnson probably got his rent at a discounted rate. "Better turn off the phones," he said, grateful Caroline had come through on a phone charger. He would need his phone later.

"I'll go to the door," Charlie said while doing as he asked with her phone. "As long as I don't have a gun pointed in his face, he'll think I'm harmless."

"Fool that he is."

She smirked. "If anyone else is there, I'll make an excuse to leave."

A few minutes later, Charlie stood at Johnson's door, just aside from the peephole, gun drawn. Remy positioned himself off to the side, weapon ready. If she had any trouble, he'd be right there, and if Johnson balked at letting her in, Remy's standard issue Smith & Wesson could be very persuasive. He signaled her to go.

She rang the bell, then knocked hard a couple of times.

After a moment, a man's voice shouted, "Fuck off. I don't buy nothing from losers who come to my door selling shit."

"It's Charlie Street, Joey. I want to talk to you."

The door opened a crack.

"Surprised to see me?" she said. "I wasn't very happy you set me up like that and I think we need to talk."

"Set up? What're you talkin' about?"

Remy's adrenaline surged.

"Don't give me that crap, Joey. You know exactly what I'm talking about and I need to talk to you now."

Remy gritted his teeth, tightened his grip on his gun, signaled Charlie to move to the side, then came around and using his full body weight, crashed into the door, shoulder first, breaking the puny chain and sending Johnson flat on his back on the floor. Standing over Johnson, Remy aimed at his forehead.

Johnson's eyes bugged out.

"The lady said she needed to talk to you now." In his peripheral vision, he saw a bed in the middle of the room. The place was a studio with no place for anyone to hide except... "Check the bathroom," he told Charlie who'd already shut the outer door and was on her way.

"It's empty," she said, then sidled up next to him, gun in hand.

"You wanted to talk to this douchebag?" Remy said.

"I do, but I think we'll be more comfortable sitting. What do you think, Remy?" She walked to the small kitchenette table, grabbed two chairs and brought them over. Remy sat, but kept his gun aimed at Johnson's head. "Thanks, Charlie. Now where were we?"

Charlie sat next to him, leaned forward, arms crisscrossed on her thighs, her gun waving in Johnson's face. "I believe we left off with the conversation at the Stuben Warehouse. Nick here—" she turned to look at Remy—"was telling me that I had to be careful, because some very bad people would do me some bodily harm if I didn't mind my own business."

"Very interesting," Remy said, never taking his eyes

off Johnson. "Whose business were you minding that made him feel the need to warn you about these very bad people?"

"You know, that's what I can't figure out. Because that's exactly what I was doing…minding my own business." She waved the Ruger in Johnson's face, again.

"Hey, be careful with that thing." Sweat beaded on Johnson's forehead.

Facing Remy, she said, "I guess he just doesn't understand what my business is, because if he knew, I'm sure he'd tell me."

"I don't know what you fucking want from me," Johnson yelled. "And I'm going to be late for work." He leaned to sit up, but Remy shoved him back with the barrel of his gun. Hard.

"I didn't hear anyone tell you to get up, Johnson."

"What we want—" Charlie said, each word crisp and clear "—are answers. We want you to tell us what you know about the undercover cop who was in the bar talking to you."

"I don't know nothin' about him. Just that he was there."

Charlie squinted as she leaned forward, her face only a foot from Johnson's. "That's bullshit. You seemed to know a whole lot more when you were trying to get into my pants, telling me about the guys who come to you for information." She pulled back. "I want their names. And I want to know if they came to you for information on the undercover agent."

Johnson's face knotted. "I don't know what you're talking about. And I don't know no names."

"Really?" She looked at Remy, her gun waving carelessly in Johnson's face. "He's such a lying sack of crap. I'm going to give him one more chance then you can have him." She turned to Johnson again. "I said give me the names of the guys you talked to about the agent or you're going to be *very* late for work."

"I'm not lying."

"Okay, that's it." Remy held his Smith at Johnson's eye level, racked back the slide so the brass round was visible, then slowly returned the slide into position. Taking his time, he slowly thumbed the safety to OFF position. He turned to Johnson again. "Your choice, asshole."

Johnson curled into a fetal position. "No," he whined. "Please don't hurt me, I can't tell you anything. If I do, they'll kill me. First they'll torture me, beat me to a bloody pulp, then dump me in the river with concrete around my ankles."

"Like they did Adam Bentley?" Charlie said.

Uncurling himself, Johnson said, "I don't know nobody by that name."

Remy chimed in. "That's the name of the man you fingered as the agent. A man who has a wife and three kids." He gritted his teeth. "I should just pull the damned trigger right now."

"Nooo!" Johnson screeched. "I didn't know that. They just asked me what I thought, that's all."

"Oh, one more thing," Charlie said. "If you don't tell me their names, those guys that sit in the corner of the bar...then another couple of guys you might know, Tony Carlozzi and Frankie Falcone...all those guys will know real soon how you spilled your guts about what really happened at the Stuben Warehouse and that you gave up information on The Partnership's involvement in human trafficking. So, unless you give us some names, you're friggin' toast."

"Oh, man," Johnson whimpered. "Oh, man. Okay, okay. Can I at least get up to talk? There's bugs and shit on this floor and I've got a bad back."

Remy motioned Johnson to sit up. With great effort,

Johnson pulled to a sitting position, then bent to stand, got partway up and tripped forward, and in the flash of a second, he fell into Charlie, rolled over and crouched behind Charlie with her gun in his hand…and pointed at her head. Charlie didn't move.

"Drop the gun or I'll kill her."

Remy's pulse thundered in his ears. He tightened his grip.

"Shoot him, Remy," Charlie spat out.

Johnson was behind Charlie. Remy couldn't risk hitting her. "Hurt her and you're a dead man," he ground out, struggling to hold back the volcano of anger inside. He'd done hostage negotiations enough times to know he had to stay in control. Empathize. "You can't have it both ways."

"Back against the wall," Johnson yelled.

"Just shoot him," Charlie said. "You're the pistol expert—three years running." Her eyes flashed. She was saying one thing, but trying to tell him something else.

Keeping his gun on Johnson, Remy stepped back. He'd actually have a better shot if he were farther away. "Okay, take it easy," Remy said, maintaining calm, his voice low and smooth. "I'm going."

Johnson swung an arm around Charlie's neck, kept the gun at her temple. "Stand up," he said and yanked her up with him. His arm tightened so hard her eyes bulged nearly out of their sockets.

"What are you going to do, Joey?" Charlie rasped. "You can't kill both of us. Make one move to kill me and Remy will take you out in the blink of an eye."

Johnson's mouth twitched. "Not if I shoot him first."

CHAPTER TWENTY-NINE

"IT WON'T MATTER. You're a liability, a loose end. The mob doesn't like loose ends. But I can get you protection," Charlie said. She had to talk him down, say anything to get him to think, not react.

The look in Remy's eyes said he thought she was crazy.

Johnson pulled her toward the door. "I know who can protect me and it ain't no cops. My mother's dead because of them. They never protected me or her."

Held tight against his chest, she felt Johnson's body vibrate as he spoke, his anger deep. "I know, Joey," she said softly, using his real name. "I know because that happened to me, too. But I'm not talking about cops protecting you. I'm talking about federal protection. I can get that for you. I know people. The attorney general, the Wayne County prosecutor, judges, the head of the FBI. I can help you start a new life."

The look in Remy's eyes said he was ready to take the guy out if he so much as twitched a muscle. But she needed Johnson alive.

"Judges?" Johnson scoffed in her ear. "Judges like good ol' Judge Malone? Oh, yeah, he'd protect me all right. You think I was kidding when I told you he was on the take? Guys like him are the worst. Carlozzi. Falcone. Those guys are real. They don't pretend to be the good guys."

Charlie looked at Remy, saw his hands tighten on his gun. "Never mind that," she said. "What's important is that I can get you federal protection if you just give us the names of the guys you talked to about the agent." The pressure on her back eased, so she kept her voice smooth and calm. "That's all you have to do. Give us a couple of names and you'll get a whole new life."

Just as she said the last word, Johnson yanked her toward the door. "Reach back and open it," he ordered.

She did as asked and at the same time, stomped on his instep. He screamed and the second his grip eased, she dropped down, swiveled around and caught him with a sharp kick to the groin. In the fraction of a second it took for her to wind up to take him down, Remy crossed the room and swung a punch that blasted Johnson against the wall so hard she thought he might go through it. Blood splattered. Johnson doubled over. Remy kneed him in the chest, drew him up, pinned him against the wall and shoved his gun under his chin.

"I've got a better deal for you," he said through gritted teeth. He shoved the gun even harder. "Start talking."

Johnson groaned. Blood ran from his nose into his mouth, his face bunched in pain. "Okay," he gasped. "Okay."

"Right pants pocket," Remy said. "Let's cuff this bastard."

Breathing heavily, adrenaline pumping like a geyser, Charlie stuffed a hand inside Remy's pocket, felt for the flex cuffs. Her senses kicked into overdrive and for one fraction of a second, she thought what else she might like to do while feeling around for the cuffs. She gave herself a mental shake. How impossible was it that she could get aroused in a situation as testy as this?

She pulled out two sets of flex cuffs, one larger than the other, shoved an arm between the two men to grab Johnson's hands in front of him and hurrying, slipped on the smaller of the two cuffs, tightening as far as they would go.

"Nice moves," Remy said to her with a flick of his head.

She grinned. "I told you I had skills."

He laughed then shoved the gun hard under Johnson's chin again. "You're not talking."

Charlie gave one final yank on the cuffs. "Detective Malone asked you a question."

"Ow! Okay, okay. But you gotta promise to help me…get me protection. And give it to me in writing."

Remy snarled. "Slime like you don't get to call the shots. We don't *gotta* promise you anything."

"No." Charlie eyed Remy to stop. "We will. I promise we will." She took out her tape recorder, turned it on and said, "This is Charlie Street. I'm here with Nick Johnson, also known as Joseph Drakar. I have promised Mr. Johnson physical protection and participation in WITSEC, the federal witness protection system in exchange for complete information on the disappearance of undercover police officer, Adam Bentley, who went missing approximately six months ago. Mr. Johnson is going to answer questions and then willingly, and without coercion, give an account in his own words of the events surrounding the last time he saw Officer Bentley."

Remy glared at her. If eyes were guns, she'd be double dead. His mouth twisted. It was obvious he hated the idea of Johnson getting any kind of protection. But then, a second later, he told Johnson he was under arrest and continued with, "You have the right to remain silent…"

At the same time, Remy motioned Johnson to sit in a chair. When he finished reciting the Miranda Rights, Charlie clicked off the recorder and Remy, still holding his gun on Johnson, said to Charlie, "Now secure his feet."

She used the larger set of flex cuffs and once Johnson was secured, Remy removed the man's belt, went into the closet and came out with two more belts which they used to secure him to the chair.

"Geez. You don't need to keep me tied up like a hog," Johnson whined.

"Yes, we do," Remy said.

Sitting at the table with Johnson trussed up between her and Remy, Charlie turned on the recorder again and began the deposition with name, date and other pertinent information. When done, she found a tablet and wrote down the date and information discussed and repeated in writing that everything he'd said was true and given willingly without coercion. Then she stuck the pen in Johnson's hand. "Sign it."

"Like this?" He held out his cuffed hands.

"Like that."

Remy signed as a witness, and she turned the recorder on again. "Now please give me your verbal account of the events surrounding Adam's disappearance."

"It was a while ago, so it's hard to remember exactly," Johnson said.

"Not going to cut it," Remy said, half out of his chair. "Working as a stoolie for the mob isn't something anyone forgets."

"Start from the day you first saw the undercover officer."

"Tom. He said his name was Tom and we didn't talk all that much, but he came in with the other guys that I told you about before."

"What other guys? What are their names?"

"Manny and Vinnie. When Tom stopped comin' in, there was just Manny and Vinnie. Then a couple months ago, this other guy, Carl, started hanging out with them."

Charlie exchanged glances with Remy. Manny Warzynski and Vinnie Zizzo were on her list, but not anyone named Carl. "What's Carl's last name?"

"I dunno. Something like Duran...Durante. That was it."

"You never saw him before?"

"He's a new guy."

Durante could be the federal agent. "So, let's go back to Tom. Who told you Tom might be an undercover agent?"

"He used to come in sometimes alone and hang out at the bar and ask me lots of questions about the other guys, so I knew something was funny. I told Manny and then Vinnie started asking me shit, so I told him. I didn't do nothin' except answer questions."

"Nothing except sign a man's death warrant. You knew that's what you were doing," Remy gritted out.

"Hey, you play with fire, you get burned. Better him than me."

Remy launched to his feet, grabbed Johnson's shirt by the neck and lifted him off the floor, chair and all. "Keep it up you little prick—" Charlie clicked off the recorder "—and I'll feed you to your gangster buddies piece by piece. Or maybe I'll just let them take care of you instead." He dropped the chair, it wobbled and fell forward landing Johnson face first on his grimy carpet.

She glared at Remy. "The sooner we do this, the sooner we get the hell out of here." She reached to pick up Johnson and Remy reached, too, setting the guy right side up.

"So," she said, clicking on the recorder again. "When did Tom stop coming into the bar?"

Joey groaned, scrunching his nose, now red from carpet burn. "After that night. He never came back."

Charlie looked at Remy, who averted his gaze, probably so he wouldn't do something he'd regret.

"Did you ever see him again or did anyone talk about him?"

"No," Johnson answered. "I asked about him once, asked where he was, and they laughed. Manny said, 'He must've been real thirsty 'cause he's been drinking lots of water…and Vinnie's gonna do the same to you if you keep askin' stupid questions.' Scared me shitless. I knew it wasn't Manny just talking big because of what happened when they brought in some girls a few times."

"What happened?"

"The girls…they were too young to be at the bar… I mean really young, like thirteen…so I said something, cuz I didn't want no police coming down on me for that shit."

"And?"

He hung his head. "They waited for me after work. Beat me up bad. Kinda like right now." He looked at her through one eye. The other was already puffed shut.

"The girls? What happened to them?"

"Same thing as the others, I guess."

He could be talking about the sting Adam was working undercover on. Or not. Dammit, she was getting pissed at having to draw out every freaking answer.

Be tough. Act tough. Gabe's training rang in her ears. Yet her hand trembled as she took out her gun again and jammed it up under his nose. "I'm getting tired and you're getting on my nerves, so let's make this quick. I'm not going to ask any more questions because you're going to tell me everything about what's going on…everything about the sting, the girls, the people coming in from Mexico, or wherever. Tell us where they go, who takes them and what happens after they get there." She nudged the gun again to make her point.

"Ow. Jesus, that hurts."

"Good. Now spit it out. All of it."

"You mean about the houses they go to?"

Remy rounded on the guy, his fists at ready to bust Johnson again. She stopped him with a hand on his chest. Good cop, bad cop wasn't going to work when both wanted to tear the guy from limb to limb.

"Let him talk, Remy. Let's give him one more chance before we deposit him in front of Frankie Falcone's house with a note on his chest saying he squealed like a little piggy about The Partnership's human trafficking operation." She glanced at her watch. "You got five minutes, or we're outta here."

It didn't take that long, and the information was more extensive than they imagined they'd get from him—information on how The Partnership got their victims, most of them from Mexico through the drug cartels via coyotes, but they got other victims from the streets or group homes paid to pinpoint easy victims, drug them and hand them over.

"Everybody on the street knows that stuff," Johnson said. "But they trusted me after all that other stuff went down." He glanced at Charlie. "Because of before," he said.

She knew exactly what he meant. They trusted him because he'd kept quiet about ratting out her dad twenty-five years ago.

And since they trusted him, Johnson said he'd been given the job of delivering supplies and food to a couple of houses he thought were being used for the trafficking operation.

"If you didn't see anyone there, why do you think that?" Charlie prompted.

"Because it was a lot of food. And when I delivered stuff, they had me bring it inside to the kitchen and leave it there. All the windows were boarded from the inside."

Johnson continued then without much prompting, saying the detached garage connected to the house through an extra room that looked as if it had been recently constructed, probably so they could move people inside without being seen.

He'd taken a look beyond the kitchen when one of the guys had left the interior door open, but all he saw was a guy with a gun sleeping in a chair by the front door. Like a guard. That's when he saw more boarded windows. "But you couldn't guess from the outside that anything was going on," he said. All the windows were dark.

"Write down the addresses," she said.

"I don't remember. It's on my phone."

She picked up Johnson's phone from the table where Remy had deposited the contents of the guy's pockets and handed it to him. "Find them."

Two minutes later, she had addresses, one in Ferndale, one in Birmingham, and the third in Hamtramck. Like many meth labs, the hostages were being held in plain sight.

"Now," Charlie said, "you're going to do the same thing and tell us every detail about what happened twenty-five years ago in the Stuben Warehouse."

"Oh, man. I'm thirsty and I really gotta pee."

Charlie found a dirty Big Gulp cup in the filthy kitchen, filled it with water, and set it on the table in front of him…far enough away so he couldn't reach it. "Sorry dude. I can help you with the thirst problem once you start talking, but the other, you're on your own until you're finished."

The side of Remy's mouth tipped up. That he could find anything humorous in any way, about any of this, was ridiculous. But she couldn't squelch the feeling of satisfaction that coursed through her. They now knew what happened to Adam Bentley. They didn't have proof Vinnie Zizzo had killed Adam, but they had a name.

They also had the name of someone who was possibly the FBI mole. A man they had no idea how to find. Finding proof to verify Johnson's testimony on the human trafficking operation wasn't going to be easy, but it looked like it might be the only way to nail the guys at the top. And time was running out. They had to do it before the mob's hit man found them.

She sat again, gun in hand on the table. She looked at Johnson and flipped on the recorder. "Now let's talk about what happened at the Stuben Warehouse."

"Oh, man," Johnson whined some more.

"We gotta move," Remy said. "When this clown's gangster friends realize he's a no-show at work, they're going to come looking."

She nudged Johnson with the gun. "C'mon. We're on the clock here."

"That was so freaking long ago, I don't remember. How can I tell you stuff I don't remember?"

"Let me refresh your memory, then," Remy said, flexing his fingers and making a fist.

"No," Charlie said, standing. "I've got this." She held up her Ruger, looked it over for a moment. Then aimed at Johnson's crotch.

He gasped. "Yeah, yeah. Okay. Someone called me and told me to go to the warehouse. I used to go there a lot to deliver the dirty gym towels and pick up the clean ones, so I figured it was about that."

"Who called?"

"Emilio."

"You're lying." Charlie bolted to her feet. She hadn't read anything about that in the court transcripts.

"No. It's true. He said his name was Emilio, and I

didn't learn until later it wasn't. I was high and not thinking, but when I got there, I saw this guy face down in a pool of blood. I got scared and when I heard someone else come, I hid. That's when I saw him. Alex. And he came over and squatted down to feel the guy's pulse on his neck or something. Then he flipped the man and leaned over him, I guess to listen to see if he was breathing."

"You didn't say anything to him?" Charlie asked. "You knew him. He was your friend. He helped you."

"I know, but it was dark and I didn't know if he did it and came back to see if the guy was dead or what. So when he left, I followed him to the gym and that's when I saw him go in and then come out and dump something in the trash."

"And then what?"

"I called the police. There was a dead man and I didn't want to have someone think I did it. They came and found the bloody clothes."

"Who was the victim? The dead guy."

"Someone who worked at the factory. The linen company supplied towels and sheets and all kinds of stuff to hotels and businesses and then the laundry people cleaned it and sent it all back again. It was a big factory. Lots of people, mostly young girls, worked there. They stayed there all the time and slept upstairs on a different floor. The girls were illegals, so they didn't have to pay them.

"They?"

"The owners."

The owners, meaning Quadrastar. The Partnership. The Detroit mafia.

Letting the information simmer, she turned off the recorder again and went to the kitchen across the room to get herself a drink There had to be more. Johnson wasn't telling everything.

Her mouth was so dry she felt as if she'd been eating cotton balls, but the kitchen was littered with so many empty fast-food boxes, dirty dishes and moldy mounds of unrecognizable leftovers, she gagged. She wouldn't put anything in that room near her lips. Not even the water.

"We need to go," Remy said.

"Soon. We're not quite done, yet." She sat at the table again. Looked at Johnson. "Are we, Joey?" She moistened her lips with her tongue, but even that was dry. "Let's talk about your court testimony."

"Oh, ma-an. I really gotta pee."

"Why did you testify in court that you found my father with the dead man when you didn't?" She sat on the chair opposite him, gun aimed strategically.

Sighing, his shoulders sagged and he dropped his chin to his chest, a passive-aggressive attempt at some sort of resistance. "Dammit. I already told you."

"I forgot. Tell me again."

He gave another resigned sigh, and she clicked on the recorder again. He went on, his voice a bored monotone. "I said it because they threatened to kill me and my mother if I didn't say what they wanted me to say."

"Who threatened you?"

"If I tell you, they'll kill me."

"You're getting protection, remember."

"You promise? Cuz if you don't, then—"

"I promise. Now talk."

"It was one of Carlozzi's guys. Some shmuck who must've gotten whacked cuz he's not around anymore."

Tony Carlozzi, second in line, carried out orders from mob boss Frankie Falcone. But the underboss could've been acting on his own. There was a whole lot more to figure out, but right now, they needed real evidence to prove Johnson's statements. "Why the setup?"

"The drugs and the factory shit, I guess." He pressed his legs together, wiggled in the chair. "I don't know…all kinds of stuff. They must've known something…your dad and the other guy."

For years she'd searched for reasons why someone would want to frame her dad, and that one reason always came up; her dad may have had information to hurt someone. But she'd never found any evidence.

Court records of her dad's testimony said Joey had been there because he always picked up the clean towels for the gym and when he went inside, he saw her father over the body. But he'd actually seen the body first, then her father came inside. What she'd never put together was that Joey had been part of the setup.

Her father's testimony stated that because of his former gang background and arrest record, he knew he'd be a suspect, so he'd fled. The evidence to convict him had been based entirely on Joey Drakar's eyewitness testimony—and very likely the fact that her father had gang history. Years old information that should never have been allowed in court.

She'd never found a connection between her father and the victim, and she'd never imagined Joey would have been part of a set-up. If he now testified to that fact, it could cast doubt on whether her father committed the murder, but it wouldn't be enough to exonerate him.

She still needed evidence. Proof on who set her father up. And why. The only reason that made sense was that the victim, and possibly her father, knew something about the illegal activities at the warehouse. Otherwise why not set up some snitch or someone else?

"Why did you leave town?" she asked. "If you did what you were told, you should have been safe."

"That's what I thought, but right after the trial, the police started arresting guys who worked for Big Eddie, and they bragged about taking down a Mexican drug cartel. But it was just for a lot of small stuff like assault and dealing drugs. Collecting money."

"Collecting money?"

"Yeah. You know. Insurance. Business people pay to have protection." He waved a hand. "I thought I'd be next to get arrested, or even worse, that Big Eddie would think I ratted them out, so I split. Then after Big Eddie croaked a coupla years ago, I figured I could come back, only I changed my name to be extra safe."

Interesting. Big Eddie was Frankie Falcone's father, but even when Eddie was mob boss, Frankie had a huge say in what went on. What she needed right now was proof that the two men—her father and/or his supposed victim—knew something that would expose illegal activities at the factory. The factory owned by Quadrastar, AKA, The Partnership.

Right now, everything was pure speculation. She needed something other than Johnson's coerced confession, because anything he said at this point would be suspect.

She'd been so eager to get the information she'd hadn't paid attention to whether it would be admissible evidence or not. A mistake she wouldn't have made if she hadn't been so personally involved.

Besides that, she noticed her phone battery was dead again, and she had no idea when it had stopped recording.

Looking at Remy she said, "If we find the houses they're using for human trafficking, we may be able to bring down Quadrastar, or at least some of the big dogs."

"Right," Remy agreed. "And I repeat. Dangerous stuff."

"Max and Gabe are on alert, waiting for instructions."

"Good. I hope it's enough."

She moistened her lips. "I need a drink."

"We'll get one on the way."

"What about me? I'm going to wet my fucking pants."

Charlie turned to Remy. "Any ideas what we should do with this weasel?"

Remy slapped his gun against his palm. "Several."

Johnson's face went white. "I won't say anything to anyone. I promise. Just leave me here, tied up, even. I don't care if I wet my pants or anything. I'll keep my mouth shut if anyone asks anything."

"Yeah, you're real good at keeping your mouth shut," Remy said. "Trustworthy son of a bitch."

"He knows our plan," Charlie said. "If he tells anyone, we're screwed."

CHAPTER THIRTY

"JUST GET INSIDE," Remy said, giving Johnson a hard shove into the back of the vehicle. "You have the whole backseat to yourself."

They'd cut off his ankle cuffs so he could pee and then walk to the car, but kept his wrists cuffed, this time behind his back and secured with another flex cuff to his belt so he was unable to do any damage from the back seat.

"Yeah, but I can't move and these things hurt."

"Exactly," Charlie said as she slid into the passenger seat.

Remy scanned the street. It was only a matter of time before someone realized their bartender wasn't showing at work and came looking for him, and he'd rat them out in the blink of an eye.

They'd used Johnson's cell phone GPS to find the addresses on the buildings owned by Quadrastar and also for directions to the houses he'd said were used as drop houses for their victims.

"The one in Hamtramck is the closest," Charlie said. "Let's begin there?"

"As good as any." Remy started the engine and shifted into gear while Charlie input the address into the car's GPS. He surveyed the area for suspect vehicles, someone poised to follow. Nada. So far.

"Take a right at the corner," Charlie said once they

were moving. She took out her Ruger and a set of large flex cuffs from her purse. Keeping her gun on Johnson, she said, "Stick your feet up and hold them together. You try to kick me and you're a dead man."

Remy raised a brow…impressed.

"How d'ya expect me to go anywhere with these on?" Johnson said.

"Very slowly." She grinned, apparently happy with her own response. Johnson complied and she looped the large circlet over his shoes and yanked it tight.

Remy had to grin, too. He liked her wry sense of humor. Liked the way she handled herself, a competent, yet very feminine woman. Something his body was immediately aware of when she'd jammed her hand into his pocket. And, damn, if he wasn't getting hard just thinking about it.

He glanced in the rearview mirror to change lanes. "Crap."

She turned. "What?"

"Black Suburban, three cars behind." They were still on the side streets, but would hit the entrance to the 75 in a few blocks. "Hold on, we need to lose him before we get on the freeway. He floored it and, tires squealing, shot down the narrow street, took a left then another quick right into an alley next to an abandoned fourplex with charred, boarded up windows. He steered straight ahead, bouncing and bumping through the overgrown yard and out the drive on the other side, ending up on the street in front of the structure.

Just as he was going to say they'd lost the tail, two vehicles headed straight at them, guns blasting from both sides. "Down," he shouted, and cranking the wheel, did a one-eighty and kept going, up and over the curb, through a vacant lot and down another alley filled with so much trash and piles of wood that used to be houses, it looked as if it was a dump.

He swung around the mountains of debris and keeping the gas floored, hit another street, barely missing a truck at the intersection, and ended on a one-way street with cars coming directly at them.

He swerved and dodged cars, then took the first opening to hop the center island and head back the other direction. Slowing enough to weave his way through traffic, he merged three lanes over, kept to his right and turned at the next street, hit the service road to the freeway for a few blocks, but instead of getting on the freeway." He turned onto another street.

Slowing, he glanced in his mirrors. Lost them. And he had no idea where the fuck they were. The GPS had gone crazy trying to reroute itself with every turn and was useless. Halfway down the block, he saw an Exxon station, pulled in back behind a dumpster and stopped.

Charlie who'd flattened herself on the seat, her head practically in his lap, pulled herself up. "Damn."

He glanced in the rear and saw Johnson curled up in a fetal position on the floor. "They'll be right behind us," he said to Charlie. "We have to move. See if you can get the GPS to reroute us back to the place in Hamtramck."

"Got it," Charlie said. "Fifteen minutes from here, north of the Edsel Ford Freeway."

He got out his cell, punched in a code.

He shifted into gear. "Watch for our friends…and hold on."

Charlie braced herself as they sped from the Exxon station, barely missing a truck turning into the drive. Seconds later they were on I-75 heading north to Hamtramck when she spotted the two black vehicles again. "They're back."

"Yeah. I see. Right now we're far enough away that they can't hit us unless they've got some high-powered weapons. And in the midst of traffic, I doubt they'd try."

"We're all gonna die," Johnson's muffled cry came from the back.

"And you might be the first," Remy snapped.

Gun in hand, Charlie turned, saw the two cars split, each taking an outside lane and coming up faster on both sides. Remy slid into the fast lane, his speed climbing. Her pulse raced triple time as she watched the two vehicles zip around traffic, getting closer and closer. "They're gaining, close enough to hit us if they shoot."

Remy eyed the Ruger in her hand. That thing was as good as a toy in this situation. "There's a better weapon under the seat," he said. "If they get close and start shooting, use it."

She bent down, pulled out a flat, army green bag. "What is it?" she asked as she unzipped the bag and pulled out the weapon. She'd had gun training using most every make and model, but had never seen a gun quite like it. It looked like Gabe's AK47 only in miniature with a stubby barrel about nine inches long. Also in the gun bag were six see-through magazines that were fully loaded.

"Custom-made SIG 552 Commando. It was stashed at my dad's. I got it when we were there. Just in case. Think you can use it?"

"Tell me what to do."

"It's a carbine with a folding stock. Basically a machine gun. Open the stock and it will lock in place. Then get a magazine and insert it."

She sat there for a moment, glad Gabe had been so adamant about her going to the range twice a week. She was comfortable with guns and targets, even moving targets. But she'd never shot at people before.

"What's wrong?"

"Nothing." She inserted the magazine. "Done."

"Okay. Now, pull back the receiver handle—"

She pointed to the place to confirm.

"Yes, there. Pull it back and let it go…and don't put your finger on the trigger. Hold it toward the window a sec," he said, then took his eyes off the road a moment to check the selector switch. "Just making sure it's on single shot."

Yeah. So she wouldn't set off a blaze of bullets and lose control. Gabe had done the same thing when she'd tried his AK47.

"And there's the safety," Remy said, indicating the spot. "You're ready, but only if necessary."

Glancing up, she saw one of their pursuers gaining. She readied the carbine and clicked off the safety just as gunshots pinged the side of the car, the window shattered and a bullet lasered past her face so close heat burned her cheek. She ducked down, glanced at Remy to make sure he hadn't been hit. Now the other vehicle was directly across on her right, one car between.

"Hit it," she said, and as soon as Remy shot ahead, she shoved the gun out the window, took aim and fired a round at the car on her right. Blood splattered against the other vehicle's window around a bullet hole and a fraction of a second later the window shattered and fell away. The car slowed. She saw the driver with a bloodied hand over one side of his face, but he wasn't dead. She turned…saw the SUV on the other side gaining on them, heard a screech and then a loud crash. Turning, she saw the vehicle with the injured driver half crushed between a pickup and a minivan in a three-car pileup. "One gone."

Remy sped ahead, shot across two lanes to the right, but the car on her left did the same, gaining until he was in the lane directly next to them and coming up fast.

From her position in the passenger seat, she didn't have a shot, so she crawled into the back, climbing over Johnson, opened the side window and fired.

The windshield on the black SUV spiderwebbed, but didn't fall away. The car slowed. "He's down, too," she said. But as soon as the words left her lips, she saw the dude with his head out the driver's side window, and the vehicle picked up speed again. She raised her gun. At the same time, a rifle barrel poked out the SUV's side window. She ducked down just as the shots whizzed past and through the back passenger window. She popped up again like a damned gopher, fired a barrage of bullets, then ducked down.

"They're backing off," Remy said.

She rose enough to peer out the rear window and saw the black vehicle lagging behind, both tires on the passenger side flattened. She may not have hit anyone, but at least she'd slowed them down. "Excellent," she said, then climbed to the front seat. "I don't think the Department is going to like the condition of the car when you return it."

Remy grinned, then sped ahead to the Holbrook Street exit. "Almost there, according to the GPS."

She smiled, too, her heart hammering like a piston. If Remy's adrenaline was pumping it out like hers, they could have some really great sex right now.

"What's our boy doing back there?" Remy glanced in the rearview mirror. "We're going to need him when we get there."

"I'm not deaf," Johnson piped up. "And what if I don't want to do it?"

"You're going to do it because we're the only option you've got in staying alive. Now tell us again what you're going to do when we get there."

He grunted, mumbled, "Sonofabitch," then rolled over and into a semi-sitting position, apparently unable to get up on the seat being trussed as he was. "I'm going to go to the door and tell them I have a delivery in the car, exactly like I've done before. Then when someone opens the garage door for the delivery, you guys take over."

"Perfect," Remy said.

Charlie wasn't so sure. Johnson was about as trustworthy as Frankie Falcone. Every instinct within her said the guy was a snake, a weasel who'd say and do anything to help himself no matter what the consequences to someone else. But, while she and Remy might be his only option, at this point in time, he was also theirs. She pointed the 552 at him. "You make one false move and I'll use this on you."

It was almost midnight when they neared the house in a quiet, residential neighborhood, far enough from the freeway that it seemed a world away. The large two-story home, that may have once been someone's pride and joy, was rundown and looked ready for foreclosure, if it hadn't already met that fate.

Located on a corner, streetlamps lit the area around the house and she could see grass and weeds three-feet high in the back. Every window was totally dark, not so unusual for the time of night, except unlike the neighboring homes, not even a pencil-thin line of light escaped around the windows.

On Remy's phone, she punched the code for her team to move in, then waited for further instructions. She cut Johnson's cuffs as they parked next to the side door of the addition connecting the house and garage. Then, as Johnson said he'd done before, and under cover of darkness, moved single file to the door. The night was eerily silent, with no sounds from passing cars, sirens blaring, or rap music cranked high enough to split eardrums.

This time, Charlie stood behind Remy to the side of

the door with her Ruger drawn, while Johnson texted the number to let them know he was making a delivery.

Waiting, her back against the scratchy siding, Charlie's heart beat a quick staccato rhythm at the base of her throat. Her mouth was so dry she could barely swallow, and everyone in the city could probably hear her knees knocking.

Remy looked like the professional he was, his stance military straight, authority and confidence oozing from his pores. He had his S&W holstered under his jacket and carried the high-powered carbine chest high, holding it with both hands. And, she noticed, he'd switched the selector to full automatic. All they needed was to get inside, find their proof and notify the police. In and out. Easy, peasy.

After texting the contact number, Johnson knocked on the door. They waited for a long minute. No answer. Remy nodded at Johnson and he knocked again.

Nothing.

Just as she was ready to knock on the door herself, she heard the *click, click, click* sound of multiple locks opening. Her hand shook as she gripped her Ruger with both hands. This was it. They had to pull this off. If they didn't, the next bloated bodies pulled from the Detroit River would be theirs.

CHAPTER THIRTY-ONE

REMY TUCKED CHARLIE behind him as the door opened. A stocky, dark-skinned man wearing shades, despite the fact that it was midnight, nodded at Johnson. Johnson took a step inside—not following the plan. Fucking idiot! Remy shoved Johnson aside and rushed the guy, hitting him chest level, shoulder first, full body force. The man stumbled backward, disoriented but he didn't fall...and the gun never left his hand.

Remy slammed into the man again, thrusting the 552 against the guy's head, heard a distinct sound, like a walnut cracking. The guy went down. Not quite as planned, but close...as long as they hadn't made enough noise to alert anyone inside.

Charlie, gun still covering him, nodded. A quick lift of her lips told him she approved.

Johnson got up and brushed himself off. "Motherfu—"

Remy slammed a hand across Johnson's mouth before he had a chance to say anything more. "Zip it," he hissed through his teeth. "One more sound and you're down there with him." Apparently the idiot had forgotten the part about keeping quiet.

They had no idea how many guards were inside and needed the element of surprise if they were going to make this work.

Charlie shut the door. Remy moved the unconscious man to the side, used one of the multiple sets of flexi cuffs he'd brought along to bind the guy's ankles and wrists and gagged him with his own bandanna. And he took his gun.

The partition connecting the garage to the house was just a shell, apparently something to allow groups of people to be moved from the transport vehicles to the house unseen.

Johnson had said he'd never been any farther inside than where they were, so he was no help with the layout. Remy had checked building records and had a vague idea of the floor plan since it was similar to most of the other homes in the area…two stories and a basement.

The passageway had one dim light with a yellowish cast that made everyone look a little ghoulish. He nodded, motioning Charlie and Johnson to move forward with him. Johnson was to stay between them so there would be no mistake that he wasn't going anywhere and it would look like he was helping them if they were caught. A little incentive in case he decided to rat them out.

It wasn't a great plan, but it was what they had.

Once they reached the inside door, Remy held up a hand for Charlie and Johnson to stay put. He could only hope that since it was late, there would be few guards and those who were there would be sleeping.

His nerves stretched taut, Remy inched open the interior door and peered into a kitchen. Empty…the only light coming from a nightlight on the stove. His stealth training kicked in and he prowled forward, catlike, as close to the wall as he could get with appliances in the way.

Ahead on his right, an archway led from the kitchen to another room with low-level lighting, but he couldn't see beyond the archway. On his left was a hallway that presumably went to the bedrooms. There had to be bedrooms upstairs, too, and that must be where they kept people, but everything was so quiet. Strangely quiet.

How could you hold a number of people hostage and keep it dead silent? It was late and people were probably sleeping, but there were no sounds coming from anywhere.

Feeling Charlie's heat behind him, he turned. Johnson was huddled at the door. Fine as long as he stayed there.

Remy noticed the walls and windows were covered with padding. Soundproofing, the kind used in music studios. If every room was like this, it was no wonder they didn't hear anything.

Moving to the archway, he crouched low and peered into the next room, a living room…a man sleeping on the couch, an AK47 slung across his chest. Soundproofing on the walls…windows boarded. He saw no other guards. Odd. There had to be more than two guards. That would be too easy.

Remy crept to the couch and just as he came up on the guy, the dude's eyes popped open. So, he cold-cocked him. Charlie came over and they tied and gagged him with his bandanna like the other guy. He had no idea how many men might be upstairs guarding their quarry. They probably took shifts, some sleeping while the others kept watch. Minimum of two, he figured. But there were no guards outside the rooms down the hall. The two they'd encountered were probably it for the lower level. He signaled for Charlie to follow him to the first room.

At the door, he put his ear against it and listened. Nothing. Tried the knob. Locked. Not from the inside, he was sure. There was a deadbolt lock, too. He reached to the ledge above the door for a key and got only dust.

Charlie sidled up next to him, shoved her hand in her jacket pocket and pulled out what looked to be a jackknife. It had several blades, one that looked like a lock picker, but he doubted it would work. If someone could pick it from the outside, it could be done from the inside. These guys were smarter than that. And it wouldn't work on a deadbolt, anyway.

He shook his head. She pulled out another blade, only it wasn't a blade, it was a mini screwdriver. Perfect.

There were two screws in the door plate and two in the deadbolt. If he could get the plates off, he could disassemble the locks and open the door. If it wasn't barricaded from the inside.

He knelt in front of the door, his breathing deepening as he put the screwdriver to the first screw. It didn't budge. Leaning forward, he put his full body weight into it and the thing still didn't budge. They had to be quick, but quick wasn't happening. He'd kick down the damned door if he had to, regardless of how many thugs were upstairs.

He tried the other screw. Same thing. Again, he put his body weight behind it and got nothing. He tried the deadbolt, gave a few good twists and the screws turned and after what seemed like a million twists later, the first screw came off in his hand. Halfway there.

He rocked back on his haunches, ran a hand through his hair, the irony of the day hitting him. They'd outrun and outgunned two sets of hit men, taken a man hostage, overcome two Mexican guards, and in the end, they'd been stymied by one fucking screw. He muffled a laugh. Paused for a breath. Yeah. That last part wasn't happening.

He rolled to his knees...braced his body against his hands, shoved again and turned. The second screw moved. He breathed a sigh of relief. He had no desire to face off with thugs carrying AK47s. Finished with the deadbolt, he went to the lower lock, worked the screwdriver a couple more times and finally took out the first screw. He wiggled the plate to see if he could loosen the other one.

A loud grunting sound came from the living room. Charlie raised a hand for him to stay, then was gone, returning in less than fifteen seconds.

"He'll be quiet now," she whispered, then raised her gun and brought the butt down hard against the palm of her other hand, a quick simulation on how to keep kidnappers quiet.

He grinned. A few more turns of the last screw and the knob fell off in his hand. He set it on the floor, pried the rest of the lock off, and pulled out the lock mechanism. Sweat rolled down his forehead as he pushed open the door.

The room was coal black inside, and the smell of urine nearly knocked him over. He gagged and heard Charlie do the same as she came to his side. She covered her mouth and held her nose.

The ambient light in the hallway wasn't enough to see well and it took a moment for his eyes to adjust to the dark and see inside. Then he saw them…bodies, dark mounds lying side to side like sardines in a can. The stench of urine burned his nostrils and he covered his mouth, too. He felt the wall to his side for the light switch, but couldn't find it. He swung the door wider.

He couldn't tell for sure, but there had to be at least forty people crammed into a room that couldn't have been more than twelve by twenty. If there were that many in each room, there were hundreds being held prisoner in one house.

From what he could see, most appeared to be young girls, but some who were huddled together looked like families, illegal immigrants maybe. A little girl cried, apparently afraid of them as they stood silhouetted in the doorway. She probably thought he was one of her captors.

"I—" Something hard bashed against the back of his head. Sharp pain shot down his neck and spine. Stars flared in front of his eyes. Dizzying blackness about to overcome him, he fought to stay upright. Wobbly, he swung around. Charlie fell against him, her body limp. She groaned and clutched his shirt. He held tight, each holding the other up.

"The guns. Get their guns," a gruff voice said, his accent one Remy didn't readily recognize. Russian, maybe, and when the voice came into focus, he saw a heavy-set, middle-aged woman with short brown hair, surrounded by three burly gangster types, one black, two white, with tats covering most of the visible parts of their bodies. All wielded high-powered weapons—trained on both he and Charlie.

After taking their weapons and phones, two men patted them down, relieved him of the gun in his holster, took Charlie's bag, then shoved them into the room with the others and closed the door.

Within minutes the light coming through the doorknob hole darkened.

A lock clicked into place. Then another.

Charlie's head felt as if it had been split with an ax. Dizzy, she gulped in the acrid air, forced it into her lungs, in and out, in and out. Remy's arms encircled her and she folded herself into his chest, tucking her face in the crook of his neck.

"Are you okay?" he asked, his voice muffled under his hand.

"I think so." She felt the back of her head where a giant lump had formed, but it wasn't wet. *No blood.*

"Just dizzy." She kept her voice soft, too. "You?"

"I'm fine. Except for the obvious. But don't worry. We'll be okay."

"Okay?" She almost choked on the words. She hadn't given her team the final to move in and now they had no phones. "How the hell is this okay?" The rise in her voice died against his chest.

The room spun. The scent of urine, feces and sweat burned her nostrils. She grabbed a handful of shirt and buried her face in it, his masculine smell and the faint scent of fabric softener the only thing keeping her from hurling her guts out.

"Just stay calm. It'll be okay," he said again.

Her hands shook, the total blackness fraying her nerves. Even in the darkest room she'd ever been in, even with a sleep mask over her eyes, she could see *something*. But here in the inky darkness, there was nothing, and for a moment, she imagined this is what it would be like to be blind.

It wasn't just black; it was a lack of light of any kind and suddenly every sound seemed amplified. People breathing, wheezing, coughing, whimpering, whispering...like a soft undercurrent of air that wafted at a level somewhere between her ankles and knees. Her stomach revolted. She gagged, then moved to step to the side so she wouldn't puke on Remy. She bumped into something soft, warm and squishy. She jerked back, clinging even harder to Remy.

"D-Did you come to help us?" a small, barely audible voice said from somewhere on her right. "My mommy said someone would come to help us."

A child. Oh, dear God. "Yes," Charlie said quickly, still in hushed tones. "We came to help." And now they were all screwed. "Is your mommy here with you?"

"Uh-huh," the disembodied voice responded. "But she's sick. She can't talk."

Charlie edged toward the voice, but Remy kept holding her hand and moved with her, feet bumping against warm bodies. Hands. Hands against her legs. Wet and sweaty. Filthy, she imagined. "Where are you, sweetie?" she whispered into the dark. The child's voice had sounded so close. "Wave your hand in the air and I'll reach out and find you."

"Wait. We know where you are," another voice said in accented English. "We will get her to you."

Her. A little girl. Charlie heard shuffling, then movement, more shuffling, something near her feet. She reached out, swept her hand in the air, touched flesh. A small hand, which she quickly clasped in hers and crouched down. "Are you okay?" she asked, clutching the child's hand with both of hers.

"I'm hungry," the girl whimpered.

Charlie's throat closed. What awful inhumane monsters were they dealing with? What kind of person could be so cruel to another human being? Could treat them like merchandise...slaves to be bought and sold. What could they possibly want with small children? The question didn't need an answer, not one she could live with. No one could be that vile.

But she knew different. She stood, picking up the child with her.

"You're going to be okay, soon," Remy said, his voice holding all the certainty of a man who knew how to take charge. "And we'll get you something good to eat. Whatever you want."

Charlie jabbed him with her other elbow, whispered under her breath, "You have some magic powers? Because right now, things aren't looking so good."

"I know, but trust me. Things are going to be fine." He took a breath...said softly but a little louder. "Did you all hear that? Everything is going to be fine."

"Todo va a estar bien," Charlie translated in

Spanish, her voice just above a whisper. She'd heard people talking, knew some would understand.

"My wife," a man said, his voice quavering. "She's hurt. Those men hurt her. She needs a doctor."

A bone-cold chill of anger gripped Charlie. "Soon," she said. A little hope was better than none. Was that what Remy was doing? Giving people hope? Because unless he had some magic tricks up his sleeve, she didn't know how they were going to get out of this.

The place was a prison with no method of escape. Maybe when the sun came up there would be some light from somewhere and they could assess the situation. Their captors couldn't keep people in the dark all the time. They had to eat something, give them water or they'd all die. It was just a matter of time. They'd figure something out.

A blood-curdling scream rent the air outside the door. Oh, no! Johnson. He'd been in the kitchen. If they knew he'd brought them here…

Another ear-splitting scream, infused with sheer pain and terror. "No, please, Noooo."

She cringed, pressed the child against her chest and placed a hand over her other ear. Even though it was dark, Charlie instinctively closed her eyes. She didn't like Johnson, hated everything he'd done, but she wouldn't wish torture on anyone. But what could they do? Not a damned thing from in this room.

They had to get out, get the guards to open the door.

But what would make them do that? The people in this room were livestock being sold to the highest bidder. A lightbulb went off. That's it. Money. Money is the answer. If anything happened to the people in the room, the guards would be responsible. They would have to answer to the mob and whatever cartel the mob was working with.

Leaving Remy's side, she bent down and softly

called out to the man who'd answered her before. "What's your name?" she asked.

"Xavier," he said.

"Xavier, do you want to get out of here?"

"Yes, of course."

"Good. I have a plan. It's dangerous, but with your help and the help of every able-bodied person in here, we can do it."

"Many are weak and not able to fight back."

"They won't need to do much. There are only five guards that I saw, and all we have to do is overpower them. My partner is a police officer. Both of us have training. But we can't do anything until we get the guards to open the door."

"Tell me what to do."

"Keep very quiet, but wake up every person in the room and tell them to send the children and sick people to the back of the room. Then have every able person come close to the door." She reached for his hand and put the little girl's hand in Xavier's.

"It will be okay," she said to the child. Just do as you're told. Okay?"

"Uh, huh," the child responded.

"Okay, Xavier, pass the word that when I start banging on the door, everyone needs to start screaming FIRE at the top of their lungs. Tell them to keep screaming like crazy until someone opens the door. When that happens, my partner and I will overcome the guards and every possible person must rush forward out the door. I'll wait to start banging on the door until you tell me everyone knows what's happening."

"What's going on?" Remy whispered.

"I'll tell you in a minute."

She turned back to Xavier. "If everyone here rushes out at once, they won't be able to stop us without hurting one of their own."

The man was silent for the longest time, so she repeated everything she'd said in Spanish.

Finally he said, "I will tell everyone. We will do everything we can."

"Good. As soon as you've told everyone what's going to happen, let me know. I don't want anyone to panic because they think there really is a fire."

"Okay. I'll do it."

She stood again. Within seconds she heard low whispers humming through the room.

"What's going on?" Remy asked, again, irritation in his tone.

"We have a plan to get out of here."

"What? I told you everything would be okay. Help is coming." His voice was stern, indignant almost. Like, how could she dare do something without consulting him?

"I alerted Sean earlier when we were in the car."

"Were you keeping that a secret?"

"Of course not. I didn't want to say anything until I was sure they were on the way."

"And when exactly is that? I don't hear anything except Johnson's screams."

"They're coming. Take my word for it."

"Before or after Johnson dies? Remember he's the one who knows what happened to Adam. And…" She cleared her throat. "You said you didn't know who you could trust. What if Sean turns out to be one of them."

Remy was quiet for the longest time. The whispers throughout the room intensified, and she heard movement, bodies shifting about. People standing close enough to feel the heat of their skin against hers.

"Okay, what's the plan?"

She quickly told him. What she didn't say was that it was going to happen whether he liked it or not.

"It could work," Remy said. "When?"

Just as he said it, she felt a tug on her hand. "Everyone is ready," Xavier said.

She took Xavier's hand and Remy's and moved to the door. "Okay. NOW!"

They banged on the door and shouted FIRE! The room came alive with blood curdling screams and more shouts of fire, in both English and Spanish and more people joined them at the door, banging and screaming FIRE! If she didn't know better, she'd believe there really was a fire.

At the same time she heard yelling and rustling at the door, so they kept banging and screaming and the children cried and wailed at the top of their lungs and for one fraction of a second, she wondered if she'd done the right thing. Until she heard the *click, click, click* of locks opening.

"Get down," she said to Remy and Xavier. "When they open the door, we tackle them from below…and hit them where it hurts."

She had only enough time to crouch before the door flew open and through blinding white light, she rushed forward into a guard and landed one swift elbow punch to his groin. He screamed, dropped his gun and fell to his knees. Her eyes adjusting, she saw Remy had another guard down and Xavier and a half dozen men and women were on top of two other guards.

Hearing more voices, she glanced to the side and saw three more guards coming down the hallway. She picked up the guard's AK47. Saw Remy do the same with another weapon.

Just about to turn her gun on the guards, a strong arm wrapped around her throat from behind in a choke hold. A stabbing pain jabbed Charlie's neck. A knife. She froze.

"One move and I will kill her."

The voice. It was the big masculine woman who'd

shoved them into the room.

At the same time, she heard a faint *thwap, thwap, thwap* above them. Then the whine of distant sirens. Her heart leaped. She glanced to Remy. Blood pounded in her ears. *Stall. Do something.*

The woman tightened her grip and jabbed Charlie's neck again. "Call off your men or I'll slice her throat right now."

"Like hell you will," a man's voice bellowed, and she heard a loud crack, like a hammer breaking a rock. The pressure around her neck eased. She ducked, launched herself forward and turned to defend herself, but instead saw the woman drop to the floor like a stone.

Standing there as big as life was Gabe. And amid the people fleeing from the room, their eyes squinting against the light, she saw Max with the other guards at gunpoint. She scooped in a lungful of air. Her guys had made it. Her chest swelled with a quick rush of pride.

"You okay?" Gabe asked.

Remy darted forward, eyes wide. "You're hurt. You're bleeding." He pulled out a clean handkerchief, drew her close and pressed it onto her neck where the woman had broken Charlie's skin with the knife. A look of relief crossed his face. "Just a scratch. Are you okay, otherwise?"

"Yes," she croaked out, glancing at Gabe. Now that her team was there, she was just fine. She gave a wobbly smile and nodded to Max across the room.

"When we didn't get the signal, I made an executive decision to move in," Gabe said.

"Thank heaven," Remy said, when a Detroit SWAT team burst into the room. And behind them, Sean and more officers.

Within seconds the room swarmed with law enforcement officers swiftly taking the guards into custody and helping hostages as they cascaded down the stairs and streamed from every available room in the house, including the basement. Many appeared too shocked to react, while others sobbed and clung to each other.

"We have several ambulances on the way," Sean said. "Many are going to need medical attention. Nick Johnson included."

One of Sean's officers directed several young girls toward the door to await the ambulance. Dressed scantily, most were bruised and dirty, and so, so young. Some couldn't be more than nine or ten years old. Charlie hurried over to help, giving the children whatever she could find to cover up.

And that's when she saw her.

She'd only seen one photo of the girl, but she'd recognize her anywhere. Ella Linski.

Charlie's heart dropped to her toes. She'd truly thought there was no hope. Thought the teenager would never be found. And even though she didn't know the girl, tears sprang to Charlie's eyes.

"Ella?" Charlie said, walking over to the teen, huddled with three other girls near the door.

The young woman looked up, her face gaunt, eyes round with apprehension.

"Ella Linski? Your mother has been trying to find you," Charlie said quickly.

"M-my mother?"

Charlie wrapped an arm around the girl, careful not to scare her. "Yes. She's been so worried about you."

An officer came over. "We have medical assistance waiting."

Charlie nodded and as he led the young woman away, Charlie said, "It's going to be okay, Ella. I'll call your mother just as soon as I can. You'll see her very soon."

Turning, Charlie saw Remy, Gabe, and Max talking with Police Chief Bouvaird, and amidst the chaos, a little girl ran over and wrapped herself around Charlie's leg and clung like sticky glue. She was about Kacey's size, four or five years old and had to be the little girl Charlie had been holding in the room earlier. She lifted the child into her arms. Small arms clamped around Charlie's neck. "It's okay, sweetie. Everything is going to be okay."

The little girl's grip tightened.

"Do you hear those sirens?" Charlie said, brushing the moisture from the girl's tear-stained cheeks, no longer whispering. "It's going to be okay." Then she repeated the statement in Spanish to the men and women standing near her. *"Todo va a estar bien."*

And for the first time in what seemed like forever, she actually believed it.

CHAPTER THIRTY-TWO

"I CAN'T THANK you enough. I almost can't believe it," Sandra Linski said.

Unable to keep a giant smile from her face, Charlie, sitting at her desk, phone at her ear, imagined the missing girl's mother smiling, too. She fingered the photo of Ella Linski and as she shuffled it aside, she uncovered the envelope with the photo at Boblo Park. The one someone had anonymously slipped under her door.

"Oh, my. Oh, my. I just can't believe it," Sandra Linski repeated between happy sobs. The first thing Charlie had done when everyone had been attended to at the Hamtramck house, was to pick up Sandra Linski and take her to the hospital to be with her daughter.

"She's been through a lot and will need some medical care and some counseling, but she'll be okay." Charlie hoped. "And she'll be home soon."

A few hours after the raid, the police learned Ella Linski, along with a dozen other teenage girls, all drugged, had spent weeks in a house in Woodbridge that had been set up to house them until they were taken to the Hamtramck house for prostitution or sold to someone else who would do the same.

The human trafficking network was huge and a lot

of arrests had already been made with more to come. They wouldn't know the depth of the corruption until all the authorities had a chance to interrogate witnesses and conduct further investigations.

"My poor baby. My poor baby." Sandra continued between her tears of happiness. "I knew you'd find her. I could tell you didn't think she was just another bad girl who'd run away. That's what those others thought."

Charlie clutched a hand to her chest. For Ella Linski, it would be a long road to normal, if there was such a thing, but the girl and her mother would have a chance to start over. Not everyone got that second chance.

"I knew you'd find her because you cared about finding her," the woman said, finally gaining more control on her emotions. "You're a good person. I knew that right away, too."

Yes, she cared. Maybe too much, because it sometimes skewed her perspective, caused her to make mistakes. She'd done that with Remy. Started caring and made a near fatal mistake.

It wasn't the first time.

"Thank you," was all she could manage. Because Sandra Linski was wrong on the second part. Dead wrong. She was not a good person, not by a Detroit mile. A good person didn't betray the people she loved. A good person didn't have a soul that was black with guilt. "Like I said, the important thing is that Ella's safe now."

The woman gushed her thanks again and after they said good-bye, Charlie sat there for the longest time, fingering the manila envelope, then slowly pulled out the old photo.

There had to be a reason someone left the photo under her door. She angled her head, ran her finger over her father's face. So handsome, so loving…and just looking at him made her smile and hurt all at once.

Would he be proud of her? Proud of what she'd done? Or would he still hate her for betraying him. How could he not? It was her fault. All of it. And that would never change. Her bottom lip quivered at the thought.

Moisture blurred her vision and the image in front of her got blurrier and blurrier until she couldn't see her daddy's face anymore. Her shoulders trembled, and then her whole body bucked…and unable to stay silent in her pain, a choked scream tore from the deepest part of her soul.

Then she laid her head in her arms on the desk and sobbed.

And sobbed.

Giving voice to the soul-searing heartache she'd kept inside for so many years, she cried until her throat was raw. Huge, gulping, chest-clenching sobs… releasing all the years of pain and guilt…and the awful knowledge that even though she'd done everything she could to prove he wasn't guilty, nothing she could ever do would bring her daddy back.

CHAPTER THIRTY-THREE

CHARLIE'S LAST DEPOSITION took so long they had to do it in two sessions to allow for bathroom breaks and then another for lunch. She'd stayed inside to eat because there seemed to be no place she could go where she wouldn't find reporters pelting her with questions and paparazzi snapping photos like she was some kind of celebrity.

When her involvement in the takedown was made public, once again, her life story had become fodder for the media, and everyone from Wolf Blitzer to Dr. Phil had been calling for interviews.

Her family had been besieged as well since it had somehow been leaked that there was evidence to exonerate her father. Charlie's mother, while pleased that her children's father might be exonerated, wasn't happy about all the notoriety and worried it might mess up things between her and her newfound love and their engagement.

Landon was happy, but mostly for Charlie's sake since it had been her passion for so long. Her brother, five-years-old when it had happened, had been just young enough that he really didn't remember much about their dad.

Her uncle Emilio couldn't contain his emotions and had broken down and cried like a baby. She'd cried right along with him. Even though her *abuela* was gone,

Charlie knew her grandmother was looking down on them and smiling because now the world would know what she'd known all along. That her son was a good man.

She'd only seen Remy a few times in passing. He'd been busy, first getting debriefed and then testifying and completing reports on what went down, and she really wanted to sit and talk with him. After working together so much, she missed him. Maybe after finalizing his case, they could get to know each other better. It could even be fun. Her chest squeezed a little inside. It had been a long time since she'd simply had fun with someone.

Finally finished and heading home for the day, she was relieved to be through the most time-consuming aspects of the case and was glad to be on to other things. She was just going through the Devonshire case in her head when she heard footsteps in the hallway behind her.

"Charlie. Hold on a minute."

Remy. She swung around. Gave him a bright smile. "Hey. What's up?"

"I just wanted to tell you to send me a bill for services rendered so we can finish up."

He seemed so business like. Definitely not as glad to see her as she was him. "Okay. I'll be happy to do that."

His somber expression didn't change.

She gave him another big smile. "I know in the beginning, I had my doubts about working with you, but I'm glad I did. I think we actually did some pretty good teamwork."

He shifted his stance. "You got the job done. That's what matters. I'm grateful for that." He stopped... pressed his lips together and crossed his arms.

"But?"

"But I can't believe you didn't tell me what Johnson said about my father."

She pulled back at the accusatory tone. Raised a hand. "Whoa." She shook her head. "I didn't tell you because it didn't have anything to do with Adam's case. Also, I had no proof of anything. I thought I should wait to find out if it was even true before saying anything."

His mouth flattened. "That's the problem. You don't get to decide those things. I hired you to investigate and report your findings and you didn't do that."

"I did exactly what you hired me to—"

"No. You played God and decided I didn't need to know something that would have a profound effect on other people's lives. On my life."

He'd taken her so off guard, words dried on her tongue. He obviously didn't get it. She did what she thought was right at the time. Period. Done. *Fini*. She wasn't going to apologize because she didn't do her job the way *he* thought she should. "From my perspective, I did my job. End of story."

"Yeah—" he said, looking at her like he had a bad taste in his mouth instead of seeing her as someone who'd just helped him do what no one else could…instead of a woman with whom he'd spent hours making love. He cleared his throat. "I think you're right. End of story."

And then he turned and walked away.

Three weeks later and finally back in her office for good, Remy's words still burned like a branding iron. A swift ache of loss compressed her chest. She closed her eyes and reminded herself to breathe. In…and…out. In…and…out. Mind over matter.

Then she sighed and pulled out sweet, old Mr.

Nelson's file.

It never would've worked, anyhow—her and Remy—so why had she even entertained the idea? Being in a normal, loving relationship was never going to happen. Because *she* wasn't fucking normal.

So, forget it, Charlie. Quit wasting time on things that can't be changed. Be happy with what you've accomplished. Accept it and move on.

Thankfully, it was Sunday and being alone, she might actually get some work done. Aside from getting deposed and dealing with her family, she'd been nose-to-the-grindstone busy since the raid on the trafficking houses.

Her business had doubled almost overnight, but she still had yet to present her final argument on the Devonshire case.

She'd received a big, fat check from Remy for services rendered, but hadn't seen him or even talked to him. The way things had ended between them, she didn't expect she'd see him again, except maybe in court if Falcone and his goons with their million-dollar counsel didn't somehow, miraculously, plead out.

Whatever relationship she and Remy had developed was irretrievably broken. Remy was furious that she'd withheld information from him about his dad and, truth be told, she had issues with him, too. He hadn't trusted her team to get the job done and without even telling her, had called in his own troops.

On the plus side, within the last three weeks the Detroit PD had raided more houses used for human trafficking. Numerous members of the Sinaloa drug cartel, Frankie Falcone, Tony Carlozzi, Vinnie Zizzo, Manny Warzynski, and a gaggle of mob underlings, had been booked and charged on more felony counts than the court had seen in decades, if ever—with murder and human trafficking at the top of the list.

She'd been impressed and surprised with the Detroit PD's swift action on the arrests and the prosecutor's office working to ensure the charges would stick. They'd even arrested the Phoenix Rising group home director and the counselor, who'd apparently profiled the girls least likely to be missed, girls like Ella Linski with a history of drugs and running away.

The corruption went far deeper with allegations of judges getting kickbacks from The Partnership and other "interested parties," to do their bidding. The FBI was involved, and a half dozen agencies, state and federal, with acronyms she didn't even recognize, seemed to want a piece of the action.

Dozens of big-name, high-powered attorneys had been engaged, but the big bads in The Partnership were deemed a flight risk, so bail wasn't an option.

Nick Johnson, aka, Joey Drakar, was still in the hospital because of his treatment at the hands of the kidnappers, and hoping to finagle some kind of plea bargain to get him off the hook so he could be gone before Falcone had him whacked.

Even from jail, the mob boss had power. Something she had to keep in mind.

Joey had flown into a rage when she'd told him everything she'd promised him was bullshit...that she had no authority and knew no one who could do anything for him. He was on his own. She reminded him she had a recording of everything, and that he might get the prosecutor's office to consider a plea if Joey agreed they could use the tape in court.

Allan had liked the idea and said the prosecutor's office would go for it if she could get Lucy Devonshire to sign a confession and plead out. She'd laughed in Allan's face and told him he'd have to settle for what he had.

Which was plenty. Joey's testimony was critical in

Adam's disappearance and in exonerating her father. His testimony, even though the evidence was clear and a number of the guards had spilled their guts or were working on deals, was also pivotal in the human trafficking case.

It would be a huge coup for Allan if he could tie up all three cases. There were so many felony counts on the table with so many of the mob going down, Allan Chenowith's bid for governor, his ultimate goal, would be all but locked in. He was so happy he'd even hit on her again with some crazy idea they could be the next Detroit power couple.

She hated that Drakar, the person whose testimony had put her father on death row, might get off easy, but she'd had to make a decision on what was more important, nailing Drakar to the wall, or bringing those responsible for her father's murder, and who destroyed countless innocent lives, to justice. Drakar would still do time and there was a point where that had to be enough.

Although Judge Dancy Malone, like a couple of judges currently on the bench, had taken kickbacks to do the mob's bidding, she doubted the prosecutor's office would ever be able to get evidence to show Judge Malone's involvement in the group home operation way back when, or would even want to. The man still wielded too much political clout.

But somehow, even with all that had been resolved, she felt edgy, like something was missing, or that she had to do something. But what? There was nothing to do now but wait for the bad guys to go to jail and for her father to be exonerated. So, why couldn't she be content with what she'd accomplished? Be proud of what she'd done.

And pay attention to what still needed to be done. Lucy's trial for one. The final arguments were coming up next week and, so far, Max and Gabe hadn't any luck finding Lucy. Any inroads she'd made during the first part of the trial to build Lucy's character, to show she could be anyone's daughter, sister, or friend—someone who'd had a hard life and made some bad decisions—would vanish like snow in the desert if Lucy didn't show soon.

If the woman skipped, it was a guaranteed guilty verdict and life in prison.

The air in the room suddenly felt stuffy. She loosened the long scarf draped around her neck and took off her cardigan sweater. Still, sweat moistened her palms and under her arms. Her fingertips tingled. No. Stop it. Dammit. She channeled Gabe's spirit…his stern voice that blotted out the noise in her head.

Panic attacks not allowed. Just do the damn job. She *needed* to do her job.

She touched the Boblo photo again. There had to be a reason someone put it under her door, something about it that someone wanted her to know. Was it the old amusement park? The land?

She remembered going there with her dad and taking one of the old steamer ships that ferried people across the Detroit River to the island from the Boblo Dock Building. How special she'd felt going to the park, just the two of them. He'd left her waiting by the ferry while he went to talk with some men in suits who were standing by the building—about business, he'd said.

He'd bought her ice cream to eat while she waited. Told her not to tell her mother.

The memory of that day was dim and fading fast with every day that passed. Would she someday forget it altogether? Forget him? A bone-deep sense of loss filled her. Maybe if she went back there? Maybe she'd remember more about that day, keep it fresh so it didn't disappear.

She wanted to always remember riding on the hand-carved carousel, sitting on her daddy's lap to drive one of the antique cars, remember eating corn dogs, ice cream and cotton candy.

A sudden, urgent need to go to the park gripped her. Only there wasn't much left to see since the park had closed somewhere in the nineties, and the last she'd seen of the steam boats, the Columbia and the Ste. Claire, they were dry-docked at Ecorse, ghost ships, rusted, empty and abandoned, their tattered awnings flapping in the wind like broken bird wings.

She'd heard one of the boats was being renovated, but she feared its ultimate fate would be like much of the inner city. Beyond repair…and demolished.

But she could still go to the park. All she had to do was drive to Amherstburg on the Canadian side of the river and take the small car ferry to the island. She hauled in a deep breath. What would be the point? To see the condos and high-end homes that had been built on one side of the island? To see the ruins of what was left of the park on the other? Nothing would be the same.

She fingered the photo again. Despite everything that had gone down, she still had a gnawing feeling she didn't have all the answers.

She needed answers.

Deciding, she tucked the photo into her messenger bag and headed out the door.

The ten-story warehouse on the Detroit River, just downriver from the Ambassador Bridge, had long been abandoned and gutted, a sad, empty shell of brick and mortar dissolving with the sands of time. She'd been sitting in her car on West Jefferson by the old Boblo

Building for a half hour, hoping to drum up some other memories, but all she could manage was the fun they'd had, the rides, the ice cream and her father.

Then, sitting there, she realized there *was* one other thing. Since she and her father were in the picture, someone else had to have taken the photo. She slipped the envelope from her bag, took out the photo, and flipped it over. On the bottom right corner there was a faint logo and what looked like a date. Yes, she remembered there was someone who took photos of everyone on the carousel so they could sell the pictures to the tourists afterward.

She turned the photo over again to see if there were any other identifiers and that's when she saw them. In the background...in the mirror in the center of the carousel. The images were faint, but nonetheless, they were there. Two men in suits.

Odd, now that she thought about it. Back then she'd never given those men a thought. Her stomach seized. *Men from The Partnership?* Had her dad... No. She couldn't go there. Joey's confession pointed to his innocence.

But what if, as Remy said, Joey was a pawn? Or what if what Joey thought was wrong?

She glanced at the photo again. Maybe under magnification she'd be able to see the men in the picture more clearly. Or her mother might recognize them. A renewed burst of energy coursed through her.

She started the vehicle and took off, slowing at the corner where two teenagers dressed in baggy jeans, oversized shirts and knit hats, sauntered across the street and flipped her off on the way. Once, she would've instantly returned the gesture, but today, she simply turned the corner. And then flipped them off.

Feeling smug as she drove away, she glanced at the boys in the rearview mirror and saw a brown van cruise across the intersection. Her heart slammed against her ribs.

She shook her head, her gaze flicking from the mirror to the street ahead and back again. Gone now. Not coming her way. Still...

She tightened her grip on the wheel. She'd gotten comfortable, thought the brown van had been a part of Falcone's efforts to stop her investigation.

But it was still there...

CHAPTER THIRTY-FOUR

"GIVE IT A REST, Charlie. It's over and done and I'm not going to talk about it anymore."

"All I want you to do is *look* at the picture," Charlie said, standing at the dining room table waving the Boblo Island photo in front of her mother because the stubborn woman refused to look at it.

"And all I want *you* to do is tell me what difference it will make." Her mother fingered the pages of a wedding magazine she'd laid out with several others. "You've done what you wanted to do, now get on with your life. Don't waste precious time like I did."

"I'm not wasting time. I do what I need to do when I need to do it, and right now, I need some answers about the two men Daddy met at the dock the day he took me to Boblo Park. The two men in this photograph."

Diana Street turned as if in slow motion, brows raised. "Two men?"

Charlie held out the photo again. "He told me not to tell you about them." At the time, she'd thought he'd meant don't tell her mother about the ice cream, but thinking about it now, he could have meant the meeting.

Her mother's mouth thinned as she snatched the photo from Charlie's fingers and stared at it. "He would never have done that. He told me everything."

"In the background, behind the dark horse next to the post." Charlie handed her mother the reading glasses she'd plucked from the table.

Putting the glasses on, Diana said, "This is silly, and I don't know what you're trying to prove anyway."

"Daddy met two men at the dock that day, right before we got on the ferry. He bought me ice cream and had me sit and wait for him while he talked to them. I thought when he was done, that was it. But then looking closely at this photo, I can see they're still there. You can see them in the mirror behind the carousel."

Her mother stared at the photo for a moment, then handed it back. "I don't know them. Never saw them before. And now I want you to forget it once and for all."

Taking the photo, Charlie grumbled, then crossed the room to sit on a paisley wingback chair in the corner. "I can't. Not when there are still questions that need answers."

Her mother came over and sat in the matching chair next to Charlie, a resigned expression on her face. "You know the answers could be ones you don't want. Have you thought about that? What if those men were getting your father to do something illegal?

"That's ridiculous."

"Is it?" One of her mother's eyebrows arched. "Not with your father. He'd always been torn between loyalty to our family…and his other one."

Charlie covered her ears. "I'm not going to listen to stupid stuff like that. "We…our family was the most important part of his life and he would never have done anything that could hurt us. I believe that with all my heart."

Her mother sighed. "I believed that, too. But one of these days you'll realize some questions will never have answers, and when you do, you'll feel a great sense of relief. You'll finally be able to forget about the past and move on."

Reminded of the boxes of her father's things her mother had wanted to dispose of, heat filled Charlie's chest and worked its way upward. "Relief? If forgetting someone I love is what it takes to get on with my life, then I don't ever want that to happen. I don't want to do that, and I don't see how you can either."

She bolted to her feet. "Thanks for no help." She turned to leave, but her mother stood—stopped Charlie with a hand on her shoulder. Firm fingers dug into Charlie's flesh.

"Stop!" her mother snapped. "Please."

Charlie swung around. "No. I can't. I can't ever stop, not when—"

"But you can." Her mother's voice was softer now. "I stopped because I had no life. I didn't want to forget someone I loved, either. I'll always love your father. But he's not here, and I am, and I have to keep living. I couldn't do that until I realized why I wasn't living. It was because I felt guilty, because I could have stopped him from going out that night—"

Charlie shook her head so hard her hair whipped across her face. Her throat constricted. "No. It was me," she said, her voice small. Tears of remorse filling her eyes, she brought her hands to her mouth. "I did it. It was my fault. All my fault."

It was. She was responsible and nothing could change that. When she spoke again, it was like a robot speaking. "I…told them… I told the police where he was hiding."

Diana's eyes flew open. "Oh, no, Charlie." Her mother pulled Charlie into her arms. "Is that what you think?" Her grip around Charlie tightened, and after a moment, her mother said, "Why didn't you tell me?"

Charlie shook her head.

"Oh, my sweet child. I feel so horrible. I can't believe that's what you thought all this time." She held Charlie at arm's length. "It wasn't you, honey. By the time the police talked to you, they already knew where your father was."

Charlie pulled away. "What do you mean?"

"I mean the officers who arrested him already knew where he was. One of the neighbors told them he saw your father going into the garage. By the time the officers you talked to got to him, the others were already there."

Charlie stood there, her mother's words not really registering.

"You weren't to blame...any more than I was. And that's what I was trying to tell you before. I spent so much time thinking that if I'd only kept him home that night—if only this, if only that—until I finally realized, I was just there. Your father made the decision to go out that night, not me. Not you. You were just there, a child doing what you were taught to do."

"I thought I was helping him. The police told me I would be helping him." A familiar anger churned inside at the thought. Seconds later, a heavy weariness enveloped her. She felt like she hadn't slept for weeks...which was probably true. "I better go," she said.

Because in the end, it didn't matter which officers had arrested her dad; what mattered was that she'd told them where he was. He'd asked her not to, and she betrayed him. Betrayed his trust.

As she reached the door, her mother said, "I don't recognize those men in the picture, but ask your uncle Emilio. I bet he knows, or would have some idea."

Remy followed the brown van for several blocks, then somehow lost it. Whoever was driving the vehicle knew what he was doing. Damnit. He banged the heel of his hand against the wheel. How the hell had he let some slimebag stalker lose him?

The guy was smart, and he had to have garnered his expertise somewhere. Military, maybe. Or he was, or had been, a cop...or a race car driver. Not the typical profile for a stalker, but then they came in all sizes and shapes. With mental health issues. Obsessive tendencies.

He hadn't talked to Charlie since they'd passed each other in the hallway during depositions, but every night since, he'd been doing a drive-by at her place and following her to make sure she was safe. He'd talked to Max and Gabe and enlisted their help to help keep an eye on her, too. Although arrests had been made, the mob's reach was long, and he wasn't going to leave anything to chance.

She must be on another job already, because he couldn't imagine what she was doing at the old Boblo building, otherwise. Especially at dusk. The crime rate rose rapidly once the sun went down.

His blood pressure had spiked the second he saw the brown van and he'd apparently been so overeager to follow, he'd been made and the guy lost him. He gripped the wheel tighter, wished it was the stalker's neck.

He pulled off Jefferson and headed toward the station. It was late, but he hoped the captain was still there and he could get him to agree to put a watch on Charlie, at least until the criminals were put away for good.

And he could catch the creep stalking her.

The captain was still pissed that Remy had been involved in the takedown, but couldn't argue the point publicly since the mega bust was giving him more kudos and airtime than he deserved, or would ever have gotten otherwise.

The chief of police had even lauded Captain Pendergast as someone who could take his position eventually, so Remy was back doing business as usual. Which, after the DNA results confirmed it was Adam's body they'd found in the river, meant talking with Adam's family, his wife, Susan, and his parents—one of the toughest things he'd ever done. Then they'd asked him to give the eulogy at Adam's funeral.

He wasn't sure he could even do it, but when it came to talking about Adam, he found he had a lot to say about the love of family and friends and loyalty, despite having to stop three times to dry his eyes before continuing.

Maybe once the trials were over, Adam's family would finally have some kind of closure. And he hoped once Alejandro Montoya Street was exonerated, Charlie would find peace as well.

But he doubted it.

She, like him, knew there were still holes that needed filling. Things that didn't add up. Like who'd left a message to tell him Charlie had gone to the Stuben Warehouse? Who was the other shooter at the warehouse that same day? Was it the same person or two different people? And who was still following her in the brown van? His guess was that it was one person, a disgruntled client of hers, or someone on the other side of a case she'd won.

A stalker. Seventy to eighty percent of stalkers had some kind of relationship, work or otherwise, with the person they were obsessed with, so it was likely Charlie knew who it was. He wanted to talk to her about it, but their working relationship had ended, and he had no right to butt into her business.

Other than he cared about her. A lot.

And a stalker, he knew from past experience, was unpredictable and could jump from the first stage to the last stage without warning. Especially when the person didn't get what he wanted. A stalker who knew how to lose a tail, was obviously experienced. A time bomb waiting to go off.

Just thinking about Charlie in danger sent a jolt of fresh fear up his spine. He tightened his grip on the wheel. Fuck it! He swung wide, made an illegal U-turn, and headed toward Corktown.

Ten minutes later, four blocks from Charlie's, he spotted the brown van again, this time parked in front of an abandoned house that was charred black on one side. He pulled to a stop behind the van, got the license number and called it in.

He didn't want the guy to take off, so he didn't wait for the information and instead, got out and walked toward the van. Through the back window it looked like the driver's seat was empty. Still, gun drawn, he moved forward until he was directly behind the driver's door. He banged on the window with his free hand. "Police. Come out with your hands raised," he said, then yanked the door open.

Empty. Crouching, he went around the back of the vehicle, then repeated the process on the other side. Still nothing. Determining the van was vacant, he skulked toward the house from the side where he wouldn't be visible. The windows and front door were boarded, so unless someone was watching through the cracks, he would be safe from view.

Reaching the dilapidated side door, blackened from the fire, he made a fist and banged as loud as he could, shouting, "Police! Open up!" He kicked in the door, and gun raised, sidestepped inside and flattened his back against the wall next to the door.

He did a quick one-eighty. The place was gutted. Boards and broken glass lay in heaps around him. All that remained was a crumbling shell, an arsonist's delight. He moved to the side, then forward to what looked like a kitchen. Empty pizza boxes with leftover crusts and soda cans littered the counter next to where a sink would've been. Still fresh. The rats hadn't gotten to the food yet, and just as he thought it, he heard a faint sound. Breathing. Directly behind him.

He ducked, swung around, came up punching and jammed his fist into a man's nose. The guy bent forward groaning an expletive in Spanish. Remy jabbed him in the kidney, got him in a choke hold from behind. "Police," he said, lifting the guy nearly off his feet. "And you're under arrest." He tightened his grip with a jerk to bring his point home.

"Wait," the man coughed out. "I haven't done anything."

"Yeah? Well, I got news. Stalking is a crime, asshole. Michigan State Statutes 750.411. You have the right to remain si—"

"No, no! Listen to me, *mi amigo*. I wasn't stalking. I was watching to keep her safe. Protecting her."

"Yeah, that's what they all say.

The streets were dark for blocks near the gym, which Charlie guessed was because the city didn't have enough money to keep them on or change the bulbs. One dingy light lit the parking lot and as she pulled in, it flickered, ready to die, too.

The lot was empty, but as she got closer, she saw her uncle's car near the back door.

Her heart warmed. Uncle Emilio had been the closest thing to a father she and Landon had had. He'd helped her mom and cared for Charlie and Landon as if they were his own children. As she got older, she sometimes wondered if her uncle might be in love with her mother and that's why he did it. She'd asked her mother once, and she'd dismissed it…way too fast.

Uncle Emilio wasn't crazy about her mother's new love interest, either. But if Emilio was in love with her mom, it was too late now. Diana was do-or-die intent on marrying stick-up-his-ass Wayne, no matter what.

Getting out of the car, she remembered her mother's words about feeling as if she were to blame. A wave of guilt swept over her. She should be happy her mother had found love again. And maybe she did need to stop blaming herself for something that happened when she was a child.

And how many times had she told herself that same thing? The problem was that logic was in her head, not her heart.

The back door was locked, so she knocked, then took out her key. "It's me, Uncle Emilio. It's Charlie." No answer. She knocked harder. Just as she did, the door opened. Her uncle stood there, his eyes wide, obviously surprised to see her.

Going in, she said, "You shouldn't be working this late, Uncle Emi. It's not good for you."

He grunted as she came inside. "I was just cleaning up some things," he said, his tone edged with annoyance. "Did you come here to chew me out?"

The man seemed to have gotten unusually cantankerous over the past few months and she didn't know why. "No, but I figured as long as I was here I might as well since you don't seem to care about us anymore."

He motioned toward his office, ignoring her teasing remark.

Shaking her head, she said, "Thanks, but I won't be

here long." She cleared her throat. "We missed you at Easter dinner. Did you have a hot date or something?" She sat on a bench next to the wall facing the boxing ring, drummed her fingers on the envelope in her hand.

"No. I just wanted to be alone."

She frowned. Arched an eyebrow. "Well, we missed you, so don't let it happen again."

At that point, he sat next to her and placed a hand over hers. "To be honest, *mi chiquita*, your mother doesn't need me there. She has someone else to take care of her now, and I would just be in the way. I would be a reminder of a past she wants to forget."

Charlie gnashed her teeth. "That is so ridiculous. You're family. Wayne is just some guy who wants to control her life and for some reason she's liking it. I hope she sees the light before it's too late."

Uncle Emilio's mouth turned down. "She thinks she's in love."

"What do you mean…thinks?"

"He's the first man she's been with since Alejandro. She likes the feeling and she wants it to continue. I don't begrudge her wanting to start a new life. She deserves to be happy."

"She told me it was guilt that kept her from moving on with her life. That she blamed herself for not keeping my dad home that night."

"Ha!" Her uncle finally smiled, head bobbing. "*Dios Mio*. I told her a many times there was nothing she could have done to keep him from going out that night. If it was anyone's fault, it was mine."

Charlie pulled back. "Yours? Don't be silly. How could that even be possible?"

"He went to the warehouse because of me. He went to see what happened and when he saw the body, he thought it was me."

"But you didn't know. You had no control over that.

Just like you said my mother had no way of keeping him home that night."

His mouth flattening, her uncle shoved a hand through his thick shock of hair that she'd watched gradually turn silver as time marched on. He was still a handsome man who looked so very much like her father—like she imagined her father would look had he lived.

He took a deep breath. "Your mother is the only one who knows how much trouble I'd been in. I was an addict, a gambling addict. And I owed the wrong people a lot of money. Your father knew it and had helped me out of jams many times. It was perfectly logical for him to believe something had happened to me. When he came back all bloody and called me, I told him to hide the evidence. To stay out of it."

He looked at her, eyes filled with anguish. "If he hadn't done that, it wouldn't have looked so bad."

The reflection of years of guilt and pain in her uncle's eyes made Charlie's chest ache. All these years he'd been carrying his own guilt, taking care of his brother's family because he felt guilty. "But it's not your fault what happened to him. You had no control over that." And for the first time, she truly realized how little control any of them had. "He made the choice to go, not you."

He shook his head. "Brothers always stand together. We do what we have to do."

"And you helped him, too." She pointed to his chest where she knew he had a long jagged scar from getting knifed in a fight where he'd saved her father's life.

His eyes lit for a second, as if remembering something from a very long time ago. He nodded. "We took care of each other."

Locking eyes with his, she said, "And you took care of your brother's widow and his children all these years because you felt you were to blame for what happened?" She hadn't meant for it to come out like that, but tensed at the thought it could be true.

Instantly he raised his hands to cup her face. "Oh, no, sweet child. No, no, no. I help because I love you. All of you. You are family. My family. I will always be there for you. Don't you ever think there was any other reason."

She gave a wobbly smile. Then a silent sigh at the irony. They'd all been carrying their own guilt, letting it fester deep inside…all feeling responsible for an act planned by someone else which, in the end, no one had any control over.

How freaking bizarre was that.

And how important was any of it now. She glanced at the envelope, remembered the reason she came. The photo. The men in the background.

And realized it didn't matter.

"Well, good," she said. "Because we love you, too, and we don't want you staying away just because my mother is having a moment of temporary insanity."

Emilio cracked a smile. "That is for sure. But she deserves to be happy, and if this man makes her happy, then we shouldn't interfere."

Maybe, he had a point. "Well, I don't have to like it."

Talking with her uncle like they used to warmed her heart, and simultaneously they relaxed against the wall behind them.

"So what did you really come over to talk about?" Emilio finally said.

A smile formed. "Nothing. Nothing except talking to you." She leaned her head on his shoulder and squeezed his hand.

Her phone chirped and she had half a notion to let it ring. Retrieving it from her bag, she saw the caller ID.

Remy. Her stomach fluttered. She hesitated...for less than a nanosecond. "Street here." Business, keep the distance. Because there couldn't possibly be any other reason for his call.

There was silence for a moment. Then, "I need to talk to you about something important. Something I just learned." His tone sounded grave.

"About?" She wasn't sure she wanted to know. For the first time since she could remember, she felt free and didn't want to corrupt the feeling with any of the past. But if it was about his case, she had to listen.

"About the man in the brown van."

Her heart stopped.

"About the man you were supposed to meet. Smith."

CHAPTER THIRTY-FIVE

CHARLIE RUSHED HOME. Remy said they should talk in person, and she was just walking in the door from the garage when her phone played "Mama Mia"…the ringtone for her mother.

Crap. Talking to her mother was the last thing she wanted to do right now, but after their guilt conversation, she'd feel guilty if she didn't. "Hey, Mom. What's up?"

Shrugging off her sweater, she climbed the stairs to her apartment, switched the phone from hand to hand, ear to ear.

"Nothing. Just wondering what Emilio had to say. Did he recognize the men?"

"I didn't ask. We talked about other stuff…like why he didn't make it for the last family dinner." She went to the kitchen and checked the fridge to see if there was anything to eat…a random gesture since she never had anything in it unless it was leftovers from her mother or a restaurant. She stared at the void inside…and as if on cue, her stomach growled.

"Oh. What did he say?"

Charlie heard disappointment in her mother's voice…in the 'Oh' as if she wanted to know more about the men at the park. Definitely getting mixed messages here. "He said he'll be at the next dinner. No big deal."

She saw no reason to go into detail and have her mother go all wonky about why Uncle Emilio didn't feel he should be there when Wayne was there.

"Did you show him the picture?"

"No, I didn't. And—" she sucked in a deep breath "—I decided you were right. It's time to forget it all and move on."

After a long silence, Charlie said, "Are you still there? I know it's probably a shock, but it's true. You were right. I've done all I can and life is too short to be living in the past."

More silence, then, "Well, I'm glad. I did begin to wonder about that picture, though. I mean…your father never lied to me. And I don't know what would make him tell you not to tell me—"

"Mom…it's in the past. Remember? I'm sorry I said anything at all. It was nothing. He was probably telling me not to tell you about the ice cream. And from now on, I'm going to stop thinking about it except for the good stuff, and so should you. You have a wedding to plan. Remember?"

She heard a big sigh on the other end, so she added, "Okay?"

Finally her mother said, "Okay. So then you won't be too busy to come over next week sometime to help me with wedding plans."

"No," Charlie said. "I mean, no, I won't be too busy. That's great. In fact, let's do it next Sunday and call Uncle Emilio and invite him to a family dinner."

"Next Sunday? Wayne will be out of town."

Yeah. She knew. "Darn. Oh, well, let's do it anyway. Landon wants us to meet his new girlfriend, too."

"What? He never—"

"Call him. He'll tell you all about her," she said, her stomach growling even louder. Mentioning something her brother was doing that her mother didn't know about was all she needed to say and Diana was on it.

Immediately after hanging up, she called Slows to have them deliver some food. She was so hungry she ordered a slab of ribs and slaw, beans and rolls and hoped she had time to scarf it down before Remy got there.

She got out a beer and pounded it down. Took a deep breath and looked at her rumpled clothes. She hadn't seen Remy in weeks and she looked like crap. On a tear, she went to the bedroom, found a black tank top, skinny jeans, a black narrow belt with a silver buckle, and a pair of sexy boots. Why, sexy, she didn't know. Her hair was a mess, too, so she smoothed it back in a ponytail and found some long silver earrings.

She brushed her teeth, splashed her face with cold water and squirted a couple drops of Visine in her eyes. A little lipstick and blush, and she still looked like crap.

Her phone buzzed with a text message. She heard a knock downstairs. She jumped. Good grief, she was acting like she was going on a first date. *Business. Remember?*

She took a deep breath and on the way downstairs, read the text. I'M HERE.

Her pulse rocketed as she unlocked and opened the door. Remy stood there, his expression something between gravity and eagerness. Like he was happy to see her, but not. "Hi," she said.

"Hi." He smiled. Sort of.

She moved aside to let him in. "Go on up." She left the bottom door unlocked for the food delivery and followed on his heels, appreciating the great fit of his well-worn Levi's.

Once inside, he went directly to the fridge. "Got a beer?"

"Sure. I'll have one, too."

He opened both bottles and then handed her one. He angled his head indicating they should sit in the living room. "So," she said on the way. "Tell me what you found out." She sat on the couch.

He sat next to her, stared for a moment. "You look great."

That was the last thing she expected him to say. She didn't remember him ever saying that before...other than saying how hot she was when they were making love. "Uhm, thank you," she said, even more confused.

"And I've missed...working with you."

She drew back to look at him. "Clearly, you've had a few drinks already."

"No, but I've had time to think, and I've thought about a lot of things and realized we were really good together. And that I didn't appreciate it."

She waited for some kind of shoe to fall...or ball to drop...or whatever other cliché might happen, because this was obviously some alien person sitting in front of her. This was not Remington Malone, the stone man who'd never admit to anything, especially having feelings of some kind. "And?"

"And nothing. I just wanted you to know that." He paused. "And I wanted to tell you that I've been having you tailed."

"What?" Her mouth fell open. "You had me followed?"

"I've been tailing you, too. I apologize, but I was worried since we hadn't tied up all the loose ends."

It was true. They hadn't tied up everything, but she was definitely more comfortable now that the right people were in jail. And for just a little while, she wanted to forget about all that. Be a normal person, live a normal life. If there was such a thing. "I know, but following me? That's a little extreme, isn't it?"

"I didn't think so. And I was right. When you were

at the dock earlier, the brown van was following you."

She drew back. "You were at the dock?"

He nodded. "And so was the brown van."

"I know. I saw it, but he didn't come my way."

"That's because he saw me following him...and he lost me. That told me he's an experienced stalker. I was sure he was some maniac."

"Was? Did the license check show you something different? Is he Smith?"

Remy took a swig of beer. "Yes and no." His phone buzzed, he looked at it, then took a moment to text back. "Sorry. Had to let someone know something."

"So, what did you mean, yes and no?" As she was speaking, a loud knock sounded at her door. "Ah, that would be my food." She got up and crossed the room. "I hope you're hungry because I was starving and ordered a whole ton of food."

Smelling the mouth-watering scent of ribs, she reached for the doorknob.

"Charlie... What I wanted to say is that Smith—"

She swung the door wide just as Remy said "—is your father."

CHAPTER THIRTY-SIX

CHARLIE STARED into the face of a man who was Uncle Emilio's perfect double.

Her stomach slammed to her toes. Blood pounded in her ears. Her knees buckled.

Both men stepped forward, and Remy grabbed her arms, keeping her from falling.

"We better sit," Remy said, directing Charlie to the couch, while the man who looked like Uncle Emilio, the man who Remy said was her father, placed a Slows Bar B-Q bag of food on the kitchen counter, then came to sit next to her.

Fifteen minutes later, her head was still spinning, only now it was spinning with information she could barely imagine, much less process or believe— information about her father and the federal witness protection program. Information that coincided with what she'd gathered where her father's murder trial was concerned, but from there on, it spun off in an entirely new direction.

Her father had been asked years earlier to become a snitch for the FBI and tell all about all his years as a gang member and what he knew about The Partnership. He'd declined for a long list of reasons, the most important being that his family had been threatened by both the gang and the Detroit mafia.

After he was framed for murder, the feds offered a

new deal...all the information he could give them in exchange for his life without bars and protection in the WITSEC program. But he couldn't do it because his family would become the mob's next target. The only way he could give the feds any information was to end up dead on paper and disappear.

So, he'd exchanged the information he had to keep his family safe, and all these years he'd been living a shadow life, watching his family from afar. But when he learned Charlie had been a target a few months ago, he said he had to come out, even though it was against his WITSEC contact's wishes.

Even now, he couldn't make himself known or his family would still be in danger because the information he'd given the police resulted in not only the takedown of Roberto 'The Slasher' Moreno, the most notorious gang member of the Highwaymen motorcycle gang, but also Big Eddie's nephew, and a few of the mob's soldiers.

Their whole family— Charlie, Landon, Emilio and Diana—would still be in jeopardy if he made himself known now. He assured her, once he was exonerated and Falcone, Big Eddie's son, was convicted, it was possible he could finally come out.

As he was talking, Charlie kept studying him, still unable to believe her father was really there...really alive. The whole thing was surreal, like a weird, crazy dream, or a story from some movie that was happening to someone else. But when he smoothed back her hair, touched her cheek and said, *Te quiero, mi dulce niña*, she knew it was real—he was real—and she threw herself into his arms and let her tears flow.

Her father simply held her, repeating, *I love you my sweet little girl.*

When she finally stopped to breathe, she rose to her feet, questions spilling out of her like a rapid-fire machine gun. Why didn't he let himself be known instead of following her? Scaring her half to death. Didn't he know she'd think it was someone wanting to take another shot at her? He rose and simply stood there, his body open and exposed as he explained that he didn't plan on her seeing him, but if somehow she did, maybe it would make her more watchful, and maybe she wouldn't do some of the crazy things he'd seen her do in her work.

As she asked question after question and he explained, her nerves ratcheted tighter and tighter under her skin, gradually building until something snapped and a jolt of anger jagged through her. Pacing, struggling for control, she rounded on him. "I can't believe I spent my entire life believing a lie. I can't believe I devoted all my time and energy trying to prove you were innocent. To the detriment of most everything else in my life." Her voice shook when she spoke, her words laced with years of pent-up hurt and anger.

But it was more than that. Her father's conviction for murder and his violent death in prison had defined her. Becoming an attorney, working pro bono to ensure others got the help he didn't get in court was all because of what had happened to him. All because she'd thought she was to blame for his arrest and, ultimately, the worst possible thing ever. His death in prison.

"It was all a lie," she said. "My whole life has been a lie. All the time I've spent…everything I've done to prove you innocent…was for nothing."

He reached out to touch her, but she backed away, clutching her hands to her chest, her chin quivering.

"No!" She shook her head. "You can't just come back and take it all away. You can't do that!" She rubbed her temples. "And what about my mother…and Landon. My mother is about to marry someone else. Did you know that, too?"

He nodded, a deep sadness in his eyes. "I never expected she wouldn't. I just didn't think it would take this long. I can't make any of that right. All I can say is that I didn't want to put your lives in jeopardy, and I didn't want to take you all away from everything you knew—your grandmother who was still alive, your friends in school, your uncle Emilio. I thought your mother would find someone better than me and you and Landon would have a happy, more secure life with someone who could take care of you and make your lives so much better than I could."

He bowed his head and studied his hands, the work-worn hands of someone who'd done a lifetime of hard labor. Then she noticed the tired lines in his handsome face, the weathered skin that attested to more hard work. His body was still muscular, but she could see a limp when he moved and wondered if he'd been badly hurt by someone or something...and had no one there to comfort him...and she wanted to cry for him and for her, and Landon and her mother and Emilio...and she wanted to strike out at him or someone or something to purge all the anger and bitterness inside of her at the unfairness of it all.

Seeing her father alive was the most wonderful thing that had ever happened to her—and the worst. All the years they'd lost. Time they would never get back.

"I know you're going to need time to absorb all this," her father finally said. "I understand your anger, but I can't change any of it. I only hope that maybe someday you can find it in your heart to forgive me."

At that, she rushed into his arms, her chest heaving with the one certainty she had in this sudden alternate universe. "There's nothing to forgive, Daddy. I love you and that's all that matters."

She felt his body tremble and then the wetness of his tears against her cheek. After a long, long moment he held her at arm's length and said, "I have to go now, and I will have to stay out of sight until I'm sure everyone will be safe. But I'll be close. Remy has the number where you can reach me if you need to."

The mention of Remy's name brought her to attention, reminded her he was still there. Without him, she would never have known her father was alive.

Apparently seeing questions in her eyes, her father added, "It's best that way. It's too dangerous for you to be involved in any way."

Her heart sank. *Not involved in any way so she wouldn't betray him, again.* That's what he thought. He had to. And how could she blame him.

"What if Remy isn't around." He'd said he was leaving, moving away, once they found Adam. She raised a hand to her head, feeling dizzy with all the questions clamoring inside. Questions she couldn't ask. Wouldn't ask, because it would hurt too much to know the truth.

But she knew. She'd always known. She wasn't loyal. Couldn't be trusted not to betray those she loved. It was better if Remy moved away.

"I'll be around," Remy said. "I've come to like it here."

She turned to Remy, her questions turning to confusion. If she hadn't been so blown away by what had just happened with her father, she might have had a positive reaction to what he'd just said, but at that moment something else hit her.

She faced her father. "It was you. It was you who texted Remy to go to the Stuben Warehouse." Her brain engaged again, she smiled. "And it was you who helped drive the shooter away."

He nodded. "I wasn't going to let anything happen to my little girl." He glanced at Remy. "Or her friends."

Her chest swelled with love and pride, and she

wanted to scream and shout and hug him and Remy and dance around like they were little kids.

And that's when she knew, no matter what happened from here on out, everything would be okay. Things wouldn't be perfect, how could they be? But they would be okay. More okay than they'd been in twenty-five years. She hugged her father again, holding on long and hard.

"I'll be in touch," her father said. "I promise." Then they parted, and her father turned to go.

Fresh panic stabbed in her chest. He'd just gotten there. He couldn't leave. Not yet. "But what about the others?" she said, stopping him at the door, a sudden desperate need infusing every cell in her body. She needed to be with him, to talk to him, to touch him.

"What about my mother and Landon? They deserve to know, too." She swallowed a fresh batch of tears. "I don't think I can keep something this huge a secret from them."

"Do what you feel you need to do," her father said, then reached out one more time and gently, lovingly, touched her cheek…ran his hand over her hair. "Just remember, whatever happens, I love you. All of you."

Remy went to the door with her father, as if ready to leave, too, but she placed a hand on his arm. "Can you please stay for a few minutes?" She didn't know why, but she wanted him stay. No, she needed him to stay.

He did. Without question.

When the door closed behind her father, she hauled in a lungful of air, then said, "My mother is not going to like this."

"Yeah," Remy agreed, his tone holding the same dire certainty as hers. "I don't think I want to be around on that one."

She held his eyes with hers. "I hope you don't mind sticking around here for a little while."

He smiled, the slow, seductive smile that sent a quiver to the pit of her stomach. He leaned in as if to kiss her. But instead, he moved her to the side, grabbed the bag of ribs from the counter, took out the box and handed her a napkin.

Was that it? Was he just going to sit down and eat ribs and pretend like nothing had happened and everything was the same? She was so jacked from what just happened, she didn't know how she could eat a thing.

Remy walked to the couch, placed the food on the coffee table. He motioned for her to sit with him, but she was so wired, she could probably conduct electricity for the whole state of Michigan. She pulled the band from her ponytail, shook out her hair, and whirled around in a circle. "Oh, my God. I think I could fly to the moon and back on my own power…and I have so many questions to ask him, so much to tell him, I—"

"All in due time, kiddo. Now come and help me eat some of these ribs or I'm going to start without you."

She walked over and sat next to him. "Okay, but I want to know everything that happened when you found him. What exactly was he doing? Did he say anything about me? Say anything about the picture? Oh, no. I should've asked him about that. I bet he was the one who put it in the stairwell. Maybe he thought I'd figure out what was going on without telling me. Did he talk about my mother?" She turned to look at him. "Oh, man. She can't get married now. She's going to have to know. I have to tell her…stop her—"

Remy stuck a rib between her teeth. Grinned when she stopped talking and licked her lips.

"Yum."

"I know." He licked a finger, then got up. "More beer?"

Taking a deep breath, she waved toward the kitchen.

Remy was right. There would be plenty of time to find out everything. She didn't need to know everything right this minute. It should be enough to know her father was alive, and they would have time to talk, and maybe she could even explain. He would understand, wouldn't he? She'd been a little girl, doing what she thought was right. He had to know that, didn't he? She glanced at Remy as he came back with two more beers.

Remy didn't understand why she'd kept things from him. But even so, he was here, acting like they were two good friends having ribs and a beer together …acting like nothing had happened. With Adam. With her father. Between the two of them. Which was why he didn't need to talk about it. Maybe she didn't either. Yeah, right.

"So," she said after he got settled on the couch next to her. "We should talk." She glanced over. "Don't you think?"

His eyes met hers. "No. I'm good."

Okay. A wave of relief swept through her. Thinking about it, she was good, too.

But there was other stuff. A lot of other stuff. "You know, just because Falcone is in jail doesn't mean we're out of danger."

"Like you said before, we make a great team."

She held his gaze for a moment longer.

"And I like you a lot."

She picked up another rib, a smile forming.

Yes. She had to agree. They did make a great team.

And it would be good to have a friend inside the Detroit PD.

And if you haven't read **STREET**,
*the prequel to DETROIT RULES, I invite you to
read the following excerpt and pick up a copy on my
website, Amazon or other book outlets to see how
Charlie Street got her start...*

STREET

The Heat is Coming...

Lucas Cabrera, playboy, undercover agent...assassin. Trained by a black-ops government agency to carry out top secret missions, Luc has his own lifelong mission. Revenge against the man who harmed his mother. Acting as a bodyguard to get to his target, he's on his way to doing just that when he discovers the one thing that can stop him. His sudden emotions for the beautiful attorney who's defending the man in his crosshairs.

Crusading lawyer Charlize Street is determined to be one of the good guys. In a city like Detroit, justice is hard to come by, especially in the halls of power. So when a senator known for doing good deeds is smeared with criminal allegations, Charlie is determined to clear his name. But she isn't prepared to handle the senator's sexy bodyguard, a man who exudes both charm and danger.

When Charlie uncovers evidence someone wants kept secret, she finds herself in danger. She's been lucky so far...but needs help. Luc insists on being that guy...and soon the heat is coming from more than just the people who want to stop her. Sensing Luc has his own agenda, she wonders if there's anyone in the Motor City she can truly trust to help her...before her luck runs out.

Danger, Desire, and betrayal explode in this high-action thriller, the exciting first book in Linda Style's **Street Law** *series.*

CHAPTER ONE

Detroit, Michigan
A while ago…

PLEASE, PLEASE, PLEASE. I'll do anything, Charlie Street promised whatever god, spirit, or the devil himself, if he could produce the means to save her.

The man across the table hid behind dark Ray-Bans and a charcoal gray hoodie, pulled so close around his face all she could see was his hooked nose sticking out.

The others were dressed in personality statements of their own—a neon orange T-shirt and hair spiked like a rhino, a dude who looked like he should be auditioning for a role on *Empire*, and a guy sporting a polyester leisure suit from the '70s, complete with mutton chops. All typical garb at a Texas Hold'em table on Saturday night at the Greektown Casino.

Charlie wore her usual. Black. Tonight it was a dress. Low-cut, short, and sexy. With five-inch red stilettos. Anything to distract.

And it looked like her ploy might've worked.

The game was down to her and Hoodie.

If she won, the money would literally save her life.

Her nerves tensed. Next up…the turn card.

She studied her opponent. Stone still. No tells.

A shuffling sound came from behind her. Body heat. Some idiot looking over her shoulder. Breaking her concentration.

The dealer turned a seven of hearts, giving her two options. Adrenaline rushed as she calculated the odds. On the table, the seven of hearts, a Jack of spades, a two of hearts and an Ace. Not even a pair. Hoodie hadn't been betting. And with the odd cards on the table, if he had anything at all he'd be shoving in the chips.

She had an open ended straight, seven high, and four hearts. Three ways to go. A straight or a flush. One card left.

She swallowed, laid a hand on her chips. "All in."

Her heart pounding a hole in her chest, she pushed what was left of her winnings forward. If Hoodie met her bet and she won, she'd rake in over fifty K. If he didn't see her bet, she'd win and still have enough to make the move she'd been working toward since she left law school.

Hoodie fingered his chips, making little *clickity click* sounds, stared at the cards, then at her. Maybe. Other than the lift of his chin, it was hard to know. But he'd be looking for tells, too, to see if she might be bluffing. Which at this point, she was. But the odds were in her favor three different ways.

He shoved in the rest of his chips.

Her heart raced. Sweat broke under her arms. One card—give her a three, an eight, or a heart. She had this!

They flipped over their cards. Hoodie had a potential straight...inside.

Damn! Not the eight. It would give him a higher straight.

Okay. A three or a heart. The percentages were still on her side.

The room hummed with anticipation.

She launched to her feet.

The dealer flipped the last card. The river.

She stared. Blood drained from her limbs. No. That.

Could. Not. Happen. No, no, no.

Her throat closed. She gulped for air.

She swung around and stumbled into the man standing behind her. Barely looking at him except to note he was much taller than she was, she shoved past him and tore through the crowd, tears suddenly streaming.

She'd lost it. Every penny of the money she'd saved for two years. Her brain stalled. She couldn't think as she pushed through a blurry sea of people.

How could it…how could she…be so stupid?

Blindly charging through the game rooms on her way to the parking garage, bile rose in her throat. She passed a restroom, backed up and stumbled inside. Unable to make it to the toilet, she hit the sink, leaned over, and puked her guts out.

Arms on the sink, she ran the water, cupped her hands to collect enough to rinse, and spit… three times.

Seeing herself in the mirror, she laughed, her voice a high cackle. Mascara ran down her cheeks and ringed her eyes. All she needed was some big red lips and she'd look like a clown. A very sad clown. An idiot clown.

Only an idiot would've made that last play. One more bet to see if he'd stay and raise. That's what she should've done. She'd lost focus. The guy behind had unnerved her, and she'd jumped the gun. Stupid. But the most stupid part was that she was there in the first place.

Pulling a tissue from her purse, a dollar bill fluttered to the floor.

She stared at it, then laughed, tearing up at the same time. Well—she hauled in a lungful of air—she wasn't totally broke.

The irony was that she'd done just the opposite of what she'd started out to do earlier in the evening. Now instead of having enough money to quit her job and work for herself, she'd have to work a long time at Reston, Barrett and Brown just to get back what she'd lost.

If she didn't kill herself first. Working for a law firm that had no conscience was akin to selling her soul.

On her way to the garage, passing several rows of quarter slots lined up like robots, she spotted a Megabucks slot on the end. She fingered the dollar, the only thing between her and poverty.

When she was little, her dad had given her a toy bank shaped like a slot machine and every time she put in a penny, the wheels would spin and lights would flash.

It was an omen of some kind, wasn't it? Her dad looking over her from above.

She stopped and not bothering to sit, shoved in the money, pushed the button and watched the reels spin. A Megabucks icon bounced to a stop. The teaser. Then another...and another.

Bells rang, lights flashed, red, blue, green, and yellow. She might have screamed. The woman sitting on the stool next to her screamed. A gaggle of white-haired seniors with name tags on their shirts huddled around her as the sound and light show continued, the slot numbers spinning crazily to total up the win, finally stopping at twenty-five thousand, four hundred and forty-four dollars.

Charlie's eyes glazed over. Her heart pounded.

"Hit the button," a man's voice came from somewhere on her right. "Someone will come and take care of you. They need to get the information from the machine before any payout."

Charlie knew. This was not her first rodeo. Still, she was stunned. One minute she'd lost it all, and the next she'd won half back. Could she actually win that much on a dollar slot?

Apparently yes, she discovered when a casino employee came over, and a sometime later, she'd cashed out. Her blood rushed. She should play more, win more. A gambler's mantra.

The smart thing to do, though, would be to leave. But…when a machine was hot, chances were it would hit again. Or maybe a different slot. Wheel of Fortune. Progressive games paid the most, didn't they?

Unbelievable. She'd gone from the lowest of lows to reclaiming her life, all in the space of a few minutes. Her nerves tingled. Her pulse raced. If she stuck around, she could break even. Get it all back…and more.

The adrenaline rush of a win pulled at her, lured her back to the slot. Seeing someone at the machine, a mix of disappointment and relief shot through her. Another omen. Half of her nest egg was better than nothing…and, no, she wasn't going to tempt fate one more second.

Charlie hadn't been to the casino in two years, not since her family conspired and subjected her to their version of an intervention. She shouldn't be here now, and if she stuck around long enough…

Pulling away before she changed her mind, she charged through the casino doors leading to the attached parking garage. Her car was on the same floor at the end of the second row. Once there she would be safe from herself.

The heat of an uncharacteristically warm October mixed with noxious gas fumes trapped in the parking garage made her stomach roil again. She got out her keys and aimed the fob. Just as she clicked the UNLOCK button something bumped her from behind. Hard. Her purse yanked from her fingers.

"No!" Charlie grasped the strap…and stared into the cold eyes of a man wearing a black beanie. He swatted at her and yanked again. She clutched even harder and screamed. No petty thief was going to ruin the rest of her life.

"Let go, bitch." Grappling over the purse, the man shouldered her into the wall, hitting and jabbing with his free hand.

"No way, asshole!" Charlie held so tight her nails dug into her palms. She screamed at the top of her lungs and butted him with her head. So much for her self-defense training.

"Crazy bitch." Another guy ran over. Burly, twice her size. "Let go, or I'll fucking kill you," he spat out and punched her in the face.

Stars flashed before her eyes. She tightened her grip. *Her money. She couldn't lose her money.*

The bigger guy pressed her face against the wall with one hand, his other went around her neck. Tightening…choking…her screams a strangled gurgle. Light and dark faded in and out. Vision blurring. The purse strap scraped across her fingers as she lost her grip.

Voices…shouting, yelling. "*Ladrón estúpido.*" *Another man's voice.*

More scuffling, shoving, a flurry of arms and fists, and then the pressure around her neck fell away, and a blurry form came into focus. Familiar. The man she'd nearly run over and shoved away when leaving the poker table. He leveled his gaze at her attacker and hissed, "You should never hit a woman, *cabrón.*"

Charlie's vision cleared enough see her savior throw a kick that sent the thief across the hood of a car five feet away. Someone's arms came under hers from behind, holding her up, but her knees wobbled, unsteady. Dizzy…

"He scared them away!" A woman's voice. "But they got your purse."

A buzz filled Charlie's ears.

And then the concrete came up to meet her.

CHAPTER TWO

"THEY SAY HE killed his wife."

"Was that before or after he swindled the taxpayers and misappropriated state funds?" Charlie teased the receptionist whose muffled voice announced her client was waiting.

The woman laughed. As much as Charlie hated working for Reston, Barrett and Brown, the largest and most prestigious law firm in Detroit, she'd made a couple of good friends at the firm and would truly miss them when she left.

Except now she'd have to stay even longer than planned. Her penance for stupidly losing all her money. It wasn't her fault she was assaulted and robbed, but she had only herself to blame for going to the casino in the first place.

"I'll be right there."

Charlie had heard all the gossip and rumors about her new client, Senator Alvin Hawker, and had dismissed them. It was hard not to feel sympathy for a man whose seven-year-old son had been abducted and, after nearly a year without a word—not even a ransom request—there was little hope the boy was still alive.

As politicians went, Senator Hawker was the only one around who seemed sincere and had done several things to fix some of the inner-city problems. Despite all the rumors planted by his opponents, already gearing up for the next election, she believed in him.

And as his attorney, her job was to provide enough evidence to keep the senator from being indicted for misuse of state money, which he'd allegedly used to fund extravagant vacations and to support his friends. Including a former mistress. Pretty much business as usual in Detroit. But she didn't believe it.

From all she'd read about the man, and from all he'd done since getting elected, he appeared to be an honest man. She'd cheered him on. For once, the people had elected a politician who was different. If given the support he needed, there was no telling how much he could accomplish. Senator Hawker could set the state on the right path again.

She went out to meet her client, as she usually did, rather than having someone bring him to her office. A more personal way to begin the relationship. As she got closer, she noticed another man standing just behind and to the side of the senator. Her stomach dropped.

He was the same man who'd rescued her last night. Shit. She'd planned to keep her ill-fated visit to the casino a secret.

"Senator Hawker." Charlie extended a hand. "Nice to meet you. I'm Charlize Street."

The senator was a tall man, with dull brown hair, graying at the temples. Distinguished, except the gray made him look older than he probably was. Late fifties. He sported a golf-course tan, and although he wasn't fat, she could tell he was soft and doughy under the designer suit.

"I know who you are, Ms. Street. And to be honest, I have to say I'm not entirely happy Douglas isn't doing this himself. But looking at your record, I was impressed. Your percentage of acquittals is to be admired." He gave her a wide, welcoming smile.

Douglas Reston was her boss, and it boosted her ego to know that maybe he really did think she was a better fit to be the lead on this case than he was.

She returned the wide smile. "Well, Senator, be assured I'm going to do everything I can to maintain those percentages." She glanced at the other man.

"Luc Cabrera, my security specialist," the senator said, motioning to the guy standing behind him.

Meaning bodyguard. She extended a hand to Cabrera. So, had the senator been checking her out, and the "security specialist's" fortuitous appearance at the casino wasn't random?

"Pleased to meet you, Mr. Cabrera."

Leaning to shake hands, she got a whiff of his cologne. *Armani Acqua di Gio.* Nice. His thumb trailed across the back of her hand.

"My pleasure, Ms. Street." He nodded, his dark-eyed gaze enveloping her, familiar, as if they shared some big secret. His slight accent made the simple repetition of her name a seductive overture. He was smooth. Very smooth.

Walking together into her office, the senator said, "I'm sure Douglas has stressed how anxious I am to get this cleared up as soon as possible."

"Of course. Mr. Reston will be working with me to do exactly that, Senator." She was just as anxious as he was. The sooner she could get this case wrapped up, the better, so he could get back to doing his job and not waste time with manufactured scandals.

The senator sat in the client chair and Cabrera, wearing a black, well-tailored suit, silver gray shirt and a dark tie, stood by the door. Charlie motioned, indicating he should sit, too.

"He's fine where he is," the senator said. "Let's get this done."

After explaining the allegations and the charges they

might be up against, should it come to that, Charlie handed the senator a list of the records to which she'd need access. All routine, standard procedure.

Reading, the man nodded his agreement. "I'll have my secretary get everything to you within a few days. Everything except my personal business records."

Charlie studied the man. He clearly didn't understand. "Excuse me, Senator. We need everything on the list."

"I'd be happy to oblige, Ms. Street," he said, now looking directly at her. "But the records for that period of time no longer exist. My former assistant left the position over a year ago, and we haven't been able to locate the records since."

Charlie perused the senator's file on her computer monitor, scrolled down to his former assistant's information. "Mia Powers was your administrative assistant during the time in question. Are you saying she destroyed all your records?"

"I don't know. She took the computer with her and disappeared."

"Do you have any idea why?"

"I suspect it was because she knew I was going to let her go and hire someone else."

"My records show she also worked for you as a nanny to your son."

"Correct. After my wife died, I needed someone to be there and Mia was one of my most trusted employees. She volunteered and it worked out very well for a time. She was able to work from home a couple days a week and that really helped out with—" his voice hitched "—my son."

"I'm sorry. I hate to bring up a sensitive issue, but we have to be able to prove the opposite of what the state wants to prove. The records are critical. Have you tried to find Ms. Powers?"

"Of course. I hired the best investigator I could find. But Mia seems to have vanished into thin air."

"We'll need the investigator's findings and even so, we'll also conduct our own search. If she can't be found, we need to show you did everything in your power to find her."

"From what I remember of the law, the burden of proof is on the prosecution, not the defense."

She steepled her hands. "Then I'm sure you also remember that while that's true, we still need to provide an airtight defense."

He sat back, grinned. "If I could do that, Ms. Street, I wouldn't be here, now would I?"

From what she'd researched, Hawker was an attorney, but had never practiced law. Not one day. He'd gone straight from law school into public service. But he was her client and despite all the flack he was getting from the press, she really did believe he was innocent. She smiled in return. "Right. And like I said, I'm going to do everything in my power to provide the best defense possible."

The man shifted in his chair, clenched his hands. "Good. I'm paying this firm a great deal of money to make this go away quickly," he said. "The longer it hangs on, the worse it looks on my resume, if you know what I mean." He winked at her.

She did know. It wouldn't be good for his chances of getting reelected.

"If you use the findings we already have things should move swiftly." He launched to his feet, his expression suddenly thoughtful. "Excuse me. I must to talk to Douglas for a moment." He swung around and loped toward the door. She got up and followed, but he was gone before she could spit out another word, leaving her and Cabrera staring at each other.

She cleared her throat. "You left last night before I

had a chance to thank you."

"It is unnecessary."

"Why? Because you were spying on me?"

A slow smile tipped his lips. "Spying is such a crass word. I was enjoying watching a beautiful woman play a killer game of poker. You are very good, *bonita*."

Bonita? She stiffened at the familiarity. "I don't know your motives, Mr. Cabrera, but it's hard to believe you just happened to be there watching me."

"It is the truth. I, too, excel at the game of poker, and I admired your skill so much I could not tear myself away."

"Are you saying you weren't there checking on me for the senator?"

"I can guarantee that was not why I was there. Although spying on you is a job I think I would like very much."

"So why didn't you tell the senator you saw me there?" If Cabrera had blabbed, the senator would have mentioned it for sure.

"I suspect for the same reason you did not report the robbery to the police."

She squelched a smile. The man was quick. Smart.

"I doubt our reasons are the same, however, I thank you again. You scared off those men and I'm grateful.

He nodded. "I'm sorry I was not able to retrieve your money."

Not as sorry as she was. Early this morning she'd had to contact her bank and credit card companies to stop any charges and get new cards. And she'd had to apply for a duplicate driver's license. "Thank you. I'm afraid it's gone for good."

"I am curious. Why did you fight with them? That can be a dangerous thing to do."

Charlie sighed. "I agree, it wasn't the wisest idea in the world. I guess I need to brush up on my self-defense skills."

"I would be happy to teach you. I have expert skills in martial arts as well."

"And you're modest, too."

But she didn't doubt his statement. The punch or kick she'd seen him throw had sent her assailant across the parking garage. She pulled her gaze from his. "You are a persistent man, Mr. Cabrera."

"Please, call me Lucas. Or Luc as my friends do."

"Okay...Luc." She looked him in the eyes again. "Let me be clear. While I'm grateful for your help last night, your boss is my client. You and I will not have any contact other than what's necessary to my work with the senator, and even then, it will be as little as possible. I'd appreciate it if we can leave it right there."

"As the lady wishes." He raised his hands.

The senator returned, stood behind Cabrera. "I spoke with Douglas. He will catch you up on our conversation. If you have any other questions about records and paperwork, please contact my administrative assistant."

Hands again clasped in front of him, Cabrera shifted his gaze from Charlie to the senator then to Charlie, again.

"Or you can get in touch with Luc." Senator Hawker motioned to the bodyguard, who produced a card from his pocket, and handed it to her, his fingers touching hers...lingering too long.

Oh, man. Was this guy full of himself or what? Dangerous came to mind. Hot. She took the card. LUCAS CABRERA, SECURITY SPECIALIST. A phone number was listed, and an email address. Nothing else.

"Thank you," she said, although she couldn't think of a single reason she'd have to call the bodyguard.

Cabrera grinned. Sexy. Masculine. Totally not her

type. Although her father was half Mexican, her experiences with macho Latino men hadn't been stellar. Actually most men she'd been involved with fit that category.

Her father had been an exception, a strong supporter of equality for all. He'd had to be. He would never have gotten even close to her mother otherwise. From the time Charlie could remember, her father had told her she could do anything...be anything she wanted. And she'd believed him.

The senator was already walking down the hall to leave, so she moved to within inches of Cabrera, his body heat like fire scorching her skin. "Can you keep a secret?" she said, her voice low.

He moved even closer, his mouth nearly touching hers, his eagerness radiating. "Of course."

"Well, just between you and me, Luc..." she paused, moistened her lips "... I think you're a player, and you don't get to play with me."

Face to face, a long moment passed. Her nerves skittered.

Then he reached up, brushed his fingertips down her cheek. "I hear the words, *bonita*. But why do I not believe you?"

Watch for **DETROIT HUSTLE**,
book three in my new Street Law series
COMING SOON

A Note from the Author

Dear Reader,

Thank you for being a reader and sharing your love of reading by purchasing my stories. Without you, my words have no voice. I hope you enjoyed Charlie Street's story as much as I enjoyed writing it and that you'll consider leaving a review or rating on Amazon, Barnes & Noble, Goodreads, or wherever you like to hang out and share information about books. If you haven't read my other books, I hope you'll want to pick them up and spend more time with characters I love and who always feel like part of my family by the time I'm done writing their stories. I love to hear from readers and also connect on social media. If you'd like to chat and keep updated on future releases, please join me on

Facebook: @LindaStyle

Twitter: @LindaStyle

I'm also on Instagram, so please stop by and join the fun.

If you'd like to sign up for my newsletter and be the first to learn about book sales and freebies, you can do so on my Linda Style Amazon page and on my website.

LindaStyle.com

Best wishes and Happy Reading,

Linda

Also by Linda Style

Fiction from LMS Press
Copyright © Linda Fensand Syle

Her Sister's Secret, 2nd edition
Cowboys Don't Dance

SECRETS OF SPIRIT CREEK series: romance
Remember Me, Book 1
Trust Me, Book 2
Rescue Me, Book 3

L.A.P.D. SPECIAL INVESTIGATIONS series: romantic suspense
The Forgotten, Book 1
The Deceived, Book 2
The Taken, Book 3
The Silent, Book 4
The Missing, Book 5

STREET LAW series: crime thriller
Street, Book 1
Detroit Rules, Book 2
Detroit Hustle, Book 3 (Coming Soon)

Fiction: Backlist from Harlequin Enterprises Ltd
Copyright © Linda Fendsand Style

Her Sister's Secret
Daddy in the House
Slow Dance with a Cowboy
The Man in the Photograph
What Madeline Wants

The Witness
His Case, Her Child
And Justice for All
Husband and Wife Reunion
Going for Broke
The Man from Texas
The Mistake She Made
The Promise He Made
A Soldier's Secret
Protecting the Witness

Non-Fiction:

BOOTCAMP FOR NOVELISTS BEYOND
THE FIRST DRAFT: Writing Techniques of the
Pros
In digital and in print.
By Linda Style Copyright © 2013, LMS Press, Gilbert, AZ
85234. (403 pages)

BOOTCAMP FOR NOVELISTS BEYOND THE
FIRST DRAFT Parts I, II, and III
Digital Only

Linda's books are available on her website, on
Amazon, and other bookstore outlets.

LindaStyle.com

About the Author

LINDA STYLE is an Award-Winning, National Bestselling author with over a million copies sold in thirteen different countries. With an education in behavioral science and in journalism, Linda has worked in a number of jobs, from social services to Director of a state mental health program, to magazine editor. She's also worked as a writing instructor at Bootcamp for Novelists, an online writing school she co-founded in 2004, but as rewarding as all that all was, she says nothing compares with writing her stories of suspense, romance, and intrigue. Her books—often described as emotional, fast-paced stories that keep you riveted to the page—have won several awards, including the prestigious Daphne du Maurier Award of Excellence, the Orange Rose award for Best Book of the Year, and the HOLT Award of Merit.

When not writing, Linda loves to travel, a passion that has taken her all over the world and allows her to indulge in her other passion…photography. A Minnesota native, she now lives with her family in Arizona, where she likes to play tennis and hike in the mountains—the best place in the world to think up more stories. She invites you to stop by her website.

LindaStyle.com

Made in the
USA
Middletown, DE